Linda Holeman is the author of six bo... ... adults, and two collections of short stories for adults, both of which have won her numerous awards in her native Canada. This is her first novel. She has three children and lives in Winnipeg, Manitoba.

The Linnet Bird

LINDA HOLEMAN

headline

First published in Great Britain in 2004
by HEADLINE BOOK PUBLISHING

First published in paperback in 2004
by HEADLINE BOOK PUBLISHING

10 9 8 7 6 5 4

ISBN 0 7553 2292 4 (A format)
ISBN 0 7553 2463 3 (B format)

Typeset in Bembo by Avon DataSet Ltd,
Bidford-on-Avon, Warwickshire

Printed and bound in Great Britain by
Mackays of Chatham plc, Chatham, Kent

HEADLINE BOOK PUBLISHING
A division of Hodder Headline
338 Euston Road
London NW1 3BH

www.headline.co.uk
www.hodderheadline.com

For Holly Kennedy,
who had faith in this story.

A LINNET IN A GILDED CAGE

A linnet in a gilded cage,
A linnet on a bough,
In frosty winter one might doubt
Which bird is luckier now.
But let the tree burst out in leaf,
And nests be on the bough,
Which linnet is the luckier bird,
Oh who could doubt it now?

Christina Rossetti
Sing-Song: A Nursery Rhyme Book, 1872

PROLOGUE

Calcutta, 1839

SMOKING OPIUM IS an art.

I look at my tray and its contents – the pipe covered in finely worked silver, the small spirit lamp, the long blunt needle, the container of *chandu*, and my row of pea-size balls of the dark brown paste. My lips are dry. I close my eyes and see it: the opium ball at the end of the needle over the flame of the lamp, the bubbling and swelling of that muddy brown until it turns golden. Then catching it on the edge of the pipe bowl, using the needle to stretch it into long strings until it is cooked through. Rolling it back into shape and pushing it – quickly, for it must be the right consistency – into the bowl. Now holding the bowl close to the lamp, the flame licking. I see my lips close around the familiar jade mouthpiece, and then a deep pull, another and another. The sound is the steady unbroken rhythm of a heartbeat.

I open my eyes, licking my lips. It is early morning. The Indian sun will not reach its zenith for a few more hours; there is time, before the copper rays bake and shrink everything, before the servants have to water the *tatties* and close all the shutters. I look back to my tray.

1

Not yet. I will not take up my pipe yet. I have something to tell you.

Through the open windows I can hear the children's voices from the garden. I go to watch. David is playing with the *dhobi*'s son. The child's game, a seemingly senseless galloping about on long sticks, is played with careless, easy motions as only six-year-olds can play. Malti sits on the top step of the verandah. Slowly she waves a horsetail whisk in front of her oval, burnished face, wreathed with the pleasure of an *ayah* watching her beloved charge.

The boys romp round the lawn of creeping *doob*. The bougainvillaea and hibiscus are in scarlet display.

I never played as my son does today. At a little older than he is now, I was employed for ten hours a day, six days a week, at the bookbinder's on Harvey Close in Liverpool. I had never felt grass under my bare feet, or heard the song of a bird, and only rarely felt the sun's warmth upon my face. My son will never know the work I did, not the work I started with or the work I did later, when I was still a child but no longer young. That part of my life will remain for ever closed to him, but not to you.

David has stopped, cocking his head as if listening, or puzzled. And then he stoops, reaching beneath the low hedge of plumbago.

He runs back to Malti, his face a portrait of sorrow, his hands cupping a bird. Even from here I recognize its green feathers, the brilliant red over its beak. It stirs feebly, but one wing hangs oddly from its body. A small, common bird, the coppersmith barbet. *Basanta bauri*. Only yesterday I heard its familiar *pok-pok* from the mango trees. David is calling now, his voice thick with emotion. I see the sun-browned texture of his skin, the way his long slender thumbs

2

crook tenderly in an attempt to hold on yet not hurt the helpless thing.

I think of my own hands when I was young, chapped from the cold wind off the grey Mersey, stained with ink, cheap glue webbing between my fingers. And then, not many years later, tainted with that which I couldn't wash away. Lady Macbeth and her own dirty hands. And finally, just before I left my youth and began my voyage, I remember my hands. Nicked with cuts from paper, dry from handling books, they appeared clean, so clean, although always, at least in my mind, bearing the smell of too many men, of the blood. How, you are wondering, have I come from that place, and arrived here?

Beside my opium tray lies the quill and paper I had Malti bring me earlier this morning.

But before I begin to write, a small time to dream. It is my last. I have made this promise before. I have thought it, whispered it, spoken it, prayed it. But this time I have sworn on my child's head, in the darkness before morning, sitting beside David's bed, listening to his shallow, sweet breaths followed by the deep answering exhalations of Malti from her pallet in the corner. I crept in, knelt by him, and swore, his thick hair under my pale fingers.

I swore that today will be my last dream that is fed by the White Smoke. And without its aid, I fear my dreams will warp into the old, familiar nightmare, the one I have tried so long to lose.

I close the shutters tightly, darkening the room, and I light the lamp. There is a whir and crackle as a moth comes to life and flutters about the soft glow. The noise hurts. I have taken opium for too long; my senses are stretched to a thin wire, vibrating in the slightest stimuli – this beat of a moth's wings,

3

the drop of hot rain on the back of my hand, the unexpected confusion of a patterned sari.

The opium can no longer make me happy. It simply allows me to carry on. And today, for the last time, it will still my hand, my mind, long enough to write what I must. So that my son will know some day. For him, I will write only what is important for his future. For you, I will write of it all – part truth, part memory, part nightmare: my life, the one that started so long ago, in a place so far from here.

CHAPTER ONE

Liverpool, 1823

I HAD BEEN PUT to work for men by Da in the winter of my eleventh year. He was dissatisfied by the small wage I earned at the bookbindery, and had recently been laid off his job at the rope-maker's for turning up tip one too many times and spoiling the hemp in spinning.

It was a wet November night when he arrived home with Mr Jacobs. I suppose he met him in one of the public houses: where else would he meet anyone? I heard Da say the man's name over and over, Mr Jacobs this and Mr Jacobs that. One or both of them were stumbling, and the knocking into the few pieces of furniture, as well as the loudness of their voices, woke me from my sleep in the blankets I laid down behind the coal-box each evening. It was warmer there, close to the fireplace, and I felt I had at least a tiny degree of privacy in the one rented room on the second floor of a sagging dwelling off Vauxhall Road, in a court on Back Phoebe Anne Street.

'She's here somewhere,' I heard Da say, 'like a wee mouse, she is, scurrying about,' and then, before I had a chance to try and make sense of why he would be looking for me, I was dragged out of my blankets and into the middle of the low-ceilinged, candle-lit room.

5

'I thought you said she were eleven.' Mr Jacobs's voice was hoarse, the words clipped with impatience.

'I told you right, Mr Jacobs. Past eleven, now. Had her birthday well before Michaelmas.'

'She's small. Not much shape to her yet.'

'But she has a quim, sir, that you'll find soon enough. It's just delicate she is, a delicate slip of a girl. And she's a right pretty lass – you can see that for yourself,' Da said, pushing back my long hair with calloused hands and pulling me closer to the candle in the middle of the table. 'Where have you last seen hair like this? Golden and rich as summer's sweetest pear. And, like I told you, she's pure. You'll be the first, Mr Jacobs, and a lucky man indeed.'

I pulled away from him, my mouth opening and closing in horror. 'Da! Da, what is it you're saying? No, Da.'

Mr Jacobs's thick bottom lip extended in a pout. 'How do I know you haven't duped a hundred men before me, you and her?'

'You'll know you're the first, Mr Jacobs. Of course you'll know. Tight as a dead man's fist, you'll find her.'

I yanked my arm away from Da's grasp. 'You can't make me,' I said, backing towards the door. 'You'll never—'

Mr Jacobs stepped in front of me now. He had only a ring of greying hair, and the top of his head shone greasily in the flickering light. There was a cut, crusted over with dried blood, on the bridge of his nose. 'Quite the little actress, aren't you?' he asked. 'You can stop all your bluster now. You'll not get a penny, you nor your father, if I find you're not what's been promised.'

In one stride, Da took my arm again and pulled me into a shadowy corner of the room. 'Now, girl,' he wheedled, 'it's bound to happen some time. And better here, in your own

6

home, than somewhere out in the rain in a doorway. Many a lass helps out her family when they've fallen on hard times. Why should you be any different?'

Of course, I knew that a number of the older girls from the bookbinder's – as well as those from the sugar refineries, the glass-makers and the potteries – worked a few hours now and then on the twisting narrow streets down by the docks to bring in extra shillings when money was short at home. But I had always known I was different. I wasn't like them, I told myself. It was in my blood, this difference.

'Come on now. He'll pay handsomely.' Da put his mouth to my ear. I smelt the sourness of his breath. 'You know we've no other way, what with me put out of the job. I've always looked after you and now it's your turn to bring something in, something more than the few pennies you earn. And it's no terrible thing. Weren't I buggered meself, over and over on the ships, when I were not much older than you? And it did me no harm, did it?'

I backed away again, arms wrapped over my chest. 'No, Da. Mother would never—'

Da grabbed my upper arms, giving me a rough shake. 'There'll be no talk of your mother.'

At an impatient snick from Mr Jacobs, Da called over his shoulder, 'Now, sir, sit yourself there, on the settle, and I'll talk some sense into my lass here.'

But of course there was no talk that made sense, only – when I screamed, *you can't make me,* and tried to run for the door – a knock across my jaw that sent me flying. I felt my cheek hit the damp cold of the floor, and then I knew nothing more until I was jarred back to consciousness by hot, urgent breath on my face. My shift was pushed up round my waist, and Mr Jacobs's body was heavy on mine. His rutting scrubbed my back painfully against the splintered wood of the settle, and the top of my head banged against the wall with each thrust. The searing inside me was a fresh explosion that matched his grunts, and I saw the corresponding throb of the blue vein that ran down his forehead, thick and raised as a great worm. Sweat gleamed on his upper lip, even though the fire was out and the room cold as a tomb.

But almost worse than the pain and horror of what was happening to me at the mercy of Mr Jacobs was that Da – when I turned my head to look for him, hoping he might be moved to come to my rescue – watched from his stool, his face fixed in an expression I'd never seen before, one hand busy under the table.

I squeezed my eyes shut, and lay limp under Mr Jacobs. I knew I should fight, but was strangely detached. My body burned raw at its centre, yet my mind tripped and ran, stumbling away from Mr Jacobs's pulsing vein and the image of Da, staring. And then I heard my mother's voice, faint but clear. She recited the second stanza of 'The Green Linnet', the poem that had been her favourite, and from where she had drawn my name:

> One have I mark'd, the happiest guest
> In all this covert of the blest:
> Hail to Thee, far above the rest
> In joy of voice and pinion!
> Thou, Linnet! in thy green array,
> Presiding Spirit here today,
> Dost lead the revels of the May,
> And this is thy dominion.

I heard it in its entirety three times, and just before the start of its fourth repetition Mr Jacobs gave a great shuddering groan and lay still until I feared I would be smothered. I wanted my mother's voice back, for while I listened my body had become numb, but now she was gone, and I grew aware of everything with a terrible clarity. I felt the position of my legs, splayed impossibly wide, of torn wetness, of pain I had never known or imagined, of Mr Jacobs's unbearable weight. I heard the fretful wail of the baby in the room next door, and Mr Jacobs's rattly breathing. I smelt the rankness of his flesh. I kept my eyes closed so that I saw dark starbursts on my inner lids. It seemed that time had stopped.

Finally he moved off and away, but I stayed as I was, eyes shut, unmoving through the rustle of clothing being fastened, the exchange of a few words and then the rasp of the door scraping along the floor as it opened and closed.

More minutes passed, and I pulled my knees together, my fingers trembling as I pulled down my shift, and, still without opening my eyes, lowered myself to the floor and crawled on hands and knees back to my little nest behind the coal-box. The only sounds in the room then were my father's muttered counting, the clink of the coins and the sputter of a dying candle. I lay on my side and twisted my blanket round me, knees brought up to my chest and hands tucking my shift into the bleeding, sticky mess between my legs, weeping for my mother, even though she'd been dead a whole year, and for what was lost for ever.

Later that night, when I lit a candle and washed away the dried blood and spunk from my thighs, I swore that I would never again cry over what a man might do to me for I knew it would do no good. No good at all.

CHAPTER TWO

I WAS BORN LINNET Gow, and known as Linny Munt. My Christian name was given to me by my soft, dreamy mother, Frances Gow, thinking of the songbird with its twenty-four variations of a note. Munt was the surname of the man who took her in four months before my birth.

Ram Munt, the man who sold me that first time – and through the next two years – wasn't my real da, and not even my step-father, for he and my mother had never married. He was, however, the only father I'd known, although I knew he never looked on me as his daughter. I was simply Frances's child, a burden, someone who needed to be fed.

Ram Munt had two favourite stories. The first was about his years aboard ship. He'd been little more than a boy, come alone to Liverpool from a small village in the north. Looking for a better life, he was caught by a press gang and hauled aboard ship for an eight-month voyage. Here he was introduced to sea life in the cruellest way. When the ship returned to Liverpool and dropped anchor he tried to run, but was caught by another press gang before he'd even left the docks, and sailed again, but by this time he was older and stronger and wouldn't be bullied. By the time his second voyage was over the sea was in his blood, and he worked on board until he had been injured too often by rolling barrels, the cruel, swinging hooks, the sudden mishaps on slippery decks, and there were younger, stronger, more agile men than he to be taken on. After that he was hired as a spinner at the rope-walk near Williamson Square, his thick, damaged fingers still able to wind the hemp fibres deftly together, and walk them down to the end of the room to wrap them round the reel, repeating the process all day. He retained his coarse shipboard language and his back bore the scars of many lashings; his hands smelt of pine tar from dipping the ropes to make them stronger.

His other story was about how he'd come to take in my mother, and he told it more often than his sailing tales, usually late on a Saturday night after he'd spent all evening at the Flyhouse or Ma Fenny's.

He'd pull my mother and me out of our bed – she preferred to share a pallet with me, although Ram still called her to him a few times a week – and make us sit at the table and listen while he recounted his tale of heroism, of how he'd found my mother one wet spring night. With a bully's thrust of his chest he'd tell us about how he'd discovered her, drenched to the skin and wandering in the rain without a penny to her name.

Mother kept her head lowered as he told his story. She was always exhausted after her fourteen-hour days at the sewing press in the Pinnock Room at the bookbinder's, surrounded by piles of schoolbooks waiting to be covered: Goldsmith's *England*, Mangnall's *Questions*, Carpenter's *Spelling* and, of course, the towering stacks of Pinnock's *Catechisms*.

'I was never one to turn away a maid in distress,' Ram would go on. 'I took her in, didn't I? Took her in and gave her a meal and a fire to warm herself. She might have been

11

proud at one point, aye, but it didn't take long to persuade her that my roof and my bed were a damn sight better than what waited for her out in the streets.'

Sometimes he changed the details; in one version he stopped her as she was about to throw herself off the miasmal bank of the Mersey into the cold grey water. In another he fought off a band of longshoremen who were trying to force themselves on her in the shadow of the old grave dock, where the ships of the slave trade had once been repaired.

'In due time I even let her use my name, so she didn't have to carry the shame of a bastard child,' he'd go on, looking into my face. 'This is where you come from,' he'd usually add at this point, glaring at me now as if I were about to argue, 'and don't you forget it. No matter what fancy tales your mother puts into your head, you were born and raised on Back Phoebe Anne Street. You've the smell of the Mersey in your nostrils, and you've been marked by the fish. There can be no mistake about the origins of one what bears the mark of the fish. You're the daughter of a sailor, any fool can see.'

He was referring to the birthmark on the soft skin on the underside of my forearm, just above my wrist: a small, slightly raised port-wine stain in an elongated oval with two small projections at one end. It did have the shape of a tailed fish, I had to admit, but I didn't believe it had anything to do with the blood that coursed through me.

While the man I then called Da ranted this tedious old story I sat, like my mother, impassive, but only because she kept her cool thin hand on my arm, her broken thumbnail, rimmed with ink, absently stroking my birthmark. It was so much harder for me to sit quietly than it was for her, and I don't believe it had anything to do with my age. I saw then, young as I was, that she had nothing left in her to stand up to him or anyone; she accepted Ram Munt and his rude manners in a way I couldn't understand. I had burned with shame for her and with hatred for him for as long as I could remember.

While I struggled with the rage that made my breath quicken, my mother's face showed nothing as she listened to Ram's chants. Had she always been so accepting, so beaten? Occasionally she tried to elicit pity for him, telling me what damage had been done to him as a boy forced aboard those ships. 'He was beaten daily, and used for the men's pleasure whenever they felt the need,' she'd said. 'It hardened him. Try to think of what he might have been like as a boy, as a child called Ramsey,' she said once. But I couldn't. Nothing would make me lose my hatred of him for how he treated her.

After he'd stumbled to bed, when his weekly tirade was done, I'd put my arms round my mother. 'Never mind him,' I'd whisper. 'Tell me about Rodney Street again.' I knew this had been her one shining moment; it was her only story. Her mouth would turn up in a faint smile, and she'd tell me the beloved tale, one more time, about her job as a lady's maid when she came to Liverpool from Edinburgh, and her liaison with a fine young man who'd spent one rainy December in the grand Georgian home on Rodney Street. Mother said she was sure he was of noble blood: so fine were his features, his back so straight and hands so gentle, his manners and way of speaking enough to make her weep just remembering them. His name, she said, was for her only to know, and it would do me no good to have knowledge of it. When his visit was over and he'd had to leave Liverpool, he promised he'd be back for her by Candlemas or, at the latest, the end of March, Lady Day. He had plans to visit America in May, and he was going to take my mother with him. To America, she said.

Here my mother's face would glow softly from within, and she would sit quietly, remembering. But the story had no further happiness. The fine young man didn't come back to Rodney Street, and eventually it was discovered what Frances Gow had been up to. She was unceremoniously dismissed, in shame, without a character to ensure her another job, and it was three weeks after this, when she was destitute and desperate, that Ram Munt had offered her shelter.

'I really had no choice, Linny, none at all,' was the way she always finished. 'I tried to find him – your father. I went back to the house on Rodney Street so many times and stood, hidden in shadows across the street, in case he might come again. He'd have had no way to find me, after all. After you were born, I had a chance to talk to the girls in the kitchen, but they swore they'd never seen him again. What else could I do, Linny? He never knew about you. If he had, he'd have married me, I know,' my mother said, 'for he really and truly loved me. There seemed no other way for me, so I did what I had to do.' Here she'd look at Da where he lay sprawled, face down across the bed, his snoring a steady, muffled drone.

Every few months she'd get down the carved fruitwood box she kept hidden in the back of the dresser. It contained a small round mirror backed with ormolu, the Wordsworth book that contained 'The Green Linnet' – the poem about my name – and a heart-shaped pendant of warm gold. Upon its surface, designed with the tiniest seed pearls, was a bird – my mother told me she thought of it as a linnet. In its beak was a branch of miniature green stones that Mother said were emeralds. Ram Munt said they were glass.

'He gave me these things, your father did. The mirror, he said, because he loved to look at my face. The book, because he loved to hear my voice as I read aloud. And the pendant, he told me, was his heart to mine,' she'd say, rubbing her fingers over the softly glowing surface. 'It will be yours one day, Linny. To remember that you may have the smell of the Mersey in your nostrils, but it doesn't run through your blood.'

I always nodded and smiled. I listened to that story, over and over, right until the day my mother died, quickly and soundlessly, taken by a rapid fever that sucked her already thin body of life. I was well past ten, and had worked alongside her at the bookbinder's since I'd turned six. I had started as a gatherer, collecting the massive piles of sheets sent from the printer and running them to where the folders sat at wide tables. Once they had flattened the foldings of each sheet with a small ivory or bone knife, the sheets were collated and taken to the sewers. My mother had worked the sewing press, joining the groups of sheets with a curious kettle stitch. She could sew two or three thousand sheets a day. Just before she died I had moved up to a folder, and owned my own bone-handled knife. If all went as planned I would become a sewer when I reached fourteen.

Every Sunday, for the first year after her death, I visited her simple grave in the low-lying area of the cemetery of what was known as the Sailors' Church – for the Mersey flowed right past it at the bottom of Chapel Street. Of course, it was really Our Lady and St Nicholas Parish Church. I would stay there for some time, hidden amid the damp, nettle-fringed headstones and poorer crosses, my fingers tracing the letters of her name – Frances Gow – carved with shallow strokes into the plain wooden cross. I always thought of how Da wouldn't pay to have the bells rung as she was buried, so there was only a sad pauper's funeral for her, with some of the other sewers from the bookbindery and a few of our neighbours to stand in the cemetery, and not even a cup of tea for them afterwards.

My mother had deserved more than that, and I hated Da anew, each Sunday, with the memories of how he hadn't treated her properly even in death.

On one of these visits, on an afternoon dark with rain, a great black bird watched me from a foot away, its cruel beak jabbing the thin grass. I saw its orange, unblinking eye, and shivered. As it rose into the air, with a snapping of wings like wet sheets being shaken, I decided I would try to find my father. A child's dream, surely, but often it is the dream that becomes reality, and necessary for hope. I set off further north than I had ever been in the city, up to Mount Pleasant and, by asking numerous times, eventually found Rodney Street.

It was a long way from Back Phoebe Anne Street but after that, if the weather was clear, I would often go there on Sunday to walk up and down the most prestigious street in Liverpool, looking at the Georgian homes with their upper balconies of fine wrought iron. I saw girls I knew to be my age, but how different they looked. Back on Vauxhall Road I looked like every other girl with my too-short, patched, stained work dress, my scuffed boots, my ragged shawl. The girls here wore beautiful dresses and velvet capes. Their stockings were clean and undarned; their shoes gleamed, sometimes with silver buckles. Their hair was tied up with satin ribbons, their skin unmarked, their eyes clear as they gazed right through me. I was nothing, a poor girl from down near the docks. No one spoke to me, except one stout matron who pushed past me on the street as I stood looking at one of the fine houses. 'Be on your way, girl,' she huffed. 'This is a respectable street. We don't need your kind here.'

I ignored her. I didn't care what she or any of the other people in Mount Pleasant thought of me. I studied each man I saw carefully, whether he was walking along the street or riding by on horseback or, if he was visible, through the windows of the polished broughams or perched on the seat of a high-wheeled phaeton, looking for the face I saw in my head, one that had golden-flecked eyes shaped like mine, that had my own fair hair.

I knew what he would look like, for I'd made him as real as my mother's story.

And at the end of each of those fruitless Sunday afternoons, I'd make my way back towards the lower end of the city. As the houses grew smaller and closer together, became miserable, squalid dwellings, I felt the pinch of my own life. The feeling was true and alive as the pain in my heels, rubbed raw with boots from the pawnshop grown too small.

Surely my mother had been a lady's maid: didn't she know how to read and write, and wasn't her voice gentle, her speech cultured – despite the soft Scottish brogue? And she knew the proper way to do things: she insisted that I sit up straight at our simple meals, a clean rag spread on my lap, and instructed me on how to hold my knife and fork, to cut small bites, chew slowly and discuss pleasant subjects at table. She helped me with my reading, and even spent a few pennies from each of her pay packets buying spoiled Pinnock's *Catechisms* from the office of the bookbinder's. She could purchase one of the little sixpenny schoolbooks for a ha'penny if it were flawed – the pages put in upside down or the cover marred. This was our secret. Da would never have allowed her to spend money on anything as unimportant as a book. I kept them hidden under my pallet, and most evenings, when my mother was asleep and Da out, I'd read until I too fell asleep.

My favourites were the dozens of volumes in the *Friend to Youth* series. There were questions and answers on subjects ranging from history to business, geography and poetry. Of course I couldn't be choosy: once, the only new one I had to study for a whole two weeks was *A Catechism of Mechanics: An Easy Introduction to the Knowledge of Machinery.*

My mother also taught me to look people in the face when I spoke to them, and she always corrected my speech: if I spoke like the people on the street and in the factories I would never rise above them, 'and you must get yourself away from here, Linny. There's more than this, more than the street and the work. I can't bear to think of you never knowing anything else.'

Da laughed at her, asked her what she meant about rising above anyone. What did she think she was getting me ready to be? Did she imagine I'd become a lady's maid, as she claimed she had been? 'She'll stay at the bookbinder's with you, a well-respected trade, then find someone to marry her, get her away from my table. Let someone else worry about feeding her.'

But my mother never stopped planning. It was as if she were determined not to let me forget she hadn't come from this place, and that I must leave it by any means. Dreams of a better life for me seemed to bring her the only moments of happiness she knew.

'She could be a governess, if given a chance. She has a fine way with reading. She would be perfect as a governess,' she'd said, one night at supper. 'If only she had the proper clothing, she might, through the Church, be sent to the right people. It need never be mentioned she's from off Vauxhall Road. She's perfected my voice. It could be said she's come down from Scotland. Her background need never . . .' Her voice trailed off. She had a dull sheen on her brow, and more than once, during the meal of bacon crumbled into boiled potatoes – which she didn't touch – she put her hand to it, then pulled away her fingers and looked at them as if in surprise. 'If she were but given a chance,' she repeated, the unusual flush on her cheeks growing deeper, 'my girl would do me proud.' There was a dangerous spark in her eyes and, interpreting it as boldness, I matched it with my own, speaking out as I never had before Ram Munt.

'I know what I'd like to do,' I said, and my mother turned to me, her mouth in a strained smile, expecting, I'm sure, my agreement with her, even though we both knew that a girl from the low end of Liverpool could never pass as a governess. 'I'd like to decorate the books at the printer's.'

The odd smile faded. 'What do you mean?'

'I'd like to be finisher, like Mr Broughton in the Extra Finishing shop.'

Her face darkened. 'When have you been up to the third floor?'

'The overlooker sometimes sends me up with messages for Mr Broughton. There are beautiful things there.' I smiled, remembering. 'I've seen him laying a book with gold, then stamping it with heated tools. There were ever so many tools – rounds, scrolls, diamonds, and all the letters. And Mr Broughton can make whatever design comes out of his head, pressing those hot shapes and letters. Oh, think of it! To create such a wondrous—' I stopped, seeing disappointment on my mother's face, hearing Ram's snicker.

'But that's not a job for a lady,' my mother said. 'No woman could ever do that. You know it's only boys brought in as apprentices to the finishers. And of course only men are clever enough for the Extra Finishing. Whatever put that idea into your head?'

I couldn't admit that Mr Broughton had let me experiment more than once in those few moments of stolen time. I had washed vellum, and coloured initials, even stamped gold tooling into a ruined piece of calfskin. He seemed to enjoy our clandestine activities – quickly showing me this and that, glancing over his shoulder all the while – as much as I did.

Da's snicker had turned to laughter, and he enjoyed himself for a full minute before telling me, as he wiped at his eyes, to do what I did best – fill his bowl with more potatoes – and never again to mention such ridiculous ideas as governesses or finishers.

Later that evening the fever that had toyed with my mother for the last twenty-four hours took a firm grip.

And less than a year after she died, Da brought home Mr Jacobs.

CHAPTER THREE

AFTER THE VISIT from Mr Jacobs, Ram kept me busy. I never again called him Da; I rarely addressed him at all, but if I did, it was by his name. Ram couldn't bring customers to our second-floor room regularly, afraid that if the landlord got wind of what was going on we'd be thrown out or, worse, he would demand a percentage. Instead, after I came home from my ten hours at the bookbinder's, he'd make me change out of my ragged work dress into a clean, childish frock and pinafore he'd bought from the pawnshop. I'd plait my hair, put on the straw bonnet with blue ribbons he'd also provided, and then he'd take me to the customers.

I never knew how he found the men. They were always old, or so they seemed. And they were men who liked what I was then: a small, delicate child, who appeared at the doors of their hotels, lodging- or boarding-houses, my hand held by the short, broad, loutish fellow. There were all manner of men. Most had come to Liverpool on business from London or Manchester, from Scotland or as far away as Ireland. Some were rough, and some were kind. Some took ages to finish, and others were off almost as soon as I lifted my skirt and sat on the edge of the bed or leaned over a table.

While I might visit two unknown men on some nights, an hour each – Ram was always waiting to collect the money when their time was up – there were regulars who paid for the whole evening. I had a Monday, a Wednesday and a Thursday. These three became quite dear to me, really, because they were the kind ones: they would rather see a child smile than cry. With them I knew what to expect, and from them I learned about myself.

Monday insisted on calling me Ophelia, and always wept after his lacklustre performance; he gave me bags of sweets and stroked my hair. He told me about Shakespeare, quoting from his plays and sonnets. Monday said he was a playwright too, like Mr Shakespeare, but could get no recognition. He said that when he'd grown obsessed with the need to have his work taken seriously, his wife had left him, taking their young daughter. At this his tears turned to deep sobs, and he would shake his head, gazing at me in the rumpled bedding as if it grieved him to have me near him, yet he couldn't keep away. 'My innocent,' he'd say, wringing his hands, 'so innocent, so pure, but one born of a need to understand life's mysteries. You have the desire to make sense of all that's around you, don't you?'

Wednesday wanted to watch me bathe, and always had a copper hip bath filled with warm water waiting for me in front of a cheery fire. After I'd washed all over, soaping my hair with sweet-smelling lavender soap (he brought a new bar each week, and let me take home the used one), he'd dry me with thick soft towels, and carry me to the bed. He found his pleasure in looking at me and cautiously touching my skin; whether he was unable to perform or ashamed of something beneath the clothing he kept tightly buttoned I never knew, but he didn't mind if I fell asleep. And I usually did: it was difficult to stay awake after a full day of work, followed by the warm bath and soft bed, the harmless caresses from hands smooth as kid leather. Wednesday was difficult to leave when I heard Ram's knock.

But Thursday was my favourite. He loved to feed me, and after our time in his room, in the beautifully appointed hotel off Lord Street, he always took me downstairs to the dining room, shimmering with candelabra, silver salvers and platters polished bright as mirrors. The walls, with their elegant muted wallpaper of blue and silver, were lined with oil paintings. There were tall windows steamed by the warmth from the generous fires and bodies heated by rich food, plentiful drink and, I suspect, thoughts of the upstairs rooms.

During our time in the hotel I was instructed to call Thursday Uncle Horace. Did the people at the elaborate front desk, or those carrying clean linen and trays of food through the wide halls, or those serving us in the dining room really believe me to be his niece? Or did they turn a blind eye to the truth, accepting the lie with polite smiles, subservient bows or curtsies, willingly taking the coins Uncle Horace pressed into every hand?

Uncle Horace was huge of girth. Although he was quickly and easily fulfilled upstairs, he seemed unable to satisfy his insatiable appetite at the table. He ordered mounds of food, with special delicacies for me – capons with sizzling golden skin, turbot with lobster sauce, potatoes mashed and swirled into golden-brown domes. He bought me sweet port too. I didn't care for the taste, but loved its beautiful deep ruby colour, which reflected off the fire. Uncle Horace insisted on a table by the fireplace.

It was there, in the gracious high-ceilinged dining room, which smelt of roasted meat and caramelized sugar, hair pomade and eau-de-toilette, wealth and confidence, that I watched and learned all I could of how men and women of his class moved about. I studied the ladies at other tables, saw how they dressed, how carefully they dabbed at their lips with their heavy damask napkins, heard how their laughter chimed like music. I memorized their language and articulation, which, I now knew, was far finer than my mother's had been. It was easy, a game to play, as I pretended to listen to Uncle Horace talk about his business, wealth and opulent home in the city of Dublin. I heard about his childhood in rural Ireland, and how he would sneak out with the stableboys on Sunday afternoon for games of hurling. He told me how he'd learned to eat to take away the emptiness when his parents left him with the house staff, sometimes for a year at a time, as they travelled the world. He often brought me a soft spicy cake filled with currants — barmbrack, he called it — his own childhood favourite. It was baked by the ancient cook of his boyhood, still alive and with him in his house in Dublin. The cake would be wrapped in one of his fine linen handkerchiefs, and he'd urge me to take it home.

'Are you really as hungry as you appear?' he'd asked me once, as I quickly but neatly sucked an oyster from its shell. 'Or do you eat because you know it pleases me?'

I'd touched my mouth with my napkin, then put my hands into my lap, choosing my words carefully before I spoke. Had he never known hunger? Had he any idea that before I was brought to him I'd spent a full day with my folding knife, my hands cramping so badly that it felt as if pebbles had lodged under the skin of my palms? That I had fifteen minutes at midday to visit the privy and bolt down the bread and cheese I'd brought with me? 'I am as I appear, I assure you, Uncle Horace,' I said, 'for how else could I be anything but hungry with such food put before me, and in the presence of such company?'

He'd studied me then. 'You're undernourished, that I see. But there's another kind of hunger, Linny, a hunger for learning, for understanding, that I also see on your face.'

I raised my glass to my lips, let the crimson liquid touch them, then I returned it to the snowy tablecloth. 'That may well be,' I answered. 'Perhaps I have a hunger of the soul itself.' I was repeating, word for word, what the anaemic young man at the table behind me had said only moments earlier. I had no idea what it meant, although of course I knew what a soul was: I still faithfully attended the Sunday services at Our Lady and St Nicholas.

He laughed then, his hair damp with sweat, pomade melting down his neck, his round face reddened by the port and brandy he'd drunk. 'You're a clever little minx, I'll give you that. Come, now, give me your best Irish voice, for I'm feeling a little homesick tonight.'

I recited a poem, then told him some silly social snippet I'd overheard, mimicking his own Irish cadence, for it came easily to me.

He nodded, smiling broadly, shaking his head as if he were amazed. 'Aren't you a wonder, then? Pure Dublin, it is. It's as if you've spent all your young days taking tea on Grafton Street.' And then he summoned the waiter and ordered a dish of pears with cream for me, and brandy pudding with hard sauce for himself, and there was no more tedious talk.

I missed spending time with my old friends. At the bookbinder's I had two whom I'd worked alongside – Minnie and Jane. Minnie was a year older than me, Jane a year younger. We had sometimes left the bookbindery together, four hours before our mothers were allowed to depart, and had lingered along the streets on the way home, talking – or perhaps pretending – about the fancy hats and beaded reticules we would some day own, or what we imagined to be the finest meal in the world. Sometimes we held hands, as true friends do.

But there was no time for friendship now: I had to rush straight home from work to prepare our plain dinner, eat and change before Ram took me out. Minnie and Jane accepted my story that I had to feed my step-father, or face the back of his hand, and they still smiled at me often, but I felt the loss of their companionship keenly.

I missed the visits to the neighbours too. Some evenings, when the weather was mild, Mother and I had stood out in the court with other women and girls who lived in Back Phoebe Anne Street. I would stand beside Mother, who would usually work on a bit of darning or sewing. Other women held or nursed their babies, or caught up on their mending, like Mother, and we all watched the younger children play their skipping, hopping and stone-tossing games. I listened to the local gossip – who had been seen with whom, what arguments had been heard through the thin walls, whose baby was sickening and whose old gran was dying. Although the other women were coarser than Mother, most with missing teeth, their cheeks or bottom lips stuffed with chewing tobacco, it had still been pleasant to lean against the walls and spend a companionable half-hour before bed.

Now I'd pass those women with my head down, following Ram, sure they knew what I was off to do. I often heard whispers and mutterings, and knew I was now a regular source of gossip, but no one ever stepped forward to speak to me or ask how I was. They knew their place, these women.

But I believe it was Mae Scat, from the cellar across the lane, who might have told the Ladies of Righteous Conduct about me. Mae had always had a soft spot for my mother and, more than once, had put an arm round her shoulders and given her a warm shake when Mother had a thick lip or a swollen eye. Six months before my mother died, Mae Scat had buried her third husband; she had six living children, and swore she'd never let another man touch her. She always said she was blessed with a fortune in having only sons, and the three oldest, strapping lads all of them, brought home the bread and coffee on which they all seemed to exist.

From the corner of my eye I had seen Mae Scat watching me as I hurried down the lane after Ram. Her thick bare arms — she never wore a shawl, no matter how cold the weather — were crossed over her low bosom as her head turned in my direction. Once I heard her exclaim, to no one in particular, 'It ain't right. It just ain't right.'

So when the well-dressed woman knocked on our door one warm autumn evening I assumed that Mae Scat had sent her.

'Are you Linny Munt?'

I nodded, and my heart began a staccato beat. No one had ever come to our door asking for me before. I was still dressed in my stained clothes from the bookbindery; we'd just finished eating and I hadn't yet changed for my evening work.

'I'm Mrs Poll, from the Society of Ladies of Righteous Conduct. Could I please come in and have a word?' she said, her narrow shoulders held stiffly in the dim, smelly passage outside our door.

I hadn't opened the door any wider, and now looked over my shoulder at Ram to take my cue from him. Sitting on the settle, he stared into the fire as if he hadn't heard the knock or the low voice.

When he made no move to object, I swung open the door, stepped back, and the woman entered. She was dressed severely, with a navy bonnet and matching poplin spencer over a lighter blue cambric dress; but although the short jacket and dress were plainly cut, they were of superior quality. Instead of a reticule, she carried a large grey cloth bag with a drawstring.

'How are you this evening, Linny?' she asked.

I nodded, twisting my hands in my skirt. I was afraid suddenly, although her voice was kind. She wore navy cotton gloves, and I thought, for no apparent reason, that she was wise not to wear white ones when she came down to Vauxhall Road.

'How old are you? I would guess ten.'

'I've just passed twelve,' I said. My voice came out as little more than a whisper. I don't know what I was afraid of: perhaps I imagined she would carry me off to the children's section of the workhouse. I had heard terrible stories of the workhouse.

She looked surprised. 'Twelve. Well, I've just come to meet you, and to bring you some information. Is this your father, then?' She looked behind me, at Ram, who still hadn't moved or spoken.

I nodded again.

'Mr Munt, is it not?' she called.

Ram answered with a grunt, then rose from the settle. 'What's your business with us, since you know our names? Who has set you on to us?'

'I assure you, Mr Munt, that I am not here to make trouble. I'm checking on the well-being of the children in the area.'

I let out my breath slowly. It didn't appear that she was here to take me away.

'Well-being? What do you mean by that?' Ram demanded.

Mrs Poll licked her lips. I saw that her temples were damp. 'Making sure they are in good health. Inviting them to partake in our Children's Hour on Sunday afternoons at the church. I have a tract you might enjoy looking at,' she said, reached into the cloth bag and pulled out a folded paper. 'There are some lovely drawings.'

As I reached for the pamphlet she looked at my bruised wrist: one of my customers had handled it roughly a few days earlier. 'How have you hurt yourself, dear?' she enquired, glancing at Ram.

I put my other hand over it. 'I – I don't remember.' But I looked up at her, wanting her to know that I couldn't tell her, that I dared not. That Ram would punish me if I spoke the truth.

'Is someone mistreating you?' she asked, although now she spoke to Ram, and not to me.

Yes, yes, I wanted to cry. *Look at me, Mrs Poll. Look at me and understand what Ram makes me do every night.*

Ram's voice went up a notch. 'She only gets wot she deserves if she don't get on to her chores quick enough. It's a father's duty to see his daughter brought up right, last time I looked.'

Mrs Poll nodded. Although colour now stained her cheeks, her voice remained firm and pleasant. 'Yes. It is a father's duty to bring his children up, to feed them and make sure they are clothed. And that no harm comes to them. I can assume, then, that you are carrying out your fatherly duties?'

'You're right,' Ram answered. 'I am. Not that it's your place to check on me. There's no such part of the law wot tells a parent how to treat his child. And the Church has no business interfering.'

I bent my head over the tract, skimming the words as Ram blustered. It held a verse of scripture, and announced Sunday afternoon classes for the children of the parish. 'All those who attend will be served a slice of bread with jam at the end of the lesson,' I read.

'And isn't that a pity, Mr Munt? That prevention of cruelty to children is a moot subject.'

'Have you finished, then? My girl here doesn't have time to dawdle. Give that back, now, Linny,' Ram told me.

As I handed the tract to her, I asked, 'There's bread and jam for all?'

Mrs Poll stepped closer. 'I see you're able to read, then, dear.'

'Oh, yes,' I told her. 'I've been reading for a long time.' *And do you hear how well I speak? Can't you see I shouldn't be here, Mrs Poll? Can you take me home with you?* My thoughts were those of a young child who didn't understand life.

'Well, then.' Her voice held a note of surprise. 'Would you be interested in assisting in some of our Bible classes for younger children on Sunday afternoons? It's very simple, really. We read a passage to them, sing a verse or two of a hymn and talk about God's plan for good works and clean living.' She reached out with an unconscious gesture to tuck a stray lock of hair behind my ear, and I felt myself lean into her gloved hand. She kept her hand against the side of my

30

head for a moment, and I shut my eyes, remembering my mother's touch.

Yes, I would like that, I thought. I would like that so much. I opened my mouth to say the words, but Ram spoke before I could: 'She ain't got no time for that business,' he said. 'I allow her to get on to church of a Sunday morning, and say her prayers over her muvver's grave, but then she's to come on home.'

'It's only a hour, Mr Munt, and I'm sure Linny would enj—'

'As her father, I think I'm a better judge of how Linny should be spending her Sundays,' he said, standing. 'Come to think of it, I'm the only judge of how my daughter spends her time. That'll be all, now. And don't be expecting to see my girl at none of yer afternoons.'

Mrs Poll moved towards the door at the obvious signal that the visit – if it could be called such – was officially over. 'Well, then, I will bid you a pleasant afternoon, Linny. I'll look forward to seeing you at least in church next Sunday.'

I nodded, sinking my teeth into my bottom lip, wanting to run to her, to put my ink-stained hands on her gloved ones and hold on tightly. I knew my life was here, but I wanted to teach Bible stories to little children, and spend an afternoon with ladies who wore gloves, and have a piece of bread and jam at the end of it all. I wanted . . . I wanted so much.

But I was silent, rooted to the spot.

'And good day to you as well, Mr Munt,' Mrs Poll said then, her pointed chin rising. She opened the door and went out. I heard the swish of her hem on each step as she walked downstairs, and wished with all my heart that I could follow her.

31

I knew I would never go to the Bible classes. I knew that neither the Church, nor Mrs Poll nor any of the other Ladies of Righteous Conduct could help me. Even if I'd had the courage to tell her about my life, what Ram had said was true. Nobody had any business telling a parent how to treat his child, or interfering. Nobody.

I turned thirteen and knew I had grown hard. I knew my mother would not be pleased – not because I was a whore, for that was not my fault, but because of my evil ways and my even more evil thoughts.

My daily reflections revolved, as I worked at my folding table, around ways to kill Ram Munt. They were varied and usually torturous, and invariably involved my bone-handled knife. I also planned the ways I could kill each of the men my father brought me to. (Except the weeping, grieving Monday and Thursday's kindly Uncle Horace. By that time fastidious Wednesday no longer came to Liverpool on business; I missed my weekly bath, and had to return to washing myself with tepid water in our dented basin.)

But the others! To me they were all the same: no matter what bearing they affected, each had the identical fascination of ensuring that the worm at the centre of his body grew to a snake, then found a home in which it thrashed and jerked until it died, with a final twitch and dribble. Immediately I entered a room where one of these men waited, I would cast my eye over the furnishings. I looked for the heavy flower urn that would cave in a skull, or the sharp silver knife on the dinner tray that would slice the jugular with one stroke. Of course, these were only fancy pictures that gave me pleasure, although I had had to defend myself from my customers.

I'd had to resort to kicking and biting to escape those who used force to contort my body into positions it was not made for. Once, I had grabbed a heavy silver paperweight and knocked it into the temple of a crippled gentleman bent on cutting the palm of my hand so he could taste my blood while receiving pleasure from me. The most frightening incident involved a man who wore a hooded cloak and smelt overpoweringly of horse liniment. When he showed me the tools he carried in a leather satchel, and I understood the depravity he expected of me, I tried to leave in spite of his grip on my arm. As it tightened, so did my resolve not to be subjected to the humiliation he had in store for me. I grabbed the poker from the fireplace and stabbed it into his belly. Although I had been forced to use my left hand, it was enough: he dropped my arm, and I escaped.

The beatings I took from Ram when I came away empty-handed were slight in comparison to what I'd saved myself from.

But in spite of an unnerving evening here and there, the majority of the men were simple and unimaginative, wanting the most basic release from what they saw as their tortured state and, like their desires, my actions were uncomplicated and mindless.

To relieve the boredom and unpleasantness of these evening visits I stole any small thing I could find that wouldn't be immediately missed — a silver buttonhook, a tiny brass compass, a teacup, small jug or miniature trinket tray in Liverpool's favourite Fazackerley colours of gaudy red, blue, yellow and green in designs of Chinese lattice fences and flowers. It was easy to slip something into a fold of my shawl, or boot, or even under my bonnet when the customer was busy with his clothing after my performance.

I always sold the objects the next day at the crowded market on Great Charlotte Street on my way home from the bookbindery. With a few of the coins I bought boiled sweets and cakes, which I ate before I got home so Ram wouldn't find me out. I didn't want him to know I was stealing from customers for two reasons: first, because he would take the money from the sale of the items; and second, which was more meaningful, because for him to know of it would rob me of that small potency. Stealing from the men who took from me made me feel powerful in an adult way: I was not only deceiving the customers, but also Ram Munt. The objects themselves were of no importance to me: this new power was the treasure.

After buying my sweets I went straight to Armbruster's Used Goods. The place seemed a graveyard – all these things had once belonged to sailors and grandparents, mothers, fathers and their children. There was a nautical section of wood and brass compasses, quadrants, spyglasses and ships' bowls of blue and white china, each painted with its ship's picture. There were dusty shelves of iron coffee mills and discoloured brass warming-pans, bellows, printed tiles carefully prised from fireplaces, and one chipped crude Delftware bowl, with 'Success to ye Prussian Hero, 1769' in poorly executed black letters. There were stale-smelling blankets and stained Welsh flannel, striped and corded black silk handkerchiefs, scraps of faded drugget and carpets with a worn track down the centre.

And the glass! Row after row of black bottles, emptied of their whisky or medicine, waited alongside rummers on short thick stems and decanters of lead crystal with a bluish hue. There was no end of them, each piece more unusual than the next. I pictured the boys from the glassworks, with their weeping eyes, damaged by the fumes from the alkali mixing with lime and sand; here were some of their efforts, which sometimes blinded them, being sold for pennies in this damp shop. The place and all its contents carried the odour of mould and despair.

I passed all these sad remnants of other lives and went straight to the books. On bowed shelves were hodge-podge stacks of books with damp-warped, foxed pages, their spines darkened, covers soiled and bubbled. They sold for a penny or two each; sometimes an entire collection by one author was marked 5*d*. I bought book after book, hid them in my bed, and when I had read them either resold or exchanged them for others. Unlike the sweets, which were a treat, the books were a necessity.

Before my mother died I read from my Pinnock's *Catechism* at night for the pleasure of learning. But since Mr Jacobs and the beginning of that life, no matter how exhausted my body was when I fell into my own bed afterwards, my mind felt as if it were racing too quickly. Ugliness crammed my brain to the point, some nights, when I thought the top of my head might burst open and the evil smells and tastes flood over my pillow in a rush of foul liquid. Reading was like a quiet balm spread by a soft hand on the inside of my skull, and I depended on it to bring me back to myself before I could fall asleep. I had to wait until the snoring from across the room assured me I wouldn't be found out, and then I would read by a rushlight until my mind was ready to drift. I read all manner of books – from Defoe and Swift to Ann Radcliffe and Elizabeth Hamilton, from adventure to romance and memoir.

The thefts – and the extras they allowed me – the delicious plans for torture and murder, my charades as a young lady in luxurious bedrooms and lavish dining rooms were devised, and served, to make life bearable.

I thought, every day, of my mother and her dreams for me. I thought of what she would think of me if she could see me now: whore, liar, thief. And I swore to her every Sunday, my hand on her listing cross at Our Lady and St Nicholas, that I would be more than this. That I would be more than the Linny Munt I was now. That I would be more than the simpering young women who emerged from carriages outside the theatres, wrapped in their furs and feathers. I would be Linny Gow and make her proud. I swore it.

CHAPTER FOUR

The LAST JOB I did for Ram Munt was six months after my thirteenth birthday. It was a cold wet February evening when he came home grinning, with something wrapped in brown paper and tied with string tucked under his arm.

'It's a top-paying job I've found for you, my girl,' he said, tossing the package on to an empty chair and motioning with his head towards the cauldron hanging over the fire. I filled his bowl with the turnip and carrot soup I'd made. I had stirred into it a palmful of mouse droppings I'd gathered from behind the settle. It pleased me to add a special ingredient to Ram's food each night after I'd eaten my share. Some nights it was a trickle from the chamber pot before I emptied it into the gutter that ran down the middle of our court; sometimes it was a smear of pigeon mess I'd scraped off the window-ledge; at others it was crushed cockroaches.

That night I was more weary than usual. One of the gatherers had fainted and I had had to do her job for the hour before she recovered, running up and down the stairs with armfuls of paper, and was still expected to have finished all my folding by shutting time. All I wanted to do was lie on my pallet, read for ten minutes, then close my eyes.

The idea of the evening's work was overwhelming. I knew there was no point in telling Ram I was too tired. He would never hit me in the face – a purple eye and swollen lip were not what my customers wanted to see. Instead, he hurt me in other ways, small, sly ways – his knuckles grinding a deep bruise into the small of my back or holding a match against the underside of my arm long enough to cause a blister; nothing that would cost me a customer, just enough to make me miserable.

'We're moving up in the world, yes, moving up,' he said, ignoring the spoon I set on the table and picking up the bowl. 'You'll be working with some of Liverpool's finest ladies.' His damp greatcoat steamed by the fire, sending up the smell of wet dog.

I stood across from him. 'Ladies?' My voice held the faintest note of contempt.

Ram slurped noisily, then hooked a chunk of carrot out of the bowl with his fingers. 'It's a party, put on for some gentlemen visiting. I heard, down at the Flyhouse, they was looking for a number of the best Liverpool had to offer, not the sailors' slags or even them from Paradise Street. "Oh," I says, "I have exactly what you're looking for," I tells 'em. "Just a girl and clean as a whistle, hair like silk." "She has to be yellow-haired," the fellow says, "only one with the palest of hair will do for the special job I have in mind." "Well, you can't get much fairer than my girl," I tells him. "And she'll do anything you please. She's a good girl, is my Linny," I tells the young gentleman what appears to be in charge. I told him that, Linny, that you'd do anything, and that's what he's expecting. So don't disappoint me. With what you'll make tonight we might start thinking about moving out of here into better lodgings.' He glanced around the spotless room, then shook the piece of carrot at me. 'If you do well, you'll be asked for again. This could be the beginning of a new life for us.' He winked then, popping the carrot into his mouth. 'Only the beginning,' he repeated, chewing, a piece of brilliant orange caught between his browning front teeth.

The package contained a green dress of Spitalfields silk with an *écru*-coloured frill. It was used, bought at the clothes market on Fox Street, and smelt faintly of cold sweat. Before I put it on I inspected the seams for fleas. It was last year's style: I had seen that none of the fashionable ladies on Lord Street wore this design any longer. But it clung softly, the fabric smooth against my skin. After I'd changed into it and stood before Ram, he nodded appreciatively. I had never before worn a dress with a low-cut bodice, and when I looked down and saw the new swell of my breasts, I had to stop myself putting up my hands to cover them.

'Brush out your hair. No plaits tonight. You have to look your best. Yes, tonight will be special.'

I did as I was told. Then, studying myself in the ormolu mirror from the fruitwood box, I took out the pendant and fastened the clasp round my neck. I admired how the gold shone against my skin, how the green stones complemented the green silk of the dress. But when I reached for my grey shawl, telling Ram I was ready, he took another look, then shook his head.

'Take off that cheap trinket,' he said, his eyes skittering from the pendant to my face and back to the pendant. 'It spoils the look.'

I closed my hand around it. It had reminded Ram of my mother. *Could he actually feel guilty about what he's forced me to become?* I returned the pendant to the fruitwood box, realizing, with a sudden sharp stab of what I knew to be my own guilt, that I should never have thought of wearing it. What a disgrace to my mother's memory, even to consider putting in on for what I'd be doing. I'll only wear it when I can feel proud of who I am, I told myself, and closed the lid of the fruitwood box with a firm click.

Ram had hired a cart, and we jerked along the streets, rising high above Liverpool's maze of lanes, alleys and courts that led up from the waterfront. Eventually I saw St Andrews, the Scottish kirk, and knew we were in Mount Pleasant. And then we were on the grand street where I had spent so many Sunday afternoons: Rodney Street. We stopped in front of one of the brightly lit Georgian houses, with a door wide enough to admit our whole cart, and Ram walked me to it, tucking my hand into his arm as if he were a proud father escorting his daughter down the aisle. I knew the exteriors of these houses well from my Sunday visits, but had never expected to step inside one.

The door was opened by a butler – a middle-aged man in velvet breeches – whose closed face didn't ask any questions. With no flicker of emotion he stepped aside, and as I pulled my arm from Ram's and hesitantly crossed the threshold, he closed the door in Ram's face. But Ram pushed it open before the latch could engage.

'I'm to be paid before I leave,' he said. 'Payment upon delivery. That was the agreement struck between me and the gentleman.'

I lowered my head and studied the tips of my shoes, brown and scuffed, incongruous against the airiness of the green dress. I looked up to see that the butler too was staring at them, a giveaway that no fine dress could disguise.

'One moment,' he said, not bothering to disguise his distaste, although his face remained impassive. He attempted to close the door again, but this time Ram pushed harder and stepped into the foyer beside me.

'I'll wait here,' he said.

The butler turned, back stiff, went up the stairs and disappeared. We stood silently under a chandelier dancing with the light of at least thirty candles. A parlourmaid walked past, carrying an urn of dying flowers – they were tall and red, spiky, with sharp-looking greenery. I knew they must be something exotic, brought up from London – I'd never seen the like of them before.

The parlourmaid glanced at us; her face, like the butler's, showed no interest or curiosity. From somewhere in the house there was a steady rhythmic beat.

Within moments the butler reappeared. He descended the stairs at a studied pace.

Ram couldn't wait to feel the coins in his hand. He hurried over to the butler, meeting him at the bottom step. The man handed him something; from my position behind him I couldn't see what it was. But Ram glanced at it, and then he was brushing past me, eyes bright, a tight smile curving his lips. Without a goodbye he left.

I turned to the butler.

He looked at me – from my unpinned hair to the hated boots – and as he held out his hand for my wrap I saw something shift in him, almost imperceptibly, some softening that disturbed me more than his imperious manner had. He took my shawl gingerly, between thumb and first finger as if it were lousy. The parlourmaid reappeared and took it from him, her nose tilted to indicate how far beneath her I was.

41

The butler started up the stairs, and I followed. I'd never been in so magnificent a house. I put my hand on the polished banister, enjoying its feel.

By the time we reached the top of the staircase, the muffled, rhythmic sound I had heard from the foyer was louder and more distinct. I could also hear an underlying sound, like someone singing. The beat stopped, and the voice called, then laughed. The laughter verged on hysteria. The butler stopped in front of a set of double doors painted a gleaming vermilion. A brass handle in the shape of intertwined snakes graced each door. He nodded once at them, then left.

Unsure of what was expected, I knocked. I knocked again, and then put my hand on one of the snakes. It was warm to the touch, as if responding to the pulse on the other side of the door. Before I had a chance to turn it, the door was opened from the other side. Hot air, scented with perfume and smoke – smoke that was dark and sweet – rushed out at me. I stepped back.

'Oh, look,' cried the boy who had opened the door. 'Look, Pompey. It's a baby girl. And I believe she's the one.' I took him to be a few years older than me, although it was difficult to be sure.

He had brightly painted lips and spots of rouge on his cheeks, and on his head was a tiara of glass beads with a drooping ostrich feather. A gown of flowered, diaphanous material floated around him. He put his hands on my shoulders and drew me into the room. 'Do you see, Pompey?'

The gaslights on the walls were set low, creating flickering shadows. Large pieces of furniture filled every corner of the room: dressers and wardrobes, sofas and chairs sat like hulking dark animals. A very large man came out of one corner. As my eyes adjusted I saw that his skin was black, and that he wore only the smallest loincloth and a white turban. He held a drum under one arm, and as he walked in my direction, he beat it with his palm, a dull, solemn sound.

I looked at the boy.

'Don't be frightened, baby girl,' he said. His pupils were huge. He waved one hand at the black man, who immediately lowered the drum to cover his groin.

The boy laughed, and I recognized the note of hysteria I had heard moments earlier. I had assumed then that it was the voice of a woman.

An unfamiliar, nutty odour filled my nostrils, so strong now that, combined with the wavering shadows in the room, I was suddenly giddy. There was something wrong here, something unknown that frightened me.

'I'm Clancy,' the boy said. 'Now, come with me. We've been waiting.' He picked up my hand.

'I don't think—' I tried to pull away, but Clancy, so willowy and slight, tightened his grip with surprising strength, squeezing my fingers until they ached.

'But of *course* you mustn't think. Thinking is such a bore,' he said. 'You must only feel.' He gave a fierce tug, and I was jerked along. Following, I saw that he had nothing on under the gown. He led me along the periphery of the room; as we walked, stepping around ottomans and low tables, I was wondering how I could escape. It would seem that I could turn and run but for Clancy's iron grip on my hand. And for the fact that the black man – who must be Pompey – had started his sonorous drumming once more, and was now close on my heels.

'Now,' Clancy said, 'we're here.' He pulled aside a heavy brocade curtain. Behind it was another door, plain wood, a sharp contrast with the rest of the ornate room. There was a brass key in the lock. 'Go on. It's unlocked. He's waiting for you.'

'Who is he?' I asked, panic making me pull back again.

But Clancy gave me a look that was suddenly intent, and the silly smile that had been on his lips from the moment I'd first seen him now fell away, replaced by something uncertain. His expression was eerily like the one I'd seen on the butler's face less than five minutes earlier.

I also realized he was much younger than I had thought; maybe he and I were the same age.

He turned the knob and pushed me through the open doorway.

Here the peculiar smell of the smoke was stronger still, and there was something else, another smell just under the sweetness. It was as if something was slowly, delicately rotting, taking its time, enjoying the journey. As the door behind me closed, the room fell into complete darkness.

'Hello?' I called. It was wrong, so wrong. I wanted nothing more than to flee.

'Come in, come in,' a voice answered. It was a soft, tremulous voice, marred by some affliction.

'Is there no light, sir?' I asked, even more fearful. The voice had not been reassuring. 'I can't see a thing.' I had entered so many rooms, had heard so many men's voices. But at least I had been able to see what was in front of me; although there had been too many unpleasant surprises to count, I had never had to stand in the dark, afraid of who or what might make itself known to me.

There was the long, slow sound of sucking, and I saw a tiny red glow of light from the bowl of a pipe. Then there was the sighing release of air and a rustle of movement. The sharp rasp of a flint was followed by a flare of light, and I saw a figure crouched in front of a marble fireplace. As the kindling caught and the fire grew, the figure moved away with a shuffling, uncoordinated gait, and sank, with a shallow sigh, into a deep winged chair, whose shadows hid his features.

'Now you must step into the light,' the man said, 'and we'll see if you're what I've been hoping for. It's so difficult to get what one asks for, these days. I've been quite disappointed in the selection here in Liverpool. Quite disappointed,' he repeated.

I walked to the fireplace and stood in front of it.

'Turn your head. I want to see your hair.'

I looked to the left, then to the right, feeling the heat of the fire behind me.

'All right, all right.' The man's voice had risen a tone, as if excited. *What's wrong with the way he speaks?* I wondered. 'Come here now. We'll have a lovely drink together, shall we?'

I went towards the chair. 'I'd rather not, sir. What is it you wish me to do?' I asked, my nose wrinkling at the sour odour, which grew stronger as I neared the chair. I'd heard all the usual requests: none surprised me now, but apart from the hooded customer I'd never felt so threatened.

'What is your name, dear?'

'Linny.'

'Would you spell that, please?'

'As it sounds, sir. L-i-n-n-y.'

'Is that your true Christian name?'

'No. It's Linnet, like the bird.'

'Ah. The little linnet bird. Do you sing sweetly as well, child?' He didn't wait for an answer. 'And yet I think I prefer

45

Linny. Linny from Liverpool. I will remember that. Now, I want to touch it,' he went on. 'Your hair.'

I knelt in front of him, and from my lowered position I could see him in the light from the fire as it danced across his features. It was hard to tell how old he was, for his face was dissipated, the eyelids heavy over the protruding, crusty eyes. They were unfocused, as if he had just woken; his nose was veined and his lips too wet, too red. His tongue, surprisingly pink, darted in and out of his mouth in an uncontrollable flicker.

'I shall pour you a drink, shall I?' His fingers strayed to a large brown bottle on a table beside his chair. 'Have you ever been to France, my dear?'

I shook my head, trying not to watch his tongue: there was something obscene in its frenzied dance that tripped each word. I put my hand under my hair and held it towards him. 'It's free of nits, you'll find, sir, as I—' Without warning the man's feet, in their dark blue prunella slippers, flew into the air, wheeling furiously. A heel caught me in the face, sending me flying on to my side. Holding my cheek, I sat up and stared in shock. The man was slipping down in the chair, on his back now and groaning, his legs working as fast as those of the knife sharpener, who pedalled his wheel over on Seel Street. His hands gripped the armrests and he cried out in short, jerky bursts of sound.

The door opened and the black man stepped into the room, bowing his head so that his turban didn't touch the lintel. He looked down at me, then walked to the chair. As he passed, the tiny loincloth swaying, I saw that his bare foot was more than three times the length of my hand.

'It's – he's – I don't know what's wrong with him,' I said. 'I didn't do anything.'

Pompey picked up the man, whose legs were slowing now, and held him against his bare chest as easily as if he were a child.

'Pompey! Pompey!' the man cried. 'Make it leave. Make the pain leave me! Give me my chloral. Hurry. It's crushing my ribs.'

Pompey lowered him back on to the seat, then picked up the brown bottle. He poured liquid into a small glass, then held the man's quivering mouth, tucking the tongue in with his long-nailed index finger as he poured the liquid down his throat. 'Soon, soon, master. It is almost over,' he murmured. His voice was deep and heavily accented.

The old man's mouth opened and closed like the beak of a baby bird.

I watched the strange scene, fingering the lump that was rising on my cheek. The thought of performing an act on this horrid man made my gorge rise.

The man's body slowed. His spine relaxed, and all that was left in his legs was a slight tremble.

As I got to my knees, Pompey poured from the brown bottle until the glass was half full, then came towards me, holding it out. 'I see you have not drunk yet, Little Mistress. Come. Take this. It is time.' His voice was even softer now, little more than a whisper.

I shook my head, staring at his face. He had marks, I saw, wide, raised marks that were even darker than the rest of his skin, running straight down both cheeks. He had no eyelashes.

'It will not happen again – his attack – this night,' he said. 'He will have no more pain, and you have nothing to fear.' I wanted to believe the soothing voice, but I couldn't.

I glanced round Pompey to the man's now still form in the chair. 'What am I expected to . . . What does he want?' I

47

whispered, having to tip my head back to look up into Pompey's face.

His gaze rested on my swelling cheek as he held out the glass. 'Just stay quiet. Do not upset him. Drink this now, please.'

'What is it?' I asked, eyeing the colourless liquid. 'I don't take spirits.'

'It will go better for you. Drink, Little Mistress,' he said.

I put my hand against the glass, saying, 'No, I said I—' but in one swift move Pompey had seized my jaw and forced open my lips in the same way he had with the old man. The liquid went down in a flaming rush, and I choked and coughed as Pompey let go of me. I swallowed, licking my lips, but there was only the faint whisper of sweetness.

'It is better this way,' Pompey repeated, setting the glass on the table and moving towards the door.

'But what's wrong with him?'

Pompey opened the door and stepped through. 'It is called the French Welcome by some,' he said, and stopped. I leaned forward to hear what he would say next. 'Although most are more familiar with it as syphilis.'

He closed the door firmly, and I heard the turn of the brass key.

CHAPTER FIVE

I SAT IN FRONT of the fire on the carpet, which swirled with rich jewel tones. I knew the sailors often carried diseases. I tried to think if I'd heard of the French Welcome, or the other word that sounded like the hissing of a snake. I was suddenly sleepy, my eyelids so heavy that I had to struggle to keep them open. Finally I lowered myself so that I was lying on my side, my back to the fire, head resting comfortably on my curled arm. The throbbing in my cheek had disappeared; there was no pain, just a lovely sleepy floating sensation. The man appeared to sleep as well, breathing heavily and noisily. His tongue was also at rest; a thick line of dried saliva crusted on his bottom lip. In the outer room Clancy was again singing to Pompey's drumming, but the sound blended into a continuous murmur that was something I couldn't recognize but inexplicably loved.

I let my eyes close, the song, the rhythm of the man's breathing and the comforting heat of the flames lulling me. And then I was dreaming, strange and somehow dark, uneasy dreams. Soon the dark was banished; the sun came out, shining with an unfamiliar brittle light that hurt my closed eyes. In the dream my eyes stayed shut, and yet I could see perfectly. I was on Salthouse Dock, walking towards the water. Gulls flew overhead with mewling cries as their wings snapped in the sunlight. They swung and dipped, swung and dipped, finally flying so low that I felt the warm flutter of their wings against my eyelids, my cheeks. One came right up to my head: its beak, pointed and sharp, snapped in my ear. I was afraid: I wanted to get away from the mechanical clacking of the beak. I ran, but the gull chased me to the end of the pier, its cries louder now as it tried to peck me with that awful horny projection. When I could run no further I looked down at the murky water. The beak came closer. There was no choice. I jumped, and as I fell towards the water, I saw, just under the surface, my mother's face, white and still, eyeless, her hair floating round her head like seaweed.

I gasped, opening my eyes.

The man knelt over me, large shears in his hand. They gleamed silver with gold handles. Strands of my hair were in the blades. His eyes glittered and his breathing was raspy. Excited, vibrating trills rose from his throat, and his tongue was even more frenetic than it had been earlier. 'Ah!' he exclaimed, in a pleased way, studying my face as I blinked, trying to clear my vision and understand what I was seeing.

I struggled to rise but he pressed me down. 'Stay still, my girl, stay still. I'm not done,' he said, around the slippery tongue. 'I had thought you dead, but it's much more pleasant with one so warm and pliant.' He laughed in delight, as if surprised by this.

Striking at him with my arm, pushing him away, for he was little more than a ghost of a man, I got to my feet. The room was brightly lit now by the gaslights on the walls, and the lamps on the tables had been turned high. I reached upward, dully fingering the short, soft tufts, all that was left on my shorn scalp. 'What have you done?' I cried, my voice muffled as if I were speaking through a pillow. 'Why have you cut off my hair?' It took me a long time to get out each of the two sentences.

I looked at the long strands, gleaming on the vibrant carpet. Still kneeling, the man lifted one and ran it across his face, where it caught on the gummy surface of his tongue. He laughed again, pointing behind me, and now I recognized the cackle of the gull.

I turned in the direction of his finger, unable to move quickly, although my instincts screamed at me, again, to run, escape. I saw a tall standing trunk, opened vertically. Shelves lined one side, and on them were large jars.

'Go and look, dear heart. Do go and look,' the man said.

As if pulled by invisible sticky threads, I walked towards the jars, not understanding why I would follow this lunatic's instructions. The image of my mother's face, floating under water, seemed more real than what was happening in this room.

I looked at the rows of jars, but couldn't understand what I was seeing. They were filled with floating shadows. Each jar had a label, written in spidery, shaky script. *Emma, Newcastle*, said one. *Loulou, Calais. Mollie, Manchester.* I kept reading the labels. *Yvette, Toulouse. Bette, Glasgow.*

'Have you ever been to France, my little Linny?' the man asked, for the second time that evening. I turned as he struggled to his feet. He came closer, limping heavily, one shoulder twisted forward. My eyes swivelled slowly in their sockets – his hands were behind his back.

'It's a beautiful, terrible place, France. I spent too long there. Too long, with all the lovely girls. Sluts, my dear. All lovely sluts, with their ripe quims, like your young self,' he said. 'You shouldn't be allowed to keep spreading your filthy diseases. Surely you've heard of Fracastoro's shepherd – do you know the poem, my lovely? "Syphilis sive morbus Gallicus".'

He was within touching distance now.' "A shepherd once – distrust not ancient fame," ' he quoted, ' "Possessed these downs, and Syphilus his name." '

I was mesmerized by his eyes. There was no colour, only round black globes, hard as coal.

'And so, of course, you must be stopped. You and all your kind, for nothing can end the agony you've inflicted upon me. Not the mercury salts, not the bromide or the chloral. Temporary, all temporary relief. So I'm keeping a collection, you see, of those I've prevented from spreading the foulness. So many colours. And I've been looking for quite some time now for an addition to my collection. It had to be the perfect colour,' I heard him say. 'And now I've found it. Linny from Liverpool.'

I looked back at the jars, stared into the one closest to my face. And then I let out a strangled gasp, and tried to move away from what I realized I was seeing. But it was as if I had joined my mother now, except my hair couldn't float like hers, not any more. I moved my arms in torpid arcs, attempting to swim through the thick air, away from the jars, with their horrible contents of disembodied hair.

Gleaming black, rich brown, deep red, bright orange, dark blonde. All floating.

The man put his hand on my shoulder, and I turned with the pressure, and then something glinted above me, and I thought of the gull, saw the shears in the air, silver and gold, moving towards me. Instinctively I put up my arm, not quick enough to stop the blades, only to deflect them. Instead of stabbing into their intended target, my neck, they slid further and slashed the soft flesh of my left breast in a long, crooked line, slicing through the green dress as if it were butter. I saw blood pouring from the gash, but there was no pain, no shock.

I was deeper in the water now. There was no sound but the turgid beat of blood in my ears. When the shears were raised over me again, I struck clumsily at the old man, and the shears flew from his hand.

I stooped and picked them up. I looked into the maddened eyes. Then my own arm rose and lowered in what I saw as slow, graceful movements that felt like a dance, and the old man fell, the shears planted into one of those terrible eyes, his mouth a round and trembling wet circle.

I looked at him lying at my feet, and my own legs gave way. I knew I was falling, falling, into the Mersey where my mother waited.

The voices grew louder. I recognized the hysteria of the boy in the flowered dress. Clancy.

'I don't know, do I? How were we to guess he wouldn't kill her first, as he's always done? Oh, Pompey, I feel terribly light-headed. Please, let me lean against you.'

'Christ. What a mess. Why the hell didn't he give her enough chloroform to kill her before he started? But she's dead now, isn't she?' asked another voice. A man, older than the boy, his voice self-assured.

'I believe so, Young Master.' Pompey's voice. I thought of the drink he had given me. Him, not the old man.

'Well, we'll never know how this happened, will we?' the voice of Young Master said, anger just beneath the surface. 'But I knew we shouldn't have let him keep on with his sordid game. I knew we shouldn't set up another. And now look at this. I should have listened to my intuition.'

I still felt nothing, although I became aware of something new, a dull, thumping surge, a minor crescendo of pain through the top half of my body. There was the fresh iron smell of blood. I felt my head being lifted and moved. I was pulled up by my wrists, and cool air blew across them as my sleeves slid back.

'Look at that mark,' Clancy squealed. 'Like a fish.'

Then I was let go, falling limply to the floor again.

'Who brought her? Was it a pimp? Will anyone come looking for her tonight?' It was the same well-bred voice, with a touch of superiority in it. A voice no one would argue with. How odd, I thought, that I could hear and understand, but felt powerless to move so much as an eyelid.

'I believe she was bought for the night, Young Master. No one will be looking for her until morning,' Pompey said.

'What should we do, then?' asked Clancy. 'Whatever shall we do about all of this? The blood. There's so much blood.' His voice dissolved into tears.

'Shut up, Clancy. Dump her in the Mersey, Pompey,' the man said. 'Now.'

'And what of your father, Young Master?'

There was silence except for Clancy's muffled sobbing.

'Clean him up as best you can,' the superior voice ordered. 'We'll leave for London as soon as humanly possible, and while it's still dark. If someone should come to fetch the girl tomorrow, there'll be no sign of her, or any of us. Anyway, one less doxy is of little importance to anyone but an irate pimp.

'When we arrive in London we'll say my father died while visiting Liverpool, and have a proper burial there. No one need know about any of this. Only the people in this room know what has happened here. And none of us will talk. Isn't that right, Clancy?'

'Oh, my goodness, oh, of course not. But — but I'll be *haunted*, positively *haunted*, by what I've seen here tonight.' Clancy's voice rose to a breathless squeak. 'I can't look, no, I can't look any longer.'

'Pull yourself together, Clancy.' Young Master's voice was thick with annoyance.

'But those dreadful scissors, his face, oh dear, I – yes, I'm going to be sick.'

I felt the floor thud with running footsteps. There was a silence, longer than the first.

And then the confident voice spoke again. 'I can trust you to do what must be done, Pompey,' it said calmly. 'I don't want anything left, especially not that cursed hair or the damn trunk. Or anyone who might speak of tonight. Anyone. You understand, don't you, Pompey?'

'Yes, Young Master.'

I heard no more voices, but the floor vibrated with a set of heavy steps again, and there was the soft click of a door.

I moved my left arm then, and the movement brought out an unexpected and shocking pain, as if the shears had just now plunged into skin and tendon and muscle. *Help me, somebody, please*, I tried to whisper. But my lips wouldn't move and, besides, there was nobody to help me, my mother gone, a man called Ram caring only about what coins I could bring to his hand. The pungent odour of burning hair filled the air.

'Pompey?' I finally found my voice and whispered into the thick stink that enveloped me, but there was no answer, and then the dark Mersey moved in, sweetly, and I let myself go to it.

★ ★ ★

55

'What was that?'

Something had brought me back to consciousness. Was it the shout of the voice, muffled, as if by distance or barrier? Or was it a sudden jarring?

I couldn't see anything, but I couldn't tell whether or not my eyes were open. The numbness was still there, and I realized I was rocking, gently, as if in a cradle.

The voice came again, closer now: 'Gib? Gib, you hear that? Gib!'

There was a grunt, as if someone had been rudely awakened. Next a moan. 'I didn't hear nuthin'. Give us a drink, Willy.'

I was cold. Wet. I knew I was on my side. There was a sound, familiar. I strained to recognize it. Oars, small slaps as wood hit water.

'We bin out all night? Near morning, is it, Willy?'

'No. It's just gone three by the bells.' The voices came closer, the sound of rowing louder. I was aware that I was growing wetter. Water was inching into my ear. 'I heared a carriage, Gib, and then something hit the water, just over yon. Something heavy.'

A burp echoed. 'My missus will skin me alive, so she will. Take me to shore, Willy. I best be off home. If I can get in without waking her, she might not—'

I felt a bump near the top of my head. 'By Jesus, you was right, you old bugger. What is it? What is it, Willy?'

Water closed over the side of my face. I felt it on my mouth, felt it snaking through my lips. I could taste it, foul and cold. I tried to swallow, or spit it out, but could do neither. Nothing – not my mouth, or my throat – worked.

'She's sinking, Gib. Quick, help me pull it up. It's a box of some kind. Help me haul 'er in, man. Put your elbow into it.'

'It's too heavy. Here, hook this rope through the handle. We'll drag it in to shore.'

The water swirled over my face momentarily, and then I felt myself lifted. My mouth was now full of water. At the next lurching movement, I grew aware of a heaviness against my back, pressure, something pushing at me.

I was in a box – was it a coffin? *Am I dead?* The water threatened to choke me – a comfort, for I knew I must be alive. But where was I, and what was I doing, moving along the river with something heavy pushing into my back? I heard the bottom of a skiff scraping the rough stones on the water's edge. Then the box was dragged up them. I felt the vibration under me, but still couldn't move, couldn't make a sound.

'It's a trunk. One of them big travelling ones. Let's get her open, Willy. Could be somethin' right valuable.'

'I'm trying.'

'Is there a lock?'

'No. But the latches are tight. That's a good sign. Maybe there wasn't a chance for too much water to get in. Here, I got the last one, and – Jesus, have mercy!'

There was a rush of freezing air, and silence. I knew now that my eyes were closed; I could see nothing.

'It's two girls,' the softer voice, the one I knew was Willy, said.

'I can see that, can't I? Lookit how they's layin'. Like spoons. And what's all them jars? They're empty. Not even lids.'

'I don't know, do I? Jesus, Gib. What are we to do?'

'They're dead for sure, ain't they, Willy?'

'Must be. Lying so still like that.' I heard the rustle of clothing, and the softer voice came almost in my face.

'Although they ain't dead by drowning. Only half their heads is under water.' I smelt the beery stench of his breath.

'You're right. That front one looks about the age of your youngest, Willy.' There was a tug on my shoulder. 'Stabbed. Right in the heart, from what I can see.'

'Same with the other?'

More rustling, more movement; this time the weight behind me shifting.

'Nope. This one has her throat cut. Maybe there's something of value on them.'

'Not likely. Nobody'd go to the bother of killing 'em and throwing 'em in the river without first taking any valuables.'

'Hey, Willy, maybe we could sell 'em to them sawbones up at the Infirmary.'

The second voice grew loud. 'I ain't about to get messed up with no body snatching.'

'Keep yer voice down, Willy. We ain't takin' 'em from the graveyard. They come floatin' to us, fair and square.'

'No, I won't do it. I ain't sellin' these girls to them with bloodied hands so they can do their dirty work. Bad business, that is, cuttin' up the dead for their own learnin'. And we've got nothin' to wrap 'em in, and nothin' to haul 'em in. No. I won't do it, Gib,' he repeated.

I heard a soft rasp that might have been a hand scrubbing over a stubbled face. 'Could be you're right. If we was to get caught with two dead girls . . .' A sigh. Now I heard the skiff rubbing on the stones in the kissing lift and fall of the shallow water on the bank. 'But them dresses might fetch us somethin', Willy.' The voice rose hopefully.

'There's a lot of blood. And it looks like the green one is cut down the front.'

'But the blood's fresh. It would wash out easy. And my

58

good woman is right handy with a needle and thread. We could sell 'em down at the market. That flowery one looks pricy. It might bring in a shillin' or two. And the trunk — surely it'd fetch a bit. Go ahead, Willy. Start on the green one. I'll get this one off. And throw out the jars.'

There were rough, jerking movements behind me, the sound of glass breaking.

'I'm a Christian man, Gib, and a father. It don't feel right, stripping these girls and throwin' them back into the river. Don't set right with me at all.'

'Don't think about yer own girls now, Willy. I bet this dress alone—' There was a low whistle. 'This ain't no girl after all. Look here.'

Silence. Then, 'You're right, by Jesus. What's he doin' all trumped up like that?'

I was pulled up again. 'Who knows? And who cares. But this front one here is. I can tell, even with her hair all chopped off.'

'She's so small.'

'Stop thinkin' about it, Willy. They's dead, and in no need of their clothes, whether they's boys or girls, young or old. A dress is a dress.'

I'm not dead. Can't you see? I'm not dead.

The movements behind me continued. 'Quit starin' like you seen a spook,' the rougher voice said, and there was a rush of cold air as the body behind me was pulled away. I knew now that it was Clancy. 'Lookit this throat, would you? Ear to ear. Like a big red smile, it is.'

There was a small splash, and then the thud as Clancy's body was dropped back behind me. 'Here. Give the dress a good shake, then take it to the edge and wash that blood out.'

My arm was grabbed, and two jars that must have been caught in the folds of my skirt clanged together. 'Why you just standin' there, Willy? Do wot I says. If you haven't the stomach for it, I'll look after it all. But the dresses is mine, then.' I was pulled up, but in the next second dropped back. 'She don't feel like the other one,' the man called Gib said. 'Not as cold. Willy? I'm not sure this one's dead.'

My waist was kicked with the toe of a boot, and at the sudden rough movement I emitted a watery gasp as the stinking Mersey trickled out of my mouth.

'Damn. She's alive, all right,' Gib said. 'But from the looks of her she'll be gone soon. She'll never miss her dress.' He pulled it off my shoulder.

'Gib. No,' Willy said.

'Wot?'

'You heard me, Gib. Leave her be.'

'Wot you talking about? Willy?'

I felt hands under my arms, pulling me out of the trunk. The jars that were still on my dress crashed on to the slimy stones. Something warm and soft pressed against my breast. 'Cold water likely slowed the bleeding,' the softer voice said. 'Could be the water that was to kill her saved her instead. Who'da done this?'

I gagged, suddenly, and with the retching movement, brought up more watery saliva. It was as if it cleared my throat. 'Pompey,' I murmured. *It must have been Pompey, following orders to throw me into the Mersey. And he thought I was already dead, so there was no reason to slit my throat, as he had Clancy's.*

'Calling for her father,' Willy said. 'She's wanting her pappy.' And then I was roughly dragged over the stones, and the pain in my breast returned, as did the blessed darkness.

60

CHAPTER SIX

I WAS SHAKEN ROUGHLY. 'Wake up, girl. It's time you were awake. Come on, now.'

The shaking brought on such an exquisite pain that I cried out, opening my eyes and looking into the drawn face of a middle-aged woman.

The pain was everywhere. I couldn't move, pinned into place by the pounding in my temples and the terrible pain in my chest.

'Raise yerself, now. You bin lyin' here the full clock round.'

'Please,' I whispered, trying to lick my lips. 'Drink. A drink, please.'

The woman appeared not to hear me. She wore a grey shift that made her look like one long, thin slice of grey – her hair, skin and covering. 'The surgeon's been in and stitched you up.' She had to shout over the screams, curses and prayers that filled the air. 'Get dressed. There are others wot need the bed. You'll go through that door, there,' she said, pointing to one side of the long room. She dropped my boots on to the floor, then threw the green dress, stiff with blood and stinking of damp, on to the edge of the bed. There was a moth-eaten brown woollen scarf stuck to the blood on the bodice. 'You had nowt else with you, although the boots are a damn sight more than we see on many. Now move yerself.'

'Surgeon?' I whispered. 'Where am I?'

'Wot?' the woman said, leaning closer.

'What is this place?' I asked again, a slow dread coming to me.

'It's the fever hospital of the Brownlow Hill workhouse.'

I raised my head, even though the movement brought a fresh wave of pain. 'No one comes out of hospital alive. Am I going to die?'

The woman shook her head. 'Idjit. The only reason your sort believe you die if you come to a hospital is because none come but those a breath away from dead. It's not our fault if they're too far gone to be helped. You was lucky. Some kind soul took it upon himself to drop you in front of the door with your wound bound up in that scarf. Otherwise you'd have bled to death. Hurry up, girl. If you've no home go on up to the workhouse. You'll be assigned a job there when you're able.' She turned and left me.

I lay still, trying to breathe round the pain, to stop the swirling in my head, to remember.

The horror of what had passed came back to me as if I'd been struck. 'No,' I said, closing my eyes again. 'No.' The room with its sweet stink. I could remember lying on the rug in the house on Rodney Street, the smell of burning hair. The hair, and the shears. And the man . . . the man I'd killed. Whom I'd murdered. Was I to be found out, hauled off to gaol and hanged, my body thrown into a pit of quicklime with those of other murderers?

What had happened after that? Another memory. It was dark, and I was wet. Was it just the dream again, the dream of my mother floating under the surface of the Mersey? But I

62

had been cold, so cold, and now I remembered thinking, Mother? Is that you, Mother? I had felt the watery push and sway of someone floating behind me. Not Mother. Clancy. The voices of the men called Gib and Willy. It was Willy who had saved my life, who had brought me here.

Moaning, I managed to sit up on the mattress, stained deep brown from an ancient combination of blood, vomit, urine and faeces. Drawing deep breaths, I tried to quell the nausea that the pain brought on. Awkwardly I pulled off the threadbare grey shift that someone had put on me, pursing my lips with the effort, not caring that the old woman in the bed less than a foot from mine was studying me with clouded eyes. There was a thick strip of blood-soaked flannel wrapped round my chest. Getting into the dress seemed an impossibility, but there was no one to help. I knew the woman who had spoken to me would have been from the workhouse herself, her face showing no flicker of compassion.

Eventually I was dressed. The old woman reached out and, with a thickened yellow fingernail, touched my green silk skirt, smiling toothlessly and muttering something incomprehensible. I dropped the brown scarf on to her bed, and she snatched it up, sniffing at it and patting it as if it were a small animal. I shoved my feet into my sodden boots, leaving them undone, and stumbled, through the long room of groaning, piteous men and women, as if still in the nightmare. I had to pass through a number of sections of the building, unconsciously reading the names of the wards: 'Insane', with its padlocked splintered doors that didn't block the desperate shrieks and garbled voices; 'Scald and Itch', with low moans and muffled weeping; 'Smallpox', which was eerily silent; and finally, somehow worse than the screams and heavy silence, the cacophony of lonely sounds that poured through the doors of the ward simply marked 'Children'.

I stepped out into the misty grey of morning, avoided the workhouse to the left of the hospital, and took the path that led down to the main road. I walked and walked, knowing that if I fell I would be hauled back to the workhouse. I walked as the mist blew away and a watery sun threw pale shafts. As I neared Vauxhall Road and the locks of the Leeds –Liverpool canal, I noticed the early-morning crowd of spectators in Lock Fields. They were watching two young men who would likely be fighting over some all-night argument in one of the many public houses that lined the area.

I walked, in my heavy boots and spoiled dress, at times bent nearly double as I struggled with the pain. People parted in front of me. I felt as old as the crone waiting to die in the next bed in the fever hospital, the crone who loved green.

Ram's mouth opened when I fell through the door.

'Wot—' he started, but I pushed myself to my feet, wove across the floor and lowered myself on to my pallet. The pain made it impossible to lie in any position but on my back. I plucked at my blanket, but couldn't get it over me. I lay with my eyes open, and Ram came to look down at me. 'Wot's happened to you?' he asked, his eyes taking in the torn dress and the dirty flannel wrapped round me, my shorn hair. I saw the familiar look of anger round his jaw. 'I thought you'd run off on me when I went round yesterday and nobody answered my knocking. Look at the state o' you. Would you not do as you were told for the gentlemen? Did they have to punish you?'

I closed my eyes.

'I should punish you as well. That dress cost me a pretty penny,' he said. 'You'll have to stitch it up as best you can, and sponge out the blood.' His voice rose, but there was a wavering to it, a tone I hadn't heard before, as if it was an effort for him to sound angry. 'They'll never take you back at the bookbindery if you lose more than a few days. And I'm out of pocket for any night work I could get you, at least for a while. If you didn't look such a mess – what the hell happened to your hair? – I'd clout you one for all the trouble you've brought. Useless cunt,' he growled. And then, a minute later, his voice dropped and the blanket fell over me. 'Best lay still awhile,' he said, and then it was his hard palm at the back of my head, lifting it, and the rim of a cup touched my lips. When I opened my mouth cool water flowed down my throat.

I swallowed and swallowed, but made no sound. If I had been a crying sort of girl, I would surely have wept then.

Eventually the festering and oozing around the dirty sutures on my breast abated, and the delirium stopped. I knew it had been some time that I'd tossed in my bed, perhaps a week or even two; all had faded into periods of pain and thirst and light, and Ram with spoonfuls of watery gruel and lifting me on to the chamber pot, all mixed with deep blackness. But that morning, an unidentifiable length of time after what I would call the nightmare, I sat on the edge of my pallet and looked around. I was alone, light-headed yet more alert than I could ever remember. My mind was clear, tight and sure, focused. I was coming fourteen, and I knew now I was old enough to make a choice. There were two: I could stay or I could leave.

If I stayed, I would go back to the exhausting tedium of

the bookbindery – if they'd still have me – or another factory for pauper's wages, taken by Ram Munt. And I'd continue to be pimped by him, receiving for those efforts nothing but the spurt of slime deposited in or on me.

If I left, my future was uncertain, but at least I would have a say in it.

The choice was simple and obvious.

I went to the fruitwood box and took out the mirror. I stared at myself, and saw that what I had felt happening, as I tossed on my damp sheet, was true. My face was thinner than usual, but my eyes were different: they had an intensity, grown darker and larger, and they glittered with something for which I had no name. My pale hair stood up around my head, but the lack of curls and new angular cheekbones had taken me from child to young woman.

I unwrapped the strip of muslin that had been exchanged for the dirty flannel. The stitching on my breast was dark. I touched it. The skin was raised and sealed in a twisted, ropy seam. It was hardening, and with it something deeper inside me had also grown dense and rigid. Resistant and unyielding.

I cleaned the green dress and stitched the rent. I hunted out and found coins Ram had hidden about the room – my money: it was what I'd earned. The only thing I was sorry about was that Ram seemed to have drunk most of it, and it was a pitiable sum for the years of work on my feet and on my back.

I ate the heel of bread I found on the table, holding my hand over my mouth as I swallowed, willing myself to keep down the first solid food I'd had for so long, drank some tinny water, and walked out. I left the miserable room on Back Phoebe Anne Street, left the miserable court with its trickle of human waste running down the shallow gutter in the middle, left the blocks of leaning, back-to-back, vermin-infested buildings.

I wore the sophisticated green gown, a clean shawl and a straw bonnet, and under my arm I clutched the fruitwood box with its mirror, book, pendant and my bone-handled knife. The bit of money was twisted in an old handkerchief, which I'd sewn on to my underskirt.

'This is my territory,' the tall, raw-boned woman said, eyeing the golden fringe poking out from my bonnet as, a few hours later, I stood along Paradise Street, filled with its sailors' lodgings and doss-houses.

'It's a free street, isn't it?' I said, my tone matching hers.

'How long you bin workin'?'

'Close to three years,' I told her.

'Not around 'ere, you ain't. I knows every girl in a square mile. But you do look as if you knows your way around.' She studied my face. 'You're young. Younger'n most. From what I can see most likely the curse ain't even on you yet.'

I didn't answer.

'How old are you?'

'Fourteen.' *Close enough to fourteen.*

'You want to work around 'ere, you work for me. What do you say to that?'

'Depends,' I answered, with a boldness of which I hadn't known I was capable. I liked it. 'How much do you take?'

' 'Alf of what ya makes each night. Rules are, I don't abide my girls drinkin' on the job. And I've me ways to find out if youse bin cheatin' me, and if you 'as, you're out of 'ere before you can tie your bonnet strings, and I'll see to it you never gits no more customers in this area again. Understand?'

I nodded.

'You clean? My girls don't work with clap or open pox. I got a name to up'old. Only clean girls, anyone wot comes to Blue's girls knows. Were the same when I run my business down in Seven Dials in London afore I come up 'ere. My girls was all clean.'

'I'm clean,' I said, then purposely let my shawl drop open, and was rewarded by the look of disgust that filmed the woman's expression.

'Bleedin' 'ell. That's fresh. You wanna work with it in that state?'

'I don't care.'

She pulled a grimy yellow scarf from round her neck. 'Cover it with this for the next little while,' she said. 'Don't want to be scarin' 'em off first fing.'

I took the scarf and arranged it over my scar.

'What's yer name?'

'Linnet,' I told her. 'Linnet Gow.' I pulled myself taller. 'Although I go by Linny.'

The woman shook her head. 'You wanna change your name? You got anyone from before lookin' for ya –' here she raised her chin at my chest '– that you don't want findin' ya? Well?' She tapped her foot, waiting for an answer.

'I'll stay with Linny,' I said. 'Linny Gow. And if anyone comes looking for me,' the unshaven face of Ram Munt filled my head, 'I'll look after myself.'

'Fine. I got rooms ya can use, and ya can work for me as long as ya prove yourself. 'Ave trouble with a customer or any of the other girls or the ol' Bill, ya come to me. Ya'll find me fair, if ya follow the rules.' When I nodded, she smiled, revealing a missing eyetooth. Otherwise her teeth were long and square, strong-looking. 'Seems like you got pluck,' she said. 'Men who come down to the streets lookin' for it, they like a bit of pluck, don't they? If they want coyness and reluctance, well, I tells 'em, stay 'ome with yer good missus.'

She laughed at her own joke, and I opened my mouth and made a sound that might have been interpreted by some as laughter.

My hair grew out and eventually I could lift my chin and straighten my shoulders without my chest pulling and aching. In exchange for a share in a cramped room to sleep in and another room, curtained into three spaces with a thin flock mattress in each, to which I could bring customers, I handed over half of my nightly earnings to Blue, as was our arrangement.

'Where'd you say you come from?' asked Lambie one night, as we sat at a greasy table in the Goat's Head.

'Back Phoebe Anne Street, off Vauxhall Road,' I told her.

'Vauxhall Road? Then how is it you got that smart talk? Them wot's from Vauxhall Road don't talk like yer does. I'm from Scottie Road meself, and I never learned no fancy talk.'

I smiled, a true smile. 'Noble blood,' I said. 'Noble blood, my dears.' I raised my glass of sugar water, and Lambie, Sweet Girl and I toasted noble blood, earning more in an hour than in a day at the glassworks, or the pottery, or the candlemaker's or the sugar refinery or the bookbinder's, and the freedom that comes from not caring what anyone thought.

'No shortage of customers for you, is there? How does she do it then, eh?' Lambie looked at Sweet Girl. 'How does she pull in the most customers? And her with that.' Lambie pointed a finger. I looked down. My right breast swelled gently above the greying lace of my bodice, the skin smooth and glowing with the dull sheen of pearl under the stinking sputter of the gaslight. But on the left side the wide, jagged, crimson ridge ran from the top of my breast to the top of my first rib. When no one was watching I rubbed the deep, puckered scar. It still ached sometimes, as if the blades that had sunk deep into the tender flesh there had left invisible poisoned barbs that nipped and stung even after the surgeon had cut away the destroyed flesh and clumsily stitched together the ragged edges. The nipple was spared, but the muscle and fat that caused the fullness of my right breast had been lost on the left.

Sweet Girl shrugged. 'I don't know, but I wish she'd send some of whatever she's got my way. Some nights are useless, with little but piss-dribbling poxy cocks.'

'I think it's because she lets 'em pretend she's a fine lady, just stepping down for a quick fuck with her pretty little cunt all powdered and fresh. Ain't that right?'

They laughed loudly, and I raised an eyebrow at them. I knew it was my blood that made me different. And there was something else. I knew I wouldn't be staying in this life: there was something different, something bigger for me. Linny Gow would be a name that people would remember.

CHAPTER SEVEN

I T WAS TRUE: I had no shortage of men. Most I took to one of the tiny cubicles containing mattresses covered with layers of cheap, coarse sheets – the top soiled one taken off after each customer – on the third floor of the house on Jack Street, one of the narrow lanes that led away from Paradise Street. Some couldn't wait: they only wanted a quick fumble in a doorway or alley.

And, of course, Ram Munt had found me not long after I'd left Back Phoebe Anne Street. I wasn't hiding, and even with Ram's muddled thinking it wasn't difficult for him to work out where I might be.

I saw him coming as I stood under a gaslight. I knew his rolling walk and the way his ears stood out from his head, and recognized that he was squiffed to the gills even in the darkness between the street-lamps. He was staring boldly into the faces of all the girls he passed, and I stepped even closer to the light, reaching under the back of my bonnet.

Ram's steps quickened to a bow-legged, lopsided run when he realized it was me. I came towards him, arms wide as if to embrace him. When he reached me I put my left hand on his shoulder. Then I slid the glinting blade of my knife, honed to a deadly point, beside the pulse in his neck.

'Hello, Ram,' I breathed into his face. 'I wondered how long it would be before I saw you here.' I pressed, and the point broke the surface of his skin; a bright crimson bead welled up.

Ram whimpered like a babe. 'Linny, my girl, that's no way to say hello to your old da,' he said, eyes shifting.

I looked at the broken veins on his cheeks, the reddened, pocked surface of his nose, grown bulbous from drinking. Of course he was stronger than I, and even in his ale-addled state could surely manage to knock down both me and the knife before I could use it to any effect – he knew it and I knew it. But I felt powerful, standing in the circle of light. I had imagined this scene – where I held a knife to Ram Munt – so many times over the last few years that I knew my face showed him I wasn't little Linny Munt any more.

'Go away, Ram. This is my home now. You don't own me any longer.' I liked the sound of my voice as I spoke up to him.

'Linny. Now, Linny. Think it over.'

One half of my mouth smiled. 'Oh, I have, Ram. I have.'

'Trouble, Linny?' It was Blue, come up behind me. Ram frowned at her.

I smiled fully now, never taking my eyes off Ram. 'No, Blue, no trouble. Just someone who thought he knew me. But he's mistaken. He doesn't know me after all.' I lowered the knife but kept it visible, the light glancing off it.

Ram's mouth opened, then closed. He glowered at me, looked at the knife one more time; then his gaze swung back to Blue. 'She'll rob you blind,' he growled, 'and put on airs. A right sly little bitch, is this one. You'll be sorry you took her on.'

'I'll be the judge, my man,' Blue said.

Ram Munt turned and left. I watched him go, and I knew he wouldn't bother me again. I was almost sorry I hadn't sunk the knife deep into that pulsing vein when I'd had the chance. I realized it would be easy to kill again. That the first killing is like losing the maidenhead – difficult, filled with pain and confusion. But once it's been done there can be no going back. There is little to prevent the next fuck. Or murder.

Summer came, and customers were plentiful. Standing outside with the warm night air on my face and arms, my feet neither cold nor wet, was quite pleasant at times. I liked the camaraderie of the other girls: we would stand, arm in arm, watching for carriages to slow, sometimes cracking peanuts as we laughed and gossiped. It reminded me, in a small way, of my old friendship with Minnie and Jane, of standing in the court with my mother after dinner. I realized how lonely I'd been for the last years, and how tightly Ram had controlled me. I liked my independence; although I rarely refused a customer, I knew I could if he was too repulsive or suspicious. I liked the freedom of knowing that I could keep half of whatever I earned. I remembered the simple girlish dreams I'd shared with Minnie and Jane as we skipped home together from the bookbinder's, and now acquired paste necklaces, beaded reticules and feather bonnets from pawn shops. I popped into a chop house for a hot pie, sometimes twice a night, and I started a collection of small, used but fairly dear leather books.

I felt quite grown-up with my purchases and at times, as I slipped a garish bauble over my wrist and admired it, revelled in a feeling that was close to happiness. And where were Minnie and Jane? They would still be at the bookbinder's, giving their earnings to their fathers or, possibly, by now, their husbands. They'd have left behind their girlish dreams of finery from shop windows, their wages going only to keep bread on the table and them out of the rain.

I was honest with Blue, thankful for her protection, and I knew she liked me. One night as I handed over half of my take, she gave me a wink. 'Yer doing just fine for yerself, my girl,' she said. 'I fink you've got yer future sewn up tight, long as ya stay clean. A girl like you can make a livin' fer a good number o' years.'

I nodded, but of course I had no intention of working the streets for ever. Although I had a freedom Minnie and Jane would never know, I didn't like the price I had to pay. I knew I would be leaving Paradise Street, leaving Liverpool, leaving all of England. I had begun to think about America – the America my mother had once dreamed of. Even if she hadn't been able to leave the hard life, I planned to.

I read about the ship to America on a blustery March night. It was down at an agent's office in Goree Piazza where the slave trade once had its offices. It was now home to various shipping companies and a few public houses. Business had been slow that night and I'd hardly made enough for it to be worthwhile to stand in the blowing rain. I wasn't as comfortable down near the water; I preferred staying closer to Paradise Street, where the gaslights afforded a shred of safety, but once in a while I took my chances.

Luck was with me, and I'd quickly found two customers, one after the other, which was enough to finish my night, and was on my way back to Jack Street when I stopped outside an agent's office to stuff a scrap of paper down the side of my boot where it chafed my ankle bone. As I straightened and glanced at myself in the darkened glass of the office, I saw a newly placed advertisement with a heading in large black letters:

The Union Line of Packets
Liverpool to New York
Fitzhugh and Caleb Grimshaw

Underneath, in smaller letters, were details: 'The *Bowditch* will sail on the 5th of April. Room for one hundred fifty to two hundred passengers steerage; as well as several first and second class cabins. No salt will be taken; the trip is guaranteed to be dry and comfortable.'

The price for a first-class cabin was twenty-five pounds – *twenty-five pounds!* I thought. I couldn't imagine anyone ever managing to save that amount of money. The steerage price was five pounds ten shillings.

Even five pounds was an amount I'd never seen. I shrugged and walked on.

But as the weeks passed, I thought about the advertisement. I thought about what it could mean – going to America. And one dark night when I was closer to sixteen than fifteen, my lip throbbing from a punch by a customer who'd refused to pay, I started to think again about the advertisement, and the picture of the tall-masted ship, its sails full and wide in an apparent sea breeze.

I thought about a new life – a different life – where nobody knew me, and where I could start again. It might be my only chance to avoid ending up like other girls I had worked with – Lambie beaten so badly she'd gone blind and ended up in the workhouse, and, just last month, Skinny Mo dead of the bloody cough after too many years on the cold, wet streets.

I started to hoard my earnings, pawning my cheap trinkets and extra bonnets and not allowing myself to purchase any more books, much as I loved to run my hands over the softness of their covers, my fingers tracing the stamped letters. I ate less, and didn't visit the drinking houses with the other girls as often. And I waited.

I knew that when the time was right for me to go, there'd be a sign. I didn't know what it would be, but it would be unmistakable.

A few months after I had made my vow to go to America I met Chinese Sally.

'Well, look who's come down in the world,' Blue had said, when a young woman, tall and slender, walked up to us as we stood on the street one summer evening. She carried a large and obviously heavy brocade carpet bag, and wore a dainty lace frock far too fine for the street. She wore high pattens on her shoes so that her hems didn't drag through the muck. Her hair was so black it shone navy where it showed beneath her stylish bonnet. She had beautiful skin, pale and unmarked, and the colour of her almond-shaped eyes shifted and reflected the light so I couldn't quite tell whether they were green or brown.

'Yer old man back in the clink again, is 'e?' Blue asked.

'Just for a bit, Blue. He's only got a tailpiece this time, just the three months,' she said. 'And he was stitched up by someone he thought was a mate. Thanks to that rotter, Louis was caught in the act.' She set her bag on the street with a tiny sigh of regret, carefully avoiding a glob of spittle. She flexed her fingers. She wore knitted gloves. 'Just goes to show you can't trust anyone.'

'Linny,' Blue said, 'this is one of my old girls, Sal. Can you make room for 'er wiff you for a few months?'

'I prefer to be called Chinese Sally,' she said.

She looked different from any of the rest of us on Paradise Street. It wasn't only her face, but her obvious style. The lace dress was new, pressed, and had been tailored to fit, not bought from a pawnshop or a market stall. And her voice was soft, cultured.

'Certainly,' I said. 'There's only Helen in the room with me now.' Did she notice that my voice matched hers?

Chinese Sally smiled, a small, wry smile.

'She 'as a fancy man, doesn't she?' Blue told me. 'A real swell. Our Sal lives with the best of 'em as long as 'er feller don't get lagged. But she's lucky she's got 'er old friends fer when times gets rough. This is the second time you've been back now, ain't it?'

The girl nodded, studying the building behind my head. 'I didn't imagine I'd ever be back. We had planned to be off to London next month.'

'What does your man do, then?' I asked.

'He's a pickpocket,' Chinese Sally told me. 'Best of the best. There isn't one in Liverpool better than my Louis.' She picked up her carpet bag, stifling a dainty yawn behind her glove. 'I'm all done in,' she said. 'I heard this morning, early, from one of Louis's men that he'd been lagged. I was nervous to go out all day in case they were watching for me, too. I thought it best to come back here and lie low until he's out.' She yawned again. 'I'll have a good sleep, then be out for a full night's work tomorrow.'

Blue nodded. 'Linny, take 'er up to the room.' She gave

the other girl a clap on the shoulder. 'Good to 'ave ya back, Sal.'

I saw Chinese Sally stiffen and her lips tighten but she didn't say anything.

'This way,' I told her. 'The room is over on Jack Street.'

She walked beside me. 'I'm Chinese Sally down on the street. But I'm Miss Sing in my true life,' she said. And then she said nothing more. I left her sitting on the rumpled bed, looking around the tiny room with distaste, the carpet bag on her lap.

This wasn't her true life, then. Like me. I thought of her words for the rest of the night. 'In my true life,' I whispered to myself, in the superior tone Chinese Sally had used. 'My true life.'

Over the next few months I got to know Chinese Sally well. You do, don't you, when you sleep beside someone, when you hear them cry out in their nightmares, when you know what kind of customer they've last had by the smell they carry on them? I knew that her eyes were brown when she was feeling her best, and that they glinted green when she was angry. She was eighteen, a few years older than me, and her life with Louis sounded exciting.

'I'm his flash girl,' she told me one evening, as I sat on the bed, putting on my powder before I started work. 'You know, dress up pretty and entertain the higher class of gentlemen. He buys me the fancy clothes and pays my rent on a lovely set of rooms. The gentlemen who come to visit me are of the upper calibre, none of the riff-raff we have to contend with on Paradise Street.' She smiled, a wistful smile, and fell silent.

'And it's not just the customers,' she went on eventually. 'The life – well, Linny, it's nothing like this.' She looked at her expensive dresses, hanging on nails on the wall, then studied my face, coming to stand in front of me, holding her gloves. 'You'd be a good flash girl,' she said.

I set my ormolu mirror and the box of powder in my lap. 'I would?'

'Of course. You've still got the freshness the gentlemen want – all your teeth, decent enough looks, your hair thick. And, more than that, you've got a few manners, and a way with a phrase.'

Even though she was complimenting me, I still felt insulted. 'A few manners? I've got more than any of the other girls here, as you well know. My mother taught me,' I said, standing, letting a disdainful tone creep into my voice. 'Manners and proper speech.'

Chinese Sally smiled her usual careful smile, keeping her bottom lip stiff. She had two missing bottom teeth, and was loath for anyone to see the dark gap. 'You may think you're quite fine, my girl,' she said, 'but if you were to spend some time with me, among the right people, you'd learn a thing or two about what you call "proper" from those born into the idle life. You're only a small step above the rest of the girls, and I guarantee you, a few more years here and you'll have fallen off that step, and realize you really are just common baggage. And then it will be too late for any opportunities.'

I stared at her. Was she right? Would I just go on, night after night, customer after customer, my dream of leaving Paradise Street and Liverpool just that – a dream? Would I end up diseased, dying alone?

Chinese Sally must have seen the confusion on my face. She reached out and ran one finger down my cheek. 'When Louis gets out, maybe I'll bring you back with me. Would you like that?'

I shrugged, stepping back. Her finger was soft: she had a jar of lavender cream that she rubbed on to her hands before putting on her gloves each evening. 'I don't know, do I?' I raised my chin and narrowed my eyes as I spoke. 'I don't know what would be expected of me. It's not so bad here,' I said, although she and I both knew I was bluffing.

'Well, I'll ask you again, then, shall I, when you've had a chance to think about it? You don't have to take it pushed up against a wall, you know. Not looking like you do. You could bring Louis in a tidy profit, and the sooner we can make enough to leave, the sooner Louis and I will be on our way to London. Did I tell you, Linny, that Louis is going to marry me — when the time is right, of course — once we've moved down to London? And then, of course, I shall stop working, for Louis will support me properly, with a fine house full of servants. I shall have my own lady's maid.'

I thought then that if I worked for Louis I could save my money even faster, and be able to book passage to America sooner than I had planned. The idea was appealing.

It was only three weeks later that I awoke one cold November afternoon to see Chinese Sally packing her carpet bag.

'He's out,' she told me, seeing me sit up. 'Louis is out. He sent word with one of his men just an hour ago.' She stopped folding a chemise, her hands poised in the air. 'Well? Are you coming? I sent the message back that I was bringing a new girl. You can't come looking like a scarecrow. If you plan to join me, you'd better make yourself smart.'

I tossed aside the patched coverlet, ran my hands over my hair. 'Do you really think I could do it?' I said.

'First of all, when we're up there remember to call me Miss Sing,' she said, answering my question in a roundabout way. 'You can call me Chinese Sally when we're on our own, but Miss Sing when we're attending the theatre, or at a fine eating establishment, or any other social occasion.' She dug through her half-packed bag, and pulled out a dress of beige watered gauze and tossed it on to the bed beside me. 'Here. Put this on. It'll be too big for you, but it will do for today. I can't introduce you to Louis in either of your street dresses — you look like a ragged peacock. Louis likes a quality look. You can keep it. Louis will buy us both more clothes.'

I picked up the frock, fingering the fabric. 'Why are you doing this for me?'

She stared at me. 'For you? I'm not doing it for you. Do you think I have that big a heart?' She made a chuckling sound in her throat. 'I told you. You'll be part of the group, and that will help Louis. Louis likes it when I bring in new girls. He trusts my judgement. And he rewards me handsomely if they work out, which they usually do. If they don't . . .' She continued to look at me, although the stare now turned hostile. 'Well, that's not good for anybody, is it?'

I recognized the warning. The watered gauze was smooth, cool beneath my fingers. I imagined having a wardrobe full of dresses such as this one.

'Just give me time for a good wash,' I told her, adding, 'Miss Sing,' and was rewarded by her nod and the small tight smile I'd come to know so well.

Blue hadn't been happy to lose both of us, but she held no grudges. Every morning, as each of us handed over half our wages, she would assure us, 'Now youse owes me nuthin', and I owes youse nuthin'.' There were always girls, and if she lost one or two, it would only be for a night. 'I guarantee you'll be back,' she said to me now, frowning. 'Just like 'er,' she continued, tossing her head in Chinese Sally's direction. Chinese Sally stood impassive, looking down the street as if she couldn't hear – and didn't care – what Blue was saying. 'Youse can't count on that kind of life, up wiff the nobs. It never lasts, believe me. Youse'll be crawlin' back to where youse can trust your mates, and where youse knows your place. A fancy dress can only cover so much.'

I gripped the now heavy fruitwood box tighter. In it was the money I'd kept hidden under a board in the room in Jack Street, as well as my bone-handled knife, the mirror, pendant and Wordsworth. I'd also packed three small books, my favourites, the ones I couldn't bear to part with.

Wearing the dress Chinese Sally had given me, the warm cape and fancy bonnet she'd lent me, I had left my old clothes behind for Helen. And, like Chinese Sally, I didn't care what Blue said. I was leaving this place, with its stink and trouble. We walked to the corner of Chester and Roper Streets and waited. Chinese Sally kept touching her hair, tying and retying her bonnet, smoothing her skirt. 'When you meet Louis, Linny, extend your hand,' she said. 'He'll say that it's his great pleasure to make your acquaintance, and you must reply, "No, oh, no, sir, the pleasure is mine." He may kiss your glove. Allow him to do this, and then say, "Why, thank you, sir." ' She glanced at me. 'If you don't make a good impression first thing, it won't go well for me. So if you don't know what to do or say, do and say nothing. Watch me.' She was speaking faster and faster. Suddenly I was nervous, frightened at what was expected of me. I hadn't known this feeling for a long time, and realized I'd fallen into a steady, easy lull on Paradise Street.

Within a few moments a fancy curricle pulled by two dappled horses drew up. A man emerged, and stood by the open door. From all of Chinese Sally's talk, I had expected Louis to be more imposing-looking. And younger. I was surprised by how short he was, and how plain. He was at least thirty; the lines round his mouth were already deep. He had a sallow complexion, longish dark hair and yellow-brown eyes with curling lashes. There was almost something of the Italian about him. Unremarkable, really. Had I passed him on the street I might not have noticed him. I suppose that was important, him being a pickpocket, working the crowds. One wouldn't want to stand out in any way.

He bowed over Chinese Sally's hand and she giggled, a sound I had never heard her make before. Then he turned to me, his eyes running over me from my bonnet to my boots.

'This is Miss Linny Gow,' Chinese Sally said. 'The one I sent word to you about with Dirty Joe. What do you think? Will she do?'

I straightened my shoulders.

Louis continued to survey me; after thirty seconds he nodded slowly and then, remembering Chinese Sally's instructions, I extended my hand. Louis looked at it and smiled, then took it in his and raised it to his lips, although he didn't touch them to my glove. 'How lovely to meet you, my dear,' he said, his head bent over my hand, although his eyes were studying me from under those long lashes.

'It's my pleasure, sir, I'm sure,' I said, with what I hoped was my prettiest smile.

He let go of my hand, as if reluctant to do so. 'Has Miss Sing instructed you of my expectations?'

I licked my lips. 'Well, not in so many words. But I've been at the game since I was only a girl, and—'

He stepped closer, and I saw the beginnings of veins on his nose. 'I'll collect all your earnings directly. You'll take the customers I bring to you, and never turn any away. You may be expected to entertain large numbers, with another girl, at one time. Do you understand?'

'Large numbers? You mean more than one customer at once?'

'Really, Sal. She looks like a scared rabbit,' he said, turning to Chinese Sally.

'She'll be fine. I'll keep her in line,' she said, as if I wasn't standing in front of her.

Scared rabbit? I pushed the wool cloak Chinese Sally had lent me back from my shoulders, suddenly too warm. 'Did I hear you correctly in that I won't be seeing any of the money I earn?'

'You'll have your own room and clothing – good clothing, like Sal's. You won't need money for anything. All your meals will be brought to you. You won't be going out except for the entertaining I plan.'

I swallowed. There was something about him that made me think of Ram and his control over me. What was I doing? I would lose the freedom I now knew. I imagined myself a prisoner in a locked room, the door opening only to allow in a man, then locked again. And if the man proved foul in his requests, or even caused me pain, there would be nobody to protect me, and no means of escape. I took a step back. 'I think not,' I said.

Louis looked at Chinese Sally, then they both looked at me. 'What do you mean?' he asked, his voice nasty.

I took off the cloak and bonnet and handed them to Sal. 'You can come back and collect the gown, if you wish,' I told her. 'I won't be any man's possession.'

'Are you mad?' she said. 'Don't you see? Nobody gives a toss about you down on Paradise Street. Nobody cares if you live or die. You're just another doxy on the street, with nothing to live for.' Her voice had become harder, angry, and she reached forward and shook my arm like a terrier with a rat in its jaws. The fruitwood box fell to the street, and I heard the tinkle of breaking glass. 'Don't make me look a fool, Linny.'

I picked up the box and held it to my chest, stepping further away from her. The November wind chilled me to the bone without the warm cloak. 'At least I work for myself, and make my own decisions. I choose my customers. I eat what I want, when I want. Blue looks after me. I do as I please. You may see your life with him,' I tossed my head in Louis's direction, 'and that's all very well, Chinese Sally, but to me it sounds as though you're little more than a bird in a cage.'

'Fine, then,' she said, hooking her arm through Louis's. 'Stay on the street. Stay there and rot. Before you know it you'll find you're nothing but a used-up old whore who can't give it away for a pint of ale.'

Louis ignored me, and helped Chinese Sally into the carriage. The door slammed and the horses moved forward. I stayed where I was, thinking about what I'd just given up, and what I had to go back to. Had I made the right decision? Chinese Sally had been right about no one caring whether I lived or died.

My feet and fingers grew numb with cold; my back ached from standing stiffly for so long in one position. Eventually I heard the cheery whistle of the gaslight man with his ladder. The lamps were illuminated, one by one. The street glowed with a soft, deceptive light, and I knew what I must do.

As I began the long walk back to Paradise Street I thought of the broken mirror in the box under my arm, and imagined the knowing wink Blue would give me when I appeared back on the corner.

And so life went on. Winter blended to spring and spring to summer, summer to autumn. I passed my sixteenth birthday, and then my seventeenth. The customers came and went like the seasons. I grew older, and my desire to leave that life grew stronger.

CHAPTER EIGHT

H E HAD HANDS that smelt of fish. He was trying to pass himself off as a gentleman, with his fine black wool coat and top hat, but I knew by the putrid odour ingrained in his thick fingers that he was no more than a fishmonger, wearing a rented outfit for the evening. Well, we both pretend, then, don't we? I thought, supporting the man's weight as he steered me into an alley, his arm draped heavily over my shoulders.

It was late October, and I went about my job with weary, practised movements. I had been with Blue for over three years now, having had my seventeenth birthday in August. I didn't enjoy my time with the other girls as I once had, and I'd even lost the joy of reading. There seemed no time or privacy, and the energy and passion I had once felt at holding beautiful books, reading their magic and studying how they were made, had trickled away.

Nor did I worry much about my appearance: none of the customers cared about it. For the last few months thoughts of my mother had come more often. Some nights as I waited for a customer to finish I closed my eyes and envisaged the life she had wanted for me, away from the filth and stench of Back Phoebe Anne Street. I tried to picture myself at a table like those I had sat at with the man

I called Uncle Horace. I saw myself among sparkling glass and china, so delicate as to be almost transparent, reaching for the fish fork, the butter knife, the soup spoon, knowing when to pour the port, the wine and the sherry.

Now, my back pressed painfully against the rough brick of a dark building in an alley off Paradise Street – there would soon be a trail of bruises dark as inky kisses up my spine – the thick fingers of the fishmonger's left hand searched high inside me while he jiggled himself against my skirt with his right hand. I thought idly how fortunate it was that he was the last for the night. Surely another customer would object to the smell he was leaving on me.

It was no good. The fishmonger gave up. He pulled out his fingers and, his elbow knocked my hip sharply as he buttoned his trousers angrily.

'That'll be sixpence, sir,' I said, straightening my skirt and kneading my sore hip. 'A tanner, please.' I held out my hand.

'You'll get nowt. I got nothing, and I'll pay for nothing,' he said, walking away.

I sidestepped a puddle of streaky vomit glinting in the light from the street and caught his sleeve. 'Now, sir,' I told him, my voice never losing its sweetness, ' 'twasn't my fault you weren't at your best tonight. And you did find a bit of pleasure, I'm sure, judging by your familiarity of me.'

He stopped, looking down at my hand on the thick wool of his sleeve. 'I'll give you twopence, and not a penny more.' He dug in the pocket of his tight striped waistcoat and took out the coins. As he handed them to me his eyes rested on the skin just above my bodice. 'Could be that yer wrong. It *were* yer fault I weren't at me best. That's horrible, a right mess. Why don't you cover yerself?'

I held the money tightly in my fist. 'And why should I? For wasn't it one very like yourself who caused it?'

The fishmonger mumbled something unintelligible and turned away. He unbuttoned his trousers again and urinated against the wall, steam rising in the cool air. I watched the puddle he created, running along the veins between the cobbles.

I tucked the coins into the slit in the underside of my waistband, then carefully stepped over the filthy, uneven surface of the alley and out on to the nearly deserted street.

'Hoi! Linny!'

I peered down the dim street, trying to see through the shadows, then waved as the other girl hurried towards me.

'Did you have a good night, then, Linny?' Annabelle asked. She was chewing gingerly on a hard roll stuffed with greasy herring. Her cheekbone shone swollen.

'It hasn't been too bad, except for the last one. He couldn't bring his fine soldier to stand at attention, and wouldn't pay what I asked,' I told her.

Annabelle nodded. 'Bugger the rotten sods and their limp cockstands. You should carry a frumper, as I do. A sturdy blade flashing against their jewels makes 'em cough up soon enough.'

I nodded, thinking of the bone-handled knife with which I'd threatened Ram Munt, and had had cause to bring out a few more times when I'd felt truly fearful. But I'd lost it last July, when my untied straw bonnet had been blown off into the street in a sudden dry gust of gritty wind. I'd run to retrieve it before it was flattened by a horse's hoof. But it had danced and twirled away from me, caught up in the persistent wind, and by the time I'd caught it, brushed off the dust and put it back on, my knife was gone. I retraced my steps over and over again, but the knife had disappeared, snatched up, most likely, by a street urchin with a magpie's eye. I hadn't wanted to spend the money to buy another. Now I realized Annabelle was right. More and more I had to fight – either for my money or to defend myself. The customers were getting rougher and cheaper.

'Comin' for a drink?' Annabelle asked.

'No.' I yawned, blinking as the chapel bells of St Peter's chimed five times. 'I'm off to get a few hours' sleep.'

Annabelle went up the street and I made my way back to the dilapidated room on Jack Street. Now I shared it with Annabelle, Helen and Dorie.

What I had told Annabelle was true; I *was* tired. But the other reason for not going to the Goat's Head was that I didn't want to spend one extra penny of my money. I'd saved seven pounds. The fare advertised on the posters had risen from five to seven pounds over the last two years, and was always dropping or rising a few shillings, depending on the season and the ship, but seven pounds was a safe bet. I planned to work one more month, just one, to save a little more so that I wouldn't be penniless when I arrived in New York.

I would never be forced on to the street again.

As I silently let myself into the foetid room on Jack Street I saw two humped, motionless figures on the narrow mattress, and was glad Annabelle hadn't come home. Only three of us could crowd on to the flock pallet; Annabelle and I, had we come home together, would have had to draw lots to see who had the bed and who the floor. There was a definite nip in the air, and if I'd pulled the short straw, with only my shawl and extra dress to cover me, it would have been unpleasant on the cold floorboards without even a strip of drugget to keep out the draught. There was a tiny grate but we didn't light a fire because of the clouds of black smoke it emitted. The walls, untouched by the whitewash brush in years, were furred a delicate green by the rising damp. Rain made the rotting beams creak, and the window rattled in even the slightest wind. The glass was so smudged with dirt and soot that the room was in a never-ending twilight.

I took off my boots and pulled off my dress so I could unhook the front stays of my corset. Then, shivering, I put my dress back on, wrapped my shawl round me and crowded on to the edge of the flattened, stained pallet. I had to shove Dorie with my hip; she pressed closer to Helen, forcing her against the wall. I was almost asleep by the time I turned on to my other side, facing into the dark room. With my eyes closed, I fingered the reassuring thickness of my waistband – my pendant and coins, all stuffed into the slit I had made in it. There was an identical opening in the waistband of my other dress, and nobody knew about my savings, not even the other girls in the room. I'd surreptitiously transfer them with the pendant when I changed my dress each week. I'd wait until the other girls were gone or, if that proved impossible, I would turn away, facing into the corner as I pulled off one dress and slipped the other over my head. I let whoever was in the room think that it was because I was ashamed of my scarred torso.

The fruitwood box, the coins and books it had contained, had been stolen over a year ago. The only reason my pendant had been spared was because Helen, without asking, had taken it and worn it that night. I'd been furious with her when I'd seen it round her neck on the street, and had demanded it back. Later, I'd returned to Jack Street and found the room turned upside down, my box gone, and I'd been grateful that Helen had decided to borrow the pendant.

After that I'd kept it and my money with me.

With sleep coming sweetly over me, I recited the rote prayer to try to keep away the nightmare, the overpowering crush of blood and hair, cold water and the plunging shears. When I was awakened by it, as was usual every third or fourth night, I'd sit up, bathed in sweat, my mouth stretched wide as I took deep, gulping gasps. The truth of that nightmare – the knowledge that I had killed a man, even though it had been to protect myself from the same fate – was like a slinking dark animal, something with sharp teeth and yellow eyes. It was always following me, sometimes close on my heels, at other times sitting some distance away, watching. Under bright gaslights or a candle's soft glow it stayed low, pushed away by the warmth and light. But it came back when I was in the dark. In the cold of this autumn it had grown larger. There were times, now, that I felt it so close I'd whirl in the darkness of the street, thinking I heard it breathing. And then I knew the nightmare would come that night.

Now it had come three nights in succession, and I'd only managed a few hours of restless sleep. My body ached with exhaustion, and I willed myself not to dream. I felt my eyelids ease, knew the line between my brows was disappearing. Just before I let myself go, I put one hand up, in the old position, over my ruined breast: it comforted me to protect it, although I don't know why. Lately I'd been moving my other hand from its usual spot, guarding my waistband. Now I moved it further down, to my belly, cradling the child furled inside.

I knew it was a girl, and that I would call her Frances. I don't know exactly when or how she was conceived; I'd always been careful with my prevention – using the bit of sponge, washed out every morning, then soaked in alum and sulphate of zinc and put in place before my first customer; after my last, I took out the sponge and used the syringe, wrapped in a rag dripping with the same witch's brew, no matter how weary I was. It had been Blue who had taught me what to do, and I'd used the sponge and syringe faithfully as soon as my first bleeding began, only three months after I'd left Back Phoebe Anne Street for good. But all the girls get caught at one time or other. It had happened to me before, just at the end of my first year with Blue, but I hadn't even been aware of it until it was almost over. It was Helen, come back to Jack Street for her cloak, who had told me what was happening. She'd found me on the bed when I should have been out working, doubled with pain, my face waxen and wet with sweat. After a few questions she slipped out and brought back two pints of ale. Then she had sat beside me, forcing me to drink it, telling me it would be over soon, and to be glad. This way, she told me, I wouldn't have to pay to get rid of it.

All I'd felt was relief when at last the cramping and clotted bleeding had stopped. Nothing else.

But this time had been different. For one thing, I'd realized fairly early that a baby had started. And I knew it was the sign I'd been waiting for.

The trip to New York would take six weeks, longer if the weather proved poor. If I left at the end of the month, I would arrive before the baby was due. She would be born there, in the great New World, and she would be an American. I would find a respectable job – for weren't there all sorts of jobs to be had in America, especially in the place called New York? Nobody would know me, and I would create a new life for my daughter, and she would never know about my life — this life — in Liverpool.

For the last few months, while I waited for each customer to finish, murmuring rote praises and moaning with fake pleasure to bring them on faster, I made up the stories I would tell little Frances about the fine gentleman who had been her father, what had happened to him, and how I had come to the United States of America.

Then, early one morning as I had walked back to Jack Street, the rain falling in torrents and the inky sky occasionally bleached by the sheet lightning that flashed from far out over the Mersey, I grasped, with a sharp pang, that my mother had done the same thing.

For the first time, I wondered if perhaps I didn't carry noble blood. My hand sought out the birthmark under my wet cuff and fingered the raised shape of the fish.

'When are you getting rid of it?'

I shook my hands over the washbasin and wiped my face with a clean rag, then looked down at Dorie. Helen had gone to buy herself a hot pie, and Annabelle hadn't returned after the night's work, but Dorie was stretched on the bed, enjoying having the space to herself before she headed out on to the street that afternoon.

I put my hands on my abdomen, wishing I'd pulled my stays tighter. 'Can you tell?'

'I can. But most others wouldn't see it — you're that small. How far gone are you?'

'I don't know.' For my own reasons I didn't want to tell Dorie that I knew it to be almost six months. 'But it's been quickening a while now,' I added, thinking of the tiny fluttering that cheered me when little else could.

Dorie made a sound of disgust. 'It's a right fool you are, then. Once it's quickening it's harder to get rid of. Means you must be at least four months along. Why didn't you do something sooner? But it's not too late – although it'll be hard on you. A lot more painful and messy, but it can be done if you find the right person, and are willing to pay.' She stuck a finger into her mouth and dug at a back molar, her face contorting; the heavy folds of her eyelids almost hid her small eyes.

'Toothache?'

She sat up, nodding. 'I'll have it yanked at the barber later today. Why don't you come with me? I'll set you up, as long as you've got the money. There's someone the barber knows; I've used him.'

I tied a dark blue ribbon in my hair, shook my head and picked up my shawl.

'What do you do with all your money, Linny? You don't buy yourself any finery, or even a frock from the pawnshop. And you hardly ever come to a tavern or chop house with us no more, and Lord knows you eat next to nothing. No fancy cakes, no fruit pies. Just the slop from the stalls, potatoes and ox cheeks.'

'I'm saving it.'

'Not for a rainy day, I hope,' Dorie said, laughing, her eyes disappearing. Then she grimaced and slapped her cheek. 'Ow. You'd have it all spent in one November if you was saving it for that.' Her tongue probed the back of her mouth. 'You'll come with me, then?'

I shook my head again, then left her to worry her throbbing tooth.

★ ★ ★

95

I knew some of the girls who had been forced to carry a baby to birth because it couldn't be got rid of. Most left their newborns on the steps of the workhouse or a church. Only one girl I knew, Elsie, had tried to keep hers and stay in the game. She left it with a toothless hag during the night when she was at work, and the little thing – a well-formed boy – had appeared to thrive for the first four or five months. But one night he wouldn't stop crying, and the old hag, trying to quieten the teething infant so the others in the room wouldn't throw her out, had overdosed him with Mother Bailey's Quieting Syrup. The baby fell into a deep, deadly laudanum-laced sleep from which he never awoke. After that Elsie slipped away from Paradise Street, and word filtered down to us that she'd hanged herself in a flooded cellar off Lime Kiln Lane.

But, of course, no one ever knew for sure.

CHAPTER NINE

I WAS MORE TIRED than I ever remembered feeling. It didn't matter how many hours I slept, I was still weary when I awoke late afternoon to prepare for the night. I knew it was the baby, taking what she needed to grow. My feet hurt more than ever. I saw, each dawn as I unlaced my boots, that my ankles were swollen, the skin marked with angry red creases where the leather bit into them.

This particular evening – 5 November, Bonfire Night – I considered not going out at all. Perhaps I would celebrate Guy Fawkes and buy myself something hot to eat, then spend the night on Jack Street, listening to the fireworks. Maybe I would even treat myself to a yellow-backed penny novel, and attempt to read.

But even as I cleared a spot in the soot-covered window and looked down at the teeming alley below, dreaming of sailing away, and of playing with my pretty baby in a sunlit patch of grass, I knew I would have to go out. I still had to give a minimum amount to Blue each night, even if I didn't have any customers. And I wouldn't dip into my savings – I was so close I could hear the ripple of sails in the wind.

I'd been pulling fewer and fewer customers this last while. I worried, foremost, that little Frances would come to harm from some of the rougher ones. As well, my body was heavier and unwieldy, my dresses uncomfortably tight even after I had let out all the seams. I found it difficult to muster the enthusiasm necessary to elicit a favourable response, and many men, perhaps reading the unconscious unwillingness in my face and posture, would glance over me and move on to another girl.

As I laced up my boots, I saw just how badly I needed to leave it all – the damp room on Jack Street, the maze of dark alleys filled with drunken customers. And the streets were becoming ever more dangerous. In the last three weeks three prostitutes had turned up dead, strangled and left down by the docks. I had known one; she was a pallid young thing, her two front teeth knocked out in a brawl with another whore a few months earlier. There were rumours that even more girls had gone missing since the summer, but if a body never materialized its owner could not be declared dead.

That evening I picked out a spot on the corner of Paradise and Cable Streets where I'd often had good luck. Ten bells had chimed, a cacophony from all the churches nearby – St George's, St Peter's, St Thomas's – but the evening was slow, only three customers. It was often eleven before business picked up, when gentlemen on their own flooded out of the theatres, the music and dance halls. But as it was Bonfire Night, many men, their faces ruddy with the night air and rum, would go home to spend the rest of the evening watching the public fireworks with their children. It was cold. That afternoon, the sky had been leaden, the smell of snow in the air. Now a thick fog descended. On the next corner I could make out the orange glow of a burning tar barrel, lit by the drunks with nowhere to doss. The street-lamps were little more than misty orbs.

A few minutes after the echo of the last bell had died, I heard the clatter of horses' hoofs behind me. I turned, blinded momentarily by the lanterns swinging on either side of a carriage. It was a fine brougham with a pair of dancing horses. I'd seen it before, although never its passenger. It had started appearing a week ago, and one of the girls – Little Eve – had been inside.

She had whispered to me, only a few evenings ago, that it was best not to get into it. 'Take it from me, I was sorry. A mean sort he is,' she told me. 'He likes to give it down the throat or up the arse, and he's brutal with his hands. He's knocked about more than me, I've heard. Look what he did.' Little Eve had pulled back her bonnet to show me a red, swollen ear with an oozing scab where the lobe joined the jaw. 'Pretty near tore it off my head. He pays well, but you'd do better to avoid him. A bit of a villain. And you never know, Linny, who's to say he's not the one what's killed those girls?'

'You're imagining too much, Little Eve. A killer wouldn't keep coming back to the same place, would he? He'd be afraid of being caught. And, besides, you're still here, aren't you?' She didn't return my smile, and rearranged her bonnet over her injured ear.

Now the carriage stopped, and when the curtain was pulled aside, an ordinary middle-aged man looked out at me. An overshot jaw, sagging skin around the eyes and mouth, but nothing sinister. Although I knew that looks meant little, I usually trusted my instincts, and more than once I'd been right. Still, I thought about Little Eve's ear, and stayed where I was.

'Good evening, lass,' the man said. 'Are ye not cold, standing in this chill?'

Scottish. Often noisy, as they came, given to huffing and groaning, but the cadence of their voices always reminded me of my mother, and I'd a soft spot for them.

'I might be a little,' I told him.

He looked me up and down, his eyes stopping on my scar. They lingered there, seeming to caress the damaged skin. 'Would ye like to come for a wee ride, then? Have a nip and warm yourself on this miserable night?' He held up a silver flask. When I still didn't come closer, he took a long drink, then put the stopper back into it. 'I pay well,' he said. 'I'll give you a sovereign.'

'A sovereign?' I repeated. That was triple what I was hoping to save over the next month. 'Did I hear you correctly, sir? You did say a sovereign?'

'I did,' the man said, smiling now. His eyeteeth were very yellow. The horses stamped their heavy feet, their tails swinging, churning the fog, and one nodded testily, impatient at being kept waiting.

'I'm sorry, sir, but I must see it before I get in with you.' I expected him to drive off then: gentlemen in fine carriages did not like to have to prove themselves — in any way — to a girl of Paradise Street.

But the man's expression didn't change. In the next instant he had held up the gold piece, glinting in the light of the carriage lantern. 'I have it here,' he said.

I didn't like his smile. But a pound! I could stop work after tonight, and look for a ship sailing earlier. It would mean baby Frances and I could be well taken care of until I could find a job. Bugger Little Eve and her warning.

It was a lucky break, I told myself, and one I deserved.

'All right, sir,' I said, and stepped up to the carriage. The man opened the door from the inside and I climbed in, sitting across from him, arranging my skirt over my knees and crossing my ankles in their thick boots.

'I fear winter is upon us early,' I said, in my best voice.

The man held out the flask as he tucked the coin into the pocket of his fustian coat and patted it. 'Later,' he said. 'Now, what's your name?' He pulled a tartan lap robe over his legs.

'Linny,' I told him. 'And I don't drink spirits, sir.'

He laughed then, a deep rumble. 'Well, I have found myself a rare bird, haven't I?' He put the flask to his mouth again and drank, until it was empty. Then he shook it, and threw it to the floor.

It landed at my feet, and I looked at it. Silver, with initials, but there wasn't enough light in the carriage to make them out.

We drove for quite a time. I couldn't see where we were going, as he'd kept the curtains drawn, but I suspected we were circling the streets, and that once he was finished with me he would drop me back where he'd found me. Even in the darkness inside the carriage I was able to see the gleam of his eyes. They never left me. I tried, at first, to make conversation, but he was uninterested in talk. Eventually he motioned for me to sit beside him. I did as he bade, and immediately he ran his index finger over my scar, over and over, finally lowering his head to lick and nibble at the puckered flesh. I ground my teeth: I had been subjected to all manner of indignities, but somehow this filled me with a different revulsion, perhaps because no one had dared touch it before. Somehow, I considered this the only part of me left unviolated, the only area of my body that had not been used for a man's pleasure.

When I felt I could not bear it another second, I tried to

pull away from him. Thankfully he lifted his head, then tossed aside the lap robe. With one hand he pushed me to my knees in front of him, while the other worked at his buttons.

Still repulsed by his saliva wet and thick on my breast, I recoiled when I was hit by the vile smell as he burst out of his trousers, more than ready. He took hold of my head on either side and pulled my face close to his groin.

I struggled, attempting to draw back, wanting to ask him if perhaps he'd prefer something else, I could suggest other ways to please him, but before I could speak he slapped the side of my head, so smartly that my ear rang.

I knew I would have to do as he wanted, and quickly, if I was to get away without a beating, but the first slap was followed by a second, harder, stunning me. He tried to stand in the swaying carriage, his wool trousers slipping to his ankles. He towered over me with his open hand raised as I struggled to right myself.

But now he was in his game, the one that all of us from the street knew too well: he couldn't find his own satisfaction without giving pain and humiliation first.

'Sir, please,' I said, 'give me a chance to—' but he hit me again, and I fell to one side, hands flailing. Inadvertently I grabbed the door handle. The door opened, I swung out, still gripping the handle, and then I was on my face on the cobbles at the side of a street.

All the air had been knocked out of me. I lay there, gasping, in the middle of a crowd. There were so many boots, horses' hoofs and wheels passing close to my head that I feared I would be trampled.

In the next moment there were hands under my arms, and I was dragged to safety in front of the buildings that lined the street. A woman with a small boy had come to my aid. 'Are you all right, miss?' she asked, and I nodded, still bent over, trying to breathe.

'We seed you,' the boy said, 'come flying out the carriage.'

I raised my head and looked down the busy street. The carriage had disappeared. I put my hand to my chest: my heart was pounding.

'Will you be all right now?' the woman asked again, and I thanked her for her help. She was well into middle age, her face badly lined, and a number of missing bottom teeth had shaped her chin into an inquisitive point. Under a faded burgundy bonnet, her white hair had the yellow cast of one who had been blonde, although her eyebrows were coarse and dark.

I looked around. Nothing was familiar. 'What place is this?' I asked her.

'You're way down Richmond Row, miss,' she said.

My heart sank. The carriage hadn't been circling the streets. We'd come far from the centre of Liverpool.

The woman reached out and brushed at my sleeve. 'Have you no reticule, my dear? No shawl?'

I cursed myself for my foolishness. As well as being shaken and losing the sovereign – if indeed the Scot had intended to give it to me – I'd lost my shawl and my skirt was marked with boot-black. My hand flew to my waistband: the reassuring thickness was there.

The woman was watching me.

'No. I suppose I've lost them.' I didn't know how to explain what had happened to her. The dark eyes were kind, almost moist, as if she were worried about me even though I was a stranger to her.

'A pretty young thing like yourself,' she said, as if she'd read my thoughts, 'so cruelly treated.' Her eyes filmed

103

further. 'I lost a daughter of my own. I know how hard life can be for a young lady.' We were pushed and jostled by the noisy crowd. 'It's not right, one so fine as yourself, so abused,' she said, raising her voice to be heard over the shouts and the boom of distant fireworks. 'You should sit and have a sup of ale to steady your nerves.' She glanced at the boy. 'Why, if we had but a penny to spare we'd buy you a drink.'

The boy licked his lips. 'I's thirsty, Ma,' he said. He looked five or six, and I was surprised that he called the woman Ma: she appeared far too old to be his mother.

'I know, my son, but times is hard. You know your ma hasn't so much as a penny.'

I knew I was being taken in, for the child had spoken up as if on cue, but I was grateful to have been helped when most would have passed me by. 'You must let me buy you and your son a drink,' I said. 'To repay your kindness.'

The woman put her hand on the boy's head. His black hair was long and stiff with dirt, his dark eyelashes crusty. He had pale blue eyes, enormous in his small face, and his features were even. He would have been a handsome lad if he hadn't been so filthy. 'I don't care for myself, but my wee boy has been walking for hours now, and is weary. We wanted to watch the fireworks over at the park. A warm drink of barley water would pick him up. But you've lost your reticule. If you've no money . . .' She left the sentence hanging.

'I've a bit put aside,' I said.

She nodded. 'There's a nice public house only a few steps up the street, if you're able.'

The thought of sitting down for a warm drink was appealing. Although I was breathing normally now, there was a sharp pain in my back. I put my hand on it and, within a few seconds, it lessened.

The woman linked her arm through mine and led me to a public house, its name – the Green Firkin – painted in fancy curled letters on the thick glass. As she pushed the door open, a burst of drunken singing rushed at us, along with the smell of spilled gin, cigar smoke and sweat. We had to work our way through the customers packed shoulder to shoulder. As we approached a table in the far corner, a woman and two older men sitting there got up, and we took their places. I saw the woman who had rescued me nod at one of the men, and he dipped his head at her as if they knew each other. 'I've stopped here once or twice before,' she explained. 'It's a friendly place.'

As soon as we seated ourselves I put my hands under the table and dug into my waistband for a few coins. The woman took no notice of me: she was licking her fingers and rubbing at the boy's face in a pathetic attempt to clean him.

'I'll take a hot lemon gin,' she said, 'and the barley water for my boy, please.'

I made my way to the bar and ordered the gin, with barley water for myself and the child.

I managed to get the full glasses back to our table, although as soon as I set them down the pain returned. I leaned forward to rub my lower back with my fist.

'Have you trouble, dear?' the woman asked, and tossed back her gin in a deft, familiar gesture. She smacked her lips with a rubbery sound, and set the empty glass on the table.

'I must have bruised my back falling from the carriage,' I told her, sat down and took a long draught from my glass. 'I'll get myself home, and once I lie down it will be fine.' I looked at her empty glass; the child's was still full.

She'd want another drink. But I needed to get away from this noisy, smoke-filled place. And I was so far from Jack Street.

What a spoiled evening, I thought, as the child took a sip of his drink. Not only had I lost my shawl and those few hours of work, but I was buying gin for this woman and would have to hire a carriage to take me back to Jack Street.

As I turned to the woman to tell her I'd be on my way, the boy knocked over his glass, and the cooling, sticky liquid had pooled in my lap before I could move. The woman grabbed her shawl off her shoulders and mopped at my skirt, shouting at the boy for his carelessness. His face screwed up and he howled in a high, feral wail, his mouth a black square.

'Please, please,' I said, as she frantically brushed at my skirt. 'It doesn't matter. It's all right,' I said to the boy, for now he was grinding grimy fists into his eyes, and his howls were even louder.

'You're going to catch it – a good clout round the ear, that's what you'll get,' the woman yelled at him, standing now, her soaking shawl rolled into a bundle.

'No, Ma, no,' the boy cried, jumping from his stool and running for the door.

'Please, it's not impor—' I tried to tell the woman, but her mouth was fixed in a grim line.

'I'll catch up with him on the street, and haul him back,' she told me, then hurried after him. 'Wait here for me,' she added, over her shoulder.

I didn't intend to spend the rest of the night buying her gin; I hoped that the boy was a fast runner, and would have his mother – if, indeed, she was his mother – chasing him far down the street so that I could slip out and into a carriage before she returned.

The pain in my back dug deeper now, and I had to steady myself with my hands flat on the table as I stood to leave. When it passed, I reached down to shake out my skirt, wet from the spilled barley water, and saw that the waistband had been turned out. I grabbed it, turned it out further. It was empty. I dropped to my knees and scrabbled on the filthy floor under the table with my hands, crying, 'No! No, no, no!' in a high, desperate shriek not unlike the child's had been. Except that his had been a well-practised act.

I fought my way through the packed room to the door and looked up and down the street, but it was impossible to see through the men, women, children, horses and carts that thronged it. I raced back inside and told the landlord what had happened. Did he know the woman and boy? I asked. Were they regulars here?

But he wasn't interested. 'Can't help you,' he said.

'But – but she stole everything I had,' I wailed, although the man had moved down the bar and was talking to a woman sitting there.

The pain in my back was so strong now that it jolted me. My knees buckled with the unexpected shock, and a young man who had been nursing a glass of dark ale grabbed me. 'Are you ill, miss?' he asked, grasping my forearm.

When the pain receded, I felt a tremor from his hand and looked down at it, the knobbly wrist emerging from too-short sleeves. He was shaking with a mild palsy. 'No, I'm not ill, just sick at being robbed. Is there nothing anyone can do?' I cried, looking into his long, plain face. His eyes – deep blue with a darker rim – were small but kind.

'Whoever robbed you will be well away. With the Guy Fawkes celebrations and the crowds, it's easy for them to do their work.'

I withdrew my arm and stood still. The enormity of what had happened was unbearable. All this time on the street, so careful with my savings, and now caught in the oldest trick. Had my brains, as well as my back, been jolted by the fall from the carriage?

'I could see you to your home, miss,' the young man said, 'if you're worried about walking out on your own.'

I raised my head. Worried about walking out on my own? Did he not see me for what I was? Or perhaps he did, and thought he could slip in a free one by pretending concern. Nobody got one for free, not from me. I'd had enough taken tonight. Almost everything. I put my hands on the swell of my abdomen. 'I can make my own way,' I told him, 'if you'll tell me which road to take for central Liverpool.' The pain in my back had a firm grip now.

'But if you've been robbed, you'll have no money for a carriage. It's a long way.'

He appeared genuinely concerned. But so had the woman who had just taken away my future. I pressed my lips together tightly to hold back the low moan that threatened to push its way out.

'My name is Shaker,' the man said, 'and I can assure you that you don't look in any condition to be walking all that distance. You're very pale. Is it your back, miss?' My fist was once more kneading at the pain, which was now coming in waves, peaking, then receding.

'I've had a fall. It will pass soon,' I said, breathing deeply as the pain ebbed.

'Could I buy you a warm drink? Would that help?' he asked.

As I opened my mouth to say no, a particularly deep

spasm struck me and I cried out. Without meaning to, I clutched at the man's lapel.

He put his arm round my waist, and held me until the sensation lessened. 'I suspect it's not your back, miss, but something else,' he said, not meeting my eyes, but fixing his stare on the top of my head.

I felt his fingers move to one side of my abdomen. They pressed gently, through my corset, as if probing. 'Please,' I said, softly now, 'I just need to get home. If I can only—' But another wave crashed into me, and this time I had to bend over. The sound that came from my lips was animal-like, almost a grunt.

He picked me up, then, and the pain was too intense for me to object. He made his way through the crush of bodies and I leaned against his chest, my eyes shut. I couldn't bear to think of what was happening. It was wee Frances, shaken loose and wanting to be born. Too early, far too early. There was no chance she would live if she came now.

CHAPTER TEN

I WAS ABLE TO stand beside him, with his support, as he hailed a carriage and helped me inside. 'Where shall I direct the driver?' he asked, leaning in at the open door. 'Where is your home?'

I thought of the cold airless closet. The girls would be out at work for the next four or five hours. I would have to do this alone on the pallet at Jack Street. I felt my lips trembling, like the hands of the man who called himself Shaker. *No. No, no, no.* My head wagged with each inner *no*.

Shaker misinterpreted what he saw. 'It's all right. Look.' He pulled a few coins from his vest pocket. 'Here. It's enough to pay the driver.'

I couldn't say anything, just kept my eyes fixed on the faded wine-coloured curtain over the window.

Shaker waited until the carriage jolted with the impatient shifting of the horses, and there was a rough question from the driver. He answered, and climbed in beside me.

Neither of us spoke. I concentrated on the swaying curtain, biting down through each fresh assault of pain. It was no longer only in my back, but at the front and radiating down my thighs. Within ten minutes the carriage had stopped, and Shaker helped me out.

'Where are we?' I asked, looking around the dimly lit

street with its row of neat two-storey terraced houses with brick façades. I recognized traces of simple elegance in the doorways and windows, which were tall and well proportioned. I could see that the doorsteps and window-sills were well scrubbed and whitened. I cupped one hand under the rise of my abdomen in an attempt to ease the pressure.

'We're in Everton, north of the city. This is where I live – Whitefield Lane.' Shaker opened the unlocked door and led me inside. All was in darkness but for the red glow of a dying fire in a room to the left. Urged by the press of Shaker's hand on my back, I made my way up a flight of narrow stairs towards a landing. A sliver of light showed under one of the two doors there. He hesitated, and in that moment the door opened. A gaunt, grey-haired woman, holding a well-thumbed Bible in one hand and a candle in the other, stared at us. 'What is all this?' she demanded querulously, holding the candle in my direction. The flames cast craggy shadows on her scowling features. 'Who is this person?' I saw her sharp eyes taking in the cut of my dress, my apolloed hair. I knew that the odours of the ale-house – spirits, tobacco and sweat – emanated from us.

'A young woman in distress, Mother,' Shaker said.

I didn't think my legs would hold me any longer. I clung, weakly, to Shaker's sleeve, and he put his arms round me to help me stand. I leaned my forehead against his chest.

'Distress?' the woman repeated. 'From where I'm standing, she's drunk. You dare to bring home a drunken whore?' I turned to look at her, and she stepped so close that I felt the fine spray of spittle that flew from her lips. 'You disappoint me, my boy – and, much worse, you disappoint the Lord, with such behaviour.'

'Mother. You don't understand the—'

'Perhaps not. But I can't abide to see such a one as her under my roof.' Her head swivelled on her thin, wrinkled neck as she bent to speak into my face. 'Fornicator.'

Shaker ignored the word. 'It's *our* roof, Mother, not yours.'

'You give me one good reason why I should allow this, Shaker.'

'Christian charity, perhaps.'

The woman's expression changed, and she stepped back.

The agony made my knees buckle, and I moaned now, feeling tremendous pressure. I held tightly to Shaker's jacket so I wouldn't fall. In his arms, I felt the tremor of his hands on my back. 'She is about to give birth, Mother. She needs help.'

'She doesn't look with child. Although it could be because she's skin and bone, worn down by frenzied fornicating.' The woman moved closer to me again, peering first at my belly, then at my ringless fingers, and then into my face. 'And why, I ask, have you brought her here? You're not . . . connected with her, are you?' Her rheumy eyes bored into mine, suspicious and fearful now. 'Do you bear some responsibility for her state? Son? Tell me you have no responsibility towards this woman. Please.' The final word was a low whisper.

'Please,' I echoed, as the pressure felt like iron tongs, forcing my very bones apart. 'Please. Help me.'

Shaker dragged me into a dark room, half carrying me. His mother followed us. Monstrous shadows, thrown by her candle, danced on the walls. 'Why doesn't she go home, where she belongs?'

'She's been robbed of all her money. The crowds tonight . . .' Shaker trailed off. 'And she needed help,' he said. 'Now go, Mother. Go back to your room.' His voice was low but strong. 'I insist. This is not your business.'

The woman said nothing more, but left, taking the candle and closing the door behind her.

My body was no longer in my control. In the darkness I heard my voice rising in a strange, warbling call, and Shaker laid me gently on a soft surface. There was the rasp of a Congreve and then the flare of light as he touched the match to the wick of an Argand lamp. In its glow I saw I was on a narrow mattress on a rope-slung frame. It seemed the pains were building on each other, the time between them shorter and shorter. Explosions in the distance signalled the height of the fireworks. I was being torn in two.

'It's too early. It's far too early,' I whispered, drawing my knees up and apart, as Shaker lit a fire in the small grate.

'Yes, I know,' he said, almost as if to himself. 'And it appears to be too far along to stop.'

'I don't know what to do,' I said, panting now. *And I'm afraid*.

Shaker's hands were jumping wildly as he washed them in a basin. Water splashed over the front of his coat, and he removed it. Booming and crashing rattled the window pane. 'I do,' he said, then came to me.

'Let me see her.'

'It will only upset you, miss.'

'I said I want to see her.'

It had been over quickly; I didn't question anything Shaker had told me to do as he pushed up my dress and undid my stays, tucked my shimmy out of the way, then placed his large-knuckled hands on my abdomen and murmured instructions. He gave me a clean pad of cotton to bite down on when the worst of the pain came. Afterwards, he pulled the stained sheet from beneath me and spread a fresh one,

113

then brought extra cloths for the bleeding, warm water and a soft flannel for washing. He left me alone and I took off my dress and corset and cleaned myself, slowly, all over. My movements were slow and heavy, and when I had finished I lay back on the bed.

Morning hadn't yet come, although the light in the lamp seemed dimmer, and the darkness was fading. Wind whistled at the window.

'She's my baby. You can't tell me I have no right to see her.' I tried to keep the command in my voice, but I shivered even with the blanket wrapped round me. Shaker had opened the window a few inches, and the cool air rushed in, bringing fresh, somehow green-smelling air. The fireworks had long been over, and there were no sounds from outside. Used to the endless clatter and shouts of Jack Street, I found this room eerily quiet.

He studied me for another moment, then went to the washstand, which held a porcelain basin. 'Wait.'

I closed my eyes and heard small splashing sounds, gentle rustling. 'What are you doing?' I asked, as I tried to find a comfortable sitting position and pulled the blanket round my shoulders.

He didn't answer, but came to the side of the bed. He squatted beside me and lowered the porcelain basin. I looked at the tiny shape under the clean linen handkerchief that had been draped over it. A miniature winding-sheet.

I moved it with my index finger.

She lay on her side. Shaker had washed her: her skin was clean, the soft grey-blue of a mourning dove's breast, and a fine down covered her body. She was perfectly formed, but tiny, with transparent eyelids and fingernails.

I reached out and stroked the cool velvety forehead, the

arm, the back. My fingers were trembling, or perhaps not: perhaps the baby was trembling with the vibration of the basin in Shaker's hand.

I wanted to weep – the lining of my throat seemed to have swelled to an unbearable size, so thick and membranous it was difficult to swallow. Saliva filled my mouth, my nose ran, but no tears came to my eyes.

'I'm sorry. I knew it would do no good for you to—'

I had to work at my throat, and my voice returned, although only as a dull croak. 'Her name is Frances.' I took my hand away from the baby and put it into my lap, where the other clasped it. 'I'm glad she didn't live. What kind of life is it in this world for a girl?'

Shaker set the basin gently on the washstand, looking down at the baby.

'You won't dump her down a midden, will you? Give her to me, and I'll bury her myself.'

Shaker continued to gaze at the dead child.

'If you want me to leave, I'll go now. I'll take her and go,' I said, angered somehow by Shaker's stooped shoulders, his trembling hands, the sorrow that seemed a part of him. What right did he have to grieve for my Frances? He knew nothing of me, nor I of him.

I tried to swing my legs to the floor, and cried out at the sharp pain. The blanket fell away.

'I'll let you do with her whatever you wish,' Shaker said, turning to me. He stood still, except for the fluttering hands, which he tucked under his arms. 'What is your name?'

'Linny Gow,' I said, sitting there, naked but for my thin chemise. I put my palms at either side of me on the bed, preparing to push myself up. 'I must go,' I said.

'Why?' Shaker asked.

I didn't have an answer. My eyes went to the basin.

'Would you like to lie here, for a few hours at least, until the worst of the bleeding stops and you have enough strength to go home?' He came closer.

When I didn't answer, he continued, 'You mustn't go straight back to work. At least, not for a few days. Your body needs time to heal.'

Of course he knew what I was. He hadn't needed his mother to point out my occupation. He'd known from the first moment I'd stepped beside him in the public house, although his manner towards me had been so respectful that I had believed he was fooled for a short time.

At his mention of work I was overcome with exhaustion. I could not go out into the cold pre-dawn and walk all the way to Jack Street. 'I'll rest for an hour at the most,' I told him. 'Only an hour.' I lay down.

Shaker rearranged the thick wool blanket over me, and his eyes flickered over my scar. I heard an almost imperceptible sigh. Then he closed the window, stoked the fire, turned out the lamp and left.

As I lay there, warm, sleepless, in the first pale rays of morning light, I looked away from the basin towards the window. A bare wet branch touched the glass cautiously in the wind, which was dying away. The sky was pearly. I thought about Shaker, and wondered that he had known what to do. I thought of the sadness on his face as he held the basin towards me, and then later as he stared down at my dead baby.

I awoke to bright sunlight streaming through a window that was as clean as any I'd ever seen. I threw back the blanket and sat up, stiff and aching, as if I'd been beaten far worse than the few blows from the Scot in the carriage. I felt skinned, both inside and out, as if even a word would produce pain. I stood slowly, my legs shaky, and dressed.

As I let down my tangled apollo and struggled with the matted tangles, I looked at the washstand. In place of the basin there was a small tin-plated box. Shaker must have come in while I was asleep. A box for storing jewellery, was my first thought, or for keepsakes. I went to it and ran my fingers over it. Then realization struck, and I opened the lid a little. I saw the crisp white of the linen handkerchief, touched it and felt the small curled contents. I closed the lid.

The room contained a broad, austere desk and a straight chair. Stacks of books were piled on the desk, and one lay open. On the wall above it there was a drawing of a man with no flesh, just muscle, sinew and veins. There were other drawings of bones, one of a skull, split in half, with a wormy mass showing on the open side. And then I saw them, on the floor beside the desk. Jars.

For one horrible moment I was back in the brightly lit room with its terrible collection.

I went closer, afraid of what I might see. But these jars didn't contain hair. At first I thought the contents to be food – shapes that I had only seen on a butcher's stall floated in them. Then I grasped that they were parts of the body, preserved. Some I didn't recognize, although I saw kidneys, a heart, a liver. I looked at the last jar, and gasped. My hand flew to my mouth to stifle the sound, but not fast enough.

The door opened and Shaker hurried in to find me backing away from the desk. 'I'm sorry, I'm so sorry. I didn't think . . .' He was stuttering, snatching up the jar so rapidly

117

that the foetal beginnings of a human surged and bobbed in the formaldehyde.

I stared at him, stricken, feeling my own face as lifeless and bleached as the contents of the jars.

'I study the human body,' Shaker said, too quickly, as if guilty. 'I – I wanted to be a physician. Of course it's impossible for me – a physician, or even a surgeon, even the most rudimentary of barber-surgeons, like the one who once attended to you.' His eyes rested on my scar. 'Impossible, being the way I am – my hands,' he continued, as if he needed to clarify, 'but it remains a passion.' He had hidden the jar behind his back as he spoke. 'I've made some beef tea,' he said, 'and you should have some tartar emetic to make the blood stronger. But you need a physician's recommendation. It's only available at the dispensary. Are you feeling terribly indisposed?' He was babbling.

I had lowered myself on to the ladder-back chair at the desk. 'I just became light-headed from standing too quickly,' I lied. 'I'll be on my way in a moment.' I looked towards the pretty box on the table. 'Will you be wanting your box back?'

'Oh, no. Please. You had said you wanted to bury it – her, and I thought . . .'

I studied the box, not wanting to look at Shaker as he backed out of the room. He reappeared, carrying a shawl. 'I'm so sorry to have upset you, Miss Gow. Please.' He handed me the shawl – his mother's, of course. I put it round me. 'At least have a cup of the beef tea I've prepared. It's across the hall, in my mother's room. She's just returned from church, and her room is warmer. The fire hasn't been laid downstairs yet. Nan will arrive shortly and see to things. Come and sit in the other room. Please,' he added, again.

118

The suggestion of the meaty drink made saliva rush to my mouth. 'All right. Thank you, Mr . . . ?'

Colour spread upwards from Shaker's neck. 'Oh, it's just Shaker, as I told you last night. Started as an unfortunate jest while I was at school, but it stuck.' He smiled briefly, revealing crooked teeth, but it was a natural smile, and it warmed his plain face. It crossed my mind that I hadn't seen this kind of smile on a man's face for a long, long time. Not from any of the men who looked at me. 'My surname is Smallpiece. But, please, I'd prefer if you'd call me Shaker. If you don't mind the informality.'

'Thank you, Shaker,' I said. 'For last night. For helping me.' I studied his trembling hands. Did they ever stop their dance? Had they shaken as he guided the tiny blue girl out of me?

He balled them into fists, then, and I was ashamed for staring.

'You must think me such a ninny,' I said, raising my eyes, 'to be robbed like that. Me, of all people. I should know the games of the street.' I shrugged. 'I'll never get my money back, I know that.'

Shaker jammed one hand into a pocket. 'It'll have been spent on cheap gin and who knows what else by now. But I went back to the Green Firkin this morning, and the publican let me in, even though it's the Lord's Day. I asked him again, as you did last night, if he knew who the woman and child were. Of course he said he didn't – likely he would be in on it, and demand his share for letting her work his place. But I did have a look round, and found this kicked into a corner. Of course, it could be anybody's.'

He brought his hand out of his pocket and held up my pendant. At the sight of it, twirling on the end of its gold chain, the grief at having my dreams stolen came out in a dry, explosive sob. I reached for the pendant, snatched it from his fingers, and held it against my cheek.

'Her name is Frances,' I said, although I had already told him that. 'After my mother.' And then, finally, it was possible to cry. After so many years. I sobbed in a noisy, unfamiliar way, with a high-pitched keening, my nose running, eyes squeezed shut, rocking back and forth on the edge of the chair. I felt Shaker's hand on my shoulder, the trembling violent now, but it was a comfort.

When at last I could control myself, Shaker removed his hand and took a step away from me. He showed great interest in the drawing of the skinless man, then in the open book, the jars, the view from the window. He looked everywhere but at me, as if seeing me cry had been more embarrassing to him than anything he had seen the night before as I lay on his bed and he knelt between my bent legs.

CHAPTER ELEVEN

O VER A CUP of steaming beef tea in the room across the hall, which was, as Shaker had promised, warm, with a hearty fire blazing, I told Shaker my plan of going to America. About how I'd been put into the business by Ram Munt, how I'd been saving every penny I could for the purpose of leaving this life in the only way open to me. How I had almost had enough. How I had planned to raise my baby in America, and live a respectable life.

I don't know why I told him all of this, other than that I felt it was my duty to explain to him who I was, perhaps to thank him in the only way I could – other than by offering my body: by being honest with him. And as I talked, and watched his face, I realized his opinion of me mattered. I'd never felt that before.

All the time his mother was there, in her cane rocking-chair, facing the long window, tatting lace. She hadn't acknowledged me when he accompanied me into the room, one hand resting lightly on my back. He pulled out a chair for me at the small deal table in front of the fire. He acted as if she wasn't there, and in time I, too, ignored her presence.

I studied the windows, clouded from the heat, framed with crisp curtains. The wide mantel boasted a round clock in an Amritsar case, crowded by a collection of china dogs. A thick fringed rug covered the floor, warm under my feet. An oak dresser beside a horsehair screen held an assortment of glass ornaments, shells, japanned trays and gaudy biscuit boxes. The room indicated decency and prosperity.

A painting hung over the dresser, a rendition of some foreign-looking temple in blues, greens and whites. Although, even to my eye, it was poorly executed, the colours were pleasing.

'What is that painting of?' I asked, when I'd finished my story.

Shaker looked from me to the picture and back at me, as if puzzled by my question. Or perhaps surprised. He said a strange name, something that sounded like 'Tajatagra', and changed the subject. 'So you'll have to begin again, then, with saving?' he asked. He pushed his untouched cup of beef tea, now grown cold, back and forth on the well-polished tabletop, just a fraction of an inch each time. He could not remain still. I suspect he didn't drink it as his palsied hands would cause the liquid to slop over the side of the cup.

I sighed. 'I can't think of it. But of course I will. What other option is open to me? I've lost everything, save my mother's pendant. What choice have I?' I repeated, and ran my fingertip round the lip of the cup.

Shaker's mother spoke then, making both of us jump. 'What choice?' She let her tatting drop into her lap and stared at me. 'Do you not know the wonders of the Lord?' Her voice was too loud — partial deafness or anger?

'I used to go to church with my mother, when she was alive, and then for a while after she died.' I tried to keep my voice respectful for Shaker's sake, but already I hated this woman, with her suspicious eyes and pious expression.

'And what would your mother, rest her soul, think of your sinning ways now?'

'Really, Mother,' Shaker said, stealing a glance at me. The flush rose on him again.

But his mother ignored his admonishment. 'Do you think she would approve? Do you think the Lord in his glory approves of your wicked ways?'

I drank the last mouthful of my beef tea, then carefully set the cup on the table. 'I'm simply a working girl, doing what I can to get by, Mrs Smallpiece,' I said, letting an imperious note creep into my voice.

The woman's eyebrows, bushy and grey, rose into her forehead. 'And proud of it, by the sound of you. You live in an underworld of prostitution and crime, making light of our concepts of respectability and purity. Trying to pass yourself off as a lady won't work with me. I know what you are, through and through. I've known others like you. For didn't I—'

'Don't, Mother,' Shaker interrupted. 'Stop. It will do no one any good. You know what may happen if you upset yourse—'

'Pride has nothing to do with it – as you must know, being so well informed of my life,' I interrupted, staring at the old woman. I didn't care what Shaker thought now. I wouldn't be bullied by this dried-out hag. 'I started in a bookbindery beside my mother as a child of six. For my work my mother was given enough pennies a week to buy an extra bit of bacon, a loaf of bread that was half chalk, and a packet of tea leaves, used ones mixed with fresh. I'm sure you know this sad story, don't you, Mrs Smallpiece?' I glanced around the cosy room. 'But really you have no idea. You sit in your comfortable house and know that each day of your life you will be cared for and watched over. If I were still working at the bookbinder's, I would now be earning enough to rent the corner of a room in a lodging-house. I would pay half of my wage to the crimp who cheated everyone under her roof, and live on the same ration of bacon, chalky bread and weak tea. Perhaps one day I would marry, and move to another corner of another room. I'd have children and still go to work at a factory, and my life would continue thus until either child-bearing or endless work killed me.'

As I spoke, I heard my voice shift wildly, like sand beneath waves. I heard my drawing-room voice swing into the rough northern tones of Back Phoebe Anne Street. I heard the inflection of my mother's soft Scottish lilt, and then it was back to the throaty tones I had tried to perfect in the candelabra-lit dining room in the hotel near Lord Street. In my distress I couldn't hold on to one voice.

'So I chose the only way I hoped might get me away from that future. I should have known it was only a dream. I should have listened to the person who told me I was just a girl with the stink of the Mersey in my nostrils, and I would never be any better than that,' I finished, my voice now unpleasantly shrill. I stood up, trying to ignore the cramping and rush of fresh bleeding. 'I'm sorry, Shaker,' I said, ignoring the old woman now. 'I should not have spoken rudely to your mother, and it's time I was off, back to where she believes I belong.'

But Mrs Smallpiece had also risen, and approached me, one shoulder lower than the other, her face, on that side, drawn down as well. I saw a dull fire in her faded, deep-set eyes. 'I could offer you salvation. One so young as you, perhaps it hasn't set fully yet. The evil.'

'Salvation?' I asked. 'Salvation?' A derisive snick of laughter slipped from between my lips. I looked at Shaker, but he was studying his cup.

'If you take the Lord Jesus into your heart, offer up your soul to Him, there may be a chance for you to renounce your ways.' Mrs Smallpiece tried to lift her shoulder, and her chin stuck forward. 'For I also was once guilty of lustful thoughts and performed lewd acts of the flesh, yet the Lord saw fit to shine his light on me, and I was pulled from the claws of the devil. Yes, I was pulled from those claws, although not before they had sunk deep within me.' Here she flung her head in Shaker's direction. 'And my punishment for my sinning was him, there, born little better than a cripple. A son useless in body, unable to provide a daughter-in-law to care for me, unable to give me grandchildren.' She turned her oddly glowing eyes to Shaker. 'Useless,' she repeated, her voice rising to the beamed ceiling with a high, hollow echo.

I refused to look at Shaker. I kept my eyes fixed on the old woman.

Saliva bubbled on her bottom lip, and her eyelids fluttered rapidly, as if the fire I had seen there threatened to burn her. 'I accepted my punishment, kept him when others would have left him to die. And for that I was saved. The Lord in his mercy is all knowing and all seeing, Hallelujah, sayeth the Lord, Hallelujah, oh, Lord, oh, Lord, save us.' Her words came louder and faster, suddenly tripping into each other until they were merely a cacophony of grunts and garbled syllables, a speaking-in-tongues that sent a chill up my spine. In the next instant her eyes rolled heavenward and her knees buckled. She fell to the floor and her body shook with tremors, her heels beating a staccato rhythm on the floorboards.

As the acrid smell of urine filled the room I bit so hard on my bottom lip that the skin split.

Shaker knelt beside his mother, his hand under her head, turning it to one side as her tongue protruded, then forcing a smooth piece of wood he had pulled from his pocket between her clenched gums. Eventually the tremors lessened, and ceased. Shaker lowered her head to the floor, removed the wood, then took a handkerchief from his pocket and wiped her face. With a practised motion he lifted her as if she were no more than a husk and laid her on the narrow bed along one wall, tucking a large piece of flannel under her wet skirt.

He opened the window to rid the room of the smell of piss and sweat. 'I'm sorry,' he said, not meeting my eyes. 'She hasn't had one in a long while. These fits occur only when she's greatly agitated. They started after her apoplexy, a few years ago. I urge her not to excite herself,' he added. There was something in his face, some quiet desperation, that made me pity him. 'She'll be calm when she wakes. It's as if these occasional cataclysms allow her to return to her normal state for a long time afterwards,' he went on, as if assuring himself that it was all actually normal, that his life with this needy and overbearing woman was fine, that he was in some way grateful for her not abandoning him, even though it was clear it was he who had to care for her.

I looked at his mother, the line of drool shimmering down her bristled chin, and reached for the chair behind me. I sat down heavily.

Shaker sat across from me, his mother's still body stretched out a few feet from us. 'I told you, you can rest here as long as you wish. And then I'll help you get home.' He was looking at me. 'How old – do you mind if I ask? How old are you?'

'Seventeen.'

I saw surprise flicker across his face before he could stop it. 'Seventeen?'

'I've always looked younger—' I started, then understood that I had misinterpreted his surprise. 'How old did you think I was?' I knew, even after this brief time, that it was difficult for Shaker to hide his thoughts.

'I assumed you were closer to my age – twenty-three.'

I went to the gilt-framed mirror that hung on the wall beside the window, and looked at myself in bright daylight. For years I had seen myself only in the forgiving flicker of candlelight, the softening rosiness of gaslight, always in my thick layer of powder and rouge. And now I saw that I had truly become a creature of the night.

My skin, untouched by the sun for so long, had the pallor and texture of a two-day mushroom. The moon-shaped scar at the side of my mouth, from the heavy blow of a ringed hand, stood scarlet. My hair, which I had always thought of as golden, was now dry and somehow bleached of its depth of colour, like winter straw. My eyelids were shadowed purple, as were the bruised-looking pouches beneath my eyes, emphasized by caked traces of powder. And as for my eyes . . . The golden flecks that had once glinted in the brown irises, lighting them, were gone. The gold had disappeared from my hair and my eyes.

I saw Shaker's face behind me, watching me. It held the same pinched, defeated look as mine.

I backed away. 'What's happened to me?' I whispered. I was not asking Shaker, but myself. I didn't know the hollow-eyed woman in the mirror. She bore a resemblance to the ruin I had called Mother. Where was Linny, little Linny Gow, the child with the clear eyes and hair like the ripest of summer's pears?

'You've had a shock,' Shaker said quietly. 'I expect that once you feel better—'

'No,' I said, sitting again. 'No. That's not it.'

We sat in silence, listening to the quiet ticking of the clock. The sky was darkening, and the breeze from the open window lifted the strands of hair around my face. 'I don't know what I mean,' I finished limply.

Mrs Smallpiece gave a low murmur, then turned her head from side to side. Shaker helped her to her feet and settled her in her chair. Her chin slumped against her chest, but Shaker took her Bible from a shelf and put it into her loosely curled hands.

'Do you believe in signs, Miss Gow?' he asked.

He was tall. I had to tip my chin to look at him. 'Signs?' I thought of the baby. She had been my sign. But how did you interpret it when the sign didn't mean what you thought it had? Was that a sign in itself?

Although the room was still quiet, the sounds from outside grew louder: the urgent barking of a dog, the far-off lowing of cattle, the closer chiming of church bells. The breeze turned to wind, causing the curtain to billow in an arc, reminding me of the sail of a ship.

'I believe in signs,' I said.

Shaker lowered the window with a thud. Then, leaning against the sill, the light behind him, he stared at me. 'I do too, Miss Gow,' he said.

'Linny. Please call me Linny.'

The slow flush rose once more up his neck. 'I believe you are my sign, Linny Gow.'

It seemed odd and yet, somehow, I did not think it so. I simply stayed there, in the house on Whitefield Lane, with no discussion, no plan. After our conversation Shaker had disappeared, perhaps for an hour, possibly two. I had no notion of the time. I felt detached, sitting at the polished table, as if my mind were somewhere above my body, floating loose and confused. After her bout of religious fervour and the convulsive fit, Mrs Smallpiece appeared exhausted, almost as dazed as I, as if something had fled and left her empty. Eventually she made her way to the screen in the corner and went behind it, to emerge in a fresh dress. Then she returned to her chair and flipped the pages of her Bible endlessly, but didn't read from it. The two of us sat there – waiting, I felt, but for what I didn't know.

There were footsteps, two sets, on the stairs, one heavy, the other lighter, almost scampering. A stout woman clattered in with an ash pail. She stopped at the sight of me, and a young girl, with a milky, blind eye, bumped into her. Mrs Smallpiece scolded her for being late. The woman dropped the empty pail. 'How was I to know you were having company?' she demanded. 'Does that mean extra for dinner as well? That beef might not stretch. Does Merrie have to set the table for three?'

When she didn't get an answer, she turned on her heel and stalked out of the room, her ample backside swaying. The girl ran after her. In a moment I heard thumps and knocks from the staircase, as if the woman were dusting or polishing with more noise than was necessary.

Shaker returned, carrying a rolled-up flock mattress and crisp sheets, a new-looking pillow and blankets, which he arranged along the wall opposite his mother's bed. Mrs Smallpiece watched but said nothing.

Then he carried in the small tin-plated box, and took up the coal shovel from against the fireplace. I rose, holding the shawl tightly round me, and together we went down the stairs.

'Good day, Nan,' he said, as we passed the stout woman, on her knees sweeping out the sitting-room fireplace. 'And to you as well, Merrie.' The woman stared at me without replying. The girl held a figurine in one hand and a dusting rag in the other. Like the woman, she stopped what she was doing and looked at us, with her one dark blue eye, the milky one turned inward.

I walked beside Shaker through a number of streets. The sun had come out and it was warmer than it had been for several days. We stopped at a muddy lane that led to a small church surrounded by dark yews.

'There's a graveyard here, but we would have to seek permission. The Church's rules, of course.'

I nodded. 'And what would the rule for an unbaptized bastard child be?' In the next sentence I answered my own question. 'A shallow grave in unhallowed ground, among unclaimed paupers. No. I don't want to think of Frances in a place like that.'

'There's somewhere else,' he said. 'I didn't know what you wanted.' He turned, and I stuck to him like a shadow as we walked through the small village of Everton. I'd heard of Everton. Beyond the houses and shops was countryside. I'd never been in the country.

After a ten-minute walk we emerged on to a quiet road. Shaker stopped, parted a hedgerow and I stepped through. We stood in a small copse. The ground was soggy with fallen leaves, and twigs snapped under our feet when we moved. There was no sound but the dripping of the darkened boughs. There was the unfamiliar smell of grass after rain. I breathed it in: my smells were the oiliness of the docks, rotting food,

130

animal and human excrement in the streets, and the overpowering odours of the men – either the pungent unwashed smell of one class or the cologne and pomade of another. In front of us, a brave holly bush showed the beginnings of scarlet berries in the wintry air, and the long grass was soft and only now beginning to lose its rich green. 'I thought perhaps here,' Shaker said.

'Yes,' I said. 'This is a good place. This is the right place for her.'

Using the coal shovel, Shaker helped me bury Frances under the holly bush, and then backed away. I found a small, pink-streaked rock and nestled it into the freshly turned earth at the top of the small mound, then said a prayer for her. I knelt there for a time – again, time that had no length or breadth. I was aware of Shaker somewhere behind me. Finally he put his hand under my elbow to help me up, saying, 'I like to come here and think. Nobody else seems to bother with it. She won't be disturbed.'

We walked back together in silence, slowly, because I was still weak. When we entered the dining room Nan and Merrie were leaving, and a large bowl of savoury stew was on the table. The three of us had our dinner in the narrow but comfortable dining room. The wallpaper featured elaborate tea-rose clusters; it was only slightly faded, and broken horizontally by a white dado rail. We sat at a table that smelt of beeswax polish and ate from delicate plates. Although their pattern was unrecognizable from decades of washing, and there were a few nicks in the edges, the china retained an unmistakable elegance. We sat and ate without speaking, each in our own thoughts, as if we had done this all our lives.

131

CHAPTER TWELVE

THAT NIGHT I slept on the pallet in Mrs Smallpiece's room, a deep, dreamless sleep, a sleep I hadn't had for months, or maybe years, maybe since I was a child sleeping beside my mother. When I woke the next morning, I put my hand through habit to my waistband and then my belly. My eyes opened wide in the morning light as I rememberd both were empty, and all that had happened.

'Where is Shaker?' I asked, when I saw Mrs Smallpiece working on a piece of needlework in front of the fire. My voice startled me: it was almost timid.

'He's at work, good, honest work, as all God–fearing people should be.'

I rose and smoothed the sheets, then folded the blankets and patted the pillow into shape.

'Chamber pot's behind the screen,' she said, her voice pinched. 'Best do something with that hair – you're a sight. There's a comb by the washbasin.'

'Where does he work?' I asked.

'At the Lyceum,' she answered shortly.

'The Lyceum on Bold Street?' I knew the place well. It was right on the corner of Bold and Ranelagh Streets, a gentlemen's club, an impressive building with a small, grassy, semicircular area in front enclosed by an open iron fence. I had passed it often, admiring its columns and the broad marble steps leading to its grand, recessed entrance.

She nodded. 'Hurry yourself. Then take the pot down and empty it in the privy at the back. Afterwards you can come back up here and help me with my hair. I dismissed that useless Nan – she and her lazy daughter expect to be paid good money for next to nothing. Now that you're here you can take on their jobs.' I opened my mouth to protest, but she didn't give me a chance to speak. She put down her needle and held up her hands. The joints were swollen and twisted; it must have been painful for her to sew. 'More suffering for my sins,' she said. 'You'll be afflicted by something for your own wickedness, if you haven't been already. And the child was better born dead. It would have been an idiot, fathered by hundreds.'

I took a deep breath to stop myself hissing something at her – all trace of timorousness had disappeared with her wicked words. I stepped behind the screen, thankful to be out of her view for even the time it took to relieve myself. I had no intention of staying: I would never be servant to a miserable old woman with an eye cold as a haddock's.

Shaker arrived home for the evening meal looking somehow different from when I'd first seen him in the Green Firkin. It was something more than being clean-shaven, his long hair neatly combed. It went deeper than that.

We said hello to each other when he came in, both of us suddenly shy.

'I don't think she's prepared a proper meal in her life,' Mrs Smallpiece complained. 'I had to instruct her in every step. At least she has strength in her hands, so she was of some use in fetching and carrying.'

Shaker cleared his throat. 'Did Nan not come in to help today, Mother? And what of little Merrie? Who is serving dinner?'

When his mother didn't answer, I spoke up: 'Your mother told me you work at the Lyceum, in the gentlemen's club,' I said. 'I'll serve.'

He lowered himself on to his chair, and I took the plates of mutton and boiled potatoes from the sideboard and set one in front of Shaker, one in front of his mother and one at my place. I passed the gravy boat, aware of a heavy pall of awkwardness. Was it because I was serving him? Or because I was no longer in distress? Or was it because I no longer resembled the rouged and apollooed whore who had clung to him in the public house – or even the bedraggled creature who had blustered out her pathetic story of lost dreams, then hunched beside the tiny grave marked only by a pink-streaked rock?

I had combed my hair and secured it at the back of my head, my face was scrubbed clean, and I had pinned Mrs Smallpiece's shawl primly over my chest. Did I frighten him more now as an ordinary young woman?

He picked up his fork. 'Please, Miss Gow. Linny. Sit down. I work in the library. As well as the News Room that's in the Club, there's a subscription library upstairs, owned by the members.' Then he lowered his head over his food, and I was careful not to look at his attempts to get a full forkful to his mouth without losing half of it. Long minutes passed, broken only by the chink of silver on china, chewing and swallowing.

Suddenly he looked up. 'Do you read?'

'She does,' Mrs Smallpiece answered. 'I had her read to me. You know that my eyes can barely make out the print now. I chose scriptures that she needed to read. "Thou art weighed in the balance, and art found wanting" was one I thought applied to her, after her immoral life. "Ye have ploughed wickedness, ye have reaped iniquity, ye have eaten the fruit of lies—" '

'I suspected you might,' Shaker interrupted her. 'And you can write as well?'

'I haven't, not for a long time, but as a child I could. My mother taught me.'

'I see,' he said, and I recognized what was different in his face. His expression no longer reflected empty melancholy.

The next morning Mrs Smallpiece dug through her wardrobe and unceremoniously threw one of her old frocks across my pallet. The cheap, badly made and low-cut dress I'd been wearing – my garish working dress – was, I knew, unsuitable for Everton. I put on the drab brown broadcloth, eyed with chagrin the much-darned shawl and out-of-style bonnet she had also unearthed for me. The dress was a poor fit, hanging loosely. I felt as dull as it looked.

Once again I followed Mrs Smallpiece's instructions as she put me to work after breakfast, polishing the mismatched silver, then peeling vegetables delivered to the back door by the costermonger. I made biscuits and the pastry for a beef pie. A gilt-edged card was delivered, and after reading it and mumbling, 'How pleasant,' Mrs Smallpiece deposited it on a silver tray that sat on a small mahogany table near the front door. She made me read to her again, from the Bible, but after five minutes her head was nodding and she slept. I wrapped her shawl closely round me and slipped away to the clearing with its holly bush to sit tracing the smooth grooves of the pink-streaked stone. The pain in my body was healing, but a deep sadness throbbed through me. If I was to return to

Paradise Street, it would have to be tomorrow – the third day that I had been away – or Blue would give my spot, both in the room and on the street, to someone else.

But that night Shaker came home smiling broadly. He had secured a job for me in the library. I could start the following week.

I set a plate of biscuits on the table with a thud. 'You did what?'

My tone made Shaker's smile disappear. 'I said I was able to get you—'

'Did you think to ask me if I would like a job in a library? I haven't made up my mind as to what I plan to do next. You are very kind, but I've stayed until now to get my strength back, as you suggested. I haven't made up my mind about anything.'

'Haven't you?' he asked.

I fidgeted with the bread knife. 'Besides, who would hire me without meeting me? Who would hire a complete stranger?'

'I told my employer – Mr Ebbington – that my cousin, Linny Smallpiece, the daughter of my father's brother, has come from Morecambe to live under my roof and is in sore need of a position.' His voice had taken on an unfamiliar, cold quality, which I recognized as indignation. Somehow it shamed me, although I refused to show it. ' "No," I told him, when he asked, "she has no letter of character, as she's spent her life caring for her invalid father," but I told him I could vouch for you, and would assume full responsibility. I don't make a habit of lying, Linny,' he said, 'but I chose to lie today.'

I looked down at the biscuits.

'Mr Ebbington has put his faith in me. I have worked for him for seven years, my own position assured for me by my father before he died. He and Mr Ebbington were good friends. The only truth in all of this is that my father did have a brother in Morecambe, although he died four years ago and had no children.' His trembling had increased so that his whole body now shook.

'What would I be expected to do?' I asked, after a long moment, meeting Shaker's stare.

'There wasn't a position available, but Mr Ebbington told me he had been thinking of bringing in someone with a fine hand to catch up on the recording of the books. Although I am responsible for overseeing that the ordering, receiving and placement of books is carried out properly, I can't write with my . . .' he looked down at his hands with a sneer '. . . with *these*, and although Mr Worth, who is quite elderly, signs the books out for the members, the record-keeping is behind hand. That is what you would do – keep the records of the books up to date. *If*, of course, you don't find it beneath you.'

I lifted my chin. His last sentence, and his tone, stung. 'What is the pay?'

'A florin a week. Paid monthly, of course.'

Two shillings a week. More than factory work, but not much. And I could turn a far better profit in a few slow nights on the street. The yeasty smell of the fresh biscuits filled my nostrils. The cold November rain ticked against the front window pane, although the sound was muffled by the heavy closed curtains. A drop fell on the grate and sizzled in the fire. The dining room was heated and fragrant with the smells of cooked food; although its furniture and fittings and floral carpets were well-worn and had obviously been established in their positions for many years, somehow I found a deep comfort in this.

I imagined being out in this weather, hoping the rain wouldn't convince the customers inside the music halls to go straight to their warm beds and cold wives instead of having a quick one for less than the price of the carriage ride home. I thought of the putrid odour of the Scot in his brougham, of the rough, probing fingers of the fishmonger. I thought, with a queasy lurch, of the syphilitic lunatic's face in Rodney Street, of my knife at Ram Munt's throat under the gaslight on Paradise Street.

I thought of baby Frances, and her tiny curled fingers. I never wanted to carry another stranger's child.

I thought of the tall masts of the sailing ships down at King's Dock, and knew I would never set foot aboard one.

I also knew I had fooled myself, as perhaps my mother had fooled me, with stories of being more than I was, of expecting more than I should. I knew I was giving up, but I was too weary to fight any longer.

'I'll take the job.' The rain lashed against the window now, the accompanying wind moaning around the sash. 'Thank you, Shaker.' I wondered when he would come to me for payment.

After dinner, Shaker asked me to come to his room, his eyes not meeting mine. I remained expressionless, nodding once. So the payment was to be immediate. His mother behaved as if she hadn't heard his request. I wondered how he would face her afterwards, and also why he didn't wait at least until she was asleep. I was surprised at his boldness and wondered how my healing flesh would accept him.

But I could not turn him down – no matter how often he wanted to take me. I owed him that much.

When I followed him through the door he went to his

desk and I straight to his bed – the same bed I had bloodied only a few days earlier. I lay on my back and turned my face to the wall as I hiked up the brown skirt. There was silence, and I looked back at Shaker to see why he hadn't begun to unbutton his trousers.

'No,' he said, in a hushed, shocked voice. He had turned scarlet and was still standing by his desk. 'No,' he repeated. 'I – I wanted you to write something for me. I'm unable to hold a quill, as you know.'

I felt an unfamiliar heat in my cheeks, and knew that, for the first time, I was flushing as Shaker had. I hadn't known I was capable of it. I twitched down my skirt and went to the table where a large book lay open.

'This is by Bernard Albinus,' he told me. His cheeks still held that high colour, but he spoke in a normal tone, as if he had not just seen my nakedness. 'He was the most important descriptive anatomist of the last century. As well as the human skeleton, he's illustrated the muscles of the body and the complete system of the blood vessels and nerves. I've taken the book from the library many times. If I could have a set of notes of the most pertinent areas of my study – those on the nervous system – I wouldn't have to keep taking it out and trying to memorize passages. I wondered . . . if you would write out the information I show you.' He pulled out the chair for me.

'But won't your mother think . . . What will she think of me being here, in your room?'

'Never mind about her. Much of her is no more than noise.' He made the rough clearing sound in his throat. It was a habit, I now knew, which he indulged when he was uncomfortable. 'She wasn't always as you see her now. I remember her laughing and enjoying herself while my father was still alive.' His face softened, and his eyes took on a far-away look.

I tried to imagine Mrs Smallpiece laughing, Shaker as a boy, and his father, the three of them sitting at the dining-table we'd just left.

'My father was a physician,' Shaker volunteered, 'although he did more than prescribe drugs. He also chose to do the work of a surgeon, even though that was beneath him in the medical hierarchy. Instead of the expected – taking the pulse and dealing with the hysterics and melancholy of the more affluent – he dealt with the body and all its frailties. He set bones, found remedies for skin diseases, performed surgery at the Infirmary. Sometimes he allowed me to accompany him to the homes he visited, to listen and watch. That was where I found my love of the profession. He was a kind man, my father. He knew I couldn't follow his path but never spoke of it. He treated many of Liverpool's needy, usually for no payment but their gratitude. Because of that, my mother was forced to live a more frugal life than she would have if my father had provided physic to the wealthy. However, even though we live a fairly simple life, my father's reputation was such that my mother can still consider herself included in what she sees as the grander social scene.'

'She's mentioned her friends,' I told him. 'I fear my presence has prevented her inviting any of them to call.'

Shaker smiled at me. 'I'm pleased that she can still enjoy small pleasures as Dr Smallpiece's widow, with her acceptance in that milieu, and the invitations she receives.' He stopped, and in that moment I realized that Shaker took after the father he had described.

'Shortly after my father died – seven years ago – my mother suffered that terrible apoplexy, and afterwards she began to seek God.' He frowned, studying the illustration over his desk, as if he'd forgotten I was there. 'I've read of these cases more than once. It seems there may be a connection between the two – the onset of seizures and the beginning of unnatural religious fervour.'

I made a small sound, an acknowledgement, and he jumped, then focused on me. 'I tried to help her. I followed all the prescribed medical treatments – restricting her fluid intake, giving emetics and purgatives. I even bled her, trying to equalize her circulation. But none of it has helped. Although, as I told you, the fits are rare, at times her behaviour is such that I hardly recognize her.' He sighed. 'You need not worry about her demands on you. Nan, who has always worked for us, and her daughter Merrie, who looks after my mother's clothes and hair, will return. My mother dismisses them regularly for one infraction or another. Nan and Merrie stay away two or three days, long enough for my mother to miss them, and then they reappear. Nan is used to it, and she and my mother understand each other.'

I picked up the quill and dipped it into the ink. 'What did you mean, Shaker, when you told me I was your sign?' I asked, before I wrote the first word.

Shaker moved to the window. 'I had decided, that night in the Green Firkin, that . . .' He paused. '. . . I had decided to drink as much as I could, although I rarely consume strong drink. When I felt that I had taken enough to give me courage, I planned to go to – to the place where Frances is buried, so as not to leave my mother to deal with things, and drink a potion of hemlock I had procured.'

'Hemlock? Is it not a form of poison?'

I saw the corner of his lip lift. 'It is. It seemed the cowardly way out, yet I could think of nothing but ending my miserable existence. I felt there was no purpose for me any more. I had three emotions, as I stood at that counter in the public house.'

I waited.

'The strongest was self-pity. That because of my disability, I would never be the man I wanted to be. I would never be a physician, or even a surgeon. The one thing I wanted to do was to help people in that capacity. Although my work in the library is quietly fulfilling, I have no – no passion for it. And I despaired because I would never know the simple pleasure of my own family – for what young woman would be interested in someone like me?'

This surprised me. I had begun to see a quiet strength under Shaker's plain features, and in spite of his tremors, he carried himself with dignity. Surely he judged himself too harshly.

'The second emotion was guilt,' he continued, 'at leaving my mother on her own. But the self-pity triumphed over it. I paid for a letter to be written, which I hoped would explain, and included instructions for her welfare. I knew she wouldn't be destitute, as my father left enough to support her comfortably until she dies. And long ago, I spoke to Nan, about the possibility – should I ever be unable to care for my mother – that she and Merrie might move in and live here, care for her as long as she lives, to which Nan agreed. She is a widow herself, and although my mother considers Nan much beneath her, there is a strong friendship between them.'

He ran his fingers up and down the piping at the edge of the curtain.

'And the third?' I asked, when he had been silent too long.

'The third was a shred of hope. Hope that I would be

142

shown why I shouldn't carry out my plan. I had been waiting for something for over two weeks, from when I had decided on my course of action. If there was something I could interpret as a sign, then I would ask forgiveness for my bitter self-pity, and go on with my life. And you, Linny, were that sign.'

'In what way?'

'Because I saw I could help you.'

A drip of ink fell on to the clean paper, and I watched it spread. 'You mean because I'm a whore you thought you could justify your own life by changing mine into what you see as respectable?'

There was more silence, then Shaker's voice came low, in barely held-back anger. 'No. Because I thought – perhaps with feverfew tea, mixed with a touch of rosemary, which can alleviate cramping – that the labour might stop. When I realized it was too late for that I wanted to assist you, and make sure you weren't forced to give birth in an alley, alone, then bleed to death. That was how I hoped I could help you, even if I'm not a physician or a surgeon, only an ordinary man who cared about the welfare of a stranger. That was why you were my sign. You enabled me to rise above the mire of my own self-absorption.'

I bit the inside of my cheek; a small, hard lump had formed there from this lately acquired habit. It was something on which to concentrate so that I did not speak out to Mrs Smallpiece, or when I was at a loss for words – as now.

Shaker came back to the desk, and pointed to the passage he wanted me to start with, bringing the lamp closer. I began to copy, in my best hand. We never spoke again of what he had just told me.

CHAPTER THIRTEEN

WITHIN ANOTHER DAY Nan and Merrie were back at work, as Shaker had predicted. I suspected that part of the reason Mrs Smallpiece greeted them so pleasantly on their return was not only so that she could be pampered in the style to which she was accustomed. I deduced she wanted to be free to take up the social round – the luncheons, afternoon teas and church events – she so enjoyed. Perhaps she thought I might flee with the silver if left to my own devices, and she wasn't happy for me to be alone in her home.

When we were together, that first week, she tolerated me as long as I read to her from the Bible when she asked. She had one bad day when she complained about her aching joints: then she tried to persuade me to repent, to admit my wickedness and what she imagined to be my lustful thoughts. When I stubbornly refused, she thumped my hands with her Bible, predicting my lonely death after endless suffering. She made it clear that her Methodism had been a natural stage in her moral development, and it remained an intellectual and philosophical background.

I found it easy to accept her moods and helped her as Shaker had when she was seized with a fit upon awakening one morning.

She was determined that I would improve my manners and decorum, and drummed into me the rules she felt a proper young lady should observe.

'If Shaker is allowing you to stay here – and it appears that you've accepted his offer of lodging – you will not embarrass me any more than you already have. I know there's no real hope for you,' here she sighed, the loud, gusty sigh of one inconvenienced, 'but I must try. See how you're sitting.'

I looked down at myself, in Mrs Smallpiece's cast-off dress: I was leaning into a corner of the horsehair sofa, my elbow resting on its arm, my palm supporting my cheek. My legs were stretched out, feet comfortably crossed at the ankle.

'Sit up straight, girl. Hands folded in your lap. Feet beside each other. You look like the slattern you are, lying about like that.'

I straightened my spine, keeping my mouth tight, clasped my fingers together and moved my feet so that my ankles touched.

'That's better. Stay so for the next hour.'

'What?'

' "I beg your pardon, Mrs Smallpiece." You will sit thus until it feels natural. Every young lady should learn to do so when she's little more than a babe.'

'It can never feel natural.'

'Maybe not to one born in a cellar and never brought up. But here, in Everton, a lady knows how to behave.'

'I was not born in a cellar,' I said, 'and my mother did bring me up. I've also learned a thing or two about proper deportment along the way.' But no matter what I believed I knew, Mrs Smallpiece, for all her odd ways, only knew the life of a middle-class lady.

She sniffed, went to the bookshelf and pulled out two books which she deposited in my lap. One was called *An Appeal to the Consciences of Christians on the Subject of Dress*, and the other *The Proper Young Lady*. 'Study the one on respectable dress when you are alone. But I shall expect you to read a chapter a day from the book on etiquette. Begin with the first. I shall question you on what you've read each evening.' She studied me, and I remained immobile in the pose she'd demanded. 'You must realize that your presence here has hampered my own entertaining,' she said. 'I cannot allow any of those ladies in my social circle to meet you until I can trust you not to humiliate me.'

'I shan't humiliate you, Mrs Smallpiece,' I said, trying to keep the fierceness I felt out of my voice. 'I can assure you of that.'

Her expression made it clear she didn't believe me. 'We'll wait and see, shall we?' she said, and left the room, managing, even in her limp bombazine dress, to give the impression of an imperious dowager.

When she was gone I relaxed into my former comfortable position, and flipped idly through the books she'd dropped on to my lap. Nevertheless, I listened for her footsteps, ready to straighten my spine, should she return.

At her son's request, Mrs Smallpiece took me reluctantly to her seamstress and had three dresses made for me. They were all of the same pattern – with rounded neckline and front buttoning bodice, which was fitted, with no boning; the skirt was wide and gathered into the waist. The only ornaments were lace-trimmed nankeen collars with a dull sheen, while a tiny strip of white lace and one crocheted button accented each sleeve. The fabric was sturdy, meant, I'm sure, to last a

146

good ten years. One dress was brown, one grey and the last navy. They were disappointing in their fit and dull colours, but I thanked Mrs Smallpiece with an enthusiasm I didn't feel.

Although she instructed Merrie to pin my hair into a severe mode, I convinced the girl to adopt a more flattering, younger style. Later Mrs Smallpiece eyed the soft ringlets, but said nothing.

As I set off with Shaker for my first day of work at the library, we climbed into a wide hackney cabriolet which ran between Everton and Liverpool a number of times a day. Its team of four horses ensured the trip was speedy. Shoulder-to-shoulder with the other passengers, my feelings swung wildly from nervousness to confusion. When we approached Liverpool's centre, I knew none of the girls I had formerly worked with would be out so early in the day. And, I told myself, even if we did pass one, it was unlikely she would recognize the plain brown bird in the crowd of other respectable men and women on their way to work at their offices and shops.

I truly suited my name now. Never mind the linnet's voice, the beautiful variations in its tone, I had the true appearance of a female linnet, a small and rather drab finch.

Had any of them — Annabelle, Helen or Dorie — missed me? Probably — at least for a day or two. And Blue might be annoyed at having lost one of her hard-working girls. I imagined that when I had failed to return to the room on Jack Street or the gaslights along Paradise Street, they would have assumed the worst: that I had ended up as another murdered whore dumped somewhere where no one would find me. Someone might have seen me getting into the carriage with the Scot, and that would have been the last they knew of me. I had been warned, and had ignored the warning, and 'She paid the price, didn't she?' they would say. Would they mourn me? Perhaps briefly, and some might raise a glass in my memory in the Goat's Head, but there were always girls waiting to slip into the place of one who had disappeared.

When Mrs Smallpiece felt I could be trusted not to embarrass her in public, she took me to church. Like Shaker, she introduced me as the daughter of her husband's brother, her niece, although the first time she did it – standing outside the church on a cold Sunday in December – I felt her arm tremble against mine through our thick woollen jackets. Whether it was caused by anger with me for having put her in this position, or because she knew she was sinning with the lie, I don't know. But to a woman like Mrs Smallpiece, the lie, I'm sure, was less of a sin than having to admit that she was harbouring a whore.

The minister – Mr Lockie, who had tangled white eyebrows and a squint – gripped my hand with an unnerving fervour as he welcomed me into his flock. After he had been introduced by Mrs Smallpiece he studied my face intently, which might have been due to the squint. But I read something in his face that was similar to the expression Mrs Smallpiece often wore when she looked at me: the hope of salvation through conversion that the Methodists embraced. Had he registered something of my past, and, like Mrs Smallpiece, thrilled at the possibility of saving a needy soul?

The first social call she invited me to attend with her was to the home of her friend Mrs Applegate. The air was so cold that we could see our breath as we walked there. We were ushered into a parlour overheated by a roaring fire and a number of seated elderly ladies. I was introduced by Mrs Applegate as Mrs Smallpiece's 'poor niece'. Once she had directed us to our seats, Mrs Smallpiece nodded, almost imperceptibly, at my hands, reminding me I was to remove my gloves since tea was being served. She lost no time in making it abundantly clear that I had lived a sheltered life with my father in Morecambe and was unaccustomed to society. 'So please forgive her if she lacks the graces on which we pride ourselves,' she added, her neck rigid.

I accepted a mince pie from the silver tray held in front of me by a young parlourmaid, and deposited it on the decorated plate I held stiffly in my other hand. My mouth was too dry to eat. One short woman, with a nasty growth above her chin, shook her head sadly at Mrs Smallpiece, as if she understood her friend's trial, the difficulty of coping with a young woman as feeble and dull-witted as Mrs Smallpiece wished to make me appear.

Although my whole body burned with shame, and with anger towards Mrs Smallpiece, I knew it would do me no good to prove her wrong. If I was to stay in Everton for at least a while, as had been my choice, instead of going back to the rough freedom of Paradise Street, I knew I had to fight my instincts, remain quiet and adopt a simpering smile. As I sat there, I tried to imagine the expressions of shock and horror that would flood these women's faces if they could see the images that still burned so brightly in the front of my own brain, of me with my customers, on my back or knees. For all their airs and graces, I knew more than they could begin to suspect about life and human nature.

Yet despite the silent games I played, my head pounded during these events, and the lump in my cheek grew larger with constant gnawing. In the gilt mirror in the bedroom I

149

shared with Mrs Smallpiece, I saw that a new line had appeared between my eyebrows.

The Proper Young Lady grew tattered. I had memorized most of it after a few months. How tedious it all was: etiquette for the parlour, for social calls, for meeting acquaintances on the street, for introductions – there appeared no end to the rules and expectations. At times my head swam with them: when to remove one's bonnet and when to keep it on, likewise for gloves, never to stoop to retrieve something one had dropped but wait for a person of lesser standing to do so and return it, and especially the strictures on dining.

'There is nothing so indicative of good breeding as manners at the table,' Mrs Smallpiece told me. 'A lady may dress with style and carry herself on the street with dignity. She may sustain a conversation, but imperfection at the table will betray her. While your manners are passable, they are lacking in finesse.'

Although wearisome, the lessons were simple, and it pleased Mrs Smallpiece that I responded well. As the months passed, and I showed her I was willing to accept her demands, she found less reason to berate me. Now and again I witnessed a small, tight smile cross her thin lips when I took over for her, pouring the tea or passing the sugar and cake to callers on Saturday afternoons, or reading aloud to her, in a pleasant voice, from *A Family Shakespeare* – the only other book in which she was interested besides her Bible. The complete works of Shakespeare had been rewritten by Thomas Bowdler to exclude all passages considered improper so there was no fear of encountering any immorality.

Mrs Smallpiece also took pleasure in watching me decorate lawn handkerchiefs in tiny, delicate stitches, as we sat before the fire in the evening. In my hands, the fabric grew wrinkled and limp, sometimes dotted with pinpricks of blood as the needle stabbed my thumb. Although I found the work numbingly dull, it had a quiet, rhythmic monotony that allowed my mind to wander far from Everton.

Mrs Smallpiece mistook my bent head for obedience. She thought she was converting me, and there is no one more sanctimonious than one who believes she has turned a sinner into a saint.

Over this time Shaker viewed me as neither sinner nor saint, or perhaps as a little of both.

He never called me to his bed, and treated me with an oddly courteous respect. I knew he watched me when he thought I wasn't looking, and I could tell, from the embarrassment on his face and his sudden turning away, that at times he grew aroused from being near me, but he behaved as a perfect gentleman. I suspected that affection for me was growing in him, but I didn't know how to feel anything for a man. I knew men in one dimension, men like Ram Munt and Mr Jacobs, and the unspeakable man at the house in Rodney Street. There had been a seemingly endless line of similar men. I knew Shaker wasn't like them in spirit, but I could feel nothing for him but a clumsy gratitude.

I had immediately loved my job at the library, surrounded by books, and felt a thread of connection between it and my life as a child, near my mother at the bookbinder's. Thoughts of her came to me often now, with the clean paper, the smell of ink, the order of one page after another: it was soothing. I knew she would have been proud of my work. But this life, no matter how I looked at it, was a lie, a posturing and deception. I did not wear the pendant.

I sat hidden behind a high screen at a desk with my quill and ink, a pile of books and recording cards, light streaming in from the small window in the wall behind me. I wasn't to come out into the public area while there were members about, Mr Ebbington had informed me, but I would be allowed, like Shaker, to borrow books as if I were a member when the library closed for the day.

Every evening I waited for that moment with anticipation. The Argand lights on the polished reading tables would be lit, sending soft shadows on to the graceful domed and pillared interior. There were scientific instruments and maps on display, as well as elegant long-case clocks and mahogany barometers. Display books, with gold and silver clasps, bound in velvet and silk, lay under glass. The library collections – purchased or donated by its members – were wide-ranging. I would wander through the sections – History, Voyages and Travel, Sciences, Government, Jurisprudence, Theology, and the largest, Polite Literature – finding encyclopedias, heraldry, topography, poetry, drama, philosophy and novels. I paused among those quiet shelves and held books in my hands, inspecting their mottled or gilded edges, and ran my fingers over their covers. I rejoiced inwardly at the cotton cloth with ornamental characters, the embossed patterns, like cameos, and lingered on costly russia-, morocco- and calf-leather bindings.

Every week Shaker and I chose three books each to take home with us. While he knew exactly what he wanted, searching out specifically those books dealing with medical science – although he also professed an interest in history – my decision always took much longer. Shaker would wait, always patient, while I roamed the aisles. At first he had recommended books to me, pointing out poetry or drama or the Gothic tales he had read and thought I might enjoy. But I had spent a long time reading Polite Literature. Now I wanted books that would teach me about the world and its people. I was especially intrigued with tales from Voyages and Travel.

'Do you ever dream of taking a voyage, Shaker?' I asked one evening, laying a book I'd chosen – Boswell's *The Journal of a Tour to the Hebrides* – on the library table. 'There is such a huge world beyond ours.'

'I often thought of adventure when I was younger,' he admitted. 'When my father was alive we would discuss the world, its many lands and inhabitants. He encouraged me to see more, and before his death I spent one summer in Paris, at his urging. I was a little younger than you are now, and journeyed with two other lads.'

I sat down across from him, putting my elbows on the table and leaning forward, twining my feet around the legs of my chair. I knew Mrs Smallpiece would have embarked on one of her lectures if she had seen me in such a vulgar posture, but Shaker and I were alone. 'What was it like? Was it as wicked as one hears?'

He smiled. 'It was new, and exciting. I felt quite alive. My friends and I roamed about day after day, taking in the sights. One friend is an artist – he did a series of sketches and gave me some. I can show you when we get home.'

'Would you go back?'

His smile faded. 'I think my days for adventure may be over.' He crossed his arms, tucking his trembling hands under them; he did this unconsciously when he spoke of himself. 'And what of you, Linny? Do you still dream of America?'

I shook my head. It seemed so far from here, further, even,

than it had when I was on the streets. 'I can't imagine it now, although I'm not sure why,' I told him. 'And yet . . .'

'And yet?'

'There is something inside me, especially when I read these,' I put my hand atop the book that lay on the table between us, 'that makes me feel unsettled. As if there is something, just beyond my grasp, waiting for me.'

Shaker looked at my hand, my fingers caressing the *moiré*-cloth cover. Then he looked up at me. 'I believe these longings are the feelings that accompany youth, Linny. But perhaps when you . . . if you . . .'

'Perhaps what?' I prompted, when he didn't continue.

He stood then. 'Nothing. I sometimes speak without thinking.'

'You don't,' I said. 'I've never heard you say anything that wasn't well thought out.'

He gathered up his books. 'We'd better hurry, or we may miss the last carriage.'

I followed, wondering what he had been about to say.

Although I was not allowed into the Club and News Room on the main floor of the Lyceum, which was for men only, I would peep into the high-ceilinged room, with its spacious windows facing Waterloo Place, whenever I had the chance. Usually I was on my way to the basement to fetch more ink or paper, or to use the new apparatus in a room discreetly marked 'Ladies' Cloaks' – a lavatory with a flush, operated by a swift tug on a rope that hung from the wall. Such luxury! I often lingered there longer than necessary, pulling the rope for the sheer pleasure of watching the water swirl to some distant hidden place. I couldn't help but smile as I compared this method to my days of emptying the chipped chamber

154

pot out of our window and directly into the court on Back Phoebe Anne Street.

In the Club and News Room I saw men relaxing in deep leather armchairs, enjoying a cigar, coffee or tea. Some read crisply ironed copies of the *Liverpool Mercury* or one of the other newspapers and periodicals available. Others discussed imminent arrivals and departures from the port. Many club members, I discovered, were wealthy shipowners. A number had been my customers, at one time or another, but I was not concerned that I might be recognized – or even noticed.

There was also a lecture hall, with grand double doors, on the main floor. Elaborately lettered signs, designed and produced by Mr Worth, stood on an easel outside the room, advertising lectures on the arts, literature or the sciences for members and their guests.

It was a beautiful, gracious place.

As I spent my days at the library and my evenings in the genteel house at Everton, under Mrs Smallpiece's strict tutelage, I knew that the old Linny Gow was being replaced with another who moved through the world with assurance. I often felt a sense of accomplishment, a warm glow that I might, after all, become the kind of young woman my mother had envisaged. But this was accompanied by a troubling awareness of loss. I no longer shared the easy laughter and camaraderie of the girls in Paradise Street. I was less spontaneous, more tightly reined in. Perhaps I saw myself as less genuine. But there can be no going forward without a glance over one's shoulder.

My life was becoming comfortable and predictable. I met Shaker's two friends, pallid, serious but courteous young men, one of whom appeared tongue-tied in my presence. They accepted me as his cousin. Every fortnight they arrived at Whitefield Lane for dinner. The meal was always solemn with Mrs Smallpiece present, but eventually she would grow weary and retire to her room. Leaving Nan and Merrie to clear the table, the four of us would retire to the drawing room, and it was here, after Shaker and his friends had had a few glasses of spirits, that the evening became informal. The more talkative of the two young men regaled me with stories of Shaker as a boy, and I saw a mischievous side to him on those evenings that I enjoyed.

I made sure I didn't get too caught up in the stories and laughter, aware that I had to live up to my created background. Shaker never lost sight of this either, often mentioning my fictitious father – his uncle – in a way that made the story more true for me. There were moments when I believed I was indeed a Smallpiece by birth.

I had been given, I told myself often, a chance at a better life, a life for which anyone from a back court off Vauxhall Road would be eternally grateful. I no longer had to spend long hours each night being cold or wet. I didn't have to squat over a chipped basin before the sun rose each morning, removing from myself a slimy piece of sponge. I didn't have to worry about being torn open by a man who had grown to the size of a horse, or be bitten, slapped or pinched to help one grow stiff. My skirts were no longer urinated or vomited on by those reeling with drink, and my pay was given to me in a folded paper, instead of being tossed on to the filthy street for me to scrabble out from among dog dirt and gobs of spittle. I had enough to eat. I had any book I desired at my disposal, and time to read. I had my own clean bed.

Why, then, could I not be content? Why, then, was I plagued by despair, by thoughts that flew out beyond the Lyceum and the house on Whitefield Lane? My dream of

America had died, but I still imagined myself in an unknown life, completely different from that which Liverpool – with its fog, gulls and grey shifting light over the windswept emptiness of the wide stretch of the Mersey – had to offer. And I was restless and uneasy with my past, the horror of what I'd done, the old nightmare still haunting me.

Why could I not accept what Shaker had offered as a gift, and be happy with this life – no, this charade – as Miss Linny Smallpiece?

CHAPTER FOURTEEN

I MET FAITH VESPRY through Celina Brunswick. Celina was dark-haired and not extraordinary in any way, but her bright blue eyes fringed with heavy dark lashes had a certain attractiveness. Shaker and I were leaving the library one evening, about two months after I came to live with him, when we came upon her, walking arm in arm with her father down Bold Street.

'Miss Brunswick, Mr Brunswick,' Shaker said, stopping before them, tipping his hat.

'Good evening, Mr Smallpiece,' the young woman said, and then she stared at me, two spots of colour appearing high on her cheekbones.

'Hello, Geoffrey,' the older gentleman said. *Geoffrey?*

'We haven't seen you for some time,' Miss Brunswick said, her eyes flickering between Shaker and me. 'I am sure you've been missed at a number of functions over these last few months.'

'Yes. I've been . . . busy,' Shaker said. 'Allow me. Mr Brunswick, and Miss Celina Brunswick, it is my pleasure to introduce you to Miss Linny Smallpiece, late of Morecambe.'

'Miss Smallpiece?' Celina asked. Her voice was cool as she took in my unfashionable outfit. She wore a long smoky blue pelisse – the colour setting off her eyes – and her hands were hidden inside a fur muff. Her hat had a matching trim. I knew by both the cut and the fabric of her clothes that they were expensive. 'She's a relation, then?'

'My cousin,' Shaker said, and the tightness in Celina's jaw relaxed a little. 'She has suffered a loss – her father – and has come to live with my mother and myself. She works with me now, at the library.'

'She works?' Celina said, then graced me with a small smile, looking at the books under my arm, tilting her head and reading their titles aloud with a questioning lilt. '*Letters on the Improvement of the Mind*, by Hester Chapone? And Hannah More's *Search After Happiness?*' She raised her eyes to mine, a challenge in them that I didn't understand. 'Ambitious reading. May I take it that you are an admirer of the Bluestockings, then, Miss Smallpiece?'

I smiled uncertainly.

'My cousin enjoys a wide variety of reading,' Shaker said, coming to my rescue. 'I can't say that your choices apply solely to women of pedantic literary taste, do they, Linny?'

'No. Certainly not,' I responded, careful to match my intonation to Celina's, although my throat was dry with nerves. 'Yet I must admit that, yes, I do have a high regard for the Bluestockings' fearlessness in flouting public opinion on the expected confines of the female. Oh – that appears to be our carriage,' I added, as it rumbled by. I wanted to get away from this woman with her superior air and critical expression.

'Yes. We should hurry. It was a pleasure to see you again, Miss Brunswick. Sir.' Again Shaker tipped his hat.

Celina gave me a long stare from between half-lowered lids, then the four of us parted company.

'She knew,' I whispered to Shaker, once we had taken our seats in the carriage and were moving in the direction of Everton.

'Knew what?' he asked, opening his book.

'About me. She knew, immediately, that I didn't belong.'

Shaker closed the book. 'Nonsense. You answered her admirably, if a trifle stiffly. But she did appear less friendly than in the past. I've known her for over a year now. We were introduced at one of the lectures – on botany, I believe. Miss Brunswick is very interested in flora and fauna.'

'She certainly appeared interested in me, as well,' I said, then added, 'Geoffrey.'

Shaker gave a wry smile. 'It's my Christian name. But anyone who is comfortable with me calls me Shaker, as I told you.'

'Geoffrey suits you. Distinguished,' I said, and opened my book to read for the rest of the ride home, but I noticed, before he turned back to his, that he had coloured.

The following week Shaker suggested that I stay after work that Friday and attend the scheduled evening lecture.

'I couldn't,' I responded.

'Why not? As a member of staff, you'll be allowed entrance. I'm sure Celina Brunswick will be there, so at least you'll know one person.'

All the more reason not to go, I thought. 'I've just . . . I've never attended anything like that.' I thought of the lettered sign set up by Mr Worth that morning. 'Butterflies of India', it announced, and then, in smaller, plainer letters underneath, 'All Members and Their Guests Welcome'. 'Would you come, as well?'

He shook his head. 'Neither India nor butterflies interests

me. But it's something you might enjoy.' His eyes travelled to his mother's old bonnet, which I still wore every day.

I knew I didn't look fashionable enough to attend the lecture. My clothes clearly announced my working position, and although they were passable for my job, I thought of Celina Brunswick and her haughty look, her trim shape in the fitted pelisse.

'Think about it,' he said.

The following day Shaker rushed out at his lunch break and returned with a bulky paper-wrapped parcel. He carried it on his lap all the way home, his fingers spread over it as if it gave him pleasure to touch it. Once we were at home in the drawing room, he handed it to me. I opened it. It contained a gown and a hooded cape. The gown was of heavily figured amber silk with gigot sleeves that tapered gradually to the wrist. The collar edge and skirt hem were scalloped. The cape was of soft wool in a darker gold.

There was a muffled sound from Mrs Smallpiece, who sat on the sofa, her hands pressing her stomach. 'Dyspepsia,' she said, more loudly than necessary. 'I had Merrie fetch me some caraway seeds today, but they haven't helped.'

'I don't know if you'll like them,' Shaker said, as we both turned from his mother, 'but I thought perhaps for the lecture . . .'

I wished I hadn't hesitated before I spoke. 'Of course. It's a lovely ensemble, Shaker.'

'The woman in the shop told me you'd also need . . . the . . . other pieces. Inside the gown.' He wouldn't look at me as he said this.

I searched through the folds, a delicate powdery lilac scent emerging from the silk, and found a set of stiffened petticoats, as well as small bustle pads to hold out the skirt from the waist.

'It's all too beautiful, Shaker,' I said. 'I don't know that I should accept it.'

'Just try it on, Linny. Please.'

It was indeed a beautiful dress. In my mind I compared it to Chinese Sally's dresses and realized now that they had been poorly made, and had far less dignity than the figured amber silk. When I came downstairs and into the drawing room Shaker was smiling, clasping his hands. 'I knew the colour would match your eyes,' he said.

Mrs Smallpiece covered her mouth to stifle a belch. 'She looks perfectly respectable in her day dresses,' she said, her voice waspish. 'You can't make a silk purse from a sow's ear. Why does she need anything new, anyway? You're spoiling her. What she's paying for her bed and food isn't enough.'

'What do you mean, Mother? Paying?'

Mrs Smallpiece's chin rose, but her voice quavered. 'I have collected her pay packet from her for the last few months, and I'll do so again at this month's end. It's only fair.'

Shaker stood in front of his mother. 'You will return that money to her,' he said. 'She earned it. And if I choose to buy her something pretty to wear, it's nobody's business but mine.'

I turned to study the plate rail as if inspecting it for dust, so that Mrs Smallpiece wouldn't see my small but satisfied smile.

I felt so pleased with my appearance in the new dress and cape that I attended the butterfly lecture. Once there, however, my confidence fled, and I was horribly nervous as I made my way through the crowd. Perspiration gathered under my stays as I held my forced poise, thinking about every move I made, every murmured nicety. I spotted Celina sitting with another young woman, smaller and slighter. She had foxy red hair and dark grey eyes, quite striking, her looks only a little spoiled by a rather long nose.

As the crowd gathered around a table of tea and cakes after the lecture, given by a Mr Prinsep, who was an elderly and alarmingly florid gentleman, Celina stood across from me. 'Hello, Miss Brunswick,' I said, trying to feel brave in my amber gown.

'Oh, Miss Smallpiece. I didn't recognize you,' she said, not returning my smile. 'Miss Smallpiece, my good friend, Miss Faith Vespry.'

Faith gave me an open smile, and I noticed her gums. Her teeth were small and even. 'So, this is the cousin,' she said, her voice high and breathless.

I saw Celina's elbow dig into Faith's side, but she appeared to ignore it. 'Celina told me that Mr Smallpiece had his cousin living with him now. How are you finding Liverpool? Where is it you're from? Was it Bristol?'

'Morecambe, Miss Vespry,' I said firmly. I was ready. As well as any of the information Shaker had passed on to me, I had read everything I could find on Morecambe and its history, and had fabricated my whole past, including dates and places. I was thankful for my ability to memorize effortlessly.

'Do call me Faith. I know Celina thinks it common, to insist on being called my Christian name, but I know we're going to be friends, don't you? Oh, I love the seaside,' she hurried on, barely stopping for breath. 'Is that charming tea-room – oh, what is it? The Archery? – still there? Mother and Father and I visited it only last year.' Faith smiled so broadly that even more of her pink gums showed.

I was amazed, not by her openness but by how I'd changed myself in these last few months. Faith saw me as a young woman of similar standing to herself. 'Yes,' I beamed, anxious to prove myself further, 'the Archery is most enjoyable. I've taken tea there too, in the conservatory, a number of times.' The lie came out easily.

'Celina,' Faith continued, her eyes not leaving me, 'Miss Smallpiece is not at all as you described. Not at all.'

'Will you never learn to keep what you're thinking to yourself, Faith?' Celina demanded, a delicate pink staining her cheeks. She looked down into her cup.

'Why don't you put some sugar in your tea?' Faith responded. 'It must be terribly bitter, judging by your expression.'

Celina tsked, then moved along the table.

'Pay no attention to her,' Faith said. 'She's not hiding it well.'

'Hiding what?'

Faith leaned closer. 'Even though you're a cousin, Celina doesn't like the idea of another woman living with Mr Smallpiece.'

I frowned, then understood. 'Ah. Miss Brunswick is . . . attracted to Shaker?'

Now it was Faith's turn to frown. 'Shaker? That seems a cruel name.'

'Oh, I must explain. It may appear cruel but it's a boyhood nickname and it's what he prefers to be called by those familiar with him.' I stopped. 'And, of course, as I am of his family, it's natural for me to use it.' I looked through the crowd to Celina, who was talking with little enthusiasm to an older woman. 'Does Mr Smallpiece know of her feelings?'

'Of course not,' Faith said. 'She knows there could be no hope of anything between them, anyway.'

'Why?'

Faith tilted her head. 'But surely you must understand the situation. Celina's father would never approve of Geoffrey Smallpiece.'

My lips pursed in annoyance. 'Because of his affliction?'

'Poor man. He's quite hung on strings, isn't he? But that's not the most troublesome fact.' She glanced around. 'Of course, it's all too delicate to discuss, don't you agree?'

'Yes,' I said, but I didn't understand what she meant.

She pulled me into a corner. 'How coarse of me to discuss financial matters. Please don't be shocked or disappointed in me. You're not, are you?'

She was waiting for an answer. I could barely keep up with her conversation. 'Disappointed? No, not at all.'

'Although I'm sure you've never met anyone quite so candid.'

Now I smiled.

'It's just that . . .' she looked over her shoulder and, seeing that Celina was still involved in conversation, continued '. . . Mr Brunswick is, of course, hoping to make a match for Celina that would benefit the family in all ways. There could be no hope of future advancement for either her or her family if she married a man like Mr Smallpiece. Not only financially, but also socially.' She fanned herself with her gloves. I had not removed mine. 'If my mother were to hear me now, I would be confined to my room for a week.'

Again I smiled. She was refreshing, but I enjoyed her company for more than that. I was still basking in the knowledge that she had assumed I was a young woman of similar standing, and was speaking to me as such.

'You must be aware,' she went on, 'that your cousin has little interest in taking part in any of the more important social events in Liverpool. He's invited to a number of gatherings – his father was so well respected, and the name Smallpiece is well received. Yet he doesn't care to take advantage of it. Certainly you must know what I mean about him.' She raised one eyebrow.

'I suppose I do,' I said.

'I've heard he's like his father before him, most charitable. Did you know your uncle well? It seemed that he was the victim of unfortunate circumstances.'

'He was indeed,' I agreed, having no idea of what those unfortunate circumstances might have been, and praying she wouldn't discuss the matter any further.

Before I could change the subject she continued, 'And, of course, you have recently suffered a loss. My condolences.'

'Thank you,' I murmured.

'What was your late father's profession, Miss Smallpiece?' she asked now.

A second of silence lapsed. 'Please, if I'm to call you Faith, would you be comfortable calling me Linny?' I said. I was stalling for time. I couldn't believe I had forgotten to create a professional life for my supposed late father, or that Shaker had never once mentioned what his uncle did. 'He . . .' I thought of the businesses and shops we passed on our way to the library, of Seel Street, which I'd walked down only the day before, of Rushworth's, and Draper and Seeger, both piano and organ manufacturers. 'He owned a business, selling pianos,' I finished.

'Oh,' Faith said, opening her reticule. 'That reminds me.

My mother often has musical evenings. We would love you to come to the next one. It's a week from Thursday,' she went on, handing me a calling card. 'It must be difficult for you to meet people, spending all day closed up with books and living in Everton, with Mr Smallpiece not trying to introduce you to society. I can't understand why he doesn't bring his mother and move closer to where everything goes on.'

I tried to keep my face composed, and took the card.

'So. A week from Thursday,' she repeated. 'And, of course, your guardian will accompany you. It will be a surprise for Celina when she notices Mr Smallpiece. I can't wait to see her face.'

I murmured something. Although I was pleased at Faith's artless acceptance of me, it was hard work to keep up with her, needing to weigh everything I said so as not to appear a fool. Or the liar I was.

'What did you think of Mr Prinsep's lecture?' she asked.

My shoulders relaxed. I had spent some time with a book on varieties of butterflies before this evening to prepare myself. Now I felt on safe territory. 'Some of his illustrations were beautiful, weren't they? I've never thought much about butterflies.' At last. Speaking the truth. 'And he made the country sound exotic and wonderful,' I said. 'I've never thought much about India either. Quite grand, from what Mr Prinsep recounted.'

'He told us only of the pretty bits. He's an artist, after all, and doesn't see the world as realists do. There are awfully wicked things in India as well as beauty.' Her voice dropped to just above a whisper. 'They worship idols, and apparently there are friezes in the temples depicting . . . Well, I can't speak of it. I've heard that some women swoon if they accidentally view some of the statues – they're so shocking. My brother's friend is a lawyer in Bombay. He came home on a visit last year, and I listened in when he and my brother were speaking in private. Of course he only told my mother and me charming stories, but I know better.'

'Really,' I said, trying to hold back a smile. Faith was delightful. Her forthright manner reminded me of my friends in Paradise Street. Also, she didn't judge me, or look at me with suspicion. She made me feel I belonged there. And for this alone my gratitude was such that had I been Linny Gow, not Linny Smallpiece, I might have hugged her.

'I sometimes think about going there!' she added breezily. 'Don't you think it would be the most wonderful adventure?'

'I wouldn't know,' I said, anxious to keep listening to her, but Celina returned, with the older woman, and interrupted our conversation. The talk was steered into idle gossip, which held no interest for me, and I was aware that my discomfort was returning now that Faith and I were no longer alone. I bade them farewell as soon as I could, and the doorman helped me into the hired carriage that was waiting to take me back to Whitefield Lane.

On the short journey my head swirled with the pretence of belonging, and the excitement of trying to keep up with Faith's questions and comments.

That night, when I had blown out the candle by my bed and was staring into the darkness, I made out the shape of the crude painting over the oak dresser, and realized I'd seen a more professional rendition among Mr Prinsep's pictures. I smiled wryly to myself. The Taj Mahal at Agra. There was so much I didn't know.

The next week Shaker and I went to the musical evening at the Vesprys'. He took little persuading. Gallantly, he invited his mother, but she declined as I'd hoped she would. He looked very smart, in a well-cut suit that he evidently kept for such occasions.

The evening was pleasant. Shaker and I sat at the back of the Vesprys' drawing room, listening to the piano and harp recital. Later we were served small plates of pastries and glasses of sweet sherry. The pastries were more delectable than any other I had ever tasted. I saw that in spite of Shaker's trembling he ate and drank with only small difficulty; in the past, he had been more nervous when he was alone with me than he was now in mixed company. Later I brushed the crumbs off his lapels and shirt front, with its delicate ivory buttons, and we mingled with the crowd. I saw Celina watching him, her face rosy, which improved her looks. Talking to Shaker so that he followed, I moved closer to her, until it appeared that she and I had bumped into each other, although I had been aware that she, too, was moving towards us. The three of us spoke in a stilted manner at first, but before long Celina and Shaker were involved in a conversation about the choices of the pianist. I left them and made a pretence of studying the family portraits that were arranged along one wall of the drawing room, glancing back at the couple occasionally. From across the room I saw that Shaker was almost handsome, his long hair thick and shining.

Faith found me and introduced me to a man – Mr Gerrard Beck – whom I assumed to be her suitor from the way she held his arm and smiled at him so that her gums remained hidden by her top lip. She presented me to a number of other people, whose names I promptly forgot.

Shaker spoke animatedly all the way home – of the music,

the food, the company. He didn't mention Celina Brunswick specifically, but I felt a sense of pleasure in knowing that he had enjoyed himself.

I saw Faith a few days later, chancing upon her and Mr Beck as they stood outside a shop on Bold Street, but both looked flushed and ill-tempered, as if they had been arguing, so I greeted them and went on my way.

Another invitation arrived at the house on Whitefield Lane, this one for Mrs Smallpiece, Shaker and me to be at a dinner party at the Vesprys'. This time, surprising me, Mrs Smallpiece agreed. I sent back a reply in my best hand, stating that Mrs Lucinda Smallpiece, Mr Geoffrey Smallpiece and Miss Linny Smallpiece would be pleased to attend.

There were sixteen people, including the Brunswicks. Faith seated me at her right. Shaker sat across from me, with Celina on his left. Mrs Smallpiece was further down, and beside a plain young woman who appeared to be a missionary, judging from her dress and her pious expression.

We ate a puréed soup, saddle of mutton, and turkey in celery sauce. There were sweetbreads in a white sauce, potatoes and kale, then an elaborate soufflé. I worried for Shaker that he was faced with this meal in public, but when I glanced at him, as we were led to the table, he winked at me. Was it an assurance that he could manage in such situations? Or was he telling me that he had complete trust in my ability to conduct myself with the necessary decorum?

Faith and I spent much of the meal talking, although twice her mother glared at Faith, making it clear that she was to converse with others.

I saw that Shaker and Celina were also caught up in

conversation. Shaker ate little, but no one noticed. At one point I heard him laugh openly at something Mr Vespry said, and was shocked: I had never before heard him do so. It made me smile.

After that, Faith and I spent more and more time together. I sensed she found it difficult to fill her days. She sometimes sent a note to the library telling me she would be coming in – her father was a member – during my lunch break, and we would sit at my desk, behind the screen, to eat whatever she produced from her bag, with the simple meal Nan had packed for me. At other times we walked up and down Bold Street for that half-hour, arm in arm, glancing into the shop windows.

I grew comfortable with her during our time alone, mainly because with me she dropped the feminine chatter and spoke of politics and her views on the Whigs, history, literature, the art movement; she would ask my opinions and wanted to hear what I thought. She was clearly better read and more knowledgeable than she cared to disclose in the presence of others; because I worked in a library she considered me of a more serious disposition than her society friends, whose concerns ran to fashion and gossip. And when I realized that Faith was not interested in asking any more about my past – or, actually, my present – I relaxed.

Eventually I began to see that, in order to fit into the conformity that was expected, she was careful to keep her true self hidden for most of the time. I also understood that she had detected this cover in me, although the genesis of our similarity could not be compared. But for all of this I felt a begrudging admiration for her, as well as friendship.

171

Six months after our first meeting – it was early June, and it had been raining heavily for hours – Faith was in the sheltered portico of the Lyceum when Shaker and I stepped out of the doors. She'd obviously been waiting some time: the hem of her skirt was soaked, and tendrils of deep red hair, curled by the moisture and bright with beads of rain-water, escaped from her bonnet.

'Linny, I'd like to invite you as my guest for dinner. I know we have no chaperone, and it's early, but could you come? I've booked a table at the tea-room on Lord Street.' Her voice was even more breathless than usual, which I attributed to her having waited for me. Later I knew it to be something else.

I looked at Shaker. Evidently the invitation didn't extend to him.

'I know you don't think it proper, Mr Smallpiece – two ladies dining alone – but I assure you that my parents have allowed me to come out. In fact, my father has just left me here. I'll see that Linny gets home safely afterwards,' Faith told him. 'I'll hire a carriage. And we won't be late. I just . . . There's something I'd like to discuss with her.'

'If she cares to join you, and your parents have agreed, I will grant her permission,' Shaker said, and bowed. When we were away from Whitefield Lane he slipped seamlessly into his role as my guardian.

'I'd love to, Faith,' I said, meaning it. Her friendship was important to me: it was the only one I had, apart from my relationship with Shaker. And I found the weight of his feelings for me too heavy; it had taken on the shape of a burdensome yoke rather than a light cloak. I knew it was difficult for him to have me so close to him, both at work and at home.

In the evenings I worried now when I felt his breath on my cheek as he leaned over me, pointing out the work I still copied for him. I worried as I passed him a plate at dinner and our fingers touched, I worried at the pressure of his thigh against mine as we rode to and from work in the crowded carriage. I accidentally overheard him, late one night, abusing himself quietly as I passed his closed door. I felt pity for him, and anger with myself for the suffering I caused him. Had he been another sort of man, I might have gone into his room when his mother was asleep, and allowed him to use me to relieve himself. For me the physical act would have been of no more significance or sensation than a fit of sneezing. But, then, had he been another sort of man, he would have claimed me months ago, either at my bidding or not. And I knew that he wanted more than a quick poke. It was clear to me, and had been from the first week of knowing him, that Shaker Smallpiece was not of the nature of most men: he would not take a whore, or a woman outside wedlock. I believe that until he met me he had accepted his celibacy with a studied grace. I had ruined that.

Many nights now, as I fell asleep, I tried to think of a way not to hurt him when he eventually must speak of his desire: he would not be able to withstand it much longer without some form of expression.

CHAPTER FIFTEEN

FAITH AND I bade Shaker goodbye and hurried along, laughing as we attempted to stay under her bobbing umbrella. As we passed a deeply recessed doorway I saw a little girl huddled there, head covered with a thin, torn shawl. There was a bulge under the shawl at her chest, which I took to be a sleeping baby. I stopped as Faith kept going.

She looked back at me. 'What are you doing, Linny?' she called.

I dug in my reticule, glad I had a few pennies. I held them out to the child and, as her bare arm came from under the shawl, Faith was there. 'Don't give her anything, Linny,' she scolded. 'Don't encourage them to come up here begging.' Her voice rang with contempt, yet I heard pity behind it.

The child's arm hesitated, half-way to my hand and the coins.

'Do you have a baby there?' I asked. She looked eight or nine.

She nodded. 'Me bruvver,' she said.

'Do you have somewhere to go?'

She nodded again. 'But me mam's got a customer in the room. She sent me out till she were done.'

Faith let out a tiny screech. 'Heaven help us! Come away, Linny.'

'Do you have any more spare coins?' I asked Faith, made bold by the child's shivering, the stillness of the tiny baby under the shawl.

Faith opened her reticule and pulled one out. 'That's all,' she said defensively, as if I were accusing her of something. In her face I saw compassion, but also fear.

I gave the coins to the little girl and, as her hand closed round them, she pulled back into the recess of the doorway.

'Now hurry, we're getting soaked,' Faith said, and started to run. I hurried after her. The wind coming from the Mersey raced ahead of us, creating ripples on the surfaces of the puddles. Faith jumped over them as if she hadn't a care in the world, but I was heavy-hearted.

We arrived at the tea-room breathless, chests heaving. Faith shook her bonnet, sending droplets flying, and a table of matrons near the door frowned. Faith laughed at their expressions, surprising both them and me. It was bad enough that we had arrived unchaperoned, but to create a display was, I knew well by now, in breach of all etiquette.

When we were seated I tried to push away the image of the tiny pair in the doorway and the memories it brought back to me. 'Faith? What is your opinion of that child, the little thing with no hope for a future?' I asked.

'Opinion? Well, obviously the rich and poor – like good and evil – will always be with us, won't they? It's as the Reverend Mr Thomas Malthus expounds with his fears of over-population. The constant tendency of populations to grow faster than the means of subsistence is evident. That urchin, along with her mother – who contributes to the great social evil – must be accepted. My father, only last year, read Malthus's *Essay on the Principle of Population*, and quoted from it often. Poverty and inequality are part of the God-given order of the universe. It's a comfort to know that there is nothing really to be done.'

'What if one were to try to change that order?'

'For one, or for all?' she questioned, but then the waiter came, and we gave our order. Faith propped her elbows on the table and cupped her face in her hands. She was delightfully unladylike at times, while I did my best to maintain my decorum in public.

'Let's talk no more of the unpleasant aspects of life,' she said. 'I have the most marvellous thing to tell you, Linny, and you must listen because you may think me mad at first. And, by the way, I do not have my parents' permission to be here, and was daring enough to come to the library on my own. They believe me to be reading in my room.'

I smiled as she confessed what she imagined to be a daring escapade. I thought of the roast lamb with mint sauce I had ordered. I knew that the few pennies we had given to the little girl would buy her a hot potato, perhaps two, if the stall-keeper was in good humour.

'It's this. I've decided I must go to India.'

'India? What—'

She held up her hand. 'Just listen. As I told you, ages ago, it's something I've been thinking of.' She fidgeted with the lace edge of her napkin. 'My life feels empty, Linny. I'm filled with . . . *ennui*, I suppose. I have my moods . . .' She stopped, her eyes suddenly blank, as if she was seeing something inside her skull.

'We all have moods, Faith,' I said, but she didn't appear to hear me. At the next moment she focused again, and smiled, but it was almost a grimace.

'And my father says I can go, as long as I have someone to accompany me,' she continued, as if she was unaware of that lost moment. 'Of course, there will be a number of chaperones on board ship, married women going back to their husbands after bringing children home for schooling, or simply after a visit, but he won't hear of me going without a companion.' Her words were rushed.

When she paused for a breath, I said, 'Why are you so interested in India?'

Faith looked around the slowly filling room, then paused as the waiter set down our leek soup with parsley dumplings. When he had left, she lowered her voice. 'Linny, Liverpool has so little to offer in the way of interesting men.'

'But what of Mr Beck? He seemed pleasant. I sensed—'

She dismissed my words with a wave of her hand. 'Oh, he took a job in London. We parted a few weeks ago. I suppose I forgot to mention it.' But there was a hint of desperation in her voice that belied her flippancy. 'And as I said, the choice of alternative escorts in Liverpool has become thin of late.'

I thought of all the men I had known in the city. She was probably right, although our opinions were based on different impressions.

'In fact, it's quite distressing. I'm sure you don't mind if I speak so openly about my . . . difficulties.'

I knew, from various things Faith had said, that she was almost twenty-one. Her time for finding a husband had come and was almost gone. She had a year left at most. I nodded.

'And although you've still time, I don't imagine you've had the opportunity to meet many eligible young men.' She took a small spoonful of her soup. 'First nursing your father, and . . . now your life with your aunt and cousin. It's not exciting, you must admit.'

I didn't reply, but she didn't notice.

'So I've decided that I must go to India to meet a suitable man.' Her upper lip quivered as she attempted a gay smile. 'If you were to join me, Linny, there's a good chance you would meet someone as well.'

My mouth remained open, my spoon partway between the soup and my lips. I closed my mouth and lowered the spoon. 'Did I hear you correctly, Faith? Do you mean join you in travelling to India?'

'Yes. Imagine! "The delightful Miss Vespry and the enigmatic Miss Smallpiece, both late of Liverpool, arrive in Calcutta in the gentle breeze of the Cool Season." It sounds like a novel, doesn't it?' She had grown ever more excited, her voice quite loud now.

I put one finger to my lips to remind her that others were watching. 'India, Faith? It's too much — too much for me to contemplate. I must have time to think, to—'

'Oh, Linny,' she interrupted, 'what is there to think about? Wouldn't you rather have an adventure than sit behind that screen at the library? And it's almost *certain* you would meet someone suitable.'

I decided the truth would be best. 'Although India sounds outrageously exciting, I'm not interested in marrying yet,' I told her. *Or ever.*

Now it was Faith's mouth that fell open with surprise. She snapped it shut. 'What can you possibly mean? What else *is* there for women like us but to marry well?' she asked, confused.

I had no answer. 'What about Celina? I'm surprised you haven't asked her to go with you.'

'Celina isn't interested. We did discuss it, briefly, but her heart belongs to another. Even if it isn't reciprocated.' She widened her eyes. 'You *know* of whom I speak, but she remains hopeful, and has no interest in leaving England.'

I realized then that Faith must have solicited all of her unmarried friends. I was her last hope.

'And your family agrees to send you?'

'Oh, yes. At least, Father does. Mother is less certain, but Father thinks it's a fine idea. He has a number of friends who work for the East India Company's civil service and understands these things better than Mother. Actually he is intending to travel to Calcutta late next autumn, but I don't want to wait that long.' She hesitated, then continued: 'It would be the wrong time to arrive if I waited for him. The best time of all – the season for entertainment – is the Cool Season. If I wait for Father it will be the end of the season, and that won't do me any good at all. Dear friends of Father and Mother's – Mr and Mrs Waterton – have extended an invitation to me and a companion. We could stay with them as long as . . . as necessary.'

I knew she hadn't finished from the way in which she played with the engraved handle of her knife.

'I do believe that Mother would prefer I *didn't* marry, although of course she would never admit it. But I know how she depends on me. She's not well, and I have only two brothers.' I thought back to the events at Faith's home, remembered her pale, oddly bloated mother.

'I think Mother believes I will look after her for as long as she needs me – which I feel would be until her last breath. Well-meaning as she can be, and I *do* care about her – with all my heart – the idea of growing old as a spinster in that house is not what I wish for myself. I want to have my own home, Linny.'

In the moment of silence that followed, I almost heard the unspoken *before it's too late*.

'In India English men outnumber women three to one,' she went on, 'and there are all sorts of events – luncheons and dinner parties, balls and soirées. It would be impossible not to find someone. India might not be the place one wants to live out one's life, but one could come home again. Oh, say you'll think about it, please, Linny!' She reached across the table and I took her hand.

She lowered her voice. 'I don't want to insult you,' she said, 'so please don't be offended. It's not difficult to understand your situation, and I know that if you were to say you'd come with me, my father would pay for your ticket, as well as a suitable wardrobe and anything else you might need. He would discuss it with your cousin, as he is your guardian, and obtain his agreement. Once we're there we would be guests in the home of the Watertons, who are more than happy to entertain young women from home, full of the English news they've been missing.' She stopped for breath, then rattled on. 'I've been finding out everything about it. The journey can take anywhere from four to five months, depending on the weather. It would be so exciting to sail round the African cape. The sights one would see! Sometimes the ships have to drop anchor at strange places, if the ship is blown off course. And the last port of call before Calcutta is Aden. Did you know that the natives at Aden have shocks of red or yellow hair? Why is that, do you think?' Her voice rose again.

Diners at other tables were watching surreptitiously, and I saw several speak behind their hands, their eyes on Faith.

'And in the warm waters of the Indian Ocean there are whales and porpoises that leap alongside the boat, as if performing for the passengers. Imagine, Linny!' In the next instant she clapped her hand to her mouth. 'I'm so sorry,' she said, from behind her palm. 'I can tell by your expression that I *have* insulted you with my overly forward offers with regards to finances. I'm too impossibly brash, I know that. Father suggests that's why no—' She stopped.

But Faith had misinterpreted my expression.

Unexpectedly, and for the first time in my life, I had understood the meaning of seduction. If Faith Vespry had attempted to seduce me with words, she had succeeded. She had touched the dead dream, which I had buried so carefully all those months ago with my wee Frances. She had touched it, and left me weak and trembling. It wasn't offence Faith had seen in my face, but awakening and hunger.

The most difficult aspect of leaving Liverpool – it was perhaps the most difficult thing I had done in my adult life – was telling Shaker of my plans. I asked him to walk with me on a sunny Sunday a few days after my final discussion with Faith. Shaker and I wandered along a wide dusty road just outside Everton. A large spreading elder grew near the side of the road, and I stopped there, in its shade, and told him about Faith's invitation, and that I wished to go. I told him that Mr Vespry would make the necessary arrangements for me to travel to India with her, if Shaker granted his permission for me to go, and to be hosted while I was there.

He was stunned. 'You're leaving?' he said. 'Leaving Liverpool? Leaving England?' *Leaving me?* I thought I heard, although he didn't speak those words.

'Yes. There's a ship, the *Margery Ellen*, sailing in just over three weeks' time. It will take us round Africa all the way to Calcutta.'

'But that journey takes months. And it's dangerous. India

is dangerous. What will you do once you're there? When do you plan to return?'

'I don't know what will happen when I'm there. I only know I can't let this opportunity pass. Thinking about it has given me the old feeling, the one I had about leaving here and travelling on a sailing ship, as I told you I had planned since I was first on the streets.'

There was silence. Then something in Shaker's face shifted. 'The Fishing Fleet, is it?' he asked, jaw clenched.

'I don't understand.' I found it difficult to look at him: emotion was playing openly across his face. It was as if I were seeing him naked.

'Nobody speaks of it, but it's well known, Linny. Desperate women make the long voyage in the hope of finding someone to marry them.'

'Well, that's what Faith is doing, without saying as much. I'm simply accompanying her.'

'And you, Linny? You won't be putting on your best airs – the new airs, the ones you've learned while you've been living with me – to find a husband?' His voice carried an unfamiliar undertone of cruelty.

'Shaker, can you really think that of me?'

He half turned so that only his profile was visible. 'What else am I to think? Isn't your life here comfortable? Do you want for anything?'

It hadn't been cruelty, but pain. 'No.' I was ashamed. 'You've given me more than I ever thought I would have. A home, a position I enjoy, security. And you ask nothing in return. But, Shaker, I want to go. I'm sorry. You've given me everything, and yet—'

'I could give you more, Linny.' He turned to face me, his voice rising. My heart plummeted, for I knew what his next words would be. 'Marry me,' he said. 'Please. You make me feel like I've never felt before, like I never dreamed possible.' He took my hand, and his was damp. 'I do love you, Linny. You must know that.'

I looked down at our hands, joined and trembling. 'I don't think you love me, Shaker. I think I . . . Perhaps I excite you, because of what I was. Of how you've seen me, and of what you know I've done.' I was choosing my words carefully, trying to make him see that if he had taken me as many times as he needed to he would have burned me out of his dreams and imaginings. How could a man who had only done good love me, soiled as I was by my past?

'What you were has nothing to do with it,' he argued. 'It's the way you make me feel. In these last nine months you've brought me back from self-hatred. You showed me I could feel like a man.' Then, as suddenly as he had taken my hand, he dropped it and stepped away. Now his face was ashen. 'Of course. All I've spoken of is the way you've made *me* feel. I've ignored how I might have made *you* feel. But now I see. All I inspire in you is pity.'

'How can you say that? I may have pitied you briefly at the beginning of our time together, but that was soon gone when I watched you, and listened to you – not only your compassion towards me but with your mother. I see you with your friends, and the members of the library, at social events and even with shopkeepers. I have nothing but admiration for the man you are.'

'How could I not have seen, all this time, that the way you smiled at me, your many small kindnesses to me, meant nothing more than gratitude edged with pity?' He backed away.

I had no argument.

'I was so lost in my own discovery of joy, Linny, that I didn't even stop to consider yours. Forgive me.' He turned and walked stiffly towards the thick copse along the side of the dusty road, and I had to admire the proud set of his shoulders.

He didn't come home until long after his mother and I had gone to bed. I couldn't sleep, worrying about him out in the dark somewhere, but eventually heard him coming up the stairs. His footsteps were slow and heavy. They stopped on the landing, and I held my breath, thinking he would open the door, unsure of what he would say or do, or how I would respond. But then there was the quiet sound of his own door opening and closing, and nothing more.

The next day Shaker didn't come to work with me. His mother came downstairs and told me he had asked me to report to Mr Ebbington that he'd caught a fever. 'He's never missed a day of work before. Never,' she told me, her eyes and mouth softened with concern. I caught a glimpse of the woman she might once have been.

'Shall I go to see if he needs anything?' I asked, rising from my breakfast.

'No. He asked not to be disturbed,' she told me, and I sat down again, pushing away the plate that Nan set in front of me, suddenly unable to swallow.

I spent an anxious day at work, but when I returned Shaker was waiting for me in the street when I got out of the carriage. My heart beat harder at the sight of him — relief and anxiety. The sky was low and grey. It had rained earlier, and now the eaves of the buildings around us dripped in a steady rhythm. 'Are you feeling better?' I asked, although of course I knew that his reported illness had not been physical.

'Walk with me,' he said, took my hand and laid it on his arm with a firmness I had never felt from him before. He looked pale but resolute as we went to a nearby shop with a few tables in one corner. It was a well-scrubbed place, its floors gleaming and the brass polished, but empty of customers. We ordered tea and slices of hazelnut cake.

'I've spent the last twenty-four hours thinking this through,' he said, as soon as we were seated. 'I'm sorry for my behaviour yesterday. I'm ashamed of myself.'

I had to close my eyes for a second before I could trust my voice. 'Please, Shaker, it's not you who should be ashamed, but I. I'm sorry. I just . . . I don't feel anything, and don't think I ever will. Not for a man.' I tried to think of a way to describe what had happened to me inside, but I didn't know the right words.

'People rarely marry for love, Linny. They marry for companionship, financial convenience, security. Convention. I'm not convinced love plays an important role for many.'

I waited, in case he had more to tell me, but his mouth closed in a firm line. The only sound in the shop was the quiet clink of a wooden spoon beating something in a bowl behind a curtained doorway.

'I'm going to India, Shaker,' I said quietly, 'and I believe I do love you. But not as a wife for a husband. I also believe that if I *were* able to love a man in that way, than you would be that man.'

The Adam's apple moved in his throat. 'Then I must accept and be satisfied with that, mustn't I?'

We sat in silence, our tea cooling.

'But will you promise me something? That if things don't go as you hoped, in India, and you have to return to England, you will come back to me?'

'I've told you, Shaker, I can't—'

Shaker didn't let me finish. 'Not to marry me, I understand that, Linny. You made your feelings clear, and I will not ask you again. But if you ever need a home, or a friend, I'll help you in any way I can.'

I reached across the table and laid my hand against his cheek. 'Some day you'll find someone far better than I, someone who can love you in the way I can't. And you'll forget about me, as you should,' I told him.

The cake lay untouched between us. We sipped our tea, but before we had finished it we rose, as if by agreement, and went out into the street. The sky had cleared, the clouds lifted, and the summer air was heavy and fragrant. The sound of children playing in the distance floated towards us. I put my arm through Shaker's, and he put his hand on mine, and we went slowly, with no more words, towards the house in Whitefield Lane.

That night I went to his room. His eyes were open, facing the door as I came through it, almost as if he were waiting for me. It crossed my mind that perhaps he had waited for me on other nights, even though the first time I had presented myself to him, to thank him – in the only way I knew – he had behaved as if he could not lower himself so.

I knelt beside his bed in my thin nightdress, stroking his brow. This time he did not turn away: instead he sat up, pulling back the coverlet, and I thought, then, that my old whore's ways might never leave me, that I would always be willing to offer my body. But in the next instant I felt a rush of confusion: suddenly I saw that it was not just I who was offering him part of me in gratitude but the other way round.

I pulled my nightdress over my head, allowing him to see me in the moonlight. He drew a deep breath and held it. I settled myself beside him, and he exhaled. We lay, facing each other, eventually breathing in unison. His bedshirt smelt of carbolic soap. When I kissed his mouth it smelt faintly of parsley, a clean, refreshing smell. My own mouth had been violated in so many ways, but I had never kissed anyone before. The feel of his lips on mine was pleasing.

Slowly, gently, trembling violently, Shaker tightened his arms round me, his lips responding to mine, and I felt him against me, ready, with only that brief, sweet contact.

I turned on my back, pulled him on to me, and used my hand – for his quivered too terribly – to guide him inside me, and lay very still, my bent knees hugging his hips. Within a short time his body ceased the uncontrollable shaking, and then, slowly, as if with a former familiarity, we moved together. His cheek, when he lowered it to mine, was wet with tears.

Afterwards he was completely still. It was as if his trembling had flowed out of him, temporarily, along with the physical release. My throat constricted, aching, as I watched him sleeping on my scarred breast, his lashes damp. He was a man of honour, to be trusted. He would keep me safe.

And I knew, with a sad certainty, that safety was not the only thing I wanted.

CHAPTER SIXTEEN

I WATCHED AS WE sailed away from Liverpool. I saw the grey smoke over the factory chimneys. Under my feet, the deck tilted. I smelt steel – the anchors, chains, clamps, hasps. The scent of tar brought back the image of Ram Munt and his hands.

My own hands held the railing, wet with fog. My heart pounded. I was sailing away, sailing, as in my dreams, from the place that had brought me such misery. '*This is not my true life.*' Chinese Sally's words rang in my head. And now I was sailing towards a new place, and what must be the beginning of my true life.

I watched the chimneypots of Liverpool grow small. I thought of Shaker, the light limning his body as he stood on the dock, one hand lifted in a final farewell.

August 1830
My dearest Shaker,
It is over a month since we left Liverpool on this tall-masted frigate, and today is my birthday. Today I am eighteen, and to celebrate the occasion I am writing to you. I know this letter cannot be posted for months, but I am feeling a strange sense of loneliness tonight, and the act of putting quill to paper always comforts

me. I daily record this life aboard ship in my journal – the one you gave me as a parting gift – but tonight I felt inclined to address my words to you. This is the first letter I have ever written.

I have taken to life at sea as if I was born to it. As I write this, I think of my step-father: because my arm bears the mark of a fish, he often told me I was the daughter of a sailor. Of course I didn't believe him; my mother's story, of my noble father, is much more compelling, and it is the one I will always believe. Yet my feeling aboard this vessel is that the sea – in all its strength and mystery – speaks to me in a language I understand.

The accommodation is cramped and less than clean; we are below deck, in a room separated from other women by strung canvas. There is little light or air; the doorway opens into the steerage. Faith and I share our tiny cubicle with a large, whey-faced woman of indeterminate age – Mrs Cavendish. She has lived in Delhi for fourteen years and has made this voyage a number of times. Having visited home, she is now returning to her husband, a general in the Indian Army. Because of her seniority, Mrs Cavendish chose the bed nearest the door. Faith and I are relegated to string hammocks. Although Faith appeared crestfallen at sleeping in a sling-bed for several months, I love the way my hammock swings with the rock of the waves, and, so cradled, feel the unravelling of the tangles of my former life as I drift to sleep each night.

I am learning card games – whist and piquet, écarté and loo. I decline to join in until I've observed each game enough to be confident of the rules.

Occasionally there is dancing, and I take these opportunities to ensure I will be able to conduct myself without embarrassment. Do you ever dance, Shaker? I don't recall you mentioning. To date I have perfected the minuet and the quadrille, and know my dos-à-dos and promenade. I sail from partner to partner – although most of us are women! – on those evenings when the sea is calm and some of the passengers can be persuaded to bring out their violins, clarinets and violas to perform.

Do you know, Shaker, that most people spend too much time preening and being watched to observe others? This has been in my favour while I have acquired these needed skills. It is all Faith chatters about on her good days – the dances, the salons and evenings of cards we will attend. Even she doesn't seem aware that I am a novice at these things, although I have come to see that she, like many of the others, enjoys being watched, and doesn't always observe keenly that which is around her.

We take our meals in the cuddy, or dining room, and are enjoying the luxury of fresh meat from the cows and sheep brought aboard, as well as root vegetables, which are still plump and tasty – although I don't know how much longer they will remain fresh.

During these first weeks on the grey Atlantic I have wrapped myself warmly and spent many hours on deck, either sitting on a bench and studying the books on India that Faith and I brought with us – the customs, the weather – and learning what I can of Hindi, or walking briskly, stepping over coiled rope and stacks of chain, breathing in the cool, salty breeze and marvelling at the endless furrow-like swells of the metallic waves.

I am sorry to report that Faith has grown wan, sighing and constantly warning me that I am looking far too ruddy-complexioned from the wind, that I should spend more time below, resting, as she does. But I have spent enough of my life in small, foul-smelling quarters.

I am filled with optimism, Shaker, an odd, cheery nudging. I am pleased by it. I do hope you are keeping well, visiting friends and accepting invitations. It's important that you spend time with others.

Yours,

Linny

September 1830
Dear Shaker,
I trust you will read these letters in order, as this one, written three weeks after the first, will tell a different tale of my life aboard ship. Although the sea is still my ally, it has shown its other face.

From the even waves and steady wind that gave us good speed during our first month, I imagined that the rest of the voyage would be uneventful and easy. But a storm blew up in our sixth week at sea. The sky grew dark and ominous mid-morning, the wind whipping and cruelly cold, and by afternoon the waves had transformed into huge jagged crags. We were sitting in the shifting cuddy when we were advised by the gruff captain to retire to our cabins and lash ourselves to our beds until it had blown itself out. Faith turned to Mrs Cavendish, who tried to console her. 'I've seen many a storm, my dear,' she said. 'They get even worse as we round the Cape. Usually it's possible to ride them through.'

'Usually?' Faith replied, and the colour round her mouth and eyes edged into a delicate yellow-green. 'You mean . . . Does a ship ever—' She couldn't finish the sentence. I stared at her. Had she not considered the possibility of dying *en route* to India, Shaker? Of the ship overturning in a storm like this one? Of pirates, in the warm Indian Ocean, looting the ship for the passengers' goods, perhaps killing anyone who got in their way? I had thought of all of these eventualities – more – and they held little concern for me. But Faith . . . For one so clever about some things, she is woefully naive about others.

Mrs Cavendish murmured into her ear, patting her arm. 'We'll get you some Jamaica ginger root. That will help settle your stomach for at least the next little while,' she said, and the two, supporting each other on the sliding floor, lurched out. But I had to stay for just a few more minutes, and watch, through a porthole in the cuddy, what was happening to the ocean.

It was the landscape of a monstrous dream. The waves had become sheer cliffs, rearing in front of us, and we rode up into that face, then plunged, sickeningly, down its other side, only to be faced with yet another and another of the endless walls of water. A deck hand, seeing me thrown violently from side to side while I hung on to the brass rail that ran around the cuddy wall, shouted at me, and I managed to get down the gangway and to our cabin, my clothes soaked.

The storm was terrible but, as I am here to write

about it, I survived! And, as you can see, I am now enjoying recounting the drama to you. I never believed myself one for drama. Perhaps the freedom I feel is loosening it within me.

Mrs Cavendish is bullying me to bed, so I shall obediently retire.

Yours,

Linny

I didn't wish to describe to Shaker in too much detail what had happened during that first storm. It was, if nothing else, rather indelicate, and not the sort of topic that a cultured young woman should transcribe on paper.

When I stumbled downstairs, Faith was in her sling-bed, a number of scarves and shawls tied round her middle and knotted into the ropes. She moaned steadily, a low, sonorous cry, and just as I was flung on to my own hammock she angled her neck over the side and vomited, a huge, splashing puddle of reeking yellow. I secured myself in my bed, heart pounding as I heard weak, muffled cries around me, my initial excitement at the wildness of the storm replaced first by apprehension and then by panic.

During the next hours I questioned leaving Liverpool and the safety and security of life with Shaker. As I breathed in the stench of tar, vomit and other bodily expulsions, unable to hear anything but the crashing waves and howling wind, I lost track of night and day. I was thrown about violently in the darkness, imagining, with every groan of the timbers, that the icy water would burst through to fill my nose and mouth, drowning me as I lay lashed to my hammock. For what felt like days I lived in my old nightmare of drowning in the Mersey. Alternately I gasped for breath in the airless cabin or shivered, my clothes damp with sweat. My stomach and bowels emptied where I lay – my body heaved until I tasted blood on my lips, and knew that the lining of my stomach was being torn away.

I longed for Whitefield Lane, for Jack Street, even for Back Phoebe Anne Street. I kept my eyes squeezed shut and waited to die; in fact, in bereft moments, I wished for it. There had only been one other time in my life when I had felt so close to death.

Eventually I became aware that I had been asleep, and was now rocking gently. I opened my eyes and saw that the door was open and secured by its hook to the wall. Dim light filtered into the foul mess of our cabin. I heard Faith's voice, pure and high as a child's, and realized it was this that had woken me.

'Linny? Answer me! Linny?'

I twisted to look at her hammock and saw that Mrs Cavendish's bed was empty, stripped of its sheets and blankets. 'Where is Mrs Cavendish?' My voice was a hoarse croak, my throat raw from vomiting.

'She went on deck to wash her bedding. I don't think I can move.'

I plucked feebly at the scarves and shawls that had held me in, then sat up, grimacing. I undid my restraints, then stood up shakily, my ribcage and abdomen feeling bruised from the spasms of my empty stomach. I helped Faith untie herself and half smiled. 'What a pair we are! The only solution is a bucket of salt water dashed over us.'

'Don't joke, Linny. I'm too weak even to cry. I don't think I'll ever recover from this.'

'You will,' I told her.

'You're awake then, girls,' came Mrs Cavendish's booming voice from the doorway. 'Come, change all your clothing, then take it and your bedding up on deck. We'll have this place cleaned in no time. Now, that storm wasn't as bad as some I've seen. Once my ship was hit astern, and the water burst over the deck then below, straight into my cabin. I make a most becoming mermaid.' She gave a hearty laugh. 'And that storm won't be the last on this voyage.'

Faith erupted into sobs, and it took us a good ten minutes to help her compose herself enough to rise.

On the west coast of Africa our ship was diverted by another storm. This one sent us close to Brazil, and it was another three weeks before we had resumed our course. During this time I studied Hindi, wrote in my journal and continued with my unposted letters to Shaker. We had been at sea for three months. The food was no longer enjoyable; the only meat left was preserved pork, which was tough, stringy and salty. All sense of order had left the dining room; food was thrown unceremoniously on to the tables and whoever had the stomach for it that day reached out and grabbed it. The water had turned the colour of strong tea, and tasted as bad as it looked and smelt. The heat grew intense, and we changed our woollen dresses for light muslin – until we approached the Cape of Good Hope, where the weather was chilly again. As we neared the imaginary line where the Atlantic and Indian Oceans meet, we saw ourselves in danger of being dashed against the shore when a shift in the wind caught the billows in a dizzying rush.

We stopped briefly at the Cape for fresh supplies, and then were off into warmer waters. But we were soon caught in a seasonal hurricane. The ship lurched and pitched;

furniture was torn from its fastenings. I silently prayed that we would withstand the battering, and this time my body did not betray me. When, at last, a day and night had passed, I arose dry-eyed and composed, but Faith would not smile.

We sat becalmed for two weeks under a blazing sun, the sails limp, their rents now visible. No one had the energy for talk or cards, and the heat made the thought of dancing incomprehensible. The only sound was the teasing lick of water against the ship's side, and the answering creak of its timbers. The sea looked like a silver plate, hard and immobile. The crew were surly, muttering as they repaired the canvas and frayed halyards, casting irritated glances at the passengers who stepped around them in an endless circle of the deck hoping for a whisper of cooling air.

Finally, one morning, I awoke to movement, and when I went up on deck, the sails were reaching for the wind. The sea was smooth and yielding as the ship cut through it and I felt such a rise in my spirits that I smiled at the most taciturn of the deck hands. He had bulging forearms and tattoos that shifted with the movement of his muscles – only the day before he had reminded me eerily of Ram Munt but now he bore no such resemblance.

It grew unbearably hot, and we moved our bedding on to the decks. The ladies slept on one side, the gentlemen on the other, and a sail was rigged between us for decency's sake. That first night on deck I couldn't sleep. I got up, stepped over Faith and the other women, and went to the rail. Standing in the dark, I watched the sea as it reflected the moon, creating a long, winding road of silver. And then the water began to glow with a bright light, as if myriad tiny candles blazed just under the water. I watched, transfixed, until my eyes hurt with staring. Was it some underwater creature? Or a sign that I was on my true path?

During the day the Indian Ocean was filled with life: flying fish swept past us like narrow silver coins and, as Faith had predicted, whales and porpoises raced alongside the ship. The sun was clean on my skin, burning deep, seeming to warm the marrow in my bones, and I wondered if I had ever before been truly warm. As I stood on deck one day, closing my eyes and turning my face to the sky, I realized that I had not had my nightmare for many nights – perhaps weeks. It was as though the sun – infinitely stronger than it was in England – had burned the terror out of my brain, had eaten into it, destroying it, just as the bold rats scurrying below deck had eaten holes in our clothes.

There was a sudden spray of warm water over the railing. It wet my face and I licked my lips, savouring the ancient, wild taste of the sea. As I did so I turned to a young couple who stood a little away from me. They had married just before we set sail, and were travelling first to Calcutta, then overland to Bombay, where the man had a position with the East India Company civil service. We'd exchanged pleasantries a number of times; now I imagined we would smile, sharing amusement at the unexpected shower. But in the moment that I looked towards them, I saw that they were lost in each other, unaware of me. The young man lowered his face and licked the salty water from the tiny hollow at the base of his new wife's throat, and she put back her head and arched her neck. In that instant I felt shock, a deep, thudding, sobering emotion. The girl's slight movement, and the look on her face, brought me down from my moment of giddy hope. That soft and yielding expression could only have been desire. I had never known or felt it, and I was filled with sorrow, and grieved. Suddenly I had lost all fascination with the sea. It now appeared nothing more than a wearying, endless distance of furrows.

November came, and we had been at sea almost four months. Swallows swooped near the rails, indicating land. Mrs Cavendish likened the busy, twittering birds to the dove with its olive branch. But she was right, and within another day we spotted villages along the coast. The water became noisy with dozens of tiny rocking boatloads of Indians. Bumboat men, Mrs Cavendish called them, shouting to be heard over their voices as they boasted of their merchandise, hoping to sell coconuts, bananas or tamarinds. I hung over the railing, watching, as the natives threw ropes with baskets attached over the ship's side. Some of the crew called down to them in a tongue I couldn't identify and put coins into the baskets, which were lowered, then came up again, filled with whatever the sailors had requested. I longed to try the fruit, but Mrs Cavendish, with a shake of her head, indicated that it was beneath us to purchase anything in this way.

During the last few days, as we drew closer to our destination, excitement grew in me. At first I attributed it to the beauty of the water and the sun, then realized it was something else. I detected a difference in the atmosphere, and whether it was in the air itself or in the degree of the heat I couldn't say. Perhaps the smells carried on the wind contributed to the unexplained breathlessness I experienced. My nose filled with the unaccustomed smells of the populace, the scents of unknown vegetation. I felt as light-headed as I had when I twirled in my first quadrille.

* * *

We stopped at the Sandheads, at the mouth of the Hooghly river, to wait for the tide to help push us into the river. This last leg of the journey, Mrs Cavendish cautioned, was hazardous. The sixty miles up the dimpled, belching brown water of the Hooghly as it cut through the green Bengal countryside had proved disastrous for many ships because of the dangerous sandbanks and shifting shoals. 'Hundreds of lives lost on one sandbank alone, the treacherous quicksand of the James and Mary,' she went on, unmindful of Faith's expression.

Faith had not done well on the journey. Like all of us, she had lost weight. There were new hollows under her eyes and the lines around her mouth had deepened. I had tried to offer company and support, but Faith had grown sullen and uncommunicative. It seemed she had receded into herself while I had grown stronger, more able. I felt as if I had even grown taller, although I knew that was impossible.

'Look, Faith, palm trees and bananas, as we saw in your book,' I said, trying to cheer her with the vision of emerald lushness a few hours from Calcutta. There were waving fields of rice. Everywhere the colour was so vibrant, so alive. England's watercolour pastels paled in comparison. I gazed idly at a dog on the riverbank, seeing its protruding ribs and scabbed flesh. It was tearing at something surrounded by bits of rotted blue cloth. At the same time as Faith I realized that its prize was a human leg and foot. She emitted a high, strangled cry and ran from the deck. As I made to follow her, Mrs Cavendish laid a hand on my arm.

'Let her be,' she advised. 'India is hard for some, who never get used to it. Others,' she puffed out her chest, reminding me of a pouter pigeon, 'do the best they can, and are the better for it. Fourteen years – and just look at me. I've survived it all – fevers, heat, monsoons, birthing, two buried in India and three alive at home, heathen customs, snake bite. And that's to say nothing of the things I've seen – stabbings in the market, executions of thuggees, suttee. Although suttee was forbidden last year.' She studied me. 'You think you have what it takes?'

I nodded.

'Better start learning, Linny. Not even a parasol, this morning, and you're quite unfashionably coloured from the sun and wind.'

The ship stopped, mid-afternoon, just before the shallow waters of the docks at Chandpal Chat. The date I had written that morning on the final page of my voyage letter to Shaker was 18 November 1830. As I looked towards the docks, all I could make out was a swarming mass of humanity. The waters were filled with every kind of vessel – fishing boats, rafts, dhows, ferries and *lorchas*, so crowded that they chafed at each other. I thought of the coasting brigs, cutters and schooners in the thick fog at Liverpool harbour, drawing comparisons with these small vessels, worked by near-naked brown-skinned men.

The outskirts of Calcutta surprised me. White Palladian villas faced the river, elegant and stately, owned, Mrs Cavendish told me, by British merchants grown rich on the East India Company's trade.

After I'd fetched Faith from the cabin, where she sat forlornly on her sling-bed, I took up my parasol and we climbed down a rough rope ladder into *masoolas* – small rocking boats that ferried passengers to shore. Ours pitched and yawed, and we held tightly to its sides. Dirty water sloshed over our boots and soaked the hems of our dresses.

Faith had been told that we'd be met by Mr Waterton, her father's friend, who had agreed to be our host for as long as we remained in Calcutta. I was glad of my pale blue frilled parasol as I sat between Faith and Mrs Cavendish, watching the crowd swell on the pier as we crossed the short span of water. Voices rose in shouts, cries and chants.

'Do you see your husband, Mrs Cavendish?' I shouted into the woman's ear. It was a foolish question: how could anyone discern anything in such a throng? Everywhere brilliant colours swarmed; I had to close my eyes for a moment to distinguish what I was seeing. Women's saris in bright pink, orange and red, carts heaped with unfamiliar fruit and vegetables. Dark faces under white turbans. As we drew nearer the pier, I breathed in scents I couldn't identify but which I was sure, from my reading, must be jasmine, sandalwood, cloves and ginger. But there was something else. Underneath it all there was a foetid, cloying odour, of urine, dirt and decay, a deep smell of rot that I recognized from the seeping cellars in Liverpool's meanest courts.

We were lifted on to the dock, and the mass of brilliance I had seen from the *masoola* now became real, and in detail that belied the dreamy beauty I had assumed from the distance. We stood in dust and heat amid the babble of the tumultuous crowd, our boots soaked, trying to say goodbye to the passengers we had come to know so well over our journey, shouting above the tinny band playing to greet the ship.

I found it difficult to stand on land after so many months on the rolling sea. My knees felt as if they were still dipping and balancing, and there was a list to one side in my head. I felt pressure on my ankle and looked down, thinking my body was playing tricks on me as it adjusted to the land under my feet. But a young woman – little more than a girl, really – was kneeling at my feet, holding an emaciated naked infant in one arm while her other hand held up a dented tin bowl. Her mouth was moving, but in the gabble surrounding us I couldn't understand whether she was speaking, crying or praying. I had no Indian money yet, no rupees or annas, to give to her, and I smiled uncertainly, pointing at my reticule and shaking my head. She appeared not to understand, and I saw now, with a shock of recognition, that the child's head – which I had assumed was covered with black hair – was swarming with flies. The girl shifted the baby to pull at my skirt with a filthy hand, and it became apparent that the tiny scalp was a mass of running sores. I swallowed and tried to step away but felt a tiny rip at my waist as the girl held on to the thin fabric of my skirt. The handful of flowered muslin she gripped was now dark with dirt, and I knew that the gauzy material on my back was damp with sweat.

Beside me, Faith looked down, saw what the girl held, and her legs gave out. I hooked my arm through hers to hold her up, struggling with my parasol and reticule, feeling a flutter of panic. My stays were suddenly too tight, I was too hot, it was difficult to breathe, and the strange odours turned my stomach.

The pointed end of Mrs Cavendish's parasol appeared at the girl's ragged shoulder. It gave her a sharp poke. She dropped my skirt and scurried away between trousered legs and flowing skirts.

I tried to drag Faith along. Her skin had the colour of parchment, her hair a bright flame round it. Mrs Cavendish followed, with Faith's dropped reticule.

The dock was smothered with human forms: men in the ragged loincloths that I knew, from my reading, were called *dhotis*, carrying bundles on their heads; sweetmeat sellers hawking their wares – from water to hot tea to betel nut; beggar children with huge, beseeching eyes; and mangy yellow dogs. Everywhere brown-skinned men, women and children sat, stood and wandered about, some eating, some sleeping. It was a mass of moving, jabbering, stinking humanity. My light-headed listing grew; I had never swooned, thinking women who did so were weak. But now I feared that the immensity of sights, sounds and smells, the bright heat that encased my body, might squeeze me senseless. I took deep breaths, biting down hard on my back teeth to drive away the hazy sense of disconnection.

A series of high squeals rang out above the general cacophony; its urgency made me search out the new source of noise. My head cleared at what I saw.

A man on a rich chestnut horse with black mane and tail sat high above the people on the hard-packed dirt and rock of the pier. Man and beast were caught in the shifting, restless crowd, and the horse whinnied in distress, eyes rolling, lifting each foot and setting it down. The man called out in a loud, demanding voice, but I didn't know whether to his horse or to the milling throngs surrounding him. He pulled with swift, upward tugs on the leather reins as if to steer the horse in another direction, but the gleaming animal kept throwing back its head, tossing its thick mane. If it reared, the heavy hoofs would surely come down on a foot or even a child. The man had long black hair oddly similar to his horse's mane. His white teeth shone in his sun-darkened face, and I could even see the ebony glisten of his long eyes. Suddenly he leaned forward, dropped his head and appeared to speak into the horse's ear, which pricked forward. Immediately the creature stopped its frantic head-tossing and stood as if mesmerized. They looked as if they had been chiselled from one piece of magnificent stone, and finally the crowd thinned enough for them to move forward. The rider edged his horse along, never glancing down, eyes fixed on some distant spot.

'Who was that?' I asked Mrs Cavendish, still supporting Faith, who sagged against me.

'Who, dear?' Shielding her eyes, Mrs Cavendish scanned the crowd.

I pointed. 'That man. The tall one on the horse.' Whether it came from exhaustion, the excitement of docking, the confusion or the feel of solid earth under my feet, that sight of the man on his horse – so alone and distinct in the crowd – had settled me.

Mrs Cavendish followed my finger. 'A Pathan – not one of the Indian people. The Pathans are from the North West Frontier, way up beyond Peshawar, on the border with Afghanistan. They ride down into India to trade their horses. Wonderful riders, the Pathans – or Pushtuns, as they call themselves. They rule most of Afghanistan, the blighters. Proud, they are, even noble, I suppose, but the Indians are wary of them. Their women are just as fierce, mutilating their enemies. Odd to see one so far south.'

'A Pathan,' I repeated. 'A Pathan from Afghanistan.'

'Thank goodness,' Faith said weakly. 'Look. That man has a sign with my name on it. It's Mr Waterton.'

Mrs Cavendish and I hugged each other, and I followed Faith as she made her way to Mr Waterton, her shoulders so high and tight I thought they might touch her ears. He greeted us formally. He was a small man with thinning hair and a twitch under his left eye, which made him appear to be continually winking. He'd brought a palanquin for the ride to his home. It had wooden rods and tattered curtains around all four sides and was carried by four brown men wearing small, dirty loincloths. Faith was flustered as she climbed in, trying not to stare at the men, yet stealing glances at them from beneath her lashes. We sat beside each other on one of the hard wooden benches while Mr Waterton gave instructions for our luggage to be taken in a second palanquin. Then he climbed in, drew the curtains on all sides and sat across from us.

'Oh, please, Mr Waterton, may we leave the curtains open? I'd like to see Calcutta.'

He looked shocked at my request and frowned.

'Of course not, Linny,' Faith said. 'I'd feel so unsafe, with all those prying eyes, and who knows what diseases might be hovering in the air? I just want to get to the Watertons'. And not only that,' she said primly, then put one hand to the side of her mouth and whispered, 'we'd be staring right at those men. They're nearly naked, Linny.'

I sighed and sat upright on the splintered bench. We lurched as the men picked up the poles and set off at what felt like a trot. I listened to the bedlam outside the swaying curtains, wishing I could see what was going on.

'A Pathan, from Afghanistan,' I said to myself.

'I beg your pardon?' Faith enquired.

'Nothing,' I told her. 'I was just remembering something.'

CHAPTER SEVENTEEN

W HEN WE STEPPED out of the palanquin, I saw that
we had come to one of the white Palladian villas I
had seen from the ship. It was set back on a wide street,
which I learned later was called Garden Reach. The entrance
and portico of the house had been transformed into a *porte-
cochère*, and this was where we stood now, under a roofed
structure that protected us from the sun.

Faith squeezed my arm. 'Isn't this the most wonderful
house, Linny?'

I was disappointed. I don't know what I'd expected, but it
wasn't a huge and elegant one-storey home more extravagant
than any I'd seen in Liverpool. I turned to see Mr Waterton
sorting through a pile of coins in his hand. He and one of the
palanquin bearers were in dispute. The man in the ragged
dhoti was holding up five fingers; Mr Waterton shook his
head and held up three. The bearer's voice grew louder and
louder, and eventually his companions joined in, creating a
high-pitched clamour. Finally Mr Waterton threw a number
of coins on to the ground and turned his back on the men
scrabbling in the red dust. Only eighteen months ago it had
been me on my knees in dirty streets, collecting my pay.

'Mustn't let them get the upper hand,' Mr Waterton said,
looking pleased with himself as he wiped his hands on the

large checked handkerchief he pulled from inside his jacket. Then he removed his solar topee, scrubbed his glistening forehead and scalp, then ruffled what remained of his lank brown hair. 'You ladies will get used to wearing one of these,' he said, holding out his helmet. 'We have to protect our brains – they can be fried, become quite liquefied, you know. Infernal sun. Our skin isn't thick enough, just not made for this country.'

The second palanquin arrived with our luggage, and by the time it was unloaded Mrs Waterton had come out of the villa, holding a parasol, and welcoming us with a kind smile to what she called our 'English home away from home'. We went inside, and she gave us a dizzying tour of the house. My head spun: I was in India, but the furnishings in the house belied this. It was as if I had stepped into a superbly decorated English house. Except, of course, for the brown servants who hovered in the corridors, in the shadowy corners of each room, some waiting, expectant, others moving along the walls with lowered eyes. It was almost as though we were in a giant hive, with a sense of humming, activity and purpose. I could tell from the widened look of Faith's eyes that she, too, found it overpowering.

'My poor girls,' Mrs Waterton said, 'you must be exhausted. I'm sure the filth and noise of the docks was upsetting. I tend to forget. I've been here too long.' She smiled again, and this time the smile was not as pleasant. 'Far too long.' I was soon to discover that this tiresome repetition was characteristic of her speech. 'I'm sure you were frightened and intimidated today. But don't worry. You will not have to witness more sights like those you saw. You are safe now, and will remain so. Come, I'll take you to your rooms. There you may wash and rest, and at dinner you'll feel more yourselves. We have another young lady, newly married – Mrs Liston – staying with us too. She's been accompanied to dinner elsewhere, and you'll meet her at breakfast tomorrow. Now, off you go. I'll send for you when dinner is ready.'

Faith and I nodded.

After Mrs Waterton had left me in my room, beside Faith's, I stood with my back to the closed door and looked at the four-poster double bed set in the middle of the large open-raftered room, mosquito netting rolled up along the thin wooden frame that was supported over the bed by the four posts. A cloth stretched across the top, like a canopy. I thought, briefly, of the beds I'd known – the tiny pallet in Back Phoebe Anne Street, the single mattress I'd shared with two other girls in Jack Street, the flock mattress in Mrs Small-piece's room in Whitefield Lane. I'd never seen such a spacious, thick-mattressed bed in the finest hotel rooms I'd been taken to in Liverpool.

There was also a rosewood escritoire, a full-length pier glass, a small dressing-table covered with bottles of lotion and perfume, a washstand with a large jug and bowl, a deep wardrobe, a chest of drawers, and two padded chairs uphol-stered in flowered fabric. The open window was covered with screens of woven grass, rolled down from the ceiling, obliterating the view.

Overhead, a large rectangular frame of light wood covered with white cotton swung back and forth, stirring the still air. I realized, with a start, that it was being operated by a boy sitting cross-legged in a corner, the string from the fan attached to his big toe. A small woman, all in white, squatted in another corner. I looked at them, opened my mouth, but didn't know what to say.

The woman rose and came wordlessly to me. She undid

the row of buttons at the back of my dress, which was still damp with sweat. She said a word to the boy, who took the string off his toe, parted the window screens and slipped out. When she had removed my dress, corset and petticoats, I stood in my chemise while she took a sponge from the washstand, dipped it into cool, rose-scented water and began slowly, almost languorously, to wash my face and neck, chest and arms. I'd never been touched like that by another woman – or anyone else since the man I remembered only as Wednesday. The pale hair on my arms rose at the unexpected attention, and I felt drowsiness steal over me in the warm, quiet room. Then she pushed me gently towards the bed, and I lay down obediently. She covered me with a thin sheet of muslin, let down the mosquito netting, spoke another word and the boy returned.

I lay on the magnificent bed, listening to the creak of the fan – which I remembered was called a *punkah* – and the woman's soft humming.

None of the books I'd read on board had prepared me for this grandeur – or the squalor I'd seen on the dock. My head ached, and I closed my eyes.

Dinner was too long; tedious. On the way to the dining room with Faith – following a male servant, who had tapped quietly on my door – I took the opportunity to look more closely at the house. Although its decoration was English, several things showed we weren't in England. The ceilings were not enclosed, but open rafters. There were *punkahs* in every room, and much of the flooring was of cool stone. I saw a small table whose legs had been made from the curling horns of some large animal, and vases of unfamiliar flowers stood on many surfaces. There were animal skins on the floors and animal trophies on the wall; I saw umbrellas in a stand that looked like – yes, it was – an elephant's foot.

Faith and I entered the gloomy dining room with its heavy, dark furniture. The table was covered with a thick white cloth; ferns and vines had been laid across it. All of the food for dinner was placed on the table at once by a tall, imposing man with a hennaed beard and a high turban.

My heart sank as I surveyed what we were expected to eat: a shoulder of lamb, some type of fowl, sliced finely and swimming in a gluey gravy, a huge bowl of something mashed that resembled the texture, but not the colour, of potatoes, three bowls of vegetables I couldn't identify, and thick slices of dark heavy bread. My stomach was bloated and uneasy from the heat and the change in my environment, and the ache in my head had not eased with lying down. When I heard a subtle noise I looked up discreetly and saw that the ceiling was covered with a suspended white cloth. A curious movement was visible through the thin material, as if something was creeping about up there.

'Were you able to rest?' Mrs Waterton asked.

Faith spoke, rubbing her forehead: 'I found it difficult to lie still after so many months on the waves. I'm experiencing the same unease on land as I first did aboard ship.'

'How unpleasant for you,' Mrs Waterton sympathized, patting Faith's arm. 'It may take you some time to regain your strength.' She looked at me. 'You appear less exhausted, Miss Smallpiece.'

'I wasn't as troubled by the journey as Miss Vespry,' I said, not knowing whether to be proud or ashamed of my hardiness.

'Well, I had a *burra khanah* – a grand feast – prepared to welcome you, young ladies.' Mrs Waterton beamed. Then the smile disappeared. 'I must warn you that these poor ignorant people will never understand how to cook properly. It's often a hodge-podge. No matter what lengths I go to to explain rudimentary recipes to the *bobajee*, his brain isn't capable of comprehending. And yet he came with the highest recommendation. It's a curse one must accept,' she finished. 'A curse.' She sighed.

When we were seated, Mrs Waterton nodded at the stately man. '*Khit*,' she said, 'the soup.'

The man she called *khit* – which I later understood was an abbreviation of the title of his job, *khitmutgar* – stepped forward with a huge silver tureen and ladled out a thin soup that tasted nutty. As soon as we had emptied the bowls he removed them, then proceeded to fill our plates from all of the serving dishes. He cut Mr Waterton's lamb and fowl, and I wondered if we were not even to do this simple thing for ourselves. But Mrs Waterton picked up her knife and fork and proceeded to use them, so Faith and I followed suit. While we ate I heard the scratchings and scurryings of what sounded like large insects and small animals overhead in the white cloth although neither Mr nor Mrs Waterton seemed aware of it; I realized the cloth was there to stop whatever moved through the open rafters falling on to the table. They also paid no heed to the small flakes of whitewash from the frame of the *punkah* that drifted on to the table. As the *punkah* swayed, I wondered if the small boy in the dark corner of the room who pulled its rope was the one from my room.

I ate what I could of the food piled in front of me, not wanting to insult the Watertons, but I had made barely any difference to it before I had to set down my cutlery. My stomach was in distress after the small, simple meals we'd eaten over the last few months.

'My dears,' Mrs Waterton exclaimed, looking from Faith to me and back to Faith – whose plate looked as untouched as mine, 'you must nourish yourselves. You're both far too thin from the journey. Come now, it won't do to languish. Do you not agree, Mr Waterton?'

He looked up from his plate, his lips shiny with lamb grease. He snapped his fingers, and the *khitmutgar* stepped up and dabbed at his lips with a white napkin, poured him a second glass of port, then stepped back.

Mr Waterton took a sip. 'Well, they will soon get used to the dining,' he said, answering his wife but looking at Faith and me. 'I expect Miss Smallpiece and Miss Vespry are looking forward to the social season.'

Faith answered. 'Oh, yes, Mr Waterton, very much.' Her voice was quiet, almost hoarse, and I knew her to be completely fatigued.

'Of course.' Mrs Waterton either didn't notice or didn't care that Faith's voice carried no enthusiasm. 'We'll give you a few days to settle in, yes, two or three days to get your legs back, and for your appetite to return. There's no rush. My goodness, you girls have at least four full months of delightful entertaining ahead before the end of the seas—' Mrs Waterton stopped. A large flake of whitewash had fallen into the gravy. 'Well, let's not think too far ahead. I'm sure lovely young ladies such as yourselves will be kept busy.'

An awkward silence fell over the table, and Mrs Waterton called sharply, '*Koi-hai*?' and another boy hurried in to take away our plates. 'The dessert,' she said, and from a long table against the wall the *khitmutgar* brought a lacquered tray of bowls. 'I had *custel brun* – I'm sorry, caramel custard – prepared in your honour,' she said. 'You must have missed your pudding while on board. It's what I always long for when forced to sail home or back again. My pudding.'

Faith and I swallowed as much of it as we could. Mr Waterton had waved it away, obviously not as fond of it as his wife. Now the servant poured Mr Waterton a cup of tea, put in sugar and stirred it for him. I wondered if he would hold the cup to the man's lips, but Mr Waterton appeared capable of this on his own.

That first night I fell into a deep, dreamless sleep almost immediately I laid my head on the pillow. When I opened my eyes to shafts of brilliant sunshine slicing through the window screens I was momentarily disoriented, and sat up in alarm, but the woman – whom Mrs Waterton had told me would be my ayah – appeared out of nowhere, pulled back the netting and handed me a glass of something milky, sweet and refreshing. After she had helped me with my dress and hair, I was rested and excited about what the day might hold.

Faith looked better than she had the evening before, although the shadows round her eyes were still dark when we met in the dining room. We were greeted by another groaning table. I nibbled a sweet bun and a plantain. As promised, Faith and I met Mrs Liston – I liked her and guessed her age to be between Faith's and mine. She had dark blonde hair in thin ringlets and wide green eyes. She laughed with her mouth open. Unfortunately her face had been badly marked by a long-ago bout of smallpox. She had been born in India, gone home as a small child, then returned three years ago to live with her parents. She had only seen her mother three times in the twelve years she'd lived in England, and her father not at all, which was, she said, only natural.

'Natural?' I'd asked. 'To see your mother three times in all those years?'

'You're new to the ways of the English in India, Miss Smallpiece,' Mrs Waterton told me. 'As it happens, my own four children are living with relatives in Cambridge, having a proper education. I accompanied my youngest two years ago, when he was five. I try to get to England every third year, but the duration and unpredictability of the voyage are, of course, restricting.'

Inwardly I wondered at the backbone of these women, that they conceded to parting with their young children. But it was only one of the sacrifices – although perhaps the greatest – that English women in India suffered to support their husbands.

'Once you start to go about, you'll notice there are no older English children here. Mothers in India must face separation,' Mrs Liston said. 'Children aren't allowed to stay here beyond five or six – they must be sent home for their education. The mother must decide if she will accompany her child or stay with her husband. Most choose the latter. I lived with an aunt and uncle and three male cousins all those years – and I'm afraid my parents were rather shocked by how I turned out. I wasn't what they had hoped for.' She laughed as she spoke the last sentence.

I smiled and glanced at Mrs Waterton, who wore a rather guarded expression, and was paying attention to her rumble-tumble, as she called it. Scrambled eggs. Already I was noticing the household jargon.

'Mr Liston and I have been married only two months. He's gone ahead to prepare our home in Lucknow, which is in the north-east. Since Father retired from the East India Company civil service a month ago, and he and Mother

214

sailed for England, well, the Watertons have been generous enough to let me stay with them until Mr Liston returns for me.'

'How did you meet your husband?' Faith asked. I was pleased to see she had regained some of the colour in her cheeks, and had done her hair in a most charming way. Her rust-coloured dress brought out the creaminess of her skin.

'Oh, through friends, shortly after I arrived, but there wasn't much romance at first.'

Mrs Waterton cleared her throat, but Mrs Liston didn't appear to notice.

'No, we were friends for quite a time. We often went riding – chaperoned, of course,' she added, perhaps for Mrs Waterton's benefit, 'out in the country. We rode through miles of mustard fields or beans with wonderful scents. We'd pass peacocks strutting about, and through villages where the dogs would bark round the horses' legs. The villagers were polite and friendly, offering us refreshments. He's full of surprises, my Mr Liston, and he introduced me to all manner of interesting and unexpected adventures, from visiting shrines in the countryside to pig-sticking. I'd never enjoyed many of the pastimes most young ladies enjoy – perhaps it was my upbringing in the country with my cousins – and never fully expected to marry. Oh, come now, Mrs Waterton,' she said, at the woman's shocked gasp, 'don't look so gloomy. You know it's true.' She smiled at me. 'I play no instrument, my singing causes the birds to fly from the trees, and dancing with me is like lurching about with a drunken goose.'

I had to laugh with her.

'Cards have remained a mystery to me,' she went on, 'and I find musical evenings, flower-arranging and poring over the goods displayed by the box-*wallahs* so tedious.' She faced

Mrs Waterton again. 'Now, please, Mrs Waterton, humour me. Agree that it isn't the end of the world that I have been unable to master the expected accomplishments.'

'Of course it's not, dear,' Mrs Waterton murmured, but it was obvious she disapproved of Mrs Liston's choices and her unabashed disclosure of them.

'And what of you girls? Are you prepared for the endless social activities of the Cool Season?' Mrs Liston asked us, and put a forkful of fried plantain into her mouth. She chewed and swallowed with gusto and I found her enthusiasm appealing.

'I most certainly am,' Faith said, cutting a tiny bite from her sausage. 'After the positively wretched months on that ship I'm looking forward to some fun. I'm sorry to have to admit, Mrs Liston, that I'm one of those young ladies who *does* enjoy dancing, cards and all the other aspects of an active social life.' Her voice, no longer weary as it had been the evening before, now held an almost haughty note, which surprised me. I had assumed she would like Mrs Liston. In fact, the other woman's straightforward speech and confidence reminded me of the Faith I had known in Liverpool. I was struck then by how much Faith had changed during the voyage. Perhaps once she was rested properly she would regain her zest for life and make me laugh with her outrageous statements and confidences. I made a pretence of spooning an orange jam on to a morsel of my bun and watched Faith from under my eyelashes.

'I intend to enjoy myself,' Faith repeated.

'As you will, my dear,' Mrs Waterton said, smiling again. 'As you will.'

I witnessed, that first day, that Mrs Waterton spoke sharply to her servants, and constantly grumbled about them. She didn't call them by name, only by the title of the job they performed. Yet she seemed to feel affection for them – and they treated her with the utmost respect.

I began to understand the hierarchy. The household was run by the *khansana*, or head bearer, who kept a stern eye on all the other servants. Then there was the *khitmutgar*, the imposing figure who had waited on us at the table, and a number of others under him. Next came the cook – the *biwarchi* or, as Mrs Waterton referred to him, the *bobajee*. He had an assortment of helpers, whom Mrs Waterton simply called the *bobajee*'s boys. Then there was the *chuprassi*, or messenger, in his fine red sash; his job was to stand at the door all day to admit guests, and accept chits or calling cards. There was the *dhobi*, in charge of washing and ironing, the *bheesti* to carry water, the *mali* to look after the gardens, and the night watchman, the *chowkidar*; Mrs Waterton shared a *durzi*, or tailor, with two other households. There was a huge cleaning staff, each with a specific job. The boy who carried the dishes from the dining room was not the boy who washed them. Another polished the silver. The boy who swept the house was not the one who swept the verandah. The boy who dusted could not touch the dishes, and so on. The youngest servants were the *punkah*-pullers and the small boys who hovered behind our chairs, waving horsetail whisks over our heads to discourage insects. The only female servants I saw were the *ayahs*: each woman in the house had one to help her with bathing, dressing, brushing and styling her hair.

There was a litany of rigid rules that were overwhelming at first. Over and over again I asked someone passing me in the hall, on the verandah or in the dining room for something, only to be met with a blank look. At first I assumed it was because they couldn't understand the few simple commands I had learned, but later realized I had asked the wrong person. As the majority of servants – apart from the *khitmutgar* and the *chuprassi* – dressed in simple white *dhotis*, shirts and turbans, their feet bare, I found it difficult to distinguish between them. Within a few days, though, I could recognize faces, height and a distinctive manner of walking.

By the end of our third day in Calcutta it occurred to me that there was nothing for any of us to do. Mr Waterton and, it would seem, every British man who wasn't in the army was a civil servant for the East India Company. Mr Waterton was a director of Land Records; he left after breakfast, returned for lunch, went back to work until dinner. The household ran itself – or, rather, was run by the *khansana*. From what I witnessed, Mrs Waterton's role was primarily to meet with her *bobajee* each morning and discuss the day's meals. Then she might inspect the rooms to see that they had been cleaned to her standards. There were the flowers – armloads of blossoms cut and laid in an enormous pile by the *mali*, with vases filled with water – that she might arrange. Sometimes she consulted with the *durzi* over what she wanted repaired. Some days a box-*wallah* came to the back door, and spread out his wares, ranging from ribbons to cooking pans to cloth to teapots. Mrs Waterton would pick what she wanted, hand the required rupees to one of the serving staff, who in turn handed it to the box-*wallah*. She would write out any chits to communicate with or reply to chits or cards left by neighbours. This was done between breakfast and lunch.

There was a large lunch, a nap, and then, perhaps, afternoon callers, dinner out by invitation or, if it was dinner in, a visit to the Calcutta Club or to a social event.

'Mrs Waterton,' I said, finding her at a small table in the drawing room, studying a book with illustrations of cakes, 'may we go for a walk?' It was our fourth day in Calcutta: as Mrs Waterton had predicted, I felt refreshed. I had continued to sleep well and was now anxious to see some of Calcutta outside the front door. Faith was reading in her room but had agreed that she would go for a stroll with me, if there was a chaperone.

'Certainly, dear. Just follow the path through the garden along the flowers. It is lovely to walk there.' She didn't look up from the book.

'I meant a walk outside the garden.'

She looked up now, her finger on the page. 'A walk? Where would you walk to?'

'I – I don't know. I wondered if Faith and I – if we were accompanied by Mrs Liston, of course, or yourself – might go for a walk.'

'Do you mean on the road?' Her face showed consternation. 'Oh, no, my dear. It just isn't done. A lady doesn't walk about the streets of Calcutta. This is not London or Cheltenham. One simply doesn't walk about,' she repeated.

'Oh,' I said. 'I'm sorry. I didn't know.'

'Well, you wouldn't. It's quite all right. You'll learn how things are done here shortly.'

'Would it be possible to go for a ride, then?'

She closed the book. Gently, but with purpose. 'A ride? At this time of day?'

I glanced at the swinging pendulum of the mantel clock. Was I showing complete ignorance? I should have conferred first with Faith. 'Oh. It's just two. I didn't realize . . .'

'Well, it's not unheard of, I suppose, but I shall have to

have the *chuprassi* summon a palanquin. Where did you wish to go?'

I looked down at the carpet. 'I don't know, Mrs Waterton. But I would so like to see some of the city.'

Mrs Waterton's lips formed a thin line. 'There's very little of interest. There is a possibility of a drive to the *maidan* after dinner, to take the cool evening air. If you are insistent, we could arrange to do that now, but I hadn't planned an outing today. I have quite a bit to do with planning meals, as there are more of us in the house than I'm used to. And I have a number of cards to answer.'

It was obvious from her tone and the steel in her voice – as well as her reference to extra guests – that I should not be asking for anything as frivolous as a ride out. 'I understand, Mrs Waterton, of course. Please, forgive my uncalled-for request.' I backed out of the room. 'I'll have a stroll in the garden.'

She opened her book again. 'Yes. That's best, my dear. That's best.'

It appeared that I must wait a little longer to find out about the country I had come to. Mrs Waterton seemed content to shut out the Indian world and concentrate on the one she knew.

On the fifth day we began to arrange our social calls. A number of cards that had been delivered were brought in by the *chuprassi*, and Mrs Waterton, Faith and I read them together. There were invitations to dances, dinner parties and evenings of cards. Mrs Waterton went through our wardrobes, studying our dresses and admiring the latest styles. 'You have a good selection, but you need more. It doesn't do to be seen in the same dress at too many gatherings. We shall purchase some material, then have the *durzi* make new ones in similar styles. They're wonderful at reproducing, down to a stitch, these Indian *durzis*. One must be careful, though – such is my *durzi*'s zealousness that if there has been a small rent, patched over, even the patch will be reproduced. Bless him!'

I was uncomfortable with the servility. I looked away when I witnessed the tall *chuprassi*, in his fine uniform, go down on his knees to dust off Mr Waterton's shoes with a tiny brush whenever the man entered the house. I noticed the burned hand of the *dhobi*, and knew how the blistered welt – caused, I deduced, by a heated iron – must sting, yet he cheerfully *salaamed* before he accepted another mound of the lightly soiled linen that Mrs Waterton piled into his outstretched arms. When I came into my room unexpectedly, tears were coursing down my *ayah*'s face, as she straightened the items on my dressing-table, but when she saw me she beamed as if overjoyed to see me. I tried to question her as to why she had been crying, but she wiped her cheeks carelessly, never losing her smile. I saw that one of the little fly-whisk boys had lost the last two toes of his right foot, and that the amputation was fairly fresh; he touched it gingerly when he thought no one watched him. I wondered if he was the son of any of the other servants, or if he had parents at all. I wondered about many things, but dared not mention them to Faith or even Mrs Liston: it might make them think strangely of me that I should bother myself with people who should not be noticed at all.

I wanted to instruct the *durzi* that all my dresses must have a neckline that covered my scar. I tried to remember the Hindi, but couldn't find the words. Finally, alone with him in my bedroom but for the *ayah*, I disclosed it, then held a piece of fabric over it. The *durzi*, his face showing nothing, said quietly, 'Missy Sahib would like her dresses to cover this? It is possible.'

'You speak English?' I cried in delight, but at the look on his face, and the violent shaking of his head, I clapped my hand over my mouth. Once more he shook his head, this time putting his finger to his lips, and I understood that I was not to mention that I knew he spoke my language.

That afternoon Mrs Waterton had left me alone with Mrs Liston, who had asked me to call her by her Christian name, Meg, on the verandah. Well, as alone as one ever is in India. The *durzi* sat cross-legged in one corner, stitching my new dress. He held the fabric straight between his toes, and in his turban he had stuck dozens of needles, threaded with assorted colours, which he pulled out as he needed them. A bearer stood waiting in case we should require something, and the little boys waved their fly-whisks over us.

The verandah was the most pleasant place in the house. Bamboo trellises, covered with creepers that yielded reddish-yellow flowers, screened it, creating a cool, green room. On the floor there were grass mats, and flower boxes of pink geraniums, white and red achimenes, rubbery begonias and fragile violets. Instead of the hard horsehair sofas and chairs in the parlour, there were wicker or bamboo chairs for the ladies, and heavy, dark teak ones with wide seats and tall curling backs for the men.

When I was alone there for a few minutes, I sometimes allowed myself to lean back with my arms over my head, smelling the cool green of the plants. Mrs Waterton had warned me that at the first breath of the hot season all the plants would shrivel and die, no matter how many times each day they were watered, and that I should enjoy them while I could.

'Meg, today the *durzi* spoke in English to me, then seemed frightened that I might tell someone,' I said to her quietly, so that he wouldn't hear.

She grimaced. 'Of course. If a servant is perceived as too stupid he is beaten and dismissed; if he shows he is clever – and an indication of that is that he has mastered English – he is viewed with suspicion and, possibly, dismissed. It's unfair, but they play this game to survive. Of course, it is much the same at home, but the rigidity of the line between master and servant is more noticeable here. Perhaps because we are not *of* this country. We are of England, and yet—' She stopped, as if aware that she was saying too much. She stood up suddenly, causing the boy with his whisk to jump out of her way, and went to one of the flower boxes to pinch off a dying blossom. 'Anyway, I can't wait to get to *mofussil* – up-country and away from all this pomposity and overbearing officiousness. I find it intolerable. It's less formal in the countryside.' She studied my face. 'Must I fear that you'll report my mutinous thoughts?' Although she asked me in seriousness, I could tell by her expression that she hoped she had seen in me an ally.

'Of course not,' I told her. 'But I do hope you're not leaving too soon.'

'I imagine I shall be here for another two weeks.' She continued to study me, and I felt a prickle of the old fear. I had stopped worrying long ago that Faith might find me out: although I knew she cared about me, she didn't study me in much depth. I often felt I was a reflecting board for her feelings and thoughts; mine were of little interest to her. Of course this had always worked in my favour, but with everyone here I was constantly on my guard, fearful of giving myself away with a wrong word, a lapse in manners.

There was a canniness in Meg's long face that worried me. 'Tell me about yourself, Miss Linny Smallpiece,' she said now. 'I would like to know where you have been, and what you have seen. You give the impression of one who knows more than they care to say – unlike most people, who say much on matters they know little about.'

I was unable to think of a proper response. My palms were wet. I hid them in the folds of my watered-silk tea-gown.

'I'm sorry. Have I offended you?' Meg asked. 'My aunt, uncle and cousins – as well as my husband – are used to my forthright outbursts. They not only tolerate my free thinking but encourage it. I may forget myself in polite company.'

Polite company. Here was young Mrs Liston, apologizing to me because she might appear vulgar. It was ironic, and I might have delighted in it, had I not been so uncomfortable. 'No, I'm not offended,' I said. 'I'm just not . . . at ease when talking about myself.'

'Of course you aren't. Most well-brought-up young ladies wouldn't be. Please ignore me and my inappropriate familiarity. I do apologize.' She smiled.

'There's no need.' I returned her smile, and felt a rush of gratitude. By asking my forgiveness, and allowing me to grant it, she had endowed me with a feeling akin to benevolence.

CHAPTER EIGHTEEN

AND SO WE began the social round in earnest. We attended dinner after dinner – it seemed that every hostess gave the same party. We would have a drink in the drawing room at precisely eight o'clock, where Faith and I and any of the other unmarried ladies from the ship – I refused to use the phrase *fishing fleet* – were introduced to the bachelors. There was polite chit-chat, which I found tedious, as I had to keep my wits about me. I despaired at telling the same fabricated story of my past night after night, of smiling politely at the same small-talk, and of feigning interest in the men's stories. It was a tiresome game that I had played so many times and in so many forms.

When I felt I would scream if I had to stand one moment longer, with my glass sticky in my glove, we were summoned to the dining room by the bearer. We filed to the room in a strict order of precedence, depending on the position of the husband within the civil service. The hierarchy was much in play, just as it was with the servants.

At many of the grander dinners a servant waited behind each chair; each place had its array of cutlery and a champagne glass – with silver cover to prevent insects falling in – and a finger-bowl with a sweet-smelling flower floating in it. The seating was planned with the utmost care: the most senior gentleman sat to the right of the hostess, and the most senior lady to the right of the host. The Watertons appeared fairly high on the social scale, while Meg – who didn't often join us – occupied a lower spot. But the very lowest were Faith and I: we had no man to lift us in rank. We ate variations of the same English food: soup, followed by fish, joints, overcooked vegetables, then puddings and savouries. And it appeared to me, that first week, like the table settings and the menus, that everyone looked similar – the gentlemen in their boiled white shirts and tails, the women in their feathers, long gloves and dresses of similar styles, made, I assumed, by the same *durzis* who had a limited supply of patterns.

There were a few times, I admit, when my thoughts strayed to a crowded, noisy chop house where I had eaten many a greasy pie with the other girls from Paradise Street. There, the stories had flowed easily, the laughter was genuine, the camaraderie honest. I knew I had experienced a freedom there that no one in these rooms had known.

When the meal was over, port and madeira were poured for the gentlemen, while the ladies gathered in the drawing room with cordial or ratafia, waiting for the men to join them. Music might be played on a piano that always sounded out-of-tune. Eventually the senior lady stood, an indication that we could all leave. Nobody, it appeared, would dare to depart until she had made her silent declaration.

As well as the dinners, we went out for tea and to more casual evenings of cards and dance salons at other homes in the affluent areas of Garden Reach, Chowringhee and Alipur.

I found the endless social chatter difficult. The voice I had used since I began at the Lyceum – the cultured one with the same inflection as Shaker and Faith used – came now with little concentration. It was the energy I needed to feign interest, appear demure and yet gay that exhausted me. Nothing ever felt right to me in those drawing rooms: I was always acting, a player on a stage. Except that the play never ended until I retired to my room at the Watertons', and even then I wasn't alone. There were always the servants – the *durzi* and the sweeper, the polisher and the boy with his fly-whisk, the *ayah* and *punkah-wallah*.

At the beginning of my time in India I felt as if I were waiting to *see* the country. I wasn't allowed to go anywhere without Mrs Waterton and Faith, although Meg was permitted to spend time with other married ladies. Our only expedition, apart from visits to other homes, all similar to the Watertons', was to the *maidan* in the centre of Calcutta. Of course, on the way the palanquin curtains were always shut. I had peeped out the first time we went there, and had seen, running in all directions off the main road, foetid alleys and torturous lanes, the twisting under-belly of Calcutta. Mrs Waterton reprimanded me for my indiscretion, and from then on I sat like Faith, gloved hands in my lap, until we arrived at the *maidan*. The huge flat esplanade of greenery boasted small orange groves and pleasant gravelled paths, and was bordered by an array of flowering trees. No Indians were allowed there, except *ayahs* with children and those who swept the paths or picked up fallen leaves or blossoms from beneath the trees. We sat on freshly painted benches and chatted as ladies of society would in England. Faith and I were assured that we should enjoy this weather, that it wouldn't last much past the end of January. The brief Cool Season was free of the intense heat and debilitating humidity that, I was told, brought out an uncomfortable heat rash as well as hordes of flying or crawling biting insects.

'It will arrive all too soon,' Mrs Waterton warned, lips pursed. 'All too soon. And then you'll have a true taste of India.'

If I only could.

15 December 1830

Dear Shaker,

India is an education. I am a tabula rasa, ready to be inscribed with all that India has to write on me. No matter what the future, I know, with some deep instinct, that I am to be marked by this land.

I am amazed by the attitude and role of the English, although I have not been here long enough to have an informed opinion. But from what I have experienced in this first month I am uncomfortable to be forced into a position of unnatural importance. Although I have been treated admirably by every brown person I have met, the English harbour underlying hostility towards the Indians. Towards *them*, Shaker — and it is their own land. The East India Company — casually referred to here as John Company — is like a stern master, forcing the people of India in directions they cannot want to go. And ordinary English men and women, shortly after settling here, don a voluminous imperial cloak as if it is their right — no, their duty.

I cannot imagine bearing this weight.

While Calcutta is, as they say, the 'city of palaces', I would call it a city of contrasts. Near to where Faith and

I are staying, with Mr and Mrs Waterton on Garden Reach, is a world of squared white buildings of classical design, all thanks to the presence of John Company. But close to the fine shops and beautiful homes there are rows of mud-thatched huts, and human bodies burning on the river's shore. Over the fragrance of jasmine hangs the stench of open drains and rotting corpses.

Shaker, you would not believe the things one sees. I discovered that the Watertons employ a servant to stand all day at the riverbank behind their home. He pushes corpses – some with vultures already at work – back into the river before they can pile up on the bank. The man looked frightened when I came upon him and his grisly job. The gamy scent of decaying flesh was in the air. He demonstrated that I was to cover my eyes and flee, as if he were responsible somehow for what I had seen and would be punished. Poor man.

There is little medical help for the Indian people. I asked Mrs Waterton, only the other day, why there are so many obviously sick and maimed people. She laughed at me, implying that I was a silly girl. I took affront, although I was careful to hide my anger from her as she is, after all, my hostess. Then she told me that these 'heathens' have their own forms of hullabaloo that they consider healing, all noise and nonsense, she assured me. I'm sure there is more to their methods than Mrs Waterton is aware of, but I knew better than to suggest it. I asked if any Indians were treated by the physicians and surgeons employed by the East India Company. At that she shook her head and said, 'Really!'

I must watch my step.

An interesting woman is staying here with Faith and me. Her name is Meg Liston. I feel I am learning much from her.

You now have an address, should you choose to correspond.

I hope and pray that you are well.

Linny

It was Meg who filled me with hope for my future in India: she was full of opinions and questions. She told me she was writing a book about Indian shrines, and making a collection of sketches she had executed of local customs; she planned to finish them while travelling to villages in the Lucknow area. She argued openly with Mr Waterton.

'It's all very easy when you have no European rivals in India, Mr Waterton,' she announced one evening, shortly before her husband was scheduled to arrive for her. 'And after the defeat – perhaps I should say the crushing defeat – of the Marathas in the Anglo-Maratha war just over twenty years ago, you have no Indian ones either. The Company is responsible for ruling ever larger parts of India, and yet you refuse to learn to communicate with her people effectively.'

Mr Waterton's left eye winked furiously. 'We have an earnest desire to teach the heathen what the Almighty has given us. Without us there is only anarchy. The good Indian is the obedient Indian, with complete dependence on us. We must have faith that our values will set things in order.'

'Our values? Ha!' declared Meg. I hid a smile behind my napkin. 'And what have we achieved so far?'

'Meg? May I offer you more fruit compote?' Mrs Waterton

asked, glancing at her husband, with a fixed wan smile. 'The cook has tried so hard to get it right. I've been working with him for the last—'

'What have we achieved?' Mr Waterton repeated. 'Achieved? Why, Mrs Liston, look around you. Do you not believe in the hierarchy of society? Do you not believe that as British men and women we are at the top, and therefore able to control and bring enlightenment?'

'Why should we think that only we are at the top?' I asked.

All heads turned towards me, and I felt a moment of trepidation.

'Good for you, Linny,' Meg said. 'You see? She agrees. We are the new generation. Linny, myself – and Faith,' she added, after a second's hesitation, 'are confident women, ready to rise to the new challenge of being part of a bigger whole.'

Faith made a sound that might have been agreement or denial. I wanted to shake her. Why didn't she speak up? She had so many opinions – too many, I'd sometimes thought. But it was as if she'd left something of herself in Liverpool. Perhaps she felt that as the old Faith had been unsuccessful in securing a proposal of marriage she must now fit into the conventional role. It might work for her more successfully. I intended to ask her.

'Oh dear,' Mrs Waterton said, having lost her smile. 'I'm afraid we must move to the verandah, where it's fresher, for our coffee. Please. We must move to the verandah.' She stood, and we were forced to rise, and follow her outside. Mr Waterton excused himself to smoke in his billiard room, and the conversation – aggressively directed by Mrs Waterton – regressed to talk of the weather and its effect on the flowers.

'All of the lovely phlox and nasturtiums will be ruined by the first blast of hot weather,' she exclaimed.

I saw that Meg's chest was rising and falling too quickly as she sat stiffly on the edge of her chair, not joining in or even appearing to take note of Mrs Waterton's attempts at a conversation. Eventually she rose, excused herself and walked towards the garden. I watched the *mali* follow her with a light chair should she wish to sit. She waved him away impatiently. He set down the chair and squatted beside it. His eyes never left Meg, as if he were hoping she would change her mind and need his services.

When she was out of earshot, Mrs Waterton shook her head. 'I wonder how her husband will deal with her. She is all too eager to show her learning. Not a desirable trait. Not desirable at all.'

I glanced at Faith, who was picking absently at a loose strand of rattan on the arm of her chair. In a gown of pale rose batiste, with matching pink satin slippers, she was lovely and languid.

That weekend Meg's husband arrived. He was a good-looking young man with a black patch over his left eye that added to his dashing attractiveness. He and Meg left, full of talk of their coming adventures. As we waved goodbye, I knew I would miss her. I envied her: there must have been other English women in India who didn't follow the lead of the others, but they were few and far between, as far as I could determine.

We had been in the country a month, and I had yet to experience anything of the real India. I was living an English life, eating English food, being spoken to by English voices, seeing only that which was carefully controlled. I knew that I could love India, and I had begun to despair: when and under what circumstances would I be able to venture further into Calcutta, or perhaps the country? I was more of a prisoner in Calcutta than I had ever been in Liverpool or even in Everton. The troubling sense of captivity grew daily.

Shortly before Meg left I had asked her if she found it difficult to wait for her husband, to spend such a quiet, passive time at the Watertons' home before she could begin her life. *Her true life*, as Chinese Sally had said so long ago in Liverpool. I had thought that this was what Meg was waiting for as well. 'I have learned patience, living in India,' she told me. 'Something that has helped me is a Pashto proverb: "Patience is bitter, but its fruit is sweet." '

I repeated it many times each day.

Faith did not seem to need a proverb. She appeared outwardly content with the staid visits to the *maidan*, helping Mrs Waterton plan the meals, writing responses to the invitations we received, or sitting in the garden. Or, of course, attending the never-ending circus of social events. Faith had been right: there were more than three men to every woman.

I thought increasingly about Faith's behaviour. At first I had believed she was simply worn out by the long journey, that she would regain her spirit after a while. But instead, as the weeks went by, it became clear that she had chosen to embrace in Calcutta the tight reins of respectability against which she had strained in Liverpool. She was snappish with me when I questioned her acquiescence to the frivolous and shallow lifestyle at Garden Reach.

'One does not come to India without purpose, Linny,' she reported. 'The social season is important.' She pushed back a strand of hair that had come loose. 'I will not suffer the indignity of being sent home as a Returned Empty.'

She did her best. I often heard her bright laughter from across the room, but it was only I who detected in it an undertone of desperation. She was regularly surrounded by men. On our return from each party, she came into my room and sat on my bed to tell me about each young man and what he had said to her. She had a favourite, a dark, shy gentleman named Mr Snow – Charles, she confided to me – who said little, but seemed mesmerized by her chatter and the lustrous colour of her hair.

I found tiresome the troops of appraising young men, none of whom interested me. I tried, but found fault easily. Some appeared tight-lipped and priggish, but more were vain. Strutting about full of themselves, they reminded me of the peacocks on the lawns, their tails in full display.

I wondered if it was because, unlike the other young women here, I had once known men too well.

It was at one of these parties, the week before Christmas, that I met Somers Ingram.

He was tall and handsome in a rather traditional way, with thick, wavy dark hair and a well-trimmed moustache. He had deep brown eyes and even features – an aquiline nose, full-lipped mouth and strong chin. His complexion was burnished by the sun. When we were introduced he bowed over my hand, held it a moment longer than necessary, and gave me a slow smile. I knew his type well, but perhaps there was something else, carefully controlled, beneath the brilliant smile and guileless expression. I smiled back, murmuring my pleasure at making his acquaintance.

'You arrived on the November ship, then?' he asked.

'Yes. How long have you lived in India?'

'Five years.'

'You must have had some memorable experiences.'

It was a game. The same questions, the same answers. Was he as bored as I?

'I have. And what are your impressions of India?'

I had been asked this question by every young man I had spoken to. I had a brief, memorized speech that I'd heard Faith and other women use, about the wonder and strangeness of it all, the exotic difference between India and England. All lies, since I hadn't been allowed any impressions of India. So far they were all of England – the endless pressure of proper behaviour, the snobbery that showed itself in the ranking of the gentlemen within the civil service, the attempts to dine strictly on English food, the disdain shown to servants. India was still a tantalizing mystery.

That evening I was weary, and in a generally bad humour. I sighed. 'I wish I could speak to the servants properly,' I said.

'You must speak Hindi well, after all this time here, Mr Ingram.'

'Only what's necessary. Command and rebuke, mainly.'

A moment of silence passed. Mr Ingram waited for my reply. Should I do the proper thing and agree with him? No. I looked straight into his eyes, and thought I saw something of substance. I deemed that his was not a nature to trifle with. He might react with interest if I spoke my mind. 'Well, I would like more than that. I'm studying the language in some depth, but it's difficult. I try to practise with the servants at the Watertons', but they seem reluctant to respond. I don't know whether I'm pronouncing the words incorrectly, or whether they're frightened to answer.'

'Probably neither.' Mr Ingram's eyes narrowed a little. 'They're not comfortable, with you coming down to their level. Confuses them. I don't know why you bother. All you need is a smattering, just enough to get them moving. They're like children, really. Best to treat them with a firm hand. And consistency. Their own world is so tumultuous, so undisciplined, that it's a comfort to them to be told what to do, and to know what to expect if they don't obey.'

I didn't answer. He was like the rest, then, with his arrogance. I tried to think of a riposte that Meg might have made but failed. I was disappointed in him: I had thought briefly that I recognized something in Mr Ingram that made him different.

My annoyance grew as we stood in the crush of silk and fine wool, with laughter and chatter all around us. I had no further wish to talk with him, and Mr Ingram must have felt the same: his eyes roamed the room. But there was no polite way for either of us to escape.

'Have you family in England, Mr Ingram?'

'There is no one. My mother died when I was a child. I lived in London until five years ago, but after my father's death I decided to venture here. Are you from London, Miss Smallpiece?' His eyes were suddenly looking into mine with intensity.

'Liverpool.'

'I've never had cause to visit the city. Your family is there, then?'

'My parents are no longer living either,' I said. 'I had been staying with an aunt and cousin.' It was easier to give simple answers.

'I suppose they live in Mount Pleasant.'

'North of the city, in Everton. But you said you hadn't been to Liverpool, Mr Ingram.'

His expression didn't change, but he blinked, then raised a knuckle to his moustache. In the split second before he responded, I knew he would lie. A good liar usually recognizes another. 'Well, one does hear of places, even if one hasn't been there.'

'I suppose so,' I said.

He cleared his throat, raised his chin over my shoulder and, in the next moment, an elderly gentleman appeared at my side. Mr Ingram introduced us and politely took his leave.

Later that evening, as I was preparing to depart with my party, I saw Mr Ingram in conversation with another young man, glass in his hand, listening intently. As I watched him, he glanced up and our eyes met. We held each other's gaze for a second too long. Neither of us smiled.

I found the handsome Mr Ingram intriguing, but discomfiting: he made me feel as if I should be ready to flee. I could not understand the combination of attraction and repulsion, and it would come back to haunt me in a double circle.

But now I am getting ahead of myself.

CHAPTER NINETEEN

T HE MORNING AFTER I had met Somers Ingram I asked Faith if she knew of him; she admitted she had met him and found him charming. 'He has an important position in the Company, I've heard,' she said. 'He's quite the talk, to have risen so far so young. And apparently there's family wealth. Some have commented that his family's influence allowed him this expeditious move forward in his career. But one can't believe all one hears.'

I nodded.

'Why do you ask, Linny?'

'I met him last night,' I told her. 'He was arrogant, I thought.'

'He's nothing of the sort, Linny. Now, if we speak of arrogance, it must be in reference to Mr Whittington. Have you been forced to spend any time with him?' She chattered on about other bachelors, and I stopped listening, wondering what Mr Ingram had to hide, and when our paths would next cross.

The opportunity arose at an elaborate ball put on at the Calcutta Club to celebrate the ringing in of 1831. Much of Calcutta's élite was in attendance, over three hundred people. My dance card had been filled for two weeks. I wore the ballgown I had had made – at Faith's insistence – before we left Liverpool; it was golden brocade and parchment silk, with a lacy fichu to cover the low neckline. As I viewed myself in the full-length pier glass, candlelight shimmering on my skirts, I felt it lent me a certain splendour.

I had changed since I had stared, aghast, into the mirror at Shaker's home after that terrible night when he had rescued me. My hair was now thick and lustrous, my eyes bright, my complexion clear. As the *ayah* arranged my hair, I knew Somers Ingram would be there. As soon as we arrived I found myself watching for him. Although I didn't see him at the reception, or as we were seated for dinner, he appeared as soon as the dancing began, and bowed before me. 'Miss Smallpiece,' he said, and I was struck anew by his posture, the smoothness of his skin, his full lips. 'May I have the pleasure of escorting Miss Smallpiece around the floor, Mrs Waterton?' He held out his gloved hand to me.

Mrs Waterton trilled giddily, holding my dance card at a distance to peer at it. 'Why, Mr Ingram, I don't see your name on her card.'

'Come now, Mrs Waterton,' he cajoled. 'It depends, of course, on whether Miss Smallpiece will grant me the pleasure.'

'Mrs Waterton?' I asked, looking at her. I wanted to dance with him – very much.

'But of course, my dear. I will extend apologies to your disappointed partner when he arrives.'

We moved smoothly around the dance floor in a waltz. Initially Mr Ingram's patter required little of me. He spoke of the fine organization of the ball, of a problem with his *khansana*, of a sporting event he had recently attended.

'You are an excellent dancer, sir,' I told him, my gloved

hand on his shoulder, the other held firmly within his own gloved hand.

'Thank you, Miss Smallpiece,' he said, and drew me a little closer. I was aware of his thigh against mine as we turned. No other bachelor had been so bold with me – most held me at a more than respectable distance. 'But I'm aware of a certain hesitancy in your step. Does dancing bore you, or do you lack accomplishment?'

I was shocked at his less than complimentary statement. I stopped in the middle of a turn. 'I find you thoughtless, sir,' I said, putting as much indignation into my voice as I could. I didn't like the implication that I might not have danced regularly in fine salons and ballrooms. I thought of Meg Liston, and her admitted lack of interest in dancing. 'We are not all as talented as you, Mr Ingram,' I said, and my voice held a saucy note now, 'and some of us prefer to spend our time in pursuing more intellectual and cultural interests than dancing.' I watched his eyes widen. 'In fact, from your expertise on the floor, I'm certain your talents run to the mechanical, and that you have little interest in the intellect.'

He laughed, an open, delighted sound. 'Well spoken, Miss Smallpiece, and I am chastised – rightly so. Of course you dance lightly and well. I spoke boldly because I sensed you were bored by all of this, and wondered how you would react to a statement that was not as safe as the usual niceties we are all forced to utter, dance after dance.'

I was charged with a bolt of surprise that he was seeing in me precisely what I'd felt. And that he had the effrontery – no, the courage – to speak of it. It meant he had heard what I thought I had concealed in my words and tone.

As one, we moved into the dance again. 'You were testing me, then. Is that it?'

He smiled. 'You might say so. And, Miss Smallpiece, I'm delighted to report that you have passed my test. You have nerve, which is lacking in many young women I meet here. Spirit too, I see – your eyes are flashing. I must compliment you on the golden arrows you send my way.'

Now he was flirting openly. In seconds he had gone from insult to compliment. I didn't know how to deal with a man like Somers Ingram.

'What is it you do for the Company, Mr Ingram?' I asked, breathing deeply.

'I am the chief auditor,' he said.

I had no idea what that was. 'How marvellous.'

'Do you think so? Why? I'm interested to know what you would find "marvellous" about my post.'

Was he again reading my mind? How dare he put me in this uncomfortable position? Most other men would have accepted the compliment and talked about the position so that I would know what it was. They wouldn't question me on my reaction.

'You have no idea what a chief auditor does, do you?'

I clicked my tongue and smiled naughtily. I realized I was as capable of flirting as he. 'Really, Mr Ingram, you are impossible.'

'Oh, come now, Miss Smallpiece. It doesn't suit you.'

'What doesn't?'

'This false air of injury. Why would you say my position is marvellous when you don't know what it is and, furthermore, don't really care?'

Before I was forced to answer, the dance ended, and he led me back to Mrs Waterton.

'Would you be so kind as to allow Miss Smallpiece to dance again with me this evening?' he asked her.

'Many young men have requested her company,' Mrs Waterton said, fanning the air with my dance card. 'Miss Smallpiece must not appear rude.'

'Of course,' Mr Ingram said, and bowed again. I felt a surge of disappointment mixed with the relief that he wouldn't confuse me again with his unsettling behaviour.

'Although,' Mrs Waterton added, 'she may be free towards the end of the evening.'

Now Mr Ingram bent over my hand, which he still held, and pressed his lips to my glove. 'I shall look forward to it,' he said, and then left.

But he didn't come back, and I didn't see him in the crowds. I felt something akin to loss – no, not loss. That would make it appear that I missed something. Perhaps the feeling I experienced when Mr Ingram did not return for a final dance was more of the same frustration that I felt imprisoned with Faith and the Watertons on Garden Reach, with India at my fingertips.

I found myself wondering when I would see Somers Ingram next – but I wasn't longing to be close to him. It was more that something about him troubled me.

We met next at a soirée at the Calcutta Club later in January. His skin was even darker, as if he had spent recent time outdoors. While surrounded by others we exchanged opinions on the expected subjects: the weather (cool and pleasant), architecture (the renovation of some of the rooms at the Writers Building), Indian politics (the rumours of difficulties with the administration of the Rajah of Mysore), and news from home (the exciting prospect of steam navigation).

As others drifted away and we found ourselves alone near

one of the high doors, I commented on his appearance. 'You're looking very well, Mr Ingram,' I said. 'Have you been taking in some sport?'

'I hunted all last week, enjoying the glorious weather, which is not to be with us much longer, I'm afraid. We must take every advantage of it. Do you enjoy riding, Miss Smallpiece?'

I ran my finger along my cuff. 'Not particularly.' I had never been on a horse.

'I would think you would like to get out into the sun and wind of the Cool Season, gallop along and explore. Have you had that opportunity yet?'

If he only knew how I longed to do that.

'Would you care to join a small party? A number of my friends, as well as ladies such as yourself, with Mr and Mrs Weymouth, are planning an outing next week.'

'I think not, Mr Ingram. Thank you so much for your invitation but—'

'Please put aside coyness, Miss Smallpiece. It doesn't suit you, as I reminded you in the recent past.'

'I'm not being coy,' I said, annoyed.

'Really? Then what is it? Do you know how clearly your expression gives you away? You're almost scowling. I can see you arguing within yourself. What stops you agreeing to join me? Come now, Miss Smallpiece. I'd like the truth. I can tell you are more than a little anxious to be in my company.'

Now I was far more than annoyed. His presumption brought angry heat to my face. 'A lady does not need to explain herself,' I said fiercely.

'A lady does not forget herself, either,' he said. 'Do I detect rudeness?' He tutted.

'I do not appreciate your manner, sir,' I said, my voice low. 'I can assure you I do not forget myself. Ever.'

He raised one eyebrow in an infuriatingly cocky manner. 'Really?' His eyes bored into mine. Then he whispered, his lips touching my cheek, 'I don't believe you.' His breath was warm, his manner far too familiar as he put his hand on my forearm and stroked my sleeve.

Blood roared in my ears. His face was only inches from mine, a small smile on his mouth. A condescending smile, one that presumed I was like all of the other silly girls, that I would grow faint at his nearness, swoon into his arms. I found him attractive, yet hated him, with his insolence and his certainty of his charm.

I moved my face a fraction closer to his. 'Mr Ingram,' I whispered, jaw tight, and he turned his head slightly so that I might speak into his ear. I was trembling with a sense of power. 'Take your damn hand off my arm.' The words burst out, hot, urgent; I used as much venom as I could muster.

He pulled back his head as if I'd slapped him. And in that instant I knew what I'd done – what Somers Ingram had driven me to do. I had spent the last two months behaving like the lady I was pretending to be – no matter how I struggled inside. This man had made me forget who I was supposed to be: he had thrown out a challenge and, stupidly, I had risen to it.

Somers Ingram looked directly into my eyes, and what I saw there made me close mine momentarily. *How could I have been so foolish? I had worked so hard.*

'Did I hear you correctly, Miss Smallpiece?' he asked, removing his hand and stepping back, triumph in his face. His expression made it clear that he had accomplished what he'd hoped for.

'I – I . . .' I raised my gloves to my burning cheeks. Perspiration trickled beneath the tight lacing of my stays.

Mr Ingram glanced around to ensure that we were still unobserved and took my fingers in his hand, lightly, but still in a manner that was far too intimate. He ran his thumb to the centre of my palm, and the pressure of his caress made me shiver. Then he said, low and pleased, 'My dear Miss Smallpiece, the last time I heard such language was in a Turkish bath house in East London.'

There was nothing for me to say.

Mr Ingram let go of my hand and stepped a respectable distance away. 'Miss Smallpiece, I find your . . . openness of expression refreshing. I'm not above plain talk myself, given the right circumstance. So, that is a firm no to the riding invitation?'

I turned on my heel and left in a rustle of skirts, hoping for the impression of dignity.

On 31 January the Clutterbucks hosted an evening of cards to which the Watertons, Faith and I were invited. I was in good spirits; I had persuaded Faith to slip away from the *maidan* with me for a full half-hour that afternoon. The usually watchful eye of Mrs Waterton had been averted because she had encountered an old friend, down from a posting in the north, and they had become lost in conversation as Faith and I sat on a bench facing them. When I interrupted politely, asking if Faith and I might stroll through the *maidan* together, she nodded absently.

As soon as we were out of Mrs Waterton's view I steered Faith towards the outside path of the *maidan*. Then, linking my arm in hers, I pulled her along through the row of waiting rickshaws and palanquins. Faith was hesitant, but I kept a firm grip on her.

'Linny! Linny, stop! Where are we going?' she asked, her face flushed and anxious.

'I don't know. That's the beauty of it.' I laughed.

'We can't, Linny. What if someone sees us? What if something happens to us? What if somebody—'

I ignored her half-hearted cries, and within a minute we found ourselves in a market. Flowers – I recognized roses and marigolds – were piled randomly together, then fruit and vegetables I'd never seen before. I stopped in front of one cart and pulled off my gloves to caress the smooth, elongated shapes heaped on it, some white as ivory and others a deep purple. The turbaned man who crouched upon his heels beside it jumped up, took a gleaming purple one and pushed it at me. I shook my head, no, no, and told him hesitantly, in Hindi, that I had no money. But he set it gently in my hands and then performed a *salaam*. I understood it to be a gift. I bowed my head, and he nodded, dignified.

'What is it? What will you do with it?' Faith asked, clinging to me.

'I don't know the answer to either,' I said, 'but I couldn't insult him by not accepting it.'

We followed narrow paths in the market, breathing in the smell of cooking oil, garlic and tobacco. I recognized ginger and cloves, but there were many other spices for which I had no name. There was the glorious scent of sandalwood one moment, the acrid odour of burning cow-dung the next, and Faith covered her nose with her gloved hand. When we passed the braziers where women cooked flat doughy shapes, I realized I was hungry, and longed to try whatever they were paddling in their hands then throwing into a flat pan to bake. I heard snatches of foreign-sounding music from

246

unknown instruments, the tinkling of bells and the creaking axles of bullock carts.

I stopped and Faith bumped into me. I stood still, closed my eyes and listened.

'Why are you stopping, Linny? Do you know how to get back to the *maidan*? Oh dear, look at that child. Is he all alone?'

I opened my eyes to see a naked boy of about two, tottering along with short steps on the hard-packed mud underfoot. A red string was attached to his wrist. I followed it and saw it was tied to the wrist of a young mother, who held an infant to her sari while she haggled with a merchant over the piece of bright yellow cotton in her other hand. 'No. Look, there's his mother.'

The child came right to my skirt, stopped, and looked up at me. He closed his small fist around the dotted poplin of my dress. I smiled and put my hand on his dark head. His hair was silky.

'Don't touch him, Linny,' Faith said, under her breath. 'You may catch a disease.'

'He's just a baby, Faith,' I said. 'Look how pretty he is.'

'It's shameful, though. He's completely without clothing.'

The child looked at the gleaming purple vegetable in my other hand. He let go of my skirt and reached both hands towards it. His eyes were huge, a luminous black, and he made the small cry that babies of all worlds make when they want something. I put the vegetable into his outstretched hands. There was a jerk on the thread at his wrist as he took it, and I looked from him to his mother, and saw her watching, her face concerned. I smiled at her, her face relaxed, and she returned the smile.

Faith tugged at my sleeve. 'We must find our way back,

Linny. Too much time has passed. Mrs Waterton may start to look for us, and it won't take her long to realize we're not in the *maidan*.'

'All right, all right,' I said, casting one more look at the child, who was toddling on little bowed legs to his mother, laughing and holding out the vegetable.

Instinctively I understood the way the market ran: it was not very different from the markets I'd hurried through every day as a child in Liverpool.

Faith sighed with relief as the tidy, carefully sculpted shape of the *maidan* came into view. 'Aren't we wonderfully wicked, Linny?' she'd said, at ease now that we'd survived what she obviously saw as a bold foray. The chaos of the market receded with only a faint memory of sounds and smells. 'Mrs Waterton would have a fit of dyspepsia if she knew what we'd been up to.'

'Let's make sure she doesn't find out,' I said, and smiled at her. The old Faith was stirring within the new one. I put my gloves back on and raised one to my face. It carried a trace of the smoky, spicy scent of the India I wanted to know. I linked my arm through Faith's and we hurried on.

Later, as we arrived at the Clutterbucks', I was still filled with pleasure from the afternoon's unexpected taste of freedom. There were several other guests, and within moments Mr Ingram and I had met before the open verandah doors. Even though I felt a tiny jab of pleasure somewhere in my chest at the sight of him, I was anxious too: I didn't wish to speak to him, didn't want him to look at me in the suggestive way that had made me react badly. I was afraid he would spoil my mood. All I wanted, at that moment, was a breath of air. The rooms were crowded, the air filled with women's scent, and that of the oleander, jasmine and Queen of the Night that stood on every surface in large vases.

But Mr Ingram would not let me pass without speaking, even though I turned my head in the other direction. 'Well, Miss Smallpiece, it is good to see you again,' he said, the picture of politeness.

'And you, sir,' I said, trying to keep my voice pleasant, not meeting his eyes. Tension hung in the air.

A slender young attendant, in crisp white trousers, jacket and turban, hovered near us with a silver tray of fluted glasses filled with crimson liquid. The glasses shivered against each other almost inaudibly. I noticed a fine line of perspiration running from under his turban. Finally he moved forward, holding the tray in my direction but looking at Mr Ingram.

'Claret? Or perhaps madeira?' Mr Ingram said to me.

'No, thank you,' I said, yet the attendant stayed where he was. Mr Ingram finally took a glass. Still the boy stayed. Mr Ingram dismissed him with a quick murmured sentence in Hindi.

At that moment our hostess clapped her meaty hands and announced that we would break into pairs for a game of whist.

'Miss Smallpiece, I shall slip out to smoke a cheroot. I'm not interested in card games that don't involve major stakes.' He flashed his practised smile and set his full glass on a nearby table.

I watched him disappear through the open doors. He had behaved as if nothing unpleasant had passed between us only ten days earlier. I breathed deeply, reassuring myself that his manners would prevent him mentioning my vulgar display.

I played a few hands of whist, but was restless and edgy. I felt I might bite through my tongue if Mrs Clutterbuck asked what were trumps one more time, or moaned that she received only the pip cards, never the court. I begged off the next game, slipped out through the open verandah doors and descended the broad stone steps into the villa's garden. It was lovely, with its array of chest-high canna lilies, and beyond, a stand of temple frangipani with delicate, almost sculpted flowers giving off the heavy fragrance that always surprised me. The full moon was white and shining, and I stopped to put a frangipani blossom behind my ear. I felt odd, suddenly, as if I might rise up into the starry night sky. It was unsettling yet pleasant. I smiled, thinking of the merchant who had given me the vegetable, the silkiness of the child's hair, and then I held out my arms and twirled in the moonlight. I felt that something cold, hard and dark within me was loosening. And I realized, with surprise, that what I felt was happiness. I am happy, I thought. I am in a garden in Calcutta. I am Linny Gow, and I am not dreaming of another life. This is my life. 'I am happy,' I said, into the tangled beauty of the garden. The words sounded full and round, silvery and bright, as if they were catching the reflection of the moon. It seemed that I had been holding my breath all my life, my chest tight with the effort. And now, when I breathed out those words, *I am happy*, it was able to expand.

I steadied myself, standing undisturbed on the moonlit grass. I couldn't go back to the loud, stuffy drawing room. I made my way slowly down the path to the servants' quarters, the simply built godowns huddled against the back wall, where there was the constant muffled thrum of voices and the slow beat of a drum. Outside one hut a young woman sat with her back against the rough wall and nursed her baby. She jumped up when she saw me, trying to cover her breasts with her sari and *salaam* at the same time, the infant losing the nipple and wailing thinly. 'Please,' I tried to tell her in stilted Hindi, 'please, continue.' As I wound my way along the path I passed men and women squatting around rush-lights set on the earth outside their huts, talking in low voices. They all rose and fell silent as I walked by. I smiled at each, knowing I had made them uncomfortable by venturing past their quarters, but I didn't care. There was one final hut and I could see in the flood of moonlight, which outlined everything as clearly as day, a narrow path beside it that would loop back in the direction of the house. I was glad I wouldn't have to retrace my steps and disturb the servants a second time.

The hut stood alone, at a distance from the others. As I passed the open doorway, the familiar sounds of coupling made me pause and look in. I made out two figures, moving in rhythm on a mat. I should have continued on my way but stopped, listening to the harsh quick breath of one, answered by the other. In that moment I saw that it wasn't a man and woman, as I had assumed, but two men. My eyes adjusted enough to see that one was on his knees, supporting himself with his elbows, his small slender body gleaming darkly. The other, larger and more strongly built, was kneeling behind him, wearing a white shirt whose pearl buttons winked as he grasped the thin hips in front of him, driving himself in with urgency.

Before I could step away, or even avert my eyes, the man performing on the other turned his head, and I stared into the face of Somers Ingram. He stopped, mid-movement, and the drumming from somewhere behind me seemed to grow in intensity. The other man – I recognized him now as the young attendant from the drawing room – also looked

251

towards the door, and cried out in alarm. Mr Ingram pulled away from him, and the youth rolled on to his side, grabbing his shirt and throwing it over his turban and face.

It was too late to pretend I hadn't seen them. 'I'm so sorry for intruding,' I said, the words stilted, almost comical, in my ears. 'I'm really terribly sorry. I . . . was lost.' Mr Ingram gazed at me, not attempting to cover himself, his arousal still obvious as he sat back on his heels.

I hurried away, finding it difficult to breathe. I wasn't sure why I felt this unnerving sense of shock at what I had seen – I, who had not only witnessed any manner of perversions but who had been a participant. I cursed myself for my boldness in wandering, my earlier elation spoiled, my mood confused and sour. I took the frangipani blossom from behind my ear and tossed it to the ground. Had I been disappointed to find Somers Ingram behaving in that manner, or was I angry that he had made me uncomfortable during our conversations, for his own pleasure, even though his taste was for boys, not women? He had never been interested in me, and I discovered that I was offended.

I had only gone a short way before Somers Ingram strode up behind me, the shells of the path crunching under his feet. 'Miss Smallpiece?'

I turned to him. He was as composed and neatly attired as he had been in the Clutterbucks' drawing room earlier. 'I don't believe we have any business, sir,' I said, raising my chin.

'Please allow me to escort you back to the house,' he said, and took my arm firmly in his.

When I attempted to pull away, he tightened his grip so that I was unable to withdraw my hand. I tried to walk quickly, but he forced me to stroll at a leisurely pace.

'Miss Smallpiece,' he said. 'I must speak frankly.'

I made a sound of disgust. 'Do you feel that I care to speak to you about anything?'

He removed his arm but now held my upper arm in his hand, and turned so that he was facing me in the moonlight. 'You see,' he said, evidently unconcerned by whether or not I wanted to speak to him, 'what has just occurred is part of what has troubled me about you, Miss Smallpiece. What you witnessed . . . You did not react as any other young lady of your class when you saw me with my Ganymede. You didn't shriek in horror or faint dead away. You didn't become a quivering, speechless wreck, as would be expected of a young English virgin, at a sight that, by the way, most would not imagine even in their most guilty dreams – such is their carefully preserved innocence. I saw the expression – or perhaps lack of expression – on your face when you saw us . . . *in flagrante delicto*, shall we say? It was nonplussed. Which leads me to believe you were neither shocked nor even dismayed. As if you'd seen sights a proper young lady from home should never have witnessed. Am I not right?' His hand burned through the thin silk of my sleeve.

I knew I was on a precipice, and that one wrong step would send me off the edge. 'I don't understand what you're saying.' A desperate note had crept into my voice, unnerving me.

'This, coupled with your surprising language the last time we spoke, makes one wonder.'

He knows, he knows, rang in my head, a clanging that was as loud as a heavy bell.

'Are you all right, Miss Smallpiece? Perhaps you are indeed suffering from shock after all. You look startled.' He had the audacity to smile.

253

I yanked my arm from his grip, picked up my skirts and ran through the damp grass, ruining my slippers. I went back to the drawing room, found a quiet corner and sat, breathing deeply and fanning myself, trying to catch my breath. I glanced constantly towards the verandah doors, expecting Somers Ingram to appear, wondering how I would stay composed. I had made too many mistakes with him now and I was terrified.

But he didn't return, and half an hour later I was thankful when Mrs Waterton suggested we took our leave.

CHAPTER TWENTY

I T WAS 5 February: Faith and I had been invited to an evening of light refreshments and chamber music at a house in Alipur where several of the bachelors — including Somers Ingram — had their quarters. The party was being held by the Senior Ladies Group of the Calcutta Club. Mrs Waterton assured Faith and me that these ladies often assisted unmarried men with entertaining until they found wives to take over. 'It's a nice change for gentlemen to be able to entertain in their homes,' she told us.

As soon as I had heard that Mr Ingram was one of the hosts, I tried to find a reason to send my regrets. But Faith was keen to go: she had been seeing more of Mr Snow, and he would be there. 'If you don't accompany me Mrs Waterton may say I can't go, Linny. Please, you must come — for my sake if nothing else.'

I finally agreed, and knew it would be uncomfortable. But I could not avoid Mr Ingram indefinitely: our paths would continue to cross at social events and I could not remain within the Waterton home for ever.

The house was airy and more sparsely furnished than the couples' homes I'd visited. Apart from the Senior Ladies, bustling about importantly, the crowd was young, the laughter

255

loud, the talk animated, and the mood this evening was less formal than usual.

Charles Snow came immediately to greet Faith, who took his arm, and they wandered off, their heads together, intent on their conversation. I chatted with a few of the other young ladies in the drawing room, sipping lime cordial. I didn't see Mr Ingram, and was relieved.

But as we were summoned to the music room, he appeared at my side as if from smoke. 'Miss Smallpiece,' he said.

'Good evening, Mr Ingram,' I said coolly. Now it was up to him to set the tone.

His face was unreadable. 'It's good of you to come. Welcome to my home.'

'Thank you.'

'I was hoping we would meet again before too long, Miss Smallpiece. In fact, I had this event moved forward so that I would have a chance to speak to you before too much time had passed. I considered sending a card to the Watertons', but thought you might turn down my offer to call. As well, Mrs Waterton would have been present even if you did accept.'

'And why would her presence be awkward, Mr Ingram?'

Without speaking, he led me down a wide hallway. I looked over my shoulder as we went, wondering whether to draw away from his grasp and join the others, wondering if anyone saw what would be interpreted as unbecoming behaviour. But everyone was filing in the other direction, their backs to us now, and I allowed myself to be led.

We went into a room and Mr Ingram closed the shuttered doors behind us. It was a bedroom with a four-poster bed and a canopy. There were doors thrown open to the terrace at the back of the house.

'Is this your room, Mr Ingram? This is entirely improper.'
I noticed the *punkah-wallah* in the corner, languidly pulling the rope. 'What kind of woman do you think I am that I can be expected to come into a gentleman's quarters and—'

He didn't let me finish. 'Let's stop this charade. You and I need to speak in complete privacy,' he said. Something in his voice made me realize that I had been right in my first estimation of him. As he turned to face me in the low light of the room, I saw that he had dropped the mask that I knew I also wore when in the company of others. And I saw, in that instant, his true nature: he carried within him the knowledge that he would get what he desired, at any expense.

'I see no point in avoiding the subject, Miss Smallpiece. The subject being, of course, your unfortunate discovery on the card evening at the Clutterbucks'.'

'I don't know what there is to speak of,' I told him. 'What you do – your preference and activity – can hardly be classified as a subject. At least not to me.'

Somers Ingram sat on a tufted stool, staring at me as he had from that moonlit hut. That he sat while I stood was an indication of how he thought of me: it was a disrespectful gesture. Uncomfortable under his scrutiny, I sat too, primly, in a small armchair.

Although the evening air outside the open windows wasn't hot, the room was airless, the atmosphere thick as the square petticoat of the *punkah* waved slowly over us. I heard the distant tinkle and scrape of the music stop: there was muted clapping, then the familiar strains of a Mozart prelude.

I waited, although my impulse was to rise with the haughty dignity I witnessed every day, and leave the room, no matter what tactics Mr Ingram chose to employ. He had no hold over me. I could leave of my own free will. Yet I didn't.

'I know what you girls from the Fishing Fleet are like,' he said. 'It's all desperate speculation. You'll do anything you can to find a husband, won't you? The idea of going home as a Returned Empty? Why, I'm assured it's the most terrible threat hanging over your lovely heads from the moment you set foot on Indian soil. I've wanted to ask you if there's anything I can do to make you forget about the business you stumbled upon. Could I, perhaps, introduce you to one of the men who haven't yet become acquainted with all you have to offer?'

'I need no help from you, Mr Ingram,' I told him. 'And, as I told you, how you conduct your life is no concern of mine. There's no need to bribe me. I can keep secrets. And I'm not the desperate creature you describe. I might not be as anxious to find a husband as you seem to believe.' There was something so condescending in his manner – his mocking tone when he spoke of the Fishing Fleet and Returned Empties – that I wanted to put him in his place, let him know that I was not like the others.

He appeared undaunted, now daring to smile. But I saw the gleam of perspiration on his brow, the quick touch of knuckle to moustache that came when he was nervous. It gave me confidence. He crossed his legs. 'There's no other point in coming to India as an unmarried woman, is there? Oh, I know there are those who use the guise of caring for a brother, or keeping a lonely mother company, but we all know the truth. No single woman comes here with any other purpose, save the occasional missionary. Might your bold statement – that you aren't desperate – arise from the fact that you haven't done well with suitors? One can't help but notice how often you sit alone.'

I didn't drop my gaze. 'I came as a companion to my friend, Miss Vespry.'

'And you plan to return to England as soon as she's found a likely match?'

I hesitated. No one had asked me about my plans. 'No. I'm not planning to return to England. At least, not any time soon.' *There's nothing for me to go back to, although I wouldn't admit that to you.*

'And?' His foot bobbed. 'You'll do what here, when the busy Miss Vespry becomes a memsahib? Surely she won't want you as a companion when she has a husband.'

'I'm not sure. I . . . I've thought about enquiring for a position. I once had a post in a library. Through my own choosing, of course.'

He cocked his head. 'You have been *employed*? And you believe it would be possible to carry on like that in Calcutta? My, my, Miss Smallpiece. I wouldn't let that get out. Such news would be the end of you. No white woman is ever employed in India. And no white women stay, unless they're married, or have the misfortune to be a spinster daughter or sister. Surely you understand that, Miss Smallpiece. Whatever are you thinking?'

I stood. 'Really, Mr Ingram, you are too rude. I don't know why I've stayed to speak with you. We'll say no more about – your indiscretion. I would never threaten you with it, even though sodomy is punishable by hanging. We'll do our best to ignore each other when we're forced together in society.'

He tilted his head to one side, narrowing his eyes. He hadn't risen when I did, choosing to stay, disrespectfully, on the stool. 'There it is again, Miss Smallpiece. You surprise me

259

more with every passing day. How would you know that sodomy is a crime? And what do you know of it, Miss Smallpiece? Even to know and utter the word—'

I raised my chin and started towards the door.

'There's something about you that's not . . .' he looked towards the open doors '. . . not exactly . . .' he paused again '. . . I can't seem to put it into words.' His smile was now little more than a slash beneath his moustache. 'I've always considered myself a good judge of character. And now I believe it all ties together. The way the men make a wide berth around you. Your insistence on not being interested. It's almost as if you don't *like* men, Miss Smallpiece. Yes, I believe that's what it is,' he said, nodding as if surprised by his intuition. 'You may try to cover it, but now that I think about it, it's quite clear. And the men sense it. There's no other reason for their reticence, is there? It's not that you don't have a certain appeal, and while you're not the picture of conventional beauty, you're certainly as passable in appearance as any of the others. Let's speak frankly, shall we, Miss Smallpiece?'

I was half-way across the room. 'Why is it that you feel you can speak to me in such a rude and familiar way?' There was a warning buzz in the back of my head. I wished Faith would come looking for me. The distant music droned on. The *punkah* swung lazily overhead, and from the darkness beyond the terrace came the scream of a peacock, followed by the longing answer of a hen.

Mr Ingram emitted a barking laugh. 'Familiar? Well, it's not as though you haven't seen me in a most familiar way, is it?'

At that moment a gecko fell from the rafters, dropping on to the sleeve of my pale lavender watered silk. I gasped with surprise, brushing at the little lizard, but it clung tightly. Mr Ingram swung into action; he behaved as a gentleman would without thinking. He crossed the floor in a few long strides and took hold of the gecko. As he attempted to pluck it from me, the tiny creature's claws remained caught in the delicate material, dragging the loose bell sleeve up to my elbow.

And then Mr Ingram was still, his hand closed round the fragile green body. I looked at his face, which bore a curious expression. He used his other hand to disengage the harmless reptile, holding it gingerly between thumb and index finger.

'Take this,' he called, and the *punkah-wallah* appeared out of the shadows and took the gecko from him.

I arranged my sleeve, and saw that Mr Ingram was still staring at my arm with that odd, thoughtful gaze. Then his sun-darkened skin grew pale, as if the blood had been sucked out of him. For one incredible moment I imagined he had been frightened by the gecko.

'Let me see that again,' he demanded. 'The mark on the inside of your arm.' A far-off whisper increased the faint buzzing in my ears to a loud bell of alarm. Pounding heat rushed to my head. It was as if there was too much blood in my veins, as if Mr Ingram's had been transferred to me. While he had blanched to the colour of suet, I was burning, flushed. My hands continued to flutter over my sleeve, smoothing and patting it as I ignored his request.

His eyes raked my hair, my face, and then, with no warning, he grabbed my hand and roughly pushed up my sleeve. He stared down at the smooth skin and my fish birthmark, then dropped my hand and took a hasty step away as if he had become aware of the putrid breath of contagion.

I put my palm on my birthmark, looking at him with

261

consternation. 'It's just a birthmark, Mr Ingram,' I said. 'Hardly unusual.'

'I know that birthmark. I've seen it somewhere before.' His voice was low, the words weighted.

'Surely not,' I stuttered. And as another moment passed, with Mr Ingram still scrutinizing me, that odd drawn look about his mouth and eyes, I knew the worst had happened. His next words confirmed it.

'I've seen you before, I realize that now. Your face isn't familiar, but that fish marks you clearly. Although I chose not to speak of it to you, I did travel to Liverpool, and I regularly had the opportunity to keep company with all manner of men – and women. Although many of my memories of those visits are less than clear, some things stay with one, don't you find?'

God, no, I prayed. His sort hadn't usually frequented Paradise Street. Had he ever been a customer? Wouldn't I have remembered him among the vast number of faces and bodies I had known? I always believed I remembered too much – in detail I wished I could forget.

I stood, waiting. I knew by the smile now playing about his still bloodless lips that he was confident he had uncovered my past, and would use it to destroy me. The smile also made it clear that it would bring him pleasure to do so. But why? I had assured him his secret was safe with me. It was true: I had no interest in anyone else's secrets. I had my own to protect.

I straightened my shoulders, and unexpectedly felt the old pull of my scar as if it were a fresh wound. I would have to play it out, deny whatever he accused me of. 'Whatever do you mean? I demand to know what you are implying, sir,' I said, trying for polite outrage, but to my horror I heard my old voice trying to edge its way out. I swallowed. Although I might be forced, by consternation, into a rough phrase, I had begun to believe that that voice – not just the inflection but the shrillness – was gone. But in that moment, when it erupted involuntarily, I knew that it – like Back Phoebe Anne and Paradise Streets, was grimly ingrained for ever, no matter how consciously I held that part of me at bay.

'I suggest you sit down, Miss Smallpiece. You're not looking well, not well at all.'

The colour had snapped back into his face, two hectic spots high on his cheekbones. 'Here. Let me help you,' he said.

He held my upper arms and walked me backwards until my calves touched the seat of a chair. I lowered myself on to it.

He watched me. Then he glanced around the room. The *punkah-wallah* had crept back in from depositing the gecko on the terrace steps, and resumed his job, but I knew that to Mr Ingram he was of no consequence. 'Now I know what secret I've been seeing on your face, reading in your body. Now I know exactly what you are.'

There was a dark rushing at the back of my head. As if from a great distance, I heard, 'You are a working girl, aren't you, my dear? Although a post in a library is not the position I remember you in.' He pushed up my sleeve and stroked my birthmark tenderly. 'Now I know what you are,' he whispered.

Not *who* but *what*. A whore.

I had been found out. It was all over.

I didn't faint. Something, desperation perhaps, drove me to fight the thickness in my head and to rise from the chair. I ran, stumbling, from the room, and from Somers Ingram. I

263

ran down the deserted hallway and passed the music room, smelt the burst of hot, scented air, heard the French horns and violas singing. I ran on, out on to the wide drive where one of the servants stopped me and understood my desperate plea to leave. His calm expression beneath the high turban betrayed no surprise that an English girl was running like a lunatic, panting and gasping, and he summoned a small palanquin pulled by one runner.

I don't remember giving the *boyee* the location, or getting back to the Watertons' house. I dismissed the servants who gathered round me as I stepped inside, and fell across my bed fully dressed. It wasn't more than a few minutes before the chill started, my teeth chattering, and I couldn't get warm even though the night was far from cool. I pulled a cover over me, but it didn't help. I heard Faith's voice in the corridor, heard the rustle of taffeta as she peeped into my room, and then the closing of my door, when she had assumed I was asleep.

Shortly afterwards I became ill.

Faith heard me as I retched into the washbasin, and came into my room, laying her smooth cool hand against my cheek. 'We all wondered where you had got to. I came back early, before they served the evening refreshments, concerned for you. I hope it's not malaria, Linny. Have you been taking your quinine?'

I nodded. 'It's not malaria,' I whispered. 'Perhaps I ate something that upset me.'

'Do you suppose it was the pea-fowl *pilau* at lunch? It was a little oily. Or even the almondine pudding. Can I fetch you anything?' She looked at the empty mat at the foot of my bed. 'Where is your *ayah*?'

'I sent her away. I want to be alone. I'll just sleep, and be well again tomorrow, I'm sure.' Again my teeth started their dance.

'I don't care what you say, I'm going to send in your *ayah*. She can help get you into your nightdress. You can't be alone when you're ill. And she can alert me should you grow worse in the night.'

I nodded, too distressed to argue, and the *ayah* came in. I let her undress me and take down my hair, slip the nightdress over my head, bathe my hands and face with cool water. But even the quiet rhythm of her breathing in the still room as she fell asleep did little to ease my illness, brought on not by food but by terror. I knew I wouldn't sleep that night, and perhaps not for many more.

CHAPTER TWENTY-ONE

A DAY PASSED, AND then another. I stayed in my room, telling Faith I was indisposed. Mrs Waterton felt we should call for the physician, but I insisted the malaise would pass with time, implying that it was simply my monthly discomfort.

I couldn't stay still, though, and wandered about my bedroom, picking up objects and setting them down, unable to sleep, eat or even read.

By the third day I was so agitated, trying to guess what Mr Ingram would do with his information, that I could not remain shut up any longer. I sat at dinner with Faith and the Watertons, trying to focus, to behave normally. I felt my mouth smile, felt food, dry as ashes, struggle down my throat, heard my voice prattle unimportant nonsense. There was a fête at the Club that evening: Mr Snow had invited Faith to be his escort, and the Watertons would also be present. I convinced everyone to go, but told them I wasn't up to a party yet. I was terrified of encountering Mr Ingram – but perhaps I should face him, discover whatever he would do. Surely that would be better than what I was suffering with now – the unknown.

The Watertons' palanquin had barely pulled away when the *chuprassi* appeared in the drawing room where I sat at a desk, holding a quill, a blank sheet of paper before me. I had thought of writing to Shaker, hoping that the act of describing trifling matters would calm me. The *chuprassi*, adjusting his distinctive red sash, announced the arrival of Mr Ingram.

The quill fell on to the paper, ruining it with a smear of ink. Had he been watching the house, waiting to ensure that I was alone before he called? How improper, I thought insanely, that he should arrive unannounced and I without a chaperone. In the next instant I made a small, bitter sound, laughter at my own hypocrisy. I was behaving in the same way as the women I secretly scorned. And it was too late to worry about improprieties with this man.

He was ushered into the drawing room by the *chuprassi* and followed by the *khitmutgar*. As the *chuprassi* bowed his way out of the room, the *khitmutgar* went to the sideboard and poured a measure of dark rum into a heavy crystal glass. He brought it to Mr Ingram on an inlaid tray, then bowed in front of me.

'No. Nothing,' I said, and he bowed again, then took up his place at the sideboard.

'Linny,' Mr Ingram said, smiling as he took a sip. It appeared to be an artless smile, but I knew better. 'No point in bothering with "Miss Smallpiece" any longer, is there? Surely – given what I know you to be – there's no need for play-acting.'

I stepped closer to him, returning his false smile with an even falser one. 'All I care about is staying here, and of course I won't be able to if you disclose what you know of me. There's no point in spoiling it for me, Mr Ingram.' I said his name with the firmness he'd used with mine. 'You won't tell my secrets, and I won't tell yours.' At least I had the tiny comfort of thinking I could also hurt his reputation. His next words dashed it.

'So, you threaten me? Can you believe that anyone would believe your tittle-tattle? Can you imagine that anyone would accept what you – a griffin, fresh off the boat – might tell them of me, established and respected throughout Calcutta? Anything you said would come across as the words of a bitter woman, rejected by her heart's desire. It's rather pathetic that you feel you can intimidate me.'

'Have you begun your campaign of slander, then? Shall I expect to be dismissed from the Watertons' this very night?'

He seemed to enjoy making me suffer. He shook his head, smiling.

'Or will you use your knowledge to satisfy yourself at will?' I cried. 'You think you will use me, as you imply you once did – although I have no memory of you. You must have performed in a lacklustre fashion indeed.'

I saw his jaw clench.

'I was not interested in such common trade then, and still am not. My interest, as you have discovered, runs towards the stronger sex. Although I would never have used you myself, I recognize that birthmark, and know it is tied in to the times I spent with the lower end of life in Liverpool.'

I still found it strange that I had no stronger recollection of him than a whisper that might have been created by my current fear.

'Have you had many offers of male companionship, Linny? Any prospects? Has any man here paid you serious attention?'

There was little point in trying to bluff with Somers Ingram. I knew I'd frightened off the young men of Calcutta. Or, if I hadn't frightened them, I'd made them so uncomfortable that they didn't approach me. I knew what they were looking for: a reserved, perhaps coy, accommodating woman – was there any other kind in these circles? But that role – of coy sweetness – was difficult for me to play: no matter how interested I appeared in their stories, with downcast eyelashes throwing what I'd seen as becoming shadows on other women's cheeks, I knew I couldn't do it. My heart wasn't in it. Now I shook my head.

'But how do you propose to stay in India, Linny, if no marriage proposal is forthcoming?'

'As I said, I – perhaps . . . Some kind of position.'

'Really, Linny. Stop dreaming.' The scent of rum wafted towards me.

I knew he was right. I think I had known, almost from my arrival, that if I were to stay I would have to find a husband, but I had refused to admit it to myself. Our time at the Watertons' might last at the most six or seven months without an engagement, and we were into the fourth. I knew I would have to fool only one man and at that moment, I realized, I didn't care who it was. Faced with the thought of leaving India, of returning to Liverpool, I knew then that I would do whatever I had to. I would marry someone – anyone. I thought of Shaker and my words to him that I would not marry in India. But if it came down to the choice of staying as a married woman or leaving . . . Here, with servants to carry out every domestic duty, there would be no demands on me other than to entertain. I could learn to do it, make endless tedious talk over the dinner table and order servants about, organize parties and plan meals. As for the rest, it would certainly be no hardship to spread my legs under the mosquito netting for a faceless husband. These things meant nothing to me: it was a small price to pay for staying here in India where my heart had unclenched for the first time in my life. If I were to be a prisoner, better a prisoner in India where I might eventually earn some freedom, some time outside the curtained palanquins, the *maidan* and the Calcutta Club.

I thought of Meg Liston, riding off into the wilds with her husband. Writing her book. Free to explore. It might be possible for me, too.

'Are you listening, Linny? I said I had a plan.'

I blinked. 'A plan?'

Mr Ingram sat on the sofa, and nodded at the chair across from it.

'I'd rather stand.'

'As you wish. But this is what I've been thinking about, these last few days.' His eyes drifted round the room, then returned to the dark liquid in the bottom of his glass. He brushed back his springy dark hair with manicured fingernails. 'Simply put, I need a wife. I cannot wait any longer. I had planned to pick someone out of this Fleet. In fact, for a while I thought I might choose that little parakeet with the high voice you came with – Miss Vespry. She looked as if she would be easy to put up with, pretty enough not to turn me off my breakfast every morning, although she appears skittish and possibly given to instability. I would venture to guess that she's also scared witless of the touch of a man, and that might help me for the first while – she would have no expectations, of course.' He continued to rake his fingers through his hair, gazing into his glass, and then he looked back at me. 'Anyway, never mind about that. It came to me, the other night, that not only is the timing perfect but that we are an ideal match, Linny.'

'A match? You and I? We're no such thing. Please don't compare us. I find it an insult.'

270

He gave a loud, spontaneous laugh. 'Very refreshing – that you, a Liverpool doxy, would be insulted to put yourself in my league.' He laughed again, gesturing at the *khitmutgar*. The tall man stepped up immediately, the silver tray ready. His hennaed beard trembled as he waited for Mr Ingram to set down the glass. He took it to the sideboard, refilled it and brought it back. Then he faded into the recesses of the room.

Mr Ingram took a delicate sip. 'But we are a match, my dear, for the simple reason that we both have a secret to hide and can use each other to fulfil our needs. There is the added benefit that neither of us has other attachments in this world.'

I watched the *khitmutgar* in his darkened corner: his eyes never lifted from the floor. 'Why must you marry so hurriedly?'

Mr Ingram drank again. 'I'm waiting to come into my full inheritance. My father made his fortune by his instincts and shrewd investments in the building trade, although in later years much of that fortune was squandered due to his . . . ungentlemanly pursuits.' He stopped and shook his head in an impatient, angry motion. 'I'm the only heir. In spite of a goodly loss, the sum of the inheritance is still pleasing. It won't allow me complete leisure for the rest of my life, but is sufficient to offer me some choices. My father's will specifies that I receive it at twenty-five, if all conditions are met. One of those conditions is that I am married. I will be twenty-five in a mere three months.' He drained the glass.

'What I'm saying, Linny, is that you and I are in a tight spot, wouldn't you agree? And the simplest solution is for us to marry. You'll be able to stay in India. I, too, like this country, in spite of its confusion, filth and idolatry. I don't know what you find attractive, but I can live in the manner I prefer – every need cared for by an embarrassment of

271

servants to jump at my slightest whim. To say nothing of the wealth of eager, fresh young boys, who throw themselves at the chance to be the paramour of what they see as a *pukka sahib*.

'India is a wonderful place for someone like me. Had I come of age half a century ago I might have been a free-wheeling trader or soldier of fortune. But the days of straightforward trading concerns are gone. Now we are responsible for ruling the Indians. No. Not just ruling them – trying to help them. India is a stagnant country.' He paused. 'My position as chief auditor for John Company affords me a respect I could never acquire in London. And by marrying you, Linny, I'll become wealthy enough to do more or less as I like, and appear as I should. A hot-blooded young man with a wife to do for him, a wife to join the English team in India, cheer it on. It's becoming embarrassing for me to stay single – the fifth Fishing Fleet in so many years has come in to shore since I've been here. People may be wondering why none of those lovely young ladies has been to my fancy, in spite of all the well-meaning match-making by over-anxious matrons who want to ensure my domestic happiness.'

The *khitmutgar* came towards him again, tray raised, but Mr Ingram waved him away with an impatient flick of his hand. 'You will admit that you would be getting the better part of the bargain, Linny. You'd remain in India, while all I would get is a dependant. But one who will allow me the money and freedom to satisfy my needs as I please. And, of course, there would be no children. I have no interest in touching you. The assumption would be, of course, that you are barren. You will garner great sympathy from the other women.'

'And if I refuse? I may find someone else, after all, who is interested in marriage.' I was clutching at straws. He knew it; I too.

Mr Ingram set his empty glass on the polished table beside the sofa. He chose a cheroot from the humidor there, and sniffed it. 'If you say no, why, then, my dear Linny, you will be on the next ship home. And everyone who is anyone in Calcutta, and much further beyond, since there is nothing more loved here than gossip, will have learned about Miss Linny Smallpiece. Somehow, by some insidiously creeping tittle-tattle whose origin will never be remembered, everyone will hear that you are not what you appear. That you are a whore of the lowest quarter. Imagine the state Miss Vespry will get herself into! The Watertons will be mortified. And the men will nod to each other, realizing what they'd smelt when they sniffed around you. Why, it would soon be heard that you'd even propositioned one or two down at the Club.' He put the end of the cheroot into his mouth. 'And the women would appear horrified, but even they would admit to each other that there was always something not quite right about Linny Smallpiece, that they'd known it all along.' He shook his head. 'And, of course, the news would arrive in Liverpool. It might be hard on your family — a cousin and aunt, was it? — or was that a fabrication too? Whatever the case, whatever you came from there would no longer be open to you.

'You've done well, haven't you, Linny, in fooling people?' He didn't expect an answer. 'What a long way you've come. I can't imagine the route that has brought you to this level. What must you have done to get here?' He sighed. 'Admirable. I almost like you for it.'

I walked to the wide windows and looked into the darkness beyond. Suddenly the country was threatening, dark and watchful. 'Even if I were to agree to this proposal, how would we keep our true relationship hidden? For there could be no pretending that we cared for one another.'

'Simple, really. We're both expert at living a lie. We'll live as man and wife under the same roof, but spend as little time together as possible. We need not even share dinner, unless we have company. My job here,' he smiled and snapped his fingers at the *khitmutgar*, who stepped forward, lighting a flint match, 'keeps me busy. I'm often away for weeks. And I like to go to the jungle, hunting. We won't have to see each other for much of the time. When we are forced together in public, or in the presence of guests in our home, your life will appear to be that of the proper bride. You'll want for nothing.

'I ask only two things of you,' he continued. 'First, you must never breathe a word about whatever it is I might do or with whom. Of course, that's understood. And second, should you ever revert to your ways, even once, and disgrace me with your whoring, you will be out of my home in less time than it will take me to smoke this cheroot. With nothing but the clothes on your back. I'll not be cuckolded.'

He sucked deeply on the cheroot as the *khitmutgar* held the match to its tip. I watched his handsome face in the glow, and in that sudden flare of light I wondered if I could rise to this daring challenge. In the next instant I shuddered, imagining the hell he would make of my life, and how I would for ever have to dance to his tune.

'Linny? Do you understand?'

'Oh, yes. Yes, Mr Ingram, I do.'

'And you're in agreement with the plan?'

When I didn't answer, he came to stand behind me. 'There's a ship, the *Bengal Merchant*, sailing for home in three days. You could be on it, in disgrace, if you don't answer carefully.'

I told Mr Ingram I needed time to weigh my decision. In the early morning of the third day I packed my trunks, then sent my *ayah* to wake Mrs Waterton and tell her I was leaving. I went to Faith's room and woke her. Sitting on the edge of the bed, I told her of my decision.

Her face registered first disbelief, followed by confusion, then disappointment and sadness. 'You're leaving Calcutta? Now? But – but *why*, Linny? I don't understand. And, well, I thought our commitment was that you would be my companion, until . . . until either I went home or, more hopefully, had reason to stay. It's only February. The season isn't officially over until the beginning of April, and there's even time after that.' She was still in her bed, now staring at the floor. 'I thought you loved it here. You told me that you loved it, Linny, that you'd never felt so happy, and now you're leaving. Do you really want to go back to Everton? Is it that you miss your cousin and aunt? You're homesick?'

Before I had a chance to answer, Faith continued: 'No one, but no one, starts the tiresome voyage home after such a short time. It's unheard of. And – and . . .' she cast around wildly for reasons to persuade me to stay '. . . and my father will be displeased. He's on his way here, aboard a ship that is due to arrive within the next few months. He only gave his consent for me to come ahead of him because I spoke so highly of you. And now if he comes, and you're not here . . . he shall report to Mr Smallpiece, your guardian, that you've broken your side of the agreement, and his embarrassment – your cousin's – will be your burden to bear. So you can't leave, Linny. You simply can't.' She scrambled out of bed and grabbed my arms so that I was forced to face her. 'Please. Say you'll stay.'

I looked at her pretty face. She had changed since we had left the docks at Liverpool. I had kept waiting for her to adjust to the strangeness of all that was India, but it seemed she had fallen out of step, somehow, even with the atmosphere of England that smothered us in Calcutta. She had become complacent, less outspoken, perhaps even fearful, while I had found my place in the world. Faith was out of her element, and I was in mine. Or had been.

'I can't explain to you why I have to go.' I prayed that once I left, without telling Mr Ingram, he would say nothing. But then again he might decide, out of spite, to spread the stories about me.

'But the season isn't over for another six weeks. Two months or more, as I said. There's still time,' Faith said.

'For what?'

'For someone to show interest.'

'Aren't you seeing Mr Snow quite regularly?'

'I meant for you, Linny. Time for someone to ask for your hand. You mustn't despair.'

'That's not it,' I said. 'I came to be your companion. It wasn't my intention to marry here. I told you that before we left. I just thought I might . . . stay . . .' Again, my reasoning was flimsy. I walked out of Faith's room. Crying, she followed me to the waiting palanquin, wearing her dressing-gown. We were followed by Mrs Waterton, her clothing thrown on in a great hurry – it was clear she wasn't wearing her stays. She wrung her hands, her face a crumpled mask of dismay. I saw Mr Waterton poke his head out of the door, looking mulish, and then he retreated inside.

'This doesn't reflect well on us, my dear. It's as if we

haven't made you happy here,' she said. 'Mr Vespry entrusted Faith and you to us. And now you're leaving, with no travelling companion, for the voyage home. I don't know of any married women on the *Bengal Merchant* at this point. It's not right – these things have to be planned.'

'I sent the *chuprassi* to book my passage, and will use the return ticket bought by Mr Vespry. I promise I can look after myself,' I told her, and thanked her for her hospitality. The palanquin runners loaded my luggage, and I left. I looked back at the two women standing outside the beautiful villa, gleaming whitely in the morning sun. Mrs Waterton fluttered a handkerchief, but Faith covered her face with her hands, her shoulders shaking as she wept.

I left the curtains open as we rode through Calcutta. It was my first and last time to ride through the city alone and take in India with all my senses. Again, as at the dock that first day, it was the vividness of colour that so astounded me. The light was yellow. I thought of the blue light of England, how it made everything appear worn – a soft, soporific light, creating a life that was standing still, accepting. Here, in the brilliance, my eyelids felt burned away; it was impossible to close them.

We passed the last house on Garden Reach, then turned up a smaller street. Here the houses were still in the European fashion, but smaller and meaner. The roofs were thatched, the walls stained with mildew. These were the homes of the employees of the uncovenanted civil service, the Eurasian men, born here and tainted with Indian blood, no matter how distant the union had been. That bloodline ensured there could never be any hope of rising above the uncovenanted rank in the Company. Half-caste children ran about – grandchildren and great-grandchildren of the pairing of native women with men from John Company, before English women had been allowed to come to this wild, dangerous country. Some were startlingly European-looking, others darker and more native.

Finally we were at the docks. They were teeming with life and noise, as they had been when we arrived. I thought of the morning when Faith and I had left Liverpool, how the dull fog had swirled about us, dampening our clothes and skin, chilling us in the silence. I imagined arriving there again, in the same fog, trudging out to find a carriage, and then the ride to Whitefield Lane, past Paradise Street, Bold Street and the Lyceum. I imagined the look on Shaker's face, the light in his eyes when he saw me. And then I imagined myself, years later, still living in Everton, a withered old woman in a black coat and bonnet turning green. I imagined my own face, my eyesight failing and my penmanship losing its firmness as I bent over the recording cards at the Lyceum, hidden behind the stacks.

I stood beside my piled luggage, ticket in my hand. From nowhere a near-naked *sadhu*, a holy man, twirled and shouted his way through a crowd of disinterested women in fuchsia, turquoise and orange saris. His body gleamed blue-black under its covering of smeared wood ash, and his dense wiry hair hung like twisted ropes, the parting on his scalp vermilion-dusted. I recognized the three horizontal lines painted with a thick white substance on his forehead, indicating that he was a follower of Shiva, the god of Death. As he leaped about, closer and closer, the layers of beads on his chest danced and clattered. He came straight at me, as if he had been searching for me, and I stared into his bloodshot eyes. He shouted something in my face, spraying me with saliva, and his breath was rank with the smell of betel and stomach rot. I didn't understand the words, but I knew the meaning. It was a warning, a premonition. A man in an army uniform and solar topee pushed him rudely away from me, then asked if I was all right. I nodded, but couldn't speak.

I understood the portent of the *sadhu*.

I returned in a palanquin. When the door was opened by the *chuprassi*, he stared at me, then behind me, with a look of modified horror at my lack of decorum in calling unchaperoned at a gentleman's house.

'I wish to speak to Mr Ingram,' I said. 'Is he still at home?'

He nodded, but stood, immobile, blocking the door.

'Come, now,' I said, pushing past him into the entrance hall. 'I must see him. Please summon him for me.' When the man still didn't move, I started through the house, to the room where Mr Ingram and I had last spoken. By the time I reached the hallway a small herd of servants trailed after me, distressed at my boldness.

I stopped in front of the shuttered door, my hand raised. But a breeze rattled it before I could knock, and there was movement inside. Perhaps my shadow had been cast into the room, my presence announced.

'Hazi? Is that you? Have you my clean collar?'

I pulled open the shuttered door. 'It's I, Mr Ingram,' I said, stepped inside the room and shut the door on the concerned servants.

Somers Ingram stood behind his desk. He wore only his trousers and an unbuttoned collarless shirt, the cuffs undone. His hair, lacking its usual pomade, curled about his ears and neck. In spite of what had passed between us, I was still struck by his appearance.

I felt the closed door at my back.

He came towards me, his face unreadable. 'To what do I owe this early-morning visit?' he asked.

'I've made my decision.'

He came closer. I smelt soap, the starch of his shirt. 'And?' I could see now that, although he was trying to hide it, there was a shallowness in the rise and fall of his bare chest that belied his attempted nonchalance.

'I agree to your terms.'

'To be my wife,' he confirmed, with less than his usual certainty. When I nodded, he raised the knuckle of his index finger to his moustache in the way I had come to watch for. And in seeing his body's involuntary reaction – his breathing, his voice, that touch of his moustache – I felt a small sense of pride, of accomplishment, for I knew then that, no matter how he tried to pretend that my decision meant little to him, my final answer had been the one he'd hoped for.

'You've made the right decision, Linny. We are the same. We both hide something, and we must stay at the level of acceptance we have attained here. It will go much easier for us this way. There need be no sham between us. We understand each other. Do you not see it thus?' he repeated.

I didn't answer. While it might be true that he found a part of me loathsome, as I did in him, there could be no denying that, for all his bluster, I held some power over him.

CHAPTER TWENTY-TWO

15 February 1831

My dearest Shaker,

It is difficult to compose this letter, only because it is one I never expected to write to you. I know that by the time you read it you will only just have received my initial packet of letters, telling you about my new life here. I wrote them with a joyful heart, with the lightness of shaking off an old life and beginning anew. This is written in a different vein, with a heavy heart. There is no other way to say it but this: I am to be married within a fortnight. Of course, by the time you read this I expect I shall have been married for months.

It was an unexpected and, as you must know, unforeseeable event. The words I spoke to you last summer, before I left Liverpool, were true. Please dismiss from your imagination romantic trysts, passion, or even the hint of friendship. This is not a marriage that involves any emotion in either the gentleman or myself. It is a marriage for convenience. I can say no more, although I know you are now thinking, A marriage for convenience? Did I not speak this phrase to her myself, suggesting that it might work for us?

But, Shaker, there is more to this, so much more. There are things I can never explain, a hard linked chain of events from my past that precipitated this union, each link rusted, for ever fixed. And it is due to that dark time that I must become Mrs Somers Ingram. He is a gentleman from London, in the employ of the East India Company.

I can write no more at this time. As is apparent from the appearance of this letter, my hand is far from steady. Please forgive me, and please, please, dictate a letter in reply. I await each posting from England with great eagerness. Should you feel that contacting me is impossible, I will understand. But again I beg you, Shaker, do not cast me from your life, for in many ways I feel I need you now more than ever.

With deepest affection,

Linny

Writing to Shaker was the most difficult aspect of marrying Somers, as I now called him, even more difficult than trying to explain my decision to Faith. After I had given my consent and we had discussed when the event would take place – as soon as possible: Somers wanted no dilly-dallying or false courtship rituals – I returned to the Watertons'. I found Faith, pale and listless, on the verandah. A servant stood behind her, wafting a peacock fan. She sat up straight and her mouth fell open as I stepped through the doors.

'You didn't go – you've changed your mind?' she asked, jumping to her feet.

I nodded.

'I knew you couldn't abandon me, Linny. I just knew it.' She gave me a hug.

'I must tell you of my plans, Faith,' I said. 'Sit down. Please.'

She lowered herself to the rattan sofa. The boy resumed fanning. 'Plans?'

I sat beside her and took her hands in mine. 'I'm to be married, Faith.'

Her fingers contracted, and I felt the bite of her nails against the back of my hands. 'Married? But – but to whom? There's been nobody—'

'I know. It's come about quite suddenly. It's Somers Ingram.'

Faith frowned. 'Somers Ingram? Mr *Ingram*?'

'Yes.'

'He's never even come to call. I've hardly noticed you speaking to him, or dancing with him more than a few times. I – I don't know what to think, Linny, what to say.'

There was silence, except for the swish of the fan.

'The wedding will be in two weeks, on February the twenty-eighth. Somers – Mr Ingram – says it must be before the approach of the Hot Season.'

At that Faith wrenched her hands from mine and stood. 'Well. You are a sly one. I see you're capable of doing quite well for yourself, after all. And I had pitied you.' She was bristling with anger. 'It appears you've been working some black Hindu magic behind my back – behind all our backs. It's well known that Mr Ingram has been unattainable – and he is certainly a handsome, charming catch, as you know. And with his senior position in the Company – well, Linny, you will find yourself quite a senior lady, won't you? You will even be above Mrs Waterton in rank.'

I swallowed. I had not thought of my own position as Somers's wife within Calcutta society.

'Apparently a number of girls have tried for a match with him, but he wasn't interested,' Faith went on. 'There is the usual rumour, of course – that he has a black mistress – and then . . . the other.'

'Which is?' Was the secret Somers Ingram thought he had kept so well hidden common knowledge after all? But Faith's next sentence assured me this wasn't so.

'That he might like a woman with a naughty edge, that he was looking for more. And perhaps there *is* more to you than meets the eye, Linny. What is it that has so attracted Mr Ingram to you where the rest of us have failed? And why did you feel you must hide everything from me? Why have you been so selfish?'

'It wasn't like that, Faith.'

'No? You didn't confide in me that you were even interested in Mr Ingram. And there I was, making a fool of myself with him only a few weeks ago, thinking that if Mr Snow was too shy to come forward, Mr Ingram certainly seemed attracted. You must have been laughing at me.' She bunched her skirt round her and swept past me, stopping at the verandah doors. 'Well, don't expect me to attend your wedding, Linny Smallpiece, for I no longer consider you a friend. I should have listened to my instincts, and to everyone in Liverpool who advised me that you might not be a suitable companion. Did you know that, Linny? That I was cautioned against becoming too close to you by more than one? And I thought they had proved me right earlier today, when you told me you were leaving India and me. But now this! Marrying before I've had a proposal! You, whom I rescued from that dreary library and even more dreary existence in Everton, bringing you here out of the goodness of my heart with my father's money. You made it perfectly clear that you had little interest in marriage, and now you dare to be the first of our Fleet to become engaged – and with a wedding date set so preposterously soon! It's as if everything you've told me is a lie. And it's too much for me, Linny. Just too much.'

She swept from the verandah, leaving me with the boy and his peacock fan, the languid rhythm never missing a beat.

Poor Mrs Waterton. She had not recovered from the shock of my departure when I went to where she reclined on a sofa in her bedroom, a wet cloth on her forehead, and told her what I had told Faith.

Predictably, she was shocked. She sat bolt upright and tossed the cloth to the floor. She kept repeating, 'Mr Ingram? Mr Ingram, well! Well, Mr Ingram!' making it clear that she thought it impossible that a gentleman such as he could have noticed one such as myself. 'But why so quickly? Why must the wedding be so immediate?' she asked, when I told her the date. 'There's a great deal to go into planning a wedding. To enjoy it fully it must be drawn out for months. The end of February is impossible.'

'I'm sorry, Mrs Waterton, but it is at Mr Ingram's insistence.'

'Can you not convince him to extend the engagement, Linny, and be married in the first glorious sweep of the Cool Season next autumn?'

I shook my head. 'I'm sorry, Mrs Waterton.'

She was silent for a moment, and I saw a veil of suspicion fall over her face. Then she took a deep breath, stood and opened her arms. 'Well, no matter what I feel, congratulations are in order, my dear. I'm sure you'll be very happy.' She embraced me stiffly.

I was grateful to her. I knew how difficult this was for her, but she was trying hard to be pleased.

She stepped away, her face composed now. Ever true to her class, I knew she would say no more to me about the strangeness of the situation, although I also knew that within hours tongues would wag throughout Calcutta society. 'There's not even time to make up proper invitations.' She sighed. 'Well, the first thing we must do is have a dress made.' She opened the drawing-room door to shout '*Koi-hai?*' – Is anyone there? – and send a servant running for the *durzi*.

Faced with the mammoth task of creating a wedding gown, the *durzi*, swaying back and forth in distress, called in a small contingent of his fellows, and between them, in just over a week of round-the-clock work, they had created one for me. Mrs Waterton oversaw it, having told me what would be most appropriate. It was as if she were informing me that I was not to be trusted and, since I was her guest – a most troublesome one at that – I would do her bidding. Of course, I was more relieved than she would ever know to let her take over the planning of dress and wedding. Instead of punishing me, as she must have imagined she was doing, she was making it possible for me to continue in my charade, for I had no knowledge of what a wedding would entail. I had never attended one. The closest I'd come to a bride and groom was in passing a church in Liverpool as they descended the steps.

The dress was of the most delicate ivory silk with wide-blown leg-of-mutton sleeves. Because a highly fashionable gown could only be low cut, Mrs Waterton came close to swooning when I first tried it on and she saw my scarred chest. I had always hidden the disfigurement with collars and lace, scarves and fichus, and not even Faith had ever seen it. The only people who knew of it in India were my *ayah* and the *durzi*.

'Oh, my dear, I didn't know – I don't quite know how we'll . . .' Mrs Waterton was flustered. As I stood in the middle of her spacious bedroom, three *durzis* kneeling around me, she fanned herself rapidly as she sank into a chair. I saw a glimmer of pity in her expression, and hoped this would lessen her anger with me.

She conferred at length with the *durzi*, and they devised a bow for the neckline. Transparently sympathetic now, she raved over the shape and creaminess of my shoulders, telling me that the small evidence of my 'trouble' that still showed could be disguised with powder.

Then she admired the tight belt and the inverted triangle of the skirt that emphasized the curve of my waist, while the wicker cage tied with straps around my hips held the dress out in what she said was a glorious example of the style in London.

What can be said of that loveless ceremony? We had been able to forgo the banns, and there appeared no need for any legal papers of birth to be in evidence. The word of Mr and Mrs Waterton as to my character seemed all that was necessary, and Mrs Waterton had, in her usual way, taken care of the details. The simple service took place in St John's Church. When the minister pronounced my name during the ceremony, Miss Linnet Smallpiece, I was aware of Somers's eyes shifting in my direction. He hadn't even known my full Christian name. I thought of my mother many times that day, and was ashamed of the falsity of it all.

The social gathering that followed, in the ballroom of

Government House, was in the finest taste, and attended by the closest acquaintances of the Watertons, Somers's friends, and the girls from the Fishing Fleet. Mrs Waterton was constantly surrounded by the bevy of matrons who had swooped in rather grimly to help her arrange this shockingly sudden event. More than one of those ladies, possibly with hopes of a match with Mr Somers Ingram for her own daughter or one of her houseguests, treated me coolly, some verging on rudeness.

But in spite of the pall that hung over the day, to all outward appearances it was a lovely celebration. The room was resplendent with mirrors and glass chandeliers, and handsome sofas of blue satin damask sat between the rows of shining white *chunam* pillars. An elaborate white cake on a stand was surrounded by a display of presents – vases, silver serving pieces, clocks, and all manner of home decoration to help set up a young couple. Did it appear strange to anyone that the groom and his bride rarely spoke after the service? While trays of dainty sandwiches were passed by immaculate attendants, my new husband was taken off to the smoking room by a crowd of friends. I was surrounded by the other girls, who told me endlessly how lovely my dress was, admired the sparkling array of gifts, and marvelled at how lucky I must consider myself. They spoke in loud, cheerful, social voices that barely concealed their true feelings, which I knew must run from disbelief that I, the odd Miss Smallpiece, had married the most eligible bachelor in Calcutta to bitter jealousy that they had not yet had the good fortune to start planning weddings of their own.

In spite of her vow, Faith did attend, but I sensed only to avoid any gossip that her absence might create. She had treated me with a careful distance for the last two weeks at the Watertons', staying in her room while Mrs Waterton fussed over me, saying she was resting or had a headache when I knocked at her door. During that long wedding afternoon, her face remained pulled by a smile that never left.

I felt as if I were floating somehow above the scene, smiling and accepting compliments, nodding. Eventually Somers was brought to my side by his cronies. His demeanour indicated that copious amounts of port and brandy had been poured down his throat over the last few hours. He put his arm round my shoulders, in what I knew was an inappropriate public display, even at our wedding, and gave my cheek a rather wet kiss.

'Mr Ingram,' I trilled, for the sake of the others watching, 'please, I believe it's time we were on our way.' Then I cupped my hand coquettishly round my mouth to speak into his ear, as if I were whispering something personal and loving: 'Don't overdo the display, Somers. I have a reputation to keep up.'

He laughed at that, and the crowd joined in, uncertain of what they had witnessed but assuming it to be a touching moment between two people in love.

I looked for Faith as Somers and I made our goodbyes, but she had disappeared. I had hoped she might soften enough at least to wish me well before I left for my new life as a married woman, but there was no sign of her.

Just before we left, Mrs Waterton hugged me. 'Be strong, Linny. Pray to the Lord for deliverance tonight, and know I shall also be praying for your ordeal to be bearable.'

I pulled back and looked into her tear-filled eyes. Did she weep with true concern, or was it fatigue – and relief that she was no longer responsible for me? 'Thank you, Mrs

Waterton,' I said, 'for all of this, and for your prayers. I am sure to need them.' Then, because I owed her a great deal, I said what I knew she would want to hear: 'You have been like a mother to me, and I shall never forget your kindness.'

She wept openly then, hugging me to her, patting my hair, and said softly, so no one else could hear: 'Permit me to speak as your own mother might then. Do keep your . . . you know, your . . .' she discreetly touched the bow at my neckline '. . . covered by your nightdress. It may be distressing for your new husband to view it immediately. Let some time pass, and prepare him, so that it isn't so shocking.'

'I will.' As if Somers Ingram would be shocked by anything about me. He would never see it anyway. 'It is a wise suggestion.'

And then Somers and I stepped into the opulent silk-curtained ceremonial palanquin, its curved pole covered in silver, and drove back to Alipur, to Somers's bachelor quarters – the other young men had moved elsewhere – where we would reside temporarily until he had found us a home.

I was exhausted from the day and the ordeal of portraying an excited, demure young bride. Somers was very drunk, although he retained his dignity. As we were ushered into the house by the *chuprassi*, the *khansana* and a small woman came forward, obviously waiting for us. The woman knelt at my feet, *salaaming*. She wore a simple white sari threaded with blue.

'Your *ayah*, Linny,' Somers said, his words running together.

The woman rose and stood in front of me, her head still lowered.

'I'm off to bed,' he said now. 'She will show you to your room. Your trunks were delivered earlier, I believe.' His eyes weren't focusing on me. They blinked heavily.

I nodded. Although I knew that he had no physical interest in me, I felt curiously empty. And in that moment I would have preferred a meaningless encounter to the disconcerting loneliness.

'Good night, then,' he said, and walked, unsteadily, down the hallway. His *khansana* followed closely, arms outstretched as if to catch him if he fell.

The *ayah* and I stood in silence, until I remembered she was waiting for me to instruct her. 'Will you take me to my room, please?'

She turned and padded softly along the hall, feet bare, in the opposite direction from Somers. She opened a door to a bedroom lit dimly by a few candles and, still without a word, helped me out of my wedding finery and into my nightdress, then took down my hair. She fetched scented water to bathe my face, hands and feet. She turned down the sheet, and when I got into bed, she pulled it over me and let down the netting. If she thought it strange that a bride should spend her wedding night alone, her face did not betray it.

'Do you speak any English?' I asked.

For the first time, she met my eyes through the fine mesh. I saw her hesitate. 'Yes, some English,' she said. Her voice was low and melodic. From the darkness outside came the distant scream of a jackal, followed by the baying of a pariah dog. 'Does Memsahib wish me to remain?'

I blinked at my new title. 'Yes,' I told her, turning my head away as my eyes burned. I wondered again, as I had constantly in the last two weeks, if the choice I had made was the right one. 'Yes, please stay,' I repeated, my face still averted, my voice firm.

But as she blew out the candles, my gaping loneliness

only increased. The *ayah* settled, almost noiselessly, on a mat in a corner of the room.

'What is your name?' I called.

'Malti.'

'Does it have a meaning in English?'

There was a moment of silence, and then she said, quietly, 'Its meaning is a small flower. Very small and very fine.'

'Oh.'

Silence. And then I said, 'Although I'm called Linny, my name is Linnet. A bird. Also small.'

'Very good, Memsahib.'

And so we lay in the darkness, a little Indian flower and a little British bird.

CHAPTER TWENTY-THREE

T HE MARRIAGE BEGAN quietly. On the first day Somers told me I was to entertain twice a week, and to accept all invitations that came our way. The couples who came to us for dinner seemed eager to be included on our invitation list – after all, Mr Somers Ingram held a senior position, and now that he was married and could entertain properly many wished to bask in his glow.

His position was unimportant to me: I cared as little about how he spent his days as he cared about how I passed mine, although occasionally his weariness on some evenings made it clear that his responsibility was great.

I found it simple to plan the menus and confer with the cook; it required no stamina. The evenings, though, required Somers and me to behave like a blissfully married couple. We were magnificent actors. There were times when I smiled at Somers across an acre of blinding white damask, the silver winking in the candlelight, amid the laughter of our guests, and could almost believe we were what we pretended to be. He was charming in company, and I felt embraced in the bright rays he so easily emitted. But at the final closing of the front door he turned off the charm and took a bottle to his room. I retired to mine, suddenly aware of how stiff my neck was, how my face ached from the tight mask I must wear.

Occasionally, if I was particularly hot or tired, I knew the mask slipped. And Somers was the first to notice, and reprimand me. Eventually I believe others saw it, too, and there were many times when I sat at my end of the table with all heads turned to Somers as if I were no longer there.

After one especially trying evening, Somers turned to me, and I tensed, waiting for his rebuke. 'Were you particularly weary tonight, Linny?' he asked, surprising me with the quiet tone of his voice.

I nodded. 'I was. Did it show?' Because he had spoken almost respectfully to me, I was willing to meet him half-way. 'I did try, Somers, but Major Cowton talked so much that it was difficult to pay attention after a while.'

'I found tonight difficult too,' he said, and sighed.

I felt a rush of something for him, that he and I could agree on this simple thing. I put my hand on his sleeve. 'Must we see so many people, so often?'

'I'm afraid there's no other way. We would be viewed oddly if we didn't follow what is expected.' His eyes rose to my hair. 'Your hair is attractive tonight.'

'It's something new Malti tried,' I said. Where was his arrogance, the usual verbal sparring in which we tried to outdo each other?

'Well, good night, then,' Somers said, but his voice held a hesitation, something I could almost – almost – interpret as loneliness. And I knew, too, how lonely I was, in the midst of the endless stream of events with people who cared nothing for me. In my moment of unexpected emotion, I put my arms round him, and laid my head on his chest.

He immediately put me from him. 'Why would you do that?' he asked, in the voice he usually reserved for me.

'I don't know,' I replied honestly. 'I felt – well, was it

wrong of me?' Was I so repulsive to him that he couldn't bear my touch?

He didn't answer, and left me at the entrance. Behind me I heard the discreet sounds of the table being cleared.

Faith married Charles Snow six weeks after my own wedding. And while hers was a hurried affair, as was mine, it was far less auspicious: a simple exchange of vows at the church, with a tiny reception afterwards. Poor Mrs Waterton — she must have regretted the day she opened her home to guests. Within less than a year she had had to extinguish the flames that the outspoken and untameable Mrs Liston had fanned, arrange my wedding, then deal with the terrible social implications that befell her due to the scandal caused by Faith and Charles.

When Faith's father arrived in Calcutta, three weeks after I was married, it was said that Mr Snow had already proposed, and Faith had accepted. I heard all of this at second hand, as Faith had not answered any of my invitations to call. Daily my thoughts went to her. I missed her, and refused to believe she would abandon our friendship so completely. I sometimes found myself thinking of how she would laugh over some small incident, or enjoy hearing about a book I was reading. I had conversations with her in my head.

When he arrived, Faith's father forbade her to marry Mr Snow. At first no one knew why, but then rumour spread like a flooding river throughout the English enclave: Charles Snow was Eurasian, although he had hidden it until he and Faith had announced their betrothal. He had already told her of his heritage, she confided to me eventually, when we had begun to speak again, but she hadn't been aware of the gossip and discrimination it would herald. It was impossible

295

to know who had mentioned it first, and once confronted, Charles, an honourable man, did not deny it. Apart from his gleaming black hair, there was nothing in his appearance to suggest that his mother, who had died in childbed, was Indian. Mr Vespry was enraged by the slur he felt his daughter would cast on his family's good name by her union with a half-caste. It was reported that he had shouted at her, on the steps of the Calcutta Club, that if she chose to marry Charles he would disown her.

That was when Faith had come back to me. Without even a calling card she stood in my hall, gloveless, asking what she should do, her eyes tear-filled. Without speaking, I opened my arms and she came into them. I hugged her, and she returned the embrace. I felt a burden lifted from me, and although I sorrowed for her trouble, I rejoiced inwardly.

Once we were seated in the drawing room, and I had sent out the servants, I felt I could speak to her candidly. 'Do you love him, Faith?'

'Linny, I do. I never thought I could feel like this. Of course no one – absolutely no one – supports me. And although I so want you to, I will understand if you don't.' Her bottom lip was flaky and she bit continually at the loose skin with her small teeth. 'But somehow I sensed you would understand, and called on you, hoping you would admit me if you found me at your door. I was afraid to send a card and be rejected.'

'I will support you, Faith,' I said quietly. I knew better than most the need to follow one's own instinct. 'If a marriage with Charles is what you want, then of course,' I told her.

Her face crumpled with relief. 'I can't bear any longer not to have you as my friend, Linny, even though I would have accepted your decision not to have me back, after the way

296

I've treated you.' She wept, and I took my handkerchief from my sleeve and handed it to her – she appeared not to have brought even a reticule. 'I must have seemed ridiculous when you announced your marriage plans. I was so afraid—' She stopped, as if unsure whether to continue, then took a breath and plunged on. 'It was fear, my darling Linny, fear that I would be sent home. I had hoped and hoped that Charles would propose, and then you announced, so unexpectedly, that you would marry, and – and I'm sorry, Linny. Please forgive me. Since Charles asked me to be his wife, and I have known the true depth of his feelings for me, I feel as if I am a new person. I'm happy, Linny, happier than I've been for – well, I don't remember. I don't care about my father's threats. And I don't care that Charles has been lowered to the uncovenanted ranks, and that our manner of living will be much reduced. I realize, as I look upon his dear face, that I don't give a fig about all of that. I love him, and he loves me.' She gave a great, shuddering sigh.

I took her hands. 'Then you must marry him, Faith. How many times, after all, does one feel love, and have it returned?'

She attempted a shaky smile. 'I knew I was right to talk to you about this. I know I've been impossible since we left Liverpool, Linny. It's you who has been so brave, and so strong. No matter what I might have said to you in anger please know that there is no one I would rather have had with me on my journey. Can you forgive me?'

I smiled. 'Of course. And I'm so happy for you, Faith,' I told her. 'We shall always be friends.'

'But you are a senior lady and Charles . . . well, I will no longer be of your standing,' Faith said.

'I won't allow us to be pushed apart because of that.' I

snapped my fingers. 'That's what I care for what anyone might say of our friendship.'

She hugged me spontaneously. 'Isn't it marvellous, Linny, to be loved so deeply and truly? Just think. Soon we will both be memsahibs in Calcutta. Would you have ever dreamed of this life?'

'No,' I told her honestly. 'I wouldn't.'

So Faith chose Charles over her allowance, her inheritance and a return to her old life in Liverpool. I liked him. He was unassuming and had a quiet appeal. He had been employed as a commissioner in one of the Company's smaller offices, but immediately after the disclosure of his heritage he had been reduced to the uncovenanted ranks, his salary a fraction of what he had formerly commanded. As soon as they were wed most of the English community snubbed Faith, and cards requesting her presence at the finer events ceased to arrive. Social rank and the invitations it brought had been important to her, but I hoped she could surmount that, buoyed by the strength she must now draw from Charles. With him I saw her blossom.

But I made a mistake in trying to include them in our circle. Somers and I had been married for four months, and he often let me draw up the invitation list, choosing from a selection of names he supplied. Tonight I had invited two former Fishing Fleet girls, whom Faith and I knew well. They were now betrothed to young men of whom Somers approved, and who had worked with Charles before his recent fall from grace. There was also an older couple Somers had known for most of his time in India, who would act as chaperones for the engaged couples. I invited Charles and Faith without mentioning it to my husband.

As Mr and Mrs Charles Snow were announced in the drawing room, where the rest of our party stood, a hush fell over the room. I hurried to greet them. Faith looked fetching in a flowered poplin dress, the underskirt a rich brown-red, which, of course, emphasized her hair. But her eyes were wide and uncertain; Charles stood, poker-straight, at her side.

'Please, please, come in,' I said, and turned to look back into the room. There were no welcoming smiles, no murmurs of greeting. Somers turned his back, and spoke loudly to one of the other gentlemen of an inconsequential matter, setting the tone for the evening.

It was miserable; I struggled to include them in the conversation at the table, but they, too, were stilted and uncommunicative. I saw Charles's dark, intelligent stare across the table, and was ashamed that I had put him and Faith in this position.

When the last of the guests had departed, Somers turned on me. 'How *dare* you do that to me?' he growled. 'Of all the asinine, inappropriate—'

'Don't tell me that you go along with the rest of them, Somers,' I said wearily. 'You told me yourself that you had even considered courting Faith when we first arrived. And it was she who brought me here, who—'

But he cut me off. 'Those bloody half-castes! They're all alike, you know, with that damn chee-chee accent, bowing and scraping and stabbing you in the back whenever they get a chance. Mixed blood,' he sneered. 'If you've been touched by the tar-brush, you can't hide it. It will come out in one way or another.'

'You had no difficulty accepting Charles before you knew,' I said. 'And he speaks no differently from you.'

'I always suspected there was something off about him,' Somers said, 'just as I knew you were concealing something when I first met you. I've a nose for deceit. You must know that about me by now.' He turned to go to his room, but stopped. 'Don't ever humiliate me like that again. Do you understand me?'

'Yes,' I answered.

He stood there a moment longer, staring at me, and then, with long, angry strides, went to his room and slammed the door.

The next day I sent a chit to Faith, asking her to call in the early afternoon, after lunch, when Somers would have returned to work. She sent it back with a large 'YES' written across it.

When she arrived, I took her hands. 'I'm sorry for last night, Faith. Please forgive me. I could not have imagined you would be so shabbily treated.'

Faith squeezed my hands. 'It's all right. Charles didn't want to come, but I convinced him, pouting and putting on an act to make him feel guilty, telling him you were my only real friend in Calcutta, and how I would never forgive him if we didn't attend. Now I wish I hadn't. Like you, I had no idea that our presence would be so inappropriate.'

We sat down together on the sofa, still holding hands. At that moment there seemed little more to say.

15 June 1831

Dear Shaker,

Thank you, thank you, thank you! When I received your letter I cannot tell you how my heart tumbled and raced. I immediately recognized Mr Worth's distinctive hand. It is kind of him to scribe for you. Does he still do all the lettering for the announcements?

I was saddened to hear of your mother's death. I can well understand how difficult this last year must have been for you, with her needing constant attention. How kind that Celina Brunswick and her mother paid a condolence call. Faith has often spoken highly of Celina, citing her many good qualities and her musical ability.

I have been a married woman – a memsahib – for all of four months. My husband, Somers, has family wealth, which allowed him to purchase a home for us in Chowringhee within two months of our marriage. The area is one of the spaciously planned districts of Calcutta, one that attempts to catch the cooling wind off the river and is shaded by natural vegetation. The house is a stucco villa set in a verdant garden. It is really quite lovely, but too large and echoing. Somers delights in the decoration, filling the rooms with English furniture, rugs and artefacts, which hold less appeal for me.

But I love the wide verandahs, at the front and back of the house. They have proved essential in the Hot Season, which is full upon us. There are blistering winds now, the precursor, I've been warned, to the monsoons that will arrive within the month. The sun, which I welcomed on my arrival in India, has now become a threatening, brutal master. The air is bright, brilliant, and washes out the colour from the trees, the roads, the gardens, the rocks and even our faces. Surfaces are impossible to touch; the hurtful edge of the sun is everywhere. I can feel its sharpness against my skin. There is debilitating humidity. I am covered with heat rash. There are insects that defy explanation. Even my words, when I have the energy to speak, seem to melt as they leave my mouth, dissolving as if made of sugar, and carrying little meaning.

But in spite of this cruel god, the more intense the heat, the sweeter the fruits, the heavier and more fragrant the blossoms.

I stay inside my lair with all manner of devices to keep cool. There are the ever-present overhead fans – the *punkahs* – although they do little but churn the thick, hot air. The *tatties* – reed screens over all the windows and doorways – are constantly splashed with water in the hope of cooling the breeze that blows through. And I also have a thermantidote – a contraption intended to dispense cooled air through a room – but for all its deafening roar it helps little.

When Somers is at home, we are kept busy with social visits. There is a kind of forced jollity in the business of calling cards and daytime visits between eleven and two – when the sun is at its highest – that I find vapid. But when Somers is away, which he is, frequently, pig-sticking in the jungle or visiting one of the other Company presidencies in Madras or Bombay, oh, Shaker, my Indian world opens, although I must keep secret my activities. And perhaps this is how I am, and how I feel most comfortable. I see clearly now that much of my life has been a secret, and may always be so.

With Somers gone, I send my regrets to all invitations that come in and instead stay at home, going barefoot, pushing aside the *dhuri* rugs and savouring the coolness of the stone floor. I read endlessly – there is a small but adequate library at the Club, and I am a frequent visitor.

I give no orders for meals, which sends the cook into deep sulks, and I know he is offended. But I prefer to avoid the ever-present meat – venison, beef, mutton, pork, veal and poultry – and the rich English food that our poor *biwarchi* tries so hard to provide, often with curious results.

The servants think me mad, I'm sure, except for my beloved *ayah*, Malti (her name means small, fragrant flower, and suits her perfectly). They pretend they are not staring at me dancing about the house barefoot, in one of Malti's saris, my hair down, living on rice and almonds, musk-melon, mangoes and an occasional curry. They have also grown bold enough to carry on – at my urging – brief conversations with me in Hindi when the 'Burra Sahib' is not at home. My command of the language has grown remarkably.

I have also learned to ride. Again, I had to do this in secret – how could I explain to the fine English ladies of Calcutta that I had never ridden? Even the smallest English child here becomes competent at an early age. I sought out a stable away from the Club, with a patient Eurasian handler who doesn't question my inexperience, and within a few months I found myself managing quite ably in the saddle. I have not yet tackled jumps or anything more ambitious than a trot, canter or gallop, but I can ride passably enough not to draw attention to myself.

At other times I creep about Calcutta on the pretext of shopping. What do I care for shopping, Shaker? You know me well enough to understand that this pastime, so precious to the English memsahib, holds no interest for me. Instead, I give Malti, my confidante, who seems to adore me for no other reason than that she has been given the task of caring for me, a shopping list, a large basket and a chit. She rides off to the Hogg market and collects what is needed for the next few meals, or goes to Taylor's Emporium, with its wide clean aisles of gleaming silverware, sparkling china, crystal, jewellery and all manner of things English. She feels important and happy doing this, and tells me she is the envy of her counterparts, whose memsahibs would never entrust to them such decisions.

And while Malti does the shopping, Shaker, I explore. I go to the open bazaars. The main one is Bow Bazaar, with its cheerful, if squalid profusion of stalls, and, oh – I have seen items I didn't know existed, items never found in all the books I studied before arriving. There are curious idols and strange fabrics, pungent, aromatic spices, rich gums, and large glass bottles of oil and rosewater encased in wicker. There is pure ivory from Ceylon and rhinoceros hide from Zanzibar. I am safe; there is an unspoken – and, I suspect, false – respect for all memsahibs here. False, because the Indians have no choice. It is not a respect born of admiration, but relates to the colour of our skin. This, to me, is disturbing, and yet I have come to understand that India is a country that links worth with the level at which one is born.

Much as life is in England. In this one respect only, there is a similarity.

I am assuming that you are aware Faith married not long after me. I know that she wrote of it to Celina, and I hope she may have passed on the news to you. I see her as much as possible. Her health appears rather fragile. Her husband, Mr Snow, is a kind, serious yet thoughtful man, and adores her. In spite of the happiness of her marriage, Faith finds the chaos of the Indian world difficult to manage. She talks about making the journey home for a visit next year, which I think would be a wise choice, although she will have to build up her physical stamina to face that challenge.

Thank you again for writing, Shaker. I had tried not to lose faith in hearing from you since I left Liverpool – close to a year ago now. Your letter feels as if a door has swung open.

Again, Shaker, my deepest condolences on the loss of your mother.

Yours, as always,

Linny

PS In future correspondence, your letter will reach me directly if sent to Mrs Somers Ingram, which is the name by which I am now addressed.

There were parts of my life that I didn't describe to Shaker. I didn't tell him of my visits to the cemetery at St John's churchyard, for fear he would think me morbid. It seemed that, for some English women, grave-visiting was a compulsive pastime. 'The Glory Here Lies All Buried' was written over the graveyard gate. I found a peacefulness there that brought me closer to memories of my mother and my little girl. Many – oh, far too many – babies were buried there: dead of cholera, dead of enteritis, dead of smallpox, dead of fever, dead of . . . the inexplicable yet terrible grasp of India. But in spite of the sadness, I felt at peace there. After the rains started, and the stones had been washed so that the lettering stood out clear of dust, and green sprouted from crevices in them, it felt a holy place.

There were other things I witnessed of which I didn't tell Shaker. One was a suttee. Although prohibited by the government the year before I arrived, I chanced upon the smouldering remains of a pyre where a widow had lit herself and burned to death. Judging by the two small boys weeping at the pile of dark ash and grisly human remains, she had been young. I looked at the children, wondering if they were old enough to understand that she had sacrificed herself not only for their father – her death ensuring his successful rebirth – but for them. With their mother gone to take her place at her husband's feet in heaven, they were assured that the whole of the family property had passed on to them. I wondered if they had any sisters and, if so, what their fate would be.

Another afternoon, as I stood in the shade between two temples, I watched a crowd of men dragging another, his arms and legs bound tightly with strips of cloth, to a clearing between the shrines. He was forced to kneel and place his head on a large wooden block. '*Choor, choor*,' murmured the quickly gathering crowd, and I knew him to be a thief.

Next, a mahout led a docile elephant, ceremonially painted, bells jangling on his massive ankles, into the clearing. An uncharacteristic silence fell over the assembly. At a word of command from the mahout, the huge wrinkled leg rose over the thief's head. Slowly, almost delicately, with a tinkling of bells, the massive foot descended and crushed the man's skull into the stained wooden block. I couldn't look away. The reverent silence continued as the elephant was led off and the crowd thinned. Immediately two *sudras*, untouchables, hurried to drag away the body, a pulpy mess attached to the neck. The remaining throng made a wide path around them in their rags. They passed in front of me, hauling their gruesome cargo, and I vomited neatly and quietly, then wiped my mouth on the edge of my skirt and walked to the alley that would lead me back to the bazaar.

There I bought a paper pack of *pan*, and chewed the ground mixture of spices, leaves and betel nuts to settle my stomach. I watched a withered blind man play a sitar: his music was unstructured, yet ethereal. When he had finished he tilted his head to the sky and I saw tears streaming down his filthy face as a wide smile creased it. I squatted beside him and pressed what was left of the *pan* into his hand. He took mine, ran his fingers over my palm and wrist, and whispered a toothless blessing. I felt a shiver of repulsion and yet – and yet I believe the other emotion was envy. Yes. He wanted nothing more than his sitar and the warmth of that patch of sunlight. He knew his place in his world, and he accepted it.

Although the course of my life had brought me to a secure place – a lovely home in which I wanted for nothing materially – I continued to feel, often, at odds with it. What was the empty ache that haunted me, despite the luxury of my life?

As I walked away from the old man, I berated myself for my selfish thoughts.

CHAPTER TWENTY-FOUR

I WORRIED ABOUT FAITH. She and Charles were forced to live in the rather run-down area for the uncovenanted civil servants that I had often passed through. Their home was at the furthest end of Chitpore Road, in a row of low, poorly constructed bungalows with weedy growth sprouting from wide cracks in the outer walls.

The Hot Season was growing intolerable when I first visited Faith. The bungalow was small but neat, filled with evidence of Charles's life in India, unlike the homes in Garden Reach, Alipur and Chowringhee I frequented. It was simple and unadorned in a pleasing way, with its rattan furniture and small brass tables, the white walls bare except for a few woven hangings, and rush matting fragrant underfoot. In spite of her step down the social ladder, Faith appeared happy in this first flush of marriage with Charles, and enjoyed playing house. There was no verandah, and the back opened on to a courtyard. With no chance of any breeze the house was suffocating.

She had the bare minimum of servants: a thin, rabbity girl of about twelve as her *ayah*, the girl's younger brother as a general cleaner, and an elderly man who shuffled about without accomplishing anything. She shared a cook, a *dhobi*, and a *durzi* with three other bungalows.

As time passed and debilitating heat descended over Calcutta, Faith's answers to my chits, asking her to visit my home during the day, or whether I might call on her, began to contain her regret and apology, citing a variety of reasons, from the heat to her feeling poorly or a problem with a servant. When I hadn't seen her for three weeks, I took it upon myself to visit her, in spite of the afternoon sun.

I was met at the door by the *ayah*, who ushered me into the tiny drawing room. She went to fetch Faith, and as I waited in the room, light-headed from lack of air, I couldn't help but notice that white ants crawled within the matting on the floor, and there was a sour odour of unwashed linen. The flounce of the *punkah* showed a layer of dust. Dirty plates and cups sat on the small round teak dining-table, visible through an open doorway. Finally Faith came in. She was pale, her clothing rumpled, her hair falling from its pins.

'Hello, Linny,' she said. 'I was trying to stay cool by lying very still. Please forgive the state of my home. We haven't been entertaining at all. It's too hot.'

'Of course. Who can deal effectively with anything in this scorching air?' I said. We sat, and she asked the *ayah* to bring us some cold tea. With it the girl produced a plate of biscuits. She smelt strongly of the *ghee* she used to oil her hair. Faith didn't glance at the plate, but I noticed the biscuits had a mealy appearance.

We attempted small-talk, but Faith seemed confused, giving the *ayah* instructions for the cook, then changing them twice. She ordered the cleaner to spend time on small, unimportant tasks while flies swarmed over the dirty dishes. When I announced that I would be leaving within the half-hour, she paced about the room, looking out of the windows.

'Are you sure you're all right, Faith?' I asked. I saw that she wore no stays or petticoats, and her *écru* dress hung limply, sweat-stained under the arms and down the back. I changed at least four times daily in this heat: Malti prepared cool baths for me, and had fresh clothing waiting.

She looked at me distractedly. 'Yes. I just thought Charles might arrive home earlier than usual. I hoped so. I don't like being here alone.'

'You're not alone. You have the servants, and the other women in the courtyard. Do you not visit them?'

She looked away from the window. 'I just meant . . . I hope he arrives before you leave.' She came closer. 'It's the servants. They're always watching me, and I feel they don't like me.'

'Perhaps you could come out more,' I said. 'I know it's hard in this heat, but it doesn't do to stay shut up alone every day.'

'I'm not invited to the same events as you, Linny.'

'But I often go out with Malti to do other things. They have a small library at the Calcutta Club.'

'Charles is not allowed to be a member.'

'But I could take you there, as a guest.'

'It's all too wearying,' Faith said then, and when I left, twenty minutes later, she was distracted, fussing about the littered table and worrying that Charles's dinner would not be to his liking.

Although there were aspects of my life in Calcutta that I chafed against, there was much that I loved. I spent many happy hours at the library. Mr Penderel, the elderly man who supervised it, came to know me – I think he was pleased to see someone come through the doors, as there was never anyone else about when I arrived, every fourth or fifth day, to take out another two books. After a few months he began to put aside for me the volumes newly arrived by ship. The first time he saw me inspecting the binding of a particularly lovely book, he frowned. 'I assure you, Mrs Ingram, there are no mites in the binding. I check each one thoroughly before I put it on the shelves, and again when someone takes it out and returns it. I care greatly about preserving the books in this climate.'

'Oh, I wasn't looking for mites, Mr Penderel. I was looking at the detail. There's a curious stitch just here,' I showed him, 'that I haven't seen before.'

'Well, now,' Mr Penderel said, his eyes lighting, 'are you interested in books for themselves?'

'Oh, yes,' I told him. 'I've studied the way in which books are created for – well, since I was very young. I've always enjoyed it.'

Mr Penderel hastened to bring out a variety, and we spent a good half-hour discussing the finishing and stamping. I found myself more stimulated by that conversation than by any other I had had in a long time.

Visits to the library, seeing Faith, and Somers's frequent departures from our home for his own pleasures made me believe – in those first months of my marriage – that I was as close to quiet contentment as I might ever be.

18 July, 1831
Dear Shaker,
The end of June brought the red hot loo – the wind from the west. It carries a fine, silty dust that is impossible to escape; it is as insidious as a smell, finding its way indoors through cracks and fissures. It lodges in

my eyes, ears, nostrils, between my teeth. It seems my senses, too, are choked with it. Even the servants appear restless.

At its most severe the force of the wind is such that flimsy buildings are torn from the ground and trees bent almost in half. It is said that it brings madness for the English, and perhaps it does – a temporary insanity, for the incessant moaning burns into the brain in what I imagine might be similar to brain fever. When it stops everyone stands still, listening, for the quiet now appears to carry a threat.

With the end of the winds come the first monsoons, which descend without warning. It's as if the skies have opened and unceremoniously dumped buckets of warm water over the city. The streets run with muddy rivers, making walking almost impossible, with the heavy, trailing skirts, the layers of petticoats and crinolines I am forced to wear when I leave the house. The daily downpours last for a few hours, then stop as abruptly as they started. The hot, saturated air is difficult to breathe, and at times I feel as if I am trying to catch my breath through a piece of soaked gauze. After a short respite of surprisingly blue sky and the appearance of a floating, shimmering sun, new clouds gather, the blue turns an ominous slate grey and within moments the monsoon returns with renewed force.

Green mould, as bright and glistening as emerald, grows overnight and covers anything made of paper, cloth or leather even in the house. I learned what the mysterious stack of tin-lined boxes I found in one corner of an empty bedroom were for, and now store my clothing in them. If no callers are expected, the servants cover all the furniture with sheets. I spend most of my time in the verandah off my bedroom.

Flies swarm through the open windows by the dozen, and an assortment of flying, creeping and whirring creatures seem born from the wet air. Last night at dinner I recognized silverfish, white ants, stink beetles, caterpillars and centipedes all working their way over and around the table. It is difficult, of course, to eat. The fluttering begins over the food the moment it is uncovered, in spite of a horde of boys with fly-whisks. A servant stands behind me with a tablespoon, with which he scoops off the larger beetles and bugs that land on my shoulders and hair. Somers has taken to having most of his meals at the scrupulously clean and almost sealed gentlemen's lounge in the civil service building.

I could never admit this to anyone but you, Shaker, but I find many of the insects fascinating. Some of the moths are graceful and delicate, with wings of spun gold. I trapped a formidable centipede, green and yellow striped and over ten inches long, and kept him in a glass jar for over a week. Every morning I dropped in leaves and watched with respectful awe as he munched his meal. Even the flies, Shaker — the flies! They are not the common bluebottle of England. Many have bodies of deep burgundy or rich green.

I have learned to swathe the bed in voluminous folds of sheer muslin, and before I climb in every night, I pull back the sheets and perform a thorough examination to make sure I won't join a sleepy scorpion. Then I check the heavy linen canopy over the bed, assuring myself that it is firmly in place. I was awakened most unpleasantly one night when a dung beetle the size of a walnut dropped on to my face from the rafters on the first and last time that I was careless in my nightly inspection. I have also discovered, with not a little dismay, that a bath sponge makes an ideal home for a scorpion.

I take my dose of quinine – a horridly large spoonful – each morning, shuddering at the bitter taste. I have been warned that malaria strikes most often in the Wet Season. Somers fell prey to the disease during his first year here (more than five years ago), and is subject to bouts of it.

When he is ill he prefers I stay away, and the servants attend to him. But I have heard his moans, his whispers that his bones are being twisted by a huge and violent hand, and of the relentless kettledrum keeping up a beat in his head until he thinks he might go mad. Although he has spoken little of his parents to me, in his delirium he cries for his dead mother as if he were a child. And in the next instant he curses a cruel father, whose memory haunts him.

During his last attack he shivered so violently that he chipped one of his teeth. Poor man!

On that note I shall close, with the promise to write again, dear Shaker.

Yours,

Linny

I avoided writing more than a few lines about Somers, for what was there to say? I didn't believe, at the start, that he was an evil man, simply one who was totally self-absorbed. We continued to treat each other as disinterested, though polite neighbours who shared the same house. Occasionally he spoke cruelly to me, hurling insults, but only after he had drunk more than usual, or perhaps was disappointed in a rendezvous. The following day he would apologize with a small gift – some trinket or a piece of jewellery, something impersonal that he could send one of his coolies to Taylor's Emporium to purchase. I saw, at these moments, that Somers understood that his behaviour had been uncalled-for, and although a genuine smile or kind word would have meant more to me than a useless novelty, it seemed the only way he knew how to tell me he was sorry.

At odd moments I would find him studying me, but he would always look away quickly, denying, when I asked him, if something were on his mind that he wished to speak of. I sensed a deep underlying unhappiness in him, which he covered with charm and bravado. Once I tried to ask him about his childhood in London, about his mother and father, but he refused to speak of his past.

It would appear that he didn't wish to discuss any aspects of his life, not only past but present as well. And, likewise, he wished to know nothing of how I spent my time. When I asked him about his work, he said it would be of little interest to me. When I tried to tell him of the books I was reading, and of my conversations with Mr Penderel at the Club's library, he appeared bored. On the odd evening when we found ourselves alone together we spoke of the household and the servants, of plans for entertaining and social occasions to which we had been invited. We never spoke about matters of the mind or heart.

It was after the monsoons abated, and we were into the delightfully temperate Cool Season, that the downward spiral of our marriage began. I had been in India almost a year.

Somers had taken advantage of the weather to accompany a few other men on a hunt, and had been gone almost three weeks. He came home burnt a plethora of shades and immensely weary, sullen at the lack of trophy, blaming the incompetence of his coolies to beat the bushes. He recounted that although there had been a rich assortment of game – tigers, panthers, samburs, pigs – the coolies had been easily frightened after one was killed by the unexpected swipe of an injured tiger. 'Damn cowards,' he added. 'They clambered up trees at the first answering rustle to their beating after that. Let the big game get away.'

'But surely they had reason to be—'

'There's no excuse, Linny. It's a job they're paid to do.' We were in the drawing room, with its hushed, formal atmosphere. He paced in front of the damask sofa where I sat with the book I had been reading before his arrival. He was in the worst temper I had ever witnessed, and I kept quiet while he ranted about his miserable trip. Finally he shouted for the servants, and many came running. He demanded that bath water be brought to his room, and gave instructions for a hearty English meal to be prepared for dinner, ordering many courses, which included a saddle of lamb, roast beef and gravy with Yorkshire pudding. He took a bottle of port from the cabinet and disappeared for the rest of the afternoon.

In the early evening he invited me to join him for dinner, and the meal was served with its usual pomp on Sèvres dishes and polished silver. Somers kept a glass of watered madeira beside his plate, sipping from it with every bite, and summoning the *khitmutgar* continually to top it up.

As he cut his meat rather clumsily, chewing slowly but with relish, I took a sip of water from my delicate crystal goblet and pushed my slab of pink beef around the plate.

Eventually Somers looked up. 'Meat not cooked well enough for you?' His words were slurred; I had never seen him quite so intoxicated. I wondered if it was the beginning of another malaria attack.

'I ate a late tiffin, and this is a heavy meal.'

'Well, call for something else. Rahul,' he said, to a boy passing through the room carrying a stack of clean napkins, 'take Mrs Ingram's plate away.'

The boy looked at the table. His eyes widened, and he lowered his head.

'Take her plate, Rahul,' Somers instructed again.

His head still down, Rahul backed away.

'Somers, you know he can't,' I said. 'Call for someone else to—'

Instantly Somers pushed back his chair with a loud scrape and jerked towards the boy. He grabbed the thin arm roughly. The napkins fluttered to the floor like released doves. 'When I tell you—'

I ran to Rahul's side and tried to pull Somers's hand off his arm. 'Leave him alone.'

'He must obey when I give him an order.' His neck and face were a dull red, and his grip tightened. 'This one doesn't like to take orders. I found that out earlier today, didn't I, Rahul?'

So it was more than the issue of the plate. My heart went out to the boy, who was no more than fourteen. His whole body was shaking with fright. I hated to think what might have happened to him only hours earlier, when I had imagined Somers to be resting. 'Somers,' I said quietly, 'leave him.'

'How dare you defy me in front of the servants?'

'He's a Hindu. He can't touch a plate that holds beef. You

317

know that,' I said, my voice still low, my fingers working at Somers's hand. 'You could beat him until he was senseless and he still wouldn't take it. Fetch Gohar, Rahul. Gohar can take the plate. Somers, let him *go*.' I said the final word with more force that I had ever used since Somers and I had married.

In the next instant Somers smiled at me. An unnatural grimace. Then he dropped Rahul's arm. The boy fled, his shirt-tails flying. In seconds another boy emerged and silently took my plate. The rest of the servants in the dining room – the *punkah-wallah*, *khitmutgar* and the boys with their fly-whisks – continued as if nothing had happened.

We sat down. Methodically Somers shovelled in forkful after forkful of his dinner. I picked a fig from the plate of fruit and nuts sitting under the soft candlelight in the middle of the table. I took a bite, but the fig was overripe, and my throat constricted. I looked at the fine spray of bloody juice from his meat on the front of Somers's cream silk waistcoat, at the perspiration trickling from his sideburns.

We sat there, in silence but for the flutter of a moth over the candelabra, until Somers had finished his meal. Then he left the table without a word.

I thought the incident was over as I prepared for bed. But just as Malti had helped me into my nightdress Somers came in and, leaning against the doorjamb, dismissed her with one barked word. She slipped away, having to turn sideways awkwardly in the doorway to avoid brushing against him. He had never come to my bedroom, nor I to his, at any time during our marriage.

'Somers,' I said, 'why . . .' I stopped. From behind his back he had pulled a riding crop.

'Should you *ever* humiliate me in front of anyone again,

318

you'll think back to this night and pray for it – for this will be only a warning.'

'What do you mean? You're not going to whip me, Somers,' I said, with confidence. There were at least twenty servants within earshot.

'I'm not?' he asked. He waited a heartbeat, then stepped closer, smiling as if reading my mind. 'You think the servants will help? Have you learned nothing about this country? Are you so blind as to believe that anyone cares what happens to you? That any of these subservient curs would stop me controlling my own wife?'

I opened my mouth, but before I could say anything he had grabbed the front of my nightdress and yanked me to him. I struck his chest with my fists, but I was no match for his strength; he was driven by a rage fuelled with alcohol. He threw me on to the bed and an unlit lamp crashed to the floor, spilling coconut oil, filling the room with its odour. My dressing-table was overturned. Effortlessly he flipped me over, his knee in the small of my back, pinning me against the mattress. Then, holding my wrist with one hand, he used the other to whip me with the stinging leather thongs of the crop. I felt the thin fabric of my nightdress shred, and my skin split. He whipped me as I screamed at him, cursing him in the worst language I knew – the language of my old friends, Helen and Annabelle, Dorie, Lambie and Skinny Mo. He stopped, suddenly, and I glanced over my shoulder at him. His heaving chest and contorted face ran with sweat. The odd, glazed look in his eyes was, I realized with a shudder, one of sensual intimacy as he stared down at my flayed, bloody back. Then he flung down the crop, unbuttoned his trousers and pulled up my hips so that I was forced on to my knees. I struggled and wrenched myself violently away from

319

him as he fumbled with his clothing. Then I crouched, facing him, as I held the bedcover to me. He looked down at himself, muttered a curse and turned away. The mattress dipped as he half fell off the bed.

'I haven't the energy to spill my seed into you,' he said, getting to his feet, then tucking in his shirt, buttoning his trousers, smoothing his hair. 'And I'd never sully myself with you. Rahul's tight little Hindu arse is a hundred times cleaner than you'll ever be. I should use the end of my riding crop instead, although I wouldn't want to pollute it either.'

He left, and I knew that the bargain we had made was more than I had foreseen. I was his prisoner, as surely as I had been Ram Munt's.

The next day Somers offered an apology in the usual way. I was sitting on my verandah when he appeared in late afternoon. It had been difficult for me to move before noon without pain. I knew the deep lashes would leave scars. Malti had hurried into my room after Somers had crashed out. She wept, moaning in Hindi, as she washed and dressed the wounds. Her hands were soothing, working with a salve that smelt of almonds. Once she had settled me she sat on the floor beside the bed and sang softly to calm me until I fell into an uneasy sleep. She was still there, her head against the side of the bed, when I woke in the shadowy early morning. Now Somers carried in a large wicker basket and set it in front of me.

'What is it?' I asked, not wanting to look at him. The basket trembled, and there were wet, snuffling sounds. In the next instant the lid was pushed open, and a young dog looked out, his wet tongue flopping out of one side of his mouth. I took his small, bony black head in my hands and stared into his amber eyes.

'He's a crossbreed of sorts. I can't pronounce the Indian word, but it means a complicated mixture of hand-picked sire and bitch. Apparently they thrive in India, with their sturdy disposition and short hair. They're not subject to mange, as our dogs here. They're ferocious but loyal.' Somers's voice was quiet, tinged with something I didn't recognize. Was it embarrassment, or remorse? 'They don't breed well,' he went on, 'and it's difficult to get one without a wait. I was lucky to find this one. Quite a bit of terrier in him, I would think, judging by his wiry build. There's a half-caste who raises them for the English here.'

I pulled the dog out of the basket and into my lap, wincing as I moved. Although the dog was small, he was leggy and awkward, his hind legs scrambling and clawing for a foothold in my skirt as he put his paws on my chest and licked my face.

'He has a Hindu name, but you can call him whatever you like. He's been weaned for a few weeks now, and will learn to obey easily, the breeder assured me.' He leaned forward and scratched the puppy's ears. 'They're wonderful trackers.'

The dog's stub of a tail wiggled with furious intensity. I looked at Somers. His eyes were veined with pink, and the skin around them was pouched. I saw that he had gained weight since we'd married, and his face was bloated. He looked truly miserable, too, which stemmed not only from the alcohol he'd consumed. I knew he was ashamed of what he'd done.

Still, I didn't thank him for the pup. I would never again thank him. I wasn't grateful for anything he had to offer, and had decided, after a minor altercation the week before when I had declined a flagon of toilet water, that I would refuse all other gifts.

But I wanted the puppy. I had never had anything of my own before.

I named him Neel, Hindi for blue: his glossy coat was so black it had a blue sheen.

CHAPTER TWENTY-FIVE

12 March 1832

My dearest Shaker,

Thank you for your last letter. I was interested to read of your growing interest in the new homoeopathic approach to healing and pleased to hear that it is being embraced in England. There is much use of plants for various ailments among the Indians. If you would be interested, I could ask Malti to give me more specific information about those she considers to have healing qualities.

I am leaving for a hill station in a few days, and want to put this letter in the post before I depart. I'm making the journey to Simla, far in the Himalayan mountains, and will stay there for the duration of the Hot Season. My first experience with it last year made me grateful that Somers suggested I spend the next few months away from the dust and heat of Calcutta. This time at a hill station, I was instructed, is the thing we memsahibs 'must' do, if one's husband can afford it and the lady's constitution is hearty enough to withstand the difficult journey – travelling 1200 miles north, first on the Hooghly, Ganges and Yamuna rivers by *budgerow*, and then a long slow march up into the mountains by *dooli*. Summer in the cool green of the mountains is, obviously, most desirable. From what I have gathered, memsahibs apparently think little of leaving their husbands to swelter in the cities and plains while they enjoy the thin, fragrant air.

I am very pleased that Faith has agreed to come. Somers was insistent that I travel with a companion. There is a certain irony in this, is there not?

But I am troubled for Faith, Shaker. She appears unwell in a profound sense. At times I wonder if she has inherited a form of melancholy from her mother, although she refuses to speak of it when I gently question her health. Although Charles is dear to her, the circumstances surrounding their marriage have only added to the considerable strain of her malaise. When I think of the lovely, laughing girl I first met in Liverpool my heart is heavy. I really do fear for her, and wish there were something I could do to help her.

I am hoping this time in Simla will revive her.

Your faithful friend,

Linny

PS Guggal (Indian bedellium) has a fragrant resin that is extracted and used for those bloated with their own fluids, and also for painful swelling of the joints.

When I had first suggested that Faith accompany me to Simla, telling her and Charles that Somers had already rented a bungalow (true), had arranged and paid for the journey (true) and agreed that Faith could accompany me (a lie), Charles urged her to take the opportunity. It was unspoken that he couldn't afford to send her. She said she couldn't bear to be apart from him, but I knew that Charles didn't want her spending another Hot Season in Calcutta. She had fallen victim to a strange ague as well as boils and then shingles during that time last year, which had only worsened during the Wet Season. Her body had been covered in sores and racked by a fever that left her weak and wordless.

She recovered physically, but had lost the ability to chatter and smile. Instead she sat, wan and unmoving, in her chair by the window for hours at a time.

Charles had confided in me, after they had accepted the invitation to Simla for her, that he had feared she might not survive the approaching Hot Season in Calcutta, having so recently recovered from the ills of the previous year. Now he was jubilant at the thought of her spending months in the cool comfort of the Simla hills. He wanted her to be happy again, to smile, to read, argue and sketch the birds she loved to watch. I also suspected he thought that she might be more accepted in Simla without his presence. A perfect, albeit temporary solution, he called it.

But Somers was furious that I'd invited Faith. I'd known all along that he would be, and I would suffer the consequences, but I accepted it. I purposely didn't tell him that Faith would join me until the night before we were to leave. He was on his way to the Club when I stopped him at the door and informed him.

He frowned. 'No. As you well know, I've already arranged for Mrs Partridge to accompany you.' He turned his hat in his hands. His thumbs made deep imprints in the soft fabric. 'You had no right to take this upon yourself. I spoke to Colonel Partridge about it a good month ago, and Mrs Partridge was going anyway, so is quite willing to share a bungalow with you and be your—'

'And watch my every move, Somers?'

'– your companion. We agreed that you go to Simla with a companion. And now you're tarnishing the Ingram name by keeping up your association with that woman. You'll have to find a way to cut her out.' He put his hand on the doorknob as if the matter was concluded.

I pulled at his sleeve. 'It can't be done. I've invited her, and she's agreed to come, so it's settled. It will have to be the three of us, and you have no further say in it.' I held my breath. I had learned that any provocation brought out Somers's violence against me. And, for some inexplicable reason, I sometimes found myself goading him purposely. I knew what I was doing when I corrected him in mixed company, or ignored his wishes in some domestic request. It was as if I wanted to see how far I could push him before he reacted. I knew from his face when he was reaching his limit, yet I found a perverse pleasure in baiting him. I think now, looking back on my behaviour, that it was a way of drawing his attention – even if it brought me nothing more than trepidation and fear of physical pain. I wanted to reach him in some way, and perhaps this was the only way I could make him respond to me.

Now he grabbed me by the arm and swung me round. He punched my jaw with his knuckles and, as I fell, he left, slamming the door so hard that a gilt-framed painting of King William IV dropped from the wall, its glass smashing on the stone floor beside me.

The next morning, 15 March – the Ides of March – was hazy and warm. Faith, Charles, Muriel Partridge and I stood on the muddy riverbank, watching the trunks and boxes being loaded on to the long flat barge that would carry the servants and supplies for the next three weeks. A makeshift tent towards the back would serve as a sleeping shelter for them and the bargemen. Faith, Mrs Partridge and I would ride on a smaller *budgerow*, a flat combination of houseboat and barge.

Mrs Partridge was a sour, affected woman, but she had been to Simla for the last two years, and although I found her officious and unlikeable, she had been helpful in advising us of what we would need for the journey as well as during our stay. Her husband was as fussy and snobbish as she; his past position in the army – he'd retired the year before – had endowed him with a pompous self-righteousness. Somers and I had entertained them occasionally, and I'd taken an immediate dislike to them both.

We had three travel trunks apiece, and our clothing was packed neatly between flannel and wax cloth. We shared a huge chest of bed linen and towels, two cases filled with cooking and kitchen utensils, a large case containing my books, writing portfolios and Faith's sketch pads. We had also organized a trunk of warmer clothing for the servants to wear in the thin mountain air. We had brought our own *ayahs*, our own *dhobi*, two household sweepers, and hired a cook and two coolies for the journey.

'Looks like an awful amount of paraphernalia,' Charles said. 'I can't imagine conveying it uphill on those narrow mountain paths.'

Mrs Partridge sniffed. 'This is only half the amount most women take.'

'You will send a message back as soon as you can, saying you've arrived safely, won't you?' he asked Faith. His eyes looked young and anxious.

'I said I would,' Faith said. 'Please try not to worry.

Everyone goes to the stations now. There's really no danger.' I saw that her gloves were buttoned incorrectly, and that her hair had lost its shine.

We all looked at Mrs Partridge, who was standing at the edge of the bank shouting at a small man sitting on one of the trunks. 'Off! Get off there! You mustn't sit on our luggage!' The man ignored her. He crossed his arms over his chest and looked the other way as Mrs Partridge ranted at him.

'Besides,' I said, 'no one would dare bother us with Mrs Partridge about.'

Charles laughed boyishly until his eyes settled on my bruised jaw. He said no more, but cupped Faith's chin in his hand. I bent and fiddled with Neel's leash, but watched discreetly while he kissed Faith a final time. His mouth was gentle on hers, and afterwards he lowered his face to the crook of her neck, as if breathing in her scent one last time before they were parted. I saw Faith's arms tighten around him, and as they stood there, uncaring that they embraced in public view, the love they shared was clearly visible. I felt a brief stab of sorrow as I thought of how Somers and I had parted.

Early that morning he had paused at my room before he left for the office. I was still in bed. He stood at the doorway, making a show of buttoning his jacket. 'Well,' he said finally, 'safe journey.'

'I'm sure it will be.'

'Right, then.'

'Right,' I echoed, and he was gone.

Standing on the slippery mud at the edge of the Hooghly now, listening to the cries of the men loading barges all along the bank, I took a deep breath, then let it out slowly, pushing away that last image of my husband. I would be away for five months — a month each way for travelling, and three months at Simla. I was almost as excited at the prospect as I had been when we'd first arrived at the docks in Calcutta. Now I would truly discover the India I longed to know more of.

For the first few days, when the riverbanks weren't too covered in *moonge*, a tall, coarse grass as high as two men, I asked the agile bargemen to pole close to the bank so I could jump off and walk briskly. Neel loved to frisk at my side, although I kept him on his leash after he had dashed into the bush after a rodent. I begged Faith to walk with me, but she seemed content to sit on a small rattan chair tied to the barge and gaze at the river. I sensed her retreating further and further into herself, and was desperate for her to return to me. She was my one true friend, and even though I'd kept my past life a secret from her this, in an odd way, made me feel even closer to her. She had always believed in me, in who I was — or had become — and her trust filled me with a pride I had never previously known. I couldn't imagine my life without her; where once she had been an anchor for me, now I was keeping her steady when she was in danger of falling into darkness. I was determined that our time in the cool green of Simla would rouse her from this sorrow. Simla was sure to remind her of home, and then, perhaps, I would recognize the vibrant girl I had met at the butterfly lecture, which now seemed so long ago.

We had left the Hooghly and were travelling through the delta of the Ganges, a vast ragged swamp forest called the Sunderbans, which, I learned from one of our bargemen, meant beautiful forest. There was a different smell to the river now, something deeper and more earthy as we travelled north, and the breeze occasionally carried the tang of a dung fire from an unseen village. I continued to walk along the riverbank when I could, but Mrs Partridge noticed a bamboo pole with a bushy branch tied to it sticking out of the marshy ground I stepped through.

'You! You!' she shrilled, pointing at the man working the pole at the front of the barge. He was the leader, able to speak some English. He turned, and she redirected her finger at the bamboo. 'What is that?' she demanded.

The man glanced at it. 'Oh, Lady Sahib, that is merely a sign.'

'A sign of what?'

'Others are telling us that on that spot a tiger has taken a man for his dinner,' he replied nonchalantly.

'Stop the barge!' Mrs Partridge roared.

I smiled at Faith, and rolled my eyes.

'I am sorry, Lady Sahib, we cannot be stopping. Barge behind will run into us. We must always move ahead.'

'Mrs Ingram!' Mrs Partridge screamed, eyes wild. 'Get back here immediately!' At her shriek, a huge flock of tree bats that had been resting in a large jungle thorn near the bank flapped up in alarm and glided away.

I picked up Neel, ran alongside the barge and leaped on to it. 'Mrs Partridge, that bamboo looked as if it had been there for months. I'm sure we were in no danger,' I said.

'You're not stepping off this barge again,' Mrs Partridge said. 'What have I been thinking? The Sunderbans are home to the Royal Bengal tiger. I will not have you fall prey to some wild beast while you're under my supervision.'

'Your supervision?' I asked.

'Mrs Ingram,' Mrs Partridge said, puffing out her bosom, 'I am the senior lady on this journey, and I have taken it upon myself to ensure that the voyage is a safe one. You young women, relatively new to India, may have difficulty in accepting that behaviour you employed in England is not appropriate here. Now, there will be no more said about it. You will stay on the barge. And please, Mrs Ingram, pull your solar topee further over your face. Your nose is quite pink.'

We continued on the twisting, turning Ganges. I watched the wiry men poling gracefully for hour after hour, seemingly tireless. As we passed villages and meagre towns, the river became briefly a busy highway of barges and boats, always crammed with men and boys. Away from the population, we slid by small ricefields, walled with mud to keep in the water necessary for the plants' growth, and I watched women with their saris tucked about their hips, tending each plant with a clumsy wooden scoop. There were larger fields, yellow with mustard, and always jute, growing high and wild. Here the brown river was deserted and lonely under the glaring sun. I sometimes saw the pointed head of a mugger – the old water turtle – or the blunt-nosed face of a crocodile watching our progress with filmed eyes. For much of the time the river's still surface was broken only by bubbles from a submerged water creature or sudden groups of furiously paddling beetles.

Faith occasionally read, but didn't bring out her sketch books. One afternoon, while Mrs Partridge slept in the shade at the far end of the *budgerow*, and Faith and I sat in our chairs, she turned to me.

'When do you expect you will have a child, Linny? You and Somers have been married over a year now.'

I reached down to rub Neel's ears. 'I don't know.'

'Are you not anxious about it?'

I thought about the English children – those who had survived in spite of the adversity of their birth, the heat and disease. They were often pale and listless. They wore their

331

little solar topees and were shrouded in layers of clothing as they went for their riding and polo lessons, as they learned to order their *ayahs* about. There were no English children beyond the age of six in India, as Meg Liston had informed me shortly after our arrival in Calcutta. I thought about all those tiny graves in the churchyard at St John's. I thought about baby Frances under the holly bush. I knew, from the choice I had made, that I would never know the feeling of a baby's movement within me again.

'Linny? Do you long for a baby?' Faith went on, when I didn't answer immediately.

'I suppose it is in the hands of Fate,' I said, and was thankful for the distraction of a village as we rounded a bend in the river.

At the end of each day, when we stopped for the night and anchored the barges, the men lined up in front of Mrs Partridge, and she placed the agreed number of rupees in each man's calloused hand. They would jump off the *budgerow* and wade to the servants' larger barge, where they would be given a wooden bowl of curry, some chapattis and a plate heaped with fruit. If we stopped in the country, the men would simply curl up on the open deck of the servants' barge and sleep, keeping the mosquitoes at bay with smoking braziers; for our safety a few *chowkidars* were posted to keep an eye on our flotilla during the night hours. If we stopped near a town, some of the men would slip away silently after their meal. The next morning, although the right number of men in *dhotis* would be standing patiently in position at the sides of the *budgerow*, I noticed that, except for the head man, they were not always the same ones who had manoeuvred the long slender poles so deftly the day before.

At the junction of the Ganges and Yamuna rivers, our barges were directed on to the Yamuna. Eventually the sun played on the gilded domes, pointed spires and towers of the temples and mosques of Delhi as we floated by. I heard sounds – muted by the distance – that I knew well from Calcutta: bells and chants, cries and laughter. The *ghats* that led down to the river held crowds, some sitting, some standing, and in the water others bathed or washed clothes. A child on his father's shoulders waved at the *budgerow*; I waved back. The ivory of the buildings gave way to shades of yellow and orange in the lowering sun as the city disappeared from view.

The river grew ever quieter, eventually taking us to a tiny village, where the *budgerow* stopped. There were carts and animals for hire, as well as men to carry us. We had been travelling on the water for three weeks, and were ready now for the last part of this journey, on land.

An hour later we stood on the narrow road that appeared to lead straight up into the hills; the servants loaded the heavy trunks and cases on to hackeries pulled by lumbering bullocks.

'Get yourself into one of the *doolies*,' Mrs Partridge instructed. She climbed on to the straw-filled mattress of a one-person palanquin, and buttoned the curtains. Faith did the same. I got into my own, but pushed aside my curtains. Immediately I was thrown backwards as a *boyee* picked up each corner. The ride was mainly uphill, so it was impossible to sit up. I lay back, Neel beside me, head resting on my bodice, and watched the rough rock that formed a low wall alongside the path. Tiny red flowers and lichen grew out of the cracks, a sure sign of cooler temperatures.

Near a dry *nulla* the *boyees* started a chanting song, their voices broken by their huffing intake of dusty air. As I listened, I grasped, with surprise, that it was about Mrs Partridge, and consisted mainly of comments on her spreading backside and her voice, like that of a hyena in heat. I wondered how much Hindi she understood.

We spent six days being conveyed mile after mile up the precarious mountain paths, camping at night in primitive tents or the simple *dak* bungalows constructed out of thatch along the way by earlier English visitors.

I loved the nights, sitting outside our tents or thatched huts, before a fire. The twilight descended rapidly, the birds quieted and the forests around us were silent. The smell of woodsmoke was sweet and drove away the mosquitoes. The simple food tasted better than anything I'd eaten in the grand dining rooms of Calcutta. I slept well and woke in the mornings with a vigour I hadn't known possible.

Finally we approached Simla. We stopped at the bottom of the serrated foothills, breezes filtering down to us. Once the *boyees* had rested, we began the climb up. I couldn't stay in my *dooli*: I got out and walked. Scarlet rhododendrons blazed, bright as fire, across the hills. When we reached the edge of the town, on a mountain road sheltered by dark pine trees, I stared in fascination at its majesty.

Seven thousand feet above sea level, the hill station's houses had been built on a high, crescent-shaped ridge running along the base of Mount Jakko. They resembled English houses, some half-timbered cottages, yet had an Indian flavour. Chattering monkeys scrambled along the tiled roofs, while mynahs and magpies called from thick copses. I could see the spires of a church and the covered stalls of an Indian bazaar. Mrs Partridge knew exactly where to find our rented bungalow. Like many of the others, it bore a displaced English name: Constancia Cottage. Unlike the fussiness of our home in Chowringhee, it was small, built of lath and plaster, with a thatched roof. Inside there were three bedrooms, a dining room and a large sitting room with a fireplace, the first I had seen since leaving England. The kitchen, as usual, was a separate small building behind the house, close to the servants' huts. I ran to each window, throwing open the wooden shutters. From the sitting room and the tiny front bedroom I looked up at the gigantic Himalayas, snow-capped and regal against a soft blue sky. The dining room and two larger back bedrooms looked down through sloping tree-covered hills to brown plains and, glinting like thin ochre ribbons in the far distance, I saw the Sutlej and Ganges.

'Isn't this marvellous?'

'Yes, yes, it is,' Faith agreed, and spontaneously I grabbed her arms and tried to dance with her. But she stood rigid, her eyes fixed on the mountains.

Mrs Partridge glanced at me in annoyance, limped into the largest back bedroom and closed the door firmly. There was a heavy groan and the creak of a wooden bed. Faith moved, as if the pressure of my hands hurt her, and I let her go. She went to the other back bedroom and noiselessly closed the door.

CHAPTER TWENTY-SIX

20 May 1832

Dear Shaker,

How shall I describe Simla? I have written at great length about it in my journal, and I pray you will be able to see, hear and smell it as I try to explain this queerest of places to you by copying out sections I have put down — so that I will always remember it — and in this way show you the shape of my life now.

Perhaps it is simplest to say that the whole town is a curiously distorted vision of England, a wavering reflection in an Indian mirror. It is most definitely Chota Vilayat — the Little England of India, as it is often referred to here.

But in spite of this familiarity in a place so foreign, I love the beauty and freedom it affords me. If I wake early enough, I rush to my bedroom window to watch the distant peaks of the Himalayas catch fire, one after another, as they are touched by the rising sun. During the day I roam the promenade, a wide centre street known as the Mall, built on the one flat stretch of ground in the area. All along it there are scores of English shops and the bustling Indian bazaar. There is even a small bandstand, where once a week an enthusiastic, if off-key, orchestra plods through its repertoire for anyone who gathers to listen.

During the day, the Mall is filled with ponies and rickshaws waiting for hire. There are side-saddles available, should any of the memsahibs wish to ride. The *jhampanis* pulling the rickshaws are to be pitied on the steep village streets, and often it requires a joint effort of one or two pulling and another pushing behind to manoeuvre some of the heftier women up the hills. Some women choose to ride in a *dandy*, a strong cloth strung between bamboo poles. It became apparent to me, after my first few days in Simla, that the ladies don't change their habits when they leave the cities: they are determined not to exert themselves. I believe this inactivity is the cause of many of their ills, real and imagined.

I have taken to hiring a pony early every morning. There is a wide, pine-framed field called Annandale, where all manner of sports, picnics and fairs take place. Beyond the field there are low hills, and it is there that I go. When I return I often sit on one of the benches positioned along the Mall and listen to the blackbirds and cuckoos while I watch Simla's population.

Well-dressed white children in English sailor suits or dresses scamper about, attended by *ayahs* in snowy saris. Every day after tiffin a kindly old elephant with a magnificently decorated *howdah* is paraded there, and the children, in squealing groups of two or three, are carefully placed in the canopied chair and led around, waving proudly to their *ayahs*.

The English women, shopping and taking tea or cherry brandy in the outdoor cafés while their children are entertained, put away their hated solar topees and fight to outdo each other in the splendour of their hats. The flowered and feathered bonnets are monstrous in comparison to the unadorned heads of the Indian women, gleaming with oil of the *Eclipta alba.*

Because of the cooler air, the fine ladies are also able to discard the limp muslin dresses of the city and wear cotton and calico with heavily starched ruffles from neckline to hem. With a huge bustled skirt, broad-brimmed hat and lacy parasol, each memsahib takes up three times as much room on the boarded walkways as the Indian women, who slide by gracefully, bracelets and anklets jangling, while ours are fettered by their armour of stays. They appear inflexible, as if frozen between neck and hip. I sometimes think their faces look as strangled as their bodies. And perhaps also their souls.

A number of gentlemen are present, although the women far outnumber them. Some work in Simla, and others are married men whose wives are at home in England. I have seen that these men, taking their own vacations, look for the company of lone bored wives. It appears that the hill station, with its carefree, festive air, makes these ladies more susceptible to the attentions of gentlemen than they would dare show in their usual domestic setting.

Soldiers, on leave from the King's Regiment of the Indian army stationed all over the country, are striking in their scarlet tunics. In Simla for the recuperative climate, it is apparent that they are notorious for leading ladies . . . astray. As in Calcutta, there is a constant and tiresome round of formal gatherings and full-dress balls, as well as lighthearted dances and picnics.

I have made my own Simla friendship, Shaker — although it is not of the sort that other memsahibs would encourage. The relationship I have forged is with our cook. He is a swarthy fellow from the west coast, given to muttering. I know he was not happy with my visits to his kitchen at first, and cast angry looks at me as he scoured his pots with sand in a big tub.

Now, instead of lingering over tea and cakes at the popular Peliti's, which Mrs Partridge — who shares our bungalow — adores, or browsing in the English shops, I go to the Indian market and buy as many tempting foods as I can find. Now I am familiar with the fruits and vegetables for which I had no names when I first arrived. There are days when I stagger home, my basket filled with okra, aubergine, yams, mangoes and lychees, and deposit them triumphantly on the earthen floor of the lopsided kitchen hut presided over by Dilip.

It's taken a few weeks, but Dilip has agreed to show me some of his tricks. That I can now speak Hindi quite fluently was, I believe, the key to winning him over. I am careful not to show surprise or dismay at anything — neither at the acrid smell of the mustard oil he cooks with, nor at the sweet reek of the *daali*, the dung-cake hearth. His stove is a square of bricks with a hole on top for a pot and an opening for the smoke at the side. If an oven is needed he has a tin box to place on the top.

Eventually he told me that everyone knows memsahibs cannot cook, so he assumed my interest was only to spy on him. Did I suspect him of atrocities? he asked me, with narrowed eyes. Did I think he might stir eggs into the rice pudding with his fingers, or strain the soup through his turban? Or worse? Did I believe the story of the offended *bobajee* who sprinkled a curry with ground glass or included belladonna in the kedgeree?

I laughed at his stories, picked up a brick and began to pound a slab of lamb on a board. He watched me for a long time, and eventually, after a number of visits, he agreed to show me how to prepare Indian dishes – but only if it remained a secret. There it is again, Shaker. My life of secrets.

And so I now make peppery mulligatawny soup, goat curries and fish kedgerees, with Dilip instructing as I stir ingredients into the shining *dechis* made of brass and cook over that brick stove.

Faith and I eat what I prepare (when Faith can be persuaded to eat) – I confided to her how I was spending my time – but we don't breathe a word of it to Mrs Partridge. She frequents the shops that sell prepared English food, and brings home cold game pies, roast chicken and tongue. She hides away her packages of Indian sweets – she can't admit to us that she has a weakness for *sumboosaks*, cakes filled with cheese and almonds, or the delicate pastry *babas* full of mashed dates, and she hotly denied that the large box of *dol-dol*, found under the sofa by the sweeper, belonged to her.

A certain peace has washed over me here, Shaker. There is simple freedom. In the afternoons, alone in the garden, I wear only a plain cotton frock; if truth be told, I have given up my corset and crinoline. Although Mrs Partridge appears disgusted with me, what do I care? Swinging in a hammock with Neel tucked beside me, I read or watch puffy white clouds gather low over the mountains, then blow away in long, scattered wisps. Overhead, fresh breezes rustle the cool green leaves and scarlet blossoms of the rhododendron trees, and a resident blackbird scolds me with the three warning notes of his trill. A disdainful peacock struts through the shady garden at least once every afternoon, a scaled foot raised daintily before each step – then I must keep my hand on Neel's quivering back.

It took me a few weeks to understand why I felt so peaceful here. Then I realized it was the lack of noise. I have always lived with noise. First in Liverpool, then in Calcutta. Calcutta! There is no louder place on earth. The chants, the constant gong of big bells and the clang of smaller ones, the high-pitched, tuneless reedy horns, the pounding of drums, and over it all the human voices. My first night here I lay in bed, wondering what I was listening for. And then I realized it was the creak of the *punkah* – unnecessary in Simla – that has accompanied me every night since I arrived in India.

I have always lived amid the sounds of life, and much as I love the heartbeat of Calcutta, here life hangs suspended. I am peaceful, but I am waiting. For what, I don't know.

Thank you for your patience in reading this over-long letter. I have written it under my favourite rhododendron. I try to imagine you receiving it at Whitefield Lane in Everton, and how you will look up at the English sky as you read, and see me under this Indian one.

Always,
Linny

PS *Eclipta alba* is sometimes known as the false daisy. As well as keeping the hair dark and lustrous, it is also used for inflammation of the skin caused by fungus, and for eye disorders. I have also discovered *manjith* – Indian madder. The root of this plant is powdered, then used as a blood purifier and to battle internal inflammations.

I saw a prisoner today. There is a small and miserable hovel at the end of town; it seems derelict and unused, and I have never paid it much heed. But today, as I rode my pony back into town, I witnessed a group of soldiers jerking and dragging a man towards it. He was a Pathan – I recognized him by his long eyes and his height, the golden earrings glinting in his ears. His hair, loose about his shoulders, was coated with thick dust, lightening its deep colour.

I instantly remembered my first view of a Pathan at the docks as we landed in Calcutta. I remembered, too, Mrs Cavendish's warnings about how fierce they could be. Similar to that Pathan, this man was indeed striking. What I also saw was that despite the harsh treatment, he maintained an admirable dignity. His face was not that of a thieving *dacoit* or cowardly thug. What had he been accused of? Surely something serious, judging by the hard kicks of the soldiers' boots at his ankles, the jabs of their rifles into his back as they forced him along. I wondered how he could appear un-affected by it – as though he was above their humiliation.

Another soldier led his horse, a huge black Arabian, snorting and whinnying as it tossed its head. When I spotted Mr Willows, one of the shop-keepers from the Mall, I reined in my pony and enquired what had happened.

'I can't speak of his crime to a lady,' said Mr Willows, 'but hopefully he'll be hanged. Although even death is too good for him,' he added. 'Now, go home, Mrs Ingram. One of ours should never have to set eyes on a fellow like that.'

As I nudged my pony forward, Mr Willows called, 'Mrs Ingram? Do your best to forget you ever saw him. He is the stuff of nightmares.'

A Pathan, from Afghanistan, I chanted inside my head, as I had on that first day in India. *A Pathan, from Afghanistan.* 'They call themselves Pushtuns,' Mrs Cavendish had said.

I heard the story about the Pathan – actually, two stories – that evening. Mrs Partridge told the first. She considered herself an authority on the Simla gossip. 'It's simply too horrible to recount,' she told Faith and me, although her eyes gleamed and she licked her lips repeatedly.

'Did he – did he murder someone?' Faith asked, glancing at me.

'Oh, worse than that, my dear, far worse.'

'What could be worse than murder?' I asked. *What could be worse than murder?*

Mrs Partridge raised her eyebrows. 'He violated young Mrs Hathaway.'

Faith covered her mouth with her hand. 'Do you mean . . . ?' she asked, her voice muffled.

'Yes.' Mrs Partridge nodded. 'She's destroyed, of course. He caught her behind the picnic grounds, although what she was doing there alone I don't know. I've been told her body will recover, but of course she will never forget what that beast did to her. Let's just hope a child doesn't result. That would surely be the death of poor Olivia. Can you imagine bearing a half-caste, a black *baba*? And think of her husband! Oh, it sickens me to imagine how he'll feel, to know that his wife has been desecrated by a native. Is there anything worse?'

343

I couldn't look at Faith. Had Mrs Partridge forgotten Charles, or did she not care, titillated by the excitement of the unexpected and lurid situation? 'This will be an end to those lonely pony rides you take on your own, Linny. It might have been you. He must have been lying in wait to catch one of us alone.'

I had no intention of stopping my rides. 'Has it happened before? A Pathan causing trouble? I thought they were quite respected.'

'They come through at times, but usually they mind their own business. And although they have some nonsense about personal honour, they're also capable of terrible violence, as is evident now.' Her nostrils were pinched and her jaw tight. 'I suppose the temptation was just too much, seeing a lovely young white woman with no one to protect her. They all want one of us. Dark is always attracted to light, you know. Never the other way round.'

'Really, Mrs Partridge,' I said. Poor Faith, to have to listen to this. I thought of Olivia Hathaway. She was a flighty thing, pleasant enough but always over-excited and over-dressed. 'What will happen to him?' I asked. 'Mr Willows suggested he would hang.'

'Of course. There'll be no bothering with judgement. It's clear that he did it, and there is no alternative but to put him to death. He shall be hanged, and his body thrown into the forest for jackals and hyenas.'

Faith stood then, and as she passed to go to her bedroom, I saw that her face was drained of colour.

Later, Malti leaned close to my ear as she brushed out my hair. 'It is not as Memsahib Partridge tells it,' she whispered.

I looked at her in the mirror. She continued with the

344

slow, long strokes of the silver brush. Her oval face was creased with worry. 'Tell me,' I said.

'Memsahib Hathaway's *ayah* knows the true story. She was witness.'

'Witness to the rape?'

Malti shook her head. 'There was no such deed. Not by the Pushtun, and not by any man.'

I had heard the theories – that the thin air caused delusions in some. I reached up to stop the brush, and turned on my stool. 'What do you mean, Malti? Is all of this Mrs Hathaway's imagination?'

Malti lowered herself gracefully to the floor at my feet. 'I know you are fair, Mem Linny. I want to tell you, for Memsahib Hathaway's *ayah*, Trupti, is my sister.'

'Your sister?' Malti never talked about her family, even when I asked her. She always shrugged and told me that her life should be of no importance to me. 'Does she live in Delhi? That's where Olivia Hathaway is from.'

'Yes.'

'When did you last see your sister?'

'Five years ago. We had imagined we would never see each other again, at least not for many years. So you can imagine my joy when we arrived and—' She stopped, swallowed and continued: 'And now, because of what has happened, Trupti has serious trouble. So serious. I am the older sister, Mem Linny. It is my duty to help Trupti.'

'Of course. Tell me what happened.'

Malti never dropped her gaze. 'Memsahib Hathaway has a business with a soldier. The man-lady business. They meet in the woods beyond the picnic grounds. Trupti always sits some distance from her memsahib, ready to warn her if anyone approaches as she lies with the soldier.' Malti fingered

345

the silver brush, picking at the few blonde strands caught in its bristles. 'But today Trupti was not careful enough. Her lady and the soldier stayed together so long. She fell asleep, to awaken only as a small party of *sahibs* walked with their rifles, looking to shoot something, perhaps the round walking birds with the piercing cry.'

I nodded.

'They did not see Trupti, and she tried to hide herself as she hurried through the bushes to warn her lady. But she was too late. The *sahibs* spotted the movement in the woods, and raised their rifles, thinking perhaps a bear had come down from the forest. They fired, and at their shots, Memsahib Hathaway screamed. The soldier, covering his red jacket with the blanket he and the lady lay on, escaped on his horse, riding further into the forest and leaving Memsahib Hathaway in disarray, her clothing unfastened. Trupti stayed hidden, afraid, and watched as her lady continued to scream, partly in fear but, Trupti believes, more so in panic at disclosure. The *sahibs* hurried to her, helping her to cover herself as she sobbed. They asked her what had happened, who had done this thing to her, and finally she told of her *ayah* abandoning her as they walked by the woods, and of a man riding a black horse. She said the man had grabbed her and taken her for his pleasure. She pointed out Trupti, crouching in the bushes, saying she had seen it all but had not helped. The *burra sahib* beat my sister soundly with his fists and rifle.

'It was the great misfortune of the Pushtun to be in the bazaar today, buying cloth as he passed through on his way back to the North West Frontier.' She stopped, and pleated the fold of her sari between her fingers.

'Did Olivia specifically say it was a Pathan?' I thought of

346

the man's face: the set of his jaw, the narrowed eyes, the way he took the blows without flinching.

'No, Mem Linny. She said she had swooned during the misery and could not describe him.'

'So they accused him because of the black horse?'

Malti nodded.

We sat in silence for a few minutes.

'Why have you told me this, Malti?' I asked. 'I cannot bear to think of the Pathan being killed so unjustly.'

'Memsahib Hathaway blames Trupti for what happened. She has already dismissed her in disgrace, saying it was because Trupti did not help her in her time of need. Tomorrow Trupti returns to Delhi. The memsahib wants her away from Simla for what she knows, even though she would never speak of what she saw – except to me. And now she will not be able to feed her children, living in Delhi with our mother.'

'What can I do, Malti?' I asked. 'I don't believe anyone within the English community would doubt Mrs Hathaway's story. And the soldier was more worried about his own reputation and future than he was for hers. Malti, what is to be done?'

Malti's face closed. 'I should not have revealed the truth to you. It was unfair of me, Mem Linny. I told my sister I would help her, but I didn't know how.'

I picked at the raised bump of darkened skin on my third finger, caused by the pressure of the quill. 'Let me try to think of something tonight, Malti. Perhaps by tomorrow I shall see it all more clearly.'

347

CHAPTER TWENTY-SEVEN

I COULDN'T SLEEP. I thought of Olivia, a weak woman looking for romance, and her soldier, a man so low he would run from the woman he had just finished jiggling rather than risk being caught. I thought of Trupti, sent back to Delhi in disgrace, her days as an *ayah* – or working for the English in any capacity – over. I thought of the look in Malti's eyes as she told me about her sister, the way her eyebrows had risen in the hope that I might intervene. But mostly I thought of the Pathan and his proud struggle with the soldiers. I thought of his death here, in this town created for our pleasure, and how his family might never know what had become of him.

As I lay there, my mind racing, there was a soft knock on my door. I sat up. 'Yes?' I whispered, in case Malti was asleep, but she had been tossing on her pallet and I doubted it. The door opened, and Faith stood in the moonlight in her night-dress, her arms wrapped round her. 'Linny? Did I wake you?'

'No. I couldn't sleep. Are you ill?'

'No. But I – but I need to talk to you.' She came to the edge of the bed, and I saw the glint of tears on her face.

'You're cold. Come, get under the covers.' I put Neel on the floor. He padded over to Malti's pallet, and curled up there.

'Oh, I couldn't,' Faith said, and I realized she had never shared a bed with anyone but Charles.

'It's all right, there's lots of room.' She looked tiny and frail, her red hair a tangle on her white cambric nightdress.

She sat down, her back to me. 'I'll just sit here. I don't want to look at you when I tell you this.'

I waited.

'It's about what Mrs Partridge was saying this evening,' she said.

'It was very rude of her, Faith. I'm so sorry. She's a thoughtless woman.'

'I'm frightened, Linny.'

'Of what?' I could see her shoulders shaking through the thin nightdress.

'I'm carrying a child, Linny,' she said.

I moved closer to her. Relief flooded through me. This, then, was the reason for her inertia, her lack of interest, her troubling vagueness. 'But that's wonderful, isn't it? Charles loves you, and—'

'We said we wouldn't have children. We agreed it would be unfair to a child. They say the next generation is always born black, Linny. And I still hope to reunite with my family. I was sure if I took Charles home, even once, and they met him properly – my father refused any contact with him in Calcutta – they would see the same things I see in him, and relent. But if there were a child, a dark child, Linny . . .' Faith's head shook slowly. 'No. Charles even took me to an Indian woman, Nani Meera – I believe she's his aunt or a distant relative. He explained, and she gave me . . . things. To use – before and after, to stop a baby. She's a midwife.'

I nodded, although she couldn't see me.

'But they didn't work,' she whispered needlessly.

'Surely Charles is pleased, though. And perhaps the child . . .' I wasn't sure what to say.

'There is no "perhaps", Linny. Charles doesn't know. I hoped that I would lose it on the trip here, and he would never have known.' She put her face in her hands. 'I've tried not to think about it, tried to pretend it isn't happening. But tonight, when Mrs Partridge went on about the horror of a black *baba* . . .' She wept. 'There is no point in anything any more, Linny. My life at home was meaningless, and my life here feels no better.'

I pulled her down beside me, and although she wouldn't face me, she let me put my arms round her. Her bones felt like those of a bird, and her hair smelt of jasmine. I hadn't slept with my arms round anyone since my mother had died, although of course I had crowded with the others on the dank mattress on Jack Street. But how different it was to share a bed with Faith, here, in comparison with those other girls, the smell of cheap powder, sweat and semen, in a room rank with damp mould, cold ashes and greasy clothes.

'Meaningless? How can you say that? You have Charles, and now—'

'Don't speak of it, Linny. I can't bear to think. I can't bear to think about anything any more.'

I stayed quiet. I breathed in the scent of Faith's hair, comforted by her warmth and closeness, and felt myself falling asleep.

I awoke before Faith and Mrs Partridge. I had fabricated my own plans and lies while I lay in bed in the early-morning light. First I called Malti and told her that when we returned to Calcutta her sister would come to our house and work there; no matter what Sahib Ingram said I would make it so.

Malti kissed my hands and then my feet, much to my discomfort. 'Go and find her, and tell her we'll call for her on our way past Delhi,' I said. I didn't want Malti to see where I was going. As soon as she was gone I dressed and hurried through the quiet town, all the way to the windowless hovel on the outskirts.

As I approached I saw a soldier slouching against the wall, but as soon as he saw me he stood at attention beside the open door, which looked surprisingly heavy. Through the opening I could see a damp earthen floor and a pile of old straw. I also saw a foot in a high black boot.

'Ma'am? M—may I help you?' the soldier stuttered. 'This is a temporary gaol, no place for a lady.' There was a tin plate of half-eaten food on the ground beside him. I wondered if the prisoner was being fed.

'I do mean to be here,' I said. Then I told him my name, and that my conscience had been troubling me all night, that it wasn't my business but as a Christian I felt it my duty to tell the truth. These lies came to me easily: my whole life was a lie. It was only when I was forced to be truthful that I stumbled. I went on to tell the soldier that I had been in the market at the time that Mrs Hathaway was defiled, and had seen the Pathan there. Then I had seen him ride off in the opposite direction from the picnic grounds. 'Where was he found?' I asked.

The soldier didn't answer, which gave me courage.

'It was on the other side of Simla, wasn't it? Because, as I told you, I saw him nowhere near Annandale. He was going towards the western hills.'

Now a shadow passed over the soldier's face. 'Why is it, Mrs – Ingot, did you say? Why is it that you care what happens to this bas— Pardon me, ma'am, to this filthy Arab?'

351

'Ingram,' I said, standing as tall as I could. 'Mrs Somers Ingram, of Calcutta. My husband is with the covenanted civil service. Although my heart goes out to poor Mrs Hathaway, there are, you must admit, a number of black horses in this area. Did she say specifically it was a Pathan?'

The soldier looked even more uncomfortable. 'Mrs Ingram, ma'am,' he said, 'I'm only in Simla on leave. I have been asked to stand guard here, although not in a military capacity.' He was very young, with a pale down over his top lip. In all probability he was only a year or two younger than I, but I had purposely dressed in a suit of navy silk, a dark blue bonnet, whose navy ribbons ended with white egret tips, and navy kid gloves. I kept my chin raised and spoke to him, eyelids lowered.

'And who is your superior? To whom may I speak about this matter?'

'That would be Major Bonnycastle, ma'am. But he's not here. As I've explained, we're not here in a military capacity, ma'am. There's never been any need for that in Simla before now.'

I glanced at the open door again. There was the clink of a chain, and the boot was no longer visible. 'So the Pathan will remain here until a commanding officer arrives?'

The soldier looked even more uncomfortable, blinking rapidly. 'I don't believe so, ma'am.'

'Then what will you do with him?'

The young man's Adam's apple bobbed in his scrawny throat. 'Please, Mrs Ingram, this is not a matter with which you should concern yourself. He will be taken care of by those of us here, and none of the ladies will have anything to fear from him again. Now I must ask you to leave. This is no place for a lady.' And, as if to prove his point, at that moment

352

an aggressive black crow flew on to the roof of the hovel with a great flapping. It opened its beak and tilted its head, looking down at the plate. Then it let out a croak and swooped low to grab a meat-covered bone, then flew off over the head of the black horse, which shied, its flanks quivering.

I tried to tell myself I had done all I could for the moment. I didn't like to think that the soldiers would simply hang the Pathan, but the young man's blinking uncertainty had not been encouraging. Surely Olivia Hathaway would not retract her story, or admit the horse wasn't black, but brown or grey, that it hadn't necessarily been a Pathan. I doubted she would say anything more, and she would never be questioned further.

When I arrived home Faith was sitting in the garden. She was clutching a sodden handkerchief, but I saw a new glow in her, something in her expression that cheered me, although she was desperately pale. Mrs Partridge had commented on her pallor only a few days before, asking if she'd eaten clay to whiten her complexion.

Neel lay on the grass at her feet, beside a pile of her books. The sight of them encouraged me further. 'You're looking better, Faith,' I said truthfully. 'You mustn't worry about the baby. No matter what, you know you have Charles and his love.'

'Yes,' she said, studying Neel. 'I do believe, now, that everything will turn out for the best.'

I smiled at her. 'Oh, Faith, I'm glad to hear you say that. I've been so worried about you.'

She looked into my face. 'I want you to have these books, Linny,' she said, touching them with the toe of her slipper.

'What do you mean?'

'I shan't read them. You love books. You take them.'

'I couldn't, Faith. Of course you'll read them. Come for a ride with me.' I stood and held out my hand.

'I don't feel like riding, Linny. I have a number of things to do.'

What could they be? 'Please, Faith. We'll take tiffin with us, and I know a place we can go. I have a map.'

'Not today.'

'Tomorrow, then?'

She was silent, but smiled eventually. I hadn't seen her smile for a long time, and it looked unnatural, more of a rictus. 'Can we ride far, Linny? Into the mountains?'

'Perhaps.'

'All right, then. Tomorrow.'

'I promise, Faith, we'll have a lovely time.'

That night I decided that when Faith and I returned from our ride I would go again to the gaol. Perhaps there would be a different soldier on duty, and I would plead with him. I felt a tiny surge of hopefulness about Faith and the small enthusiasm she had shown when she talked about riding far into the mountains. Perhaps she could be happy again, after all.

We woke just after dawn. I left Neel with Malti and went out to the kitchen. Dilip was waiting for me, clutching a woven basket with leather straps. A warm wheat fragrance filled the hut. He must have been up in the middle of the night to make fresh chapattis.

'I told you it didn't have to be anything special, Dilip. Just some cheese and fruit would have been enough.'

He tucked back his chin as if insulted, and held out the

basket. I looked inside and saw the chapattis, saffron rice, a jar of melon and ginger jam, and a container of goat's cheese with mushrooms.

I thanked him once, knowing he would be annoyed if I said too much. Then I fetched Faith and we walked up the hard-packed road to the Mall. The morning was beautiful, its stillness broken only by the shrill cry of a lone black and white hoopoe.

Because it was so early, the only person at the stables was the *syce*, wearing a threadbare tweed jacket over his long white *dhoti*. He had been squatting under a leafy tamarind, but jumped up when he saw us and led out two ponies, flowers woven into their manes. He tightened their girths and I tied the basket to the side of Uta, a pretty brown filly with white spots. Faith's mount was a grey colt, Rami.

We led the thick-haired ponies towards the outskirts of town, and once we were on our way, I pulled a wrinkled scrap of paper from my sleeve.

'What's that?' Faith asked. She appeared composed, calm. The tightness of her features had relaxed. I marvelled at the change that had come over her.

'It's a map. A boy I know – Merkeet – who works in the spice bazaar drew it for me. I talk to him when I buy food. Once, when I admired a hill woman's *burkha*, he told me that they made beautiful beaded ones in Ludhiana, and they would sell them. Ludhiana, he claims, isn't far. I thought we could visit it, then have our tiffin and ride back.' I studied the paper. 'It looks as if we follow this ridge until we come to a stream.'

Faith spread her yellow skirt neatly over her knees on the leather side-saddle. 'Are you sure?'

'Yes – look. Here are the Himalayas, and this is the road

355

back down to the river. We can't go wrong.' I felt as I had when Faith and I had slipped away from Mrs Waterton in the *maidan*, and ventured through the bazaar. This time we were to be away from the stern face of Mrs Partridge, free to explore. To gallop and not care that our skirts blew up or our hair was tangled. Free to laugh or to sing into the wind.

But after what felt like close to two hours, I doubted Merkeet's skill in cartography. We had followed the ridge to a shallow stream, then let the ponies amble through the pebbly water until thick copses reached in closer and closer on either side. Overhead, the sun grew warmer. Faith hadn't spoken since we'd left Simla.

'We'll see Ludhiana just round the next bend,' I called back to her, not yet willing to admit that I might have made a mistake in going so far from Simla.

But the stream trickled to a damp gully after the next turn and, with nowhere else to go, I guided Uta up into a narrow opening that I hoped was a path. We had to push thick scratchy branches away from our faces as the horses plodded along. And then, with no warning, we broke out into a daisy-covered field.

'It's beautiful,' I shouted, gazing at the wide clearing. Trees enclosed the field on either side, but at one end it dipped too low for me to see where it led. The other end was edged with a jumbled pile of huge rocks. 'Let's stop here and eat,' I said to Faith, as she trotted up beside me on Rami, 'and then I suppose we'll follow the stream back. I don't think we'll find Ludhiana.'

'All right,' Faith said, staring at the rocks. 'You set out the food. I'm going to explore.'

'Uta is enjoying the daisies,' I called as she left, but Faith didn't answer, urging Rami towards the rocky end of the field. I unpacked the food while my pony snuffled happily among the flowers and cropped the grass. Faith rode back, and sat beside me while I ate. It was windy in the field.

'Please, Faith, try to eat a little. You must,' I begged.

She took a chapatti, but I saw that she only crumbled it into small pieces, distractedly making a nest of it on the ground beside her. The wind lifted her skirt in a golden circle about her; her bonnet had become untied and slipped back, and her hair was tossed in all directions. Occasionally she glanced towards the rocks.

'What's beyond them?' I asked.

'Nothing, just a sheer drop over a cliff. Nothing at all.'

I lay back in the sweet-smelling flowers, looking at the blue sky and listening to the steady tearing rasp of the grazing horses. I felt a tremor under me, and sat up to ask Faith if she had felt it. A high whinny broke the stillness. It was Uta. She bolted towards the rocks at the far end of the field. Rami trotted anxiously in a small circle.

'Uta!' I called, and jumped up. Faith had grabbed Rami's reins, and pulled herself into the saddle. 'What's frightening them?' I asked.

But Faith took off, first at a trot, but then the pony was galloping. She lost her bonnet; it swirled in an updraught and disappeared.

Something made me turn away from the puzzling vision of her, galloping towards the rocks. A man on a horse rode up the field from the dip of the valley at the far end. The ground shook with the heavy pounding of hoofs. He stood in his stirrups every few seconds to look behind him. With a jolt I recognized the Pathan. I looked back to Faith, her skirt billowing out behind her like a ship's sail.

I was in the middle. The Pathan rode towards me, Faith away. Uta veered suddenly – because of the sudden ringing explosions behind me? Faith didn't stop. Instead, she rose in her saddle in a parody of what I'd just seen the Pathan do. But she did not look behind her. She appeared fixed in a straight line, heading towards the rocks. And then she urged Rami on with her crop. He tried to turn aside as they neared the outcrop, but she forced him on. I didn't understand. And then she let go of the reins – I saw them drop as she raised her hands in the air. Rami tried to stop before the edge of the outcrop, skidding, veering sideways, and Faith went over his head in a graceful arc as if pushed by an unseen hand. But she hadn't been pushed: she had thrown herself from the saddle. My mind couldn't comprehend what I'd just witnessed: that Faith had flung herself over the rocks.

Her full skirt wafted, and I saw the white of her petticoats, then the scissoring of her legs. The whole image of her flying into open air was like a pantomime, a yellow and white spinning disc, and then she was gone. I closed my eyes in horror, and in that instant pain exploded in my shoulder.

The Pathan thundered down upon me, and my legs gave way. I fell like a broken doll in that meadow, an odd scream echoing in my head. In the next instant I realized it had come from my own mouth, a long and terrible cry, because something disastrous had just occurred, and whatever happened next could only be worse.

CHAPTER TWENTY-EIGHT

I WAS ON THE ship that had brought me to India, in my sling-bed, being tossed in a storm. All my bones ached. From the passageway outside our cabin I heard voices calling something unintelligible. There was a pounding under me as if great boulders were hitting the hull; I feared they would break through and I would be drowned. I tried to hold on to my bed, but my left arm wouldn't move. The waves were relentless in their rocking rhythm, and my ribs banged, driving the pain back to my left arm and up to my shoulder. It was difficult to breathe, my face pushed against the unyielding surface of the bed. I struggled to lift my head, and cool fresh air stung my cheeks. I opened my eyes, saw my left arm hanging oddly above my head as if I were suspended.

And then it grew clear. The pounding rhythm was hoofs; I was thrown over a horse's back and saw the ground rushing by. I felt nausea from that and the growing intensity of the pain in my shoulder; I turned my head to the side, and my nose pressed against something warm and hard, moving with the rise and fall of the animal. It was a leg.

I looked up at the broad chest and carved face of the Pathan, and the last terrifying image of Faith flying into the air came back to me. Perhaps my eyes had deceived me. Perhaps she had landed on the grass of the meadow. Perhaps she hadn't intentionally committed the act I thought I had seen, perhaps she wasn't . . .

I couldn't even think the word. I had to go back and find her. I struggled, kicking, and there was a stinging lash against my calves. And that made me more distressed and furious – I must get away, must find Faith. I lifted my chest, pushing under me with my right hand, but the Pathan lifted his own hands – which I saw were bound together with thick, frayed rope – and slapped my head down as effortlessly as one swats absently at a mosquito. I heard a popping noise as my nose smashed against the horse in a shocking burst of pain. Something warm and sticky ran into my mouth. I felt I would smother: I couldn't breathe, my nose and mouth filled with blood and, once again, I fell into rocking blackness.

I was shaken into consciousness as I was dragged off the horse. I opened my eyes, but all was dark. The Pathan held me to him, his tied hands in front of my face, one arm over my mouth. His body was so still and hard that if it hadn't been for his heat and his heavy breathing in my ear I might have been leaning against stone. I heard the horse beside us, its breath whistling. As we stood there, I eventually made out a thin strip of faint brightness far ahead of us; from the smell and dankness I knew we were in a cave. The filtered light came from an opening in what must have been heavy bushes that hid the high entrance. The horse let out a low whinny, and the Pathan took his arm from my mouth – to soothe the horse, I suppose – and I took the opportunity to struggle free. I know I shouted. The Pathan yanked me back against him, his arms crushing my ribs, and then he slapped his joined hands over my mouth, bumping my throbbing nose, and there came a rush of fresh blood. The horse wheezed softly now, and the Pathan hissed quietly; it fell silent. I breathed through bubbles of blood in my nostrils.

Hoofbeats thundered by, and the light at the entrance was cut off abruptly. There was a second of light, then another shadow. I counted seven shadows: there were seven men after the Pathan. I growled, deep in my throat, as if trying to call out, knowing, as I did, that it was as useless as the buzz of a fly. Finally there were no more hoofbeats, no shadows.

We continued to stand motionless for so long that I lost track of time. And then the Pathan took his hands from my mouth and I slid through the circle of his arms, to the ground, my legs useless as pieces of stretched India-rubber.

When a dim light hit my face, I sat up, shakily. I moved my left shoulder and cried out with pain. The Pathan, who was standing so that his body held back the bushes that covered the doorway, gnawed at the knotted rope that held his wrists together. He looked at me and uttered a few terse words.

'I can't understand you,' I said. Then I repeated it in Hindi, and he responded likewise.

'Come here.'

'No.'

He stormed towards me and pulled me up by my hair.

'Let me go. Take me back to the meadow. I need to find my friend.' I twisted under his grip, my scalp burning.

'Untie this rope,' he said, letting go of my hair and holding his joined hands towards me.

His wrists were chafed and bleeding.

'Untie it,' he said again. When I still stood, unmoving, in front of him, he said it a third time.

His voice was not the voice of a madman – a murderer or

rapist. It did not carry the superiority of Somers's voice, or Ram's threatening tone. It was simply a man's voice, raspy with exhaustion. Besides, did I have a choice? I worked at the knots, although my left hand refused to obey. Finally the rope pulled free.

He breathed deeply, rubbing his wrists, then led the black horse to the entrance. He pulled out long handfuls of the grass that grew there, and rubbed the animal down with them.

'My friend,' I said. 'My friend . . . I must go to see what happened.'

'We cannot go now. The *ferenghi* still search for me.'

'But I'm no use to you. Let me go,' I begged.

'You would lead them to this spot.'

'I wouldn't.' I grimaced and looked at my shoulder, and in the light saw blood, too much blood, both dried and fresh, covering the blue calico of my dress.

'Their bullet hit you,' he said, glancing at me, his hand, filled with the sweat-soaked grass, still. 'They shot at me, but hit you.'

I looked at him. 'Why didn't you just leave me there, in the meadow?'

He rubbed again. 'I thought you might be of use to me.'

'Use?'

'For a bargain. If they caught up with me. And your friend is dead.' He murmured to the horse, which stamped a front foot.

'Dead?' Why did my voice shake with such horror, such surprise? I think I had known, from the minute I saw Faith galloping towards that rocky outcrop, rising in her saddle, what she was about to do. Perhaps I had known, for an even longer time, that there was no cure for what Faith suffered from. 'But are you sure?'

'I am sure. There is only rock there. It is a long drop to the stones below, an empty riverbed.'

'Let me go now, then.' My voice was weaker than I wished it. *Faith, why didn't I tell you I had begun to think of you as a sister? Why didn't I do more to comfort you?*

'Not yet. When I know they have returned to Simla, then you can go. It will take you most of a day to walk back. I will be too far by then for you to help them.' Dried blood flaked around his ear and down his neck. His earlobe was torn where there had been an earring.

How had he escaped, I wondered. 'I wouldn't help them. I know you didn't do what they said you did.'

We looked at each other for the first time. He had been beaten; one eye was swollen shut in a puffy purple pouch, and his bottom lip was split. His shirt was torn down the front, and there was a cluster of dark bruises on his chest. I saw the glint of the gold hoop in his other ear through his hair.

'I know you didn't do it,' I repeated. 'I know.' Why was it so important to me that he understood this?

'How do you know what I have done or not done?'

'I know the woman lied to save herself and her lover. I went to the gaol. I told the soldier there that you weren't guilty.'

The Pathan turned back to his horse, and I lowered myself to the floor, leaning against the wall. Finally he threw down the grass and let the bush close over the opening. 'It is late. We will stay here tonight. In the morning you will go back to Simla.'

I turned away. The pain in my shoulder grew to a steady pitch. *Faith. Oh, Faith.*

★   ★   ★

I had cried out. I opened my eyes to see the Pathan kneeling over me. He held a small branch, its end flaming, in my face. One small corner of my mind wondered how he had made fire – the floor of the cave was damp and cold.

Earlier I had tried to curl up into myself and find a level spot, but the pain in my shoulder was unbearable. A sickness came over me, a heat and thirst so strong that I couldn't stop the small sounds that came from my lips. I sat up at one point, but sensed I was alone in the cave. It was too dark to make out any form, but I couldn't hear breathing from either man or horse. Had he left already? I heard my teeth chattering; in spite of the heat of my body I shivered. And then he was there, with his flaming branch.

'Water,' I said, in English, but there was no water, only a tugging at my left shoulder, the sound of tearing fabric, and a strange sizzling. Then it was as if a beast had attacked my shoulder, and I screamed as it tore and chewed at the flesh. The flame grew brighter until I was lost in its light.

'Come, you must wake now,' I heard, and opened my eyes. There was a smouldering pile of twigs in the cave, which threw a dim light.

'It is almost morning. I must go before they begin to search for you again,' the Pathan said.

I stared at him, unable to focus, partly because of the near darkness, but also because my eyes were obstructed. I blinked, trying to clear them, but the lids were weighted. They closed.

'I removed the small ball from the back of your shoulder. It will heal.'

I opened my eyes again and turned my head to look at my shoulder. Even that slight movement brought fresh pain, but not the burning of the night before. A muddy poultice was smeared over my bare shoulder, front and back. My sleeve hung in torn strips.

'Come,' he said, and led his horse out of the cave.

I followed him, stumbling, put my hand to my face and felt dried blood. The sun hadn't risen, but the sky had lost its blackness. 'You must walk that way,' he said, pointing. 'Your people will find you.'

He leaped on to his horse with one easy movement. 'There is a stream, not far from here. You will come to it if you stay in the direction the sun moves.'

I nodded, my head so heavy that even that was difficult, and walked away from the Pathan. It was difficult to keep my balance. 'No,' he called. 'Look at where the lightness comes into the sky. You go in the wrong direction.'

I looked back at him, trying to understand where he wanted me to go, but in the cold dawn he and his horse shimmered as if they were under water, or being consumed by flames. I saw the ground come up to meet me. Time buzzed in my head, the noise receding as the Pathan lifted me and put me on his horse as easily as if I were a child. My skirt bunched about my thighs as my legs stretched wide over the bare back of the black Arab. I grabbed hold of its thick mane, the hair coarse in my fingers. Then the Pathan swung up behind me; his arms, on either side of me, as he held the rope tied through the horse's bit, prevented me sliding off.

We rode at a steady gallop for what felt like hours. I was so relieved to be taken back to Simla that I allowed myself to relax against him, squinting against the rising sun, which cast an orange light over everything. My head was light and yet so heavy it was an effort to stop my chin falling towards my chest. And the thirst was worst of all: my tongue was too dry even to lick my lips. I tried not to think of Faith, tried not to think of how all this would be talked of back in Simla or, worse, of Charles, who had trusted me with his wife. I grew aware of wetness on my cheeks, and was disgusted by my feebleness. I closed my eyes tightly. *You have survived worse than this, Linny. Much worse.*

Then we stopped, and I opened my eyes, expecting to see the familiar landscape around Simla. Holding me by my right upper arm, the Pathan slid me off the horse. My legs were wobbly, and there was a painful numbness between them.

We were in a long, lush valley. Flowers bloomed everywhere – wild tulips, purple and white irises, yellow mustard. The mountains, enormous and powerful, rose beyond the pine forest at the border of the meadow. A narrow strip of river lay in front of us, glimmering in the sun. I walked unsteadily to it and fell to my knees on the muddy bank, then scooped water into my mouth with my right hand. When I had drunk as much as I could, I patted water round my tender nose, flaking away the dried blood. Then I bent lower, wanting to wash the cracked poultice off my shoulder.

'Leave it,' the Pathan said, leading his horse to the water. 'It will heal faster if covered.'

I stood while his horse drank and he squatted and splashed water into his mouth, then over his neck, face and hair. Afterwards he turned to the east and performed the prayers I had seen our Muslim servants carry out.

'How near is Simla?' I asked, when he had risen, although instinctively I knew that if we had ridden this far we should have been there by now. But perhaps the fever and the unrelenting pain in my shoulder had confused me; perhaps we had been riding for only a short time.

'I have not brought you to Simla.'

My legs would hold me no longer. I crouched on the hard, damp earth of the riverbank. 'Faith,' I whispered, rocking back and forth, closing my eyes. 'Oh, Faith, what have I done?' I sat, heavily, and put up my knees. I rested my right arm on them and lowered my forehead to it. 'Where are we, then?' I asked, speaking to the ground.

'We are near Kulu.'

'Kulu.' I tried to remember if I had heard of it, but my only knowledge of India so far north was of the Himalayas, the North West Frontier and the Afghan border. 'Is it still India?' I was whispering now.

'Yes,' he said. 'Kulu is on the border of Kashmir.'

'Why have you brought me here?' I looked up at him. The sun was behind his head, and I couldn't make out his features.

He didn't answer, and I lowered my head to my knees again.

'I know you speak the truth,' he said. 'I heard your voice, while I was prisoner of the red-coated *ferenghi*, although I understood only some of your words.' He stopped, as if unsure how to continue. 'You tried to save my life, so I could not be responsible for you losing yours.

'I could not risk taking you closer to Simla. But I could not leave you, so weakened and unable to help yourself. You need water, and you are ill from the injury caused by the bullet. If the *ferenghi* did not find you within a day, or perhaps two . . .' He brushed his horse's mane with a finger. 'So I will take you to Kashmir, to a camp there. We will ride the rest of today and tomorrow. At the camp you will gain strength, and I will arrange for you to return to Simla with someone who can lead you safely.'

I did not know what to say. What did I know of Kashmir? I had read of high, snow-covered mountains, of thick pine forests.

'You have nothing to fear,' he said.

'I'm not afraid,' I said, louder than was necessary.

He dipped his head, then led his horse to a small thicket and secured the rope. I heard him call the horse Rasool. He disappeared into the bush, and returned eventually with wild mushrooms and berries in his torn shirt. I saw that the shirt had been made with tiny, careful stitches. He wore a brightly embroidered open waistcoat over it. The sash round his waist was thick, woven with bright red and orange threads. His full black trousers were tucked into high leather boots.

I considered not taking the handful of mushrooms and berries he held out to me, his fingernails broken and dirty, the hands covered with scars, then wondered why I should refuse. What good would arrogance, stubbornness, do me now? None. Better to drink water, and eat what he offered, for I was far from anywhere that was safe and familiar; was feverish and in pain. Any hope of returning to Simla lay with the Pathan.

After we had rested and Rasool had grazed, he put his hands round my waist and swung me up again. This time he rode in front of me. As he urged Rasool to a gallop, I hooked my hands over his sash to keep from falling. I tried to look around as we raced through open fields and along gentle hills, but had to concentrate on gripping with my knees and keeping my fingers in the sash. Only my thin skirt, thinner petticoat and lawn drawers were between me and Rasool. Every few hours we stopped at rushing streams to drink, and I walked a bit to try to prevent my legs stiffening. They were rubbery and uncooperative, my inner thighs chafed. Once I went behind a bush to relieve myself, not caring about the Pathan's nearness.

Finally we stopped at the edge of a dark forest. The Pathan raised his chin at a huge conifer, and I sat under it. The moss was spongy and cool. I laid my head on it and slept. When I woke a fire crackled in the small clearing. The Pathan came to me, holding out a small steaming bird on a stick. It was well cooked, its skin brown and crackly. 'What is it?' I asked.

He said a Hindi word I didn't understand. I saw a second bird, lying beside the fire; it was still feathered, and a heavy vine was wound tightly about its neck.

'I think it's a grouse,' I said in English. I bit into the savoury flesh, grease smearing my lips and running down my chin. I chewed, and watched the Pathan expertly plucking the second bird. By the time he was roasting it over the fire, I felt myself falling asleep again, the bird's bones still in my hand.

I awoke some time during the night, my legs stiff and cramped but my shoulder no longer hurting with the same intensity. The Pathan sat behind the flickering fire. The dancing flames accentuated his cheekbones and the fullness of his lips. He appeared to be staring at me, but perhaps not. Perhaps he only looked at the fire, the blaze reflected in his eyes.

I fell once more into a deep sleep, and when I woke again the next morning, I wasn't sure whether I had seen him looking at me or dreamed it.

As I stirred in the dappled sunlight coming through the low branches of the trees, every bone in my body screamed. All evidence of the fire was gone, and neither the Pathan nor

Rasool was in sight. For a second I panicked, and tried to stand.

My legs threatened to buckle, and I clutched at a fragrant branch to stop myself falling. As I straightened, I flexed my left arm. I could lift it now. I explored the crust of mud on the back of my shoulder and felt the tender wound, but when I pulled away my fingers, there was no fresh blood.

My clothes felt as stiff as my body; they were encrusted with dirt and pine needles, and the front of my dress was spotted with grease from the grouse. I tried to walk a few steps. The insides of my thighs were bruised and tender, and my drawers pulled against my body in a sticky, distressing way, as if my courses had come, but it was too early for them. I went behind the conifer to relieve myself, and realized my drawers were stuck to me with pus and blood, my skin rubbed raw with riding.

I hobbled back to the clearing, and the Pathan appeared from between two trees, leading Rasool. 'We will find water in two hours,' he said, 'and will reach the camp by nightfall.'

I nodded, coming towards him. He was watching the way I walked, my legs held stiffly apart. I didn't look at him as he put me on the horse.

By the time we reached the next stream, I didn't know how I would ride any further. I slid down and walked to the water. When I tried to squat at the water's edge to drink, I couldn't hold back a moan.

The Pathan said nothing. But as he swung me up, and I spread my legs, and came down heavily on Rasool's hard, wide back, I felt the blisters break open and weep. I sucked in my breath involuntarily and tried to shift my weight.

'Why do you cry out?' he asked. 'Does the pain of your shoulder worsen?'

'It's not my shoulder,' I said.

'You can ride?'

I nodded, but saw him studying my face.

'We have many more hours. You must tell me if you cannot ride.'

I nodded. 'Could I – I need to sit . . .' I knew no Hindi word for side-saddle. I swung one leg over, wincing. 'If I can sit like this, it will be better.'

He looked at the sky. 'We have not travelled as quickly as I hoped, because of the extra weight for Rasool. Ahead is a difficult trail. You cannot stay on in that position, with no saddle. Why do you wish this?'

I slid off. I didn't want to have to admit to this dark stranger that my flesh was oozing with blisters. I put my hands on the back of my skirt. 'I have never ridden so. Like a man. It hurts my skin.'

He made a sound of disgust. 'Take this, then, and sit on it.' He unwound his sash. 'There is no time for this behaviour, this *ferenghi* modesty,' he said, when I hesitated. He pushed the sash into my hands.

I folded it into a thick bundle, pulled up my skirt at the back and tucked the padded wool into my drawers. Then I nodded at him, and he put me back on Rasool.

The sash protected my torn skin enough to ease the worst of the discomfort, but now I had to grip the Pathan's waist. He urged Rasool on at a gallop, but only for a short while. Soon I saw the peak of a mountain against the brilliant blue sky. Its base was hidden in mist. Dots of huge fir trees and boulders grew visible. Rasool was forced to a slow climb up a stony hill, higher and higher. The air grew cooler. And then the descent was steep, although brief, and as Rasool picked his way down, his legs stiff and his hoofs loosening pebbly

371

chunks of earth that rolled down in front of us, gravity forced me to lean against the Pathan's back. I put my cheek against his waistcoat; I felt the vibration of his heart. He smelt of sweat and pine, horse and air.

I saw a patchwork of land in the plateau in front of us, and beyond, another set of foothills rose, their edges wavering, unformed. Finally the Pathan pulled Rasool to a halt. We were beside a lake ringed with willows. There was the sound of splashing, and I turned to find its source: a small waterfall at the far end of the narrow lake. Beneath Rasool's feet the ground was sheeted with wild strawberries and columbines. The western sky flamed with orange and pink streaks behind green ranges. I thought of sketches and paintings of Switzerland I had seen in the travel books at the Lyceum. Even Simla's beauty could not rival this. Yet the glorious scene was darkened by my endless thoughts of Faith. The pain of losing her shadowed every moment.

'We will go no further tonight,' the Pathan said, interrupting my thoughts. 'It is still a number of hours away, and the route too treacherous in the dark.'

I clambered down.

'Wait here,' the Pathan said, then rode away.

I drank at the river, washed my hands and face, then I stood, looking at the reflections of the rolling foothills in the still water. The Pathan returned, carrying a saddlebag decorated with porcupine quills, from which he brushed leaves and twigs. I assumed this was a familiar spot for him to camp, and that he had left a cache for himself.

Leaving Rasool to pull at the long grass, he crouched near me and took a clean white cloth out of the bag. He unwrapped it to reveal a lump of hard white cheese. Then he produced a knife, cut the cheese in half and gave a piece to me. He ate the other in a few bites. 'The water is shallow and full of fish. You gather fruit,' he told me. He dug in his bag again and pulled out a small skin, folded and tied with a thong. He handed it to me, with a word I didn't understand. I looked at it. He took it, untied it, and I saw a gleaming dark substance. 'It is for the horse, for cuts and injuries. Use it.' He pointed at my shoulder, and then at my skirt.

I took it and walked towards a grove of low trees. Some were blossoming, while others already bore small fruit. There was a gentle curve in the lake where the willow branches, with their tender young leaves, swept low over the almost transparent sapphire water. They made a natural screen.

I looked back at the Pathan, but through the lattice of leaves all I could see was a flash of his white shirt as he moved about the shoreline. The cool water lapped quietly on the grassy sand. I unbuttoned my dress and stepped out of it. It was so covered with dirt, blood and grease that it was hardly recognizable as the simple crisp periwinkle garment I had put on two mornings ago. It was as if I had lived a lifetime since then. I stood in my chemise and petticoat, unbuttoned my high leather boots and tugged them off with a sigh of relief. I rolled down my stockings and pulled them off too. I wiggled my toes in the warm loam, luxuriating in the softness.

There were still a few pins left in my hair, although it was a tangled mess. I yanked them out and dropped them into the sand. Then I pulled off my drawers, and eased the Pathan's sash away from my body. As I stood at the edge of the water, with the warm evening air on my skin, a kingfisher swooped over my head. I picked up my dress, drawers and stockings and put one foot into the water, then the other. The bottom of the lake was covered with small slimy stones and soft mud.

I walked in, slowly. I had never been in a lake, or a river. I had never had more water around me than a zinc or copper tub could hold. I went deeper, seeing my petticoat float around me. The cool water burned my raw blisters. When I was waist-deep I let my dress, drawers and stockings drift on the surface of the water and ducked my head under to try to pull the knots out of my hair. Then I took my dress and scrubbed it as thoroughly as I could. I did the same with my stockings. The drawers were harder to clean, stiff with dried blood and pus.

At last I walked back to the shore and dried myself on the Pathan's sash. I spread the smelly ointment on the crusted scab on the back of my shoulder and on my open sores. Then I wrung out my dress and put it on, with difficulty, over my wet chemise and petticoat. I left off my drawers and carried them, with my stockings, boots, the sash and the ointment, back the way I had come.

The Pathan was standing on a small boulder in the water a few feet from the shore, working at the end of a narrow branch with his knife. Several fish already flopped senselessly at his feet. As I watched, he raised the sharpened stick over his head, then stabbed it into the water with great force. Just as quickly he pulled it back, and on the end was a large wriggling fish, its iridescent scales smooth as metal. He gathered it up and hopped nimbly over the rocks to the edge of the water.

I set down what I carried and went to the spreading branches of the trees, which were covered with small, hard plums, and gathered them into my wet skirt.

The Pathan was now crouching, slicing the scaled fish into fillets on a flat rock, burying the heads and entrails in the sand. He glanced up as I walked nearer, and watched me shake my skirt. The plums rolled on to the sand like stones. He reached into his boot and pulled out a flint. He set twigs and small bits of brush round the rock, and lit a fire.

Later, we ate the flaky fish, the plums and the tiny sweet strawberries that grew all around us. He built up the fire, and darkness fell. I held my feet to the warmth, then put on my dry stockings and boots.

Suddenly I realized that I wasn't hungry. I wasn't filthy. My shoulder only throbbed if I moved my arm suddenly. I could sit almost comfortably by leaning on one hip. My only real pain came from thinking of Faith. It was all my fault. If not for me she wouldn't be dead. She would be in the garden at Constancia Cottage, reading. It was I who had allowed her to carry out her plan. I had had one true friend in life, and I had betrayed her.

Strange sounds were all around us: small animals rustling in the underbrush, something larger circling us with cautious steps. There was the far-off warning cry of a jackal, and the murmur of a night bird high overhead. Rasool gave a shuddering whinny, and the Pathan said something to him in a language I didn't understand. The horse quieted.

'What do you speak?' I asked.

'The language of my people. Pashto.'

'But you know Hindi as well.'

'Hindi, Dari, Uzbek, Urdu, Kashmiri, Bengali, Punjabi. I have travelled widely within this country, and my own. I can speak to anyone I might meet. Except the *ferenghi*. The foreigners. I choose not to learn their language, although some of their words collect within me unbidden.' He raised his eyes from the fire. The swelling of his eye and lip were diminishing. 'Your language.' He dropped his eyes again, but not before I had seen something in them. Something that made me unafraid. Had I been afraid all this time, even though I'd boasted that I wasn't? I don't know. The haunting thoughts about Faith, the fever and pain, the uncertainty of what would happen – all had been part of my life for the last two days. What did I feel now? If I could stop berating myself for not having seen the depth of Faith's despair, for not recognizing her slow decline as more serious than a failure to adjust, I believe now that I would have known I wasn't frightened at all.

The Pathan spoke again, his eyes still on the fire. 'You have been in India long? To know the language.'

He was making conversation. How strange, I thought. I am sitting before a fire somewhere near Kashmir, talking with a wild man of the North West Frontier.

'Not so long. A year and a half.'

He nodded.

I needed to stop thinking about Faith, needed a diversion to take my mind from her. 'Tell me about your people – the Pushtuns.'

He threw a stick into the fire, where it crackled and hissed. 'There is little to tell. I am of the Ghilzai. My own tribe numbers about a hundred and fifty. We live in no one place, but spend our summers in the coolness of the mountains and our winters sheltered in protected valleys. My tribe herds sheep, and we sell or trade the wool for what we need.'

He stopped, and looked up at me. 'My people love music, poetry and games. We live a simple life.'

His words belied what I saw in his eyes. There was nothing simple about this man. I pulled up my heels and wrapped my arms round my knees, resting my chin on them. 'What were you doing in Simla?'

'I catch the wild horses of the plains. When they have learned to take the rein, I sell or trade them, sometimes in Kabul, sometimes in Peshawar or further south in India. I had sold a small herd in Rajpura, and was passing through Simla on my way to collect another that waits in Kashmir.'

'I'm sorry,' I said, surprising myself.

'Sorry? Why are you sorry?'

'For how you were treated. It was unjust.'

He nodded, his face grim.

'How did you escape?'

'They took me out. To hang me.'

I heard my own sharp intake of breath.

'Rasool stood nearby. I made the sound he knows and obeys. He broke free of his bindings, and came upon the men who held me. They scattered to protect themselves from his striking hoofs. I leaped upon him. By the time they had collected and mounted their own horses I had a good lead.'

Silence.

'Do you have a family?' I asked.

'I have two wives.' He bent forward to pile additional branches on the fire, and his face was hidden by the curve of his hair. Then he leaned back and his hair fell away. 'Both have given me a son. Allah has smiled on me.' And then, unexpectedly, his teeth flashed in a quick smile – thinking, I suppose, of his children. In that moment his face changed, showing him to be younger than I had first thought. His teeth were white and even. The smile was gone as quickly as it had come.

There seemed little more to say. We studied the fire. Finally I spoke. 'I have a husband.' I don't know why I chose to tell him that.

'Of course,' he said, and he lay on his side, his head propped by his hand. Through the heat haze I could see only the outline of his body, the rise of his hip and the thrust of his shoulder.

'What is your name?' I called, across the heat.

'Daoud,' he said. 'Chief of the Ghilzai.'

CHAPTER TWENTY-NINE

I RAISED MYSELF ON one elbow and looked across the smouldering remains of the fire. In the first light, the man named Daoud slept, his lashes dark against his cheeks. His face was shadowed with stubble.

I lay back and watched the sky with its shades of layered pink. A waft of scent from the blossoms came to me, and I breathed it in. At a quiet rustle in the leaves of the overhanging *chenar*, I watched a pair of golden orioles groom themselves, pulling at their feathers with their tiny sharp beaks, fluffing up their breasts and admiring each other with bright eyes. They flew off in a rush of beating wings, and in a moment I saw why – a large green woodpecker with a crimson head had landed on a branch in the same tree, and was staring down at me with proprietary arrogance. Then he attacked the hard limb with his long pointed bill. The instant the drumming sounded, Daoud was on his feet, knife in hand. He stared around the campsite with jerky alarmed twists of his head.

I sat up, wincing at the pressure, and wordlessly pointed to the branch. At the sight of the bird's gleaming, busy head, he shrugged, as if annoyed, then tucked his knife back into the top of his trousers. He turned and looked at the still water. Then, in one swift movement, he pulled off his waistcoat and drew his shirt over his head as he walked to the edge of the lake. I saw, with surprise, that the skin not burnished by the sun was paler than I had imagined. He wet his face, hair, chest and arms, then stood and shook, sending tiny pearls of water flying in all directions. He pulled out his knife and scraped it across his cheeks. Then he walked along the shore and disappeared behind some boulders. I went to the same lacy screen of leaves where I'd bathed yesterday, and tentatively touched my blisters. They had dried during the night. I put on my drawers, washed my face and raked my fingers through my hair.

We ate the leftover fish and some handfuls of strawberries standing beside the blackened fire. Daoud covered it with sand, then whistled, and Rasool walked to him. He motioned to his sash, which I'd left beside his saddlebag. I took it, folded it into a thick pad and tucked it into my drawers, this time without thinking.

Then he lifted me on to Rasool and we travelled quickly for the next few hours, through the foothills and into a valley. As we rode, I grew aware of my breasts pressed against Daoud's back, the feel of his hips under my hands. Just that, but it was an odd awareness.

Daoud stopped to let Rasool drink at a small pool, and I looked out at the valley spread before us. It was a paradise of lushness, spring flowers blooming everywhere – tiny blue gentians and purple violets fighting for space with larger multicoloured anemones. 'Are we in Kashmir?' I asked, and Daoud nodded.

'You see it at the height of its beauty,' he said, with a touch of pride. 'Further north, winter can be very long, very cruel. The Kashmiris wait for spring as the hawk for the hare. The birth of warm weather passes quickly, but it is a sight to soothe the emptiest spirit. Every year I hope to be in Kashmir at the time of its awakening.' He pointed to a low hill, bordered with trees. 'Beyond the trees is a small Kashmiri settlement. I have my horses there, and some of my men. That is where I will leave you.'

He turned to face forward, but before he urged Rasool away from the water, he glanced back at me. 'What are you called?'

'Linny,' I said, and added, 'I am Linny Gow.' I said it without thinking, although in the next instant realized I had used my old name. Here I was Linny Gow. I was not Linny Smallpiece, or Linny Ingram. Here, there was no need for pretence. For the first time in a long, long time, I was who I was.

He repeated it, 'Linny Gow.' It sounded full of music as it came off his tongue.

In a grove of trees beside a small stream, the camp was a combination of black tents and animal enclosures built of stone or wooden rails. One of the larger fenced areas held a number of majestic horses, and small pastures held single mares with their foals. In the smallest field, surrounded by a rough stone wall, a mangy, bloated, limping goat bleated loudly and mournfully as Rasool splashed through the rushing stream.

We had arrived. It had taken us four days to reach this camp – only four days, yet we had travelled to a far different world from the one I'd left behind in Simla. My breath quickened. What awaited me? Would the people here treat me with hostility? Would Daoud protect me?

Once the horse had stepped up on to the low bank, men, women and children gathered, talking and pointing.

The men were dressed like Daoud — dark trousers, white shirts and embroidered waistcoats; some wore a white turban. They were all strongly built. Some had well-trimmed, thin moustaches. The women were lighter complexioned, their skin a soft toffee and their eyes light brown, although their hair was very black, hanging down their backs in a tight plait. They wore long, loose cotton tunics of faded blue, green, plum or crimson, and underneath the calf-length robes, full black trousers gathered at the ankle. Their shoes were of soft material, embroidered, the toes turned up. Most had small dark blue caps with a loose veil. On some the veil hung behind; it covered the faces of others. They were all adorned with an abundance of silver jewellery — bracelets, anklets, earrings, and the Muslim nose ring of the married woman.

A hush fell over them as Daoud dismounted, then reached up and swung me down. A child in his mother's arms repeated something in a shrill, reedy chirp until he was quieted with a sharp word. I didn't know where to look. No one smiled at me, or came forward. They all stared. I dropped my eyes, conscious of how odd I must appear to them, afraid to stare back but not wanting to show them how uneasy I felt.

Daoud spoke and I looked up again. A boy of twelve or thirteen, in muslin jodhpurs, a shirt, embroidered waistcoat and cap, scurried forward, and Daoud handed him Rasool's reins. The young *syce* proudly led away the huge horse, and when he was gone an older man approached Daoud. They greeted each other in a chest-to-chest embrace. Then the man asked something, his tone questioning, and all the eyes in the crowd came to me, then returned to Daoud. He spoke at length, and the eyes pivoted to me again. I longed to know what he told them; I prayed it would not turn them against me. He spoke again, and I saw some of the women nod, not unkindly, and my fears diminished.

Then Daoud looked at me. 'The women will care for you,' he said, in Hindi. 'They are the women of the *gujars* – the Kashmiri herdsmen. Their men are driving the goats to pasture, and they are hired to feed my men. Mahayna!' he called.

A young woman with a baby in a sling on her hip stepped forward. 'Mahayna speaks many Indian dialects,' he said. He addressed her in Hindi. 'This *ferenghi* is called Linny. She speaks Hindi. Give her food and fresh clothing, and let her share your tent.' He walked away with long strides, and his men followed.

The sloe-eyed woman nodded at his back, then turned to the rest of the women and chattered in a high-pitched voice. A crowd of about twenty surged forward, and I clenched my hands at my sides while their rough, reddened ones reached out to touch my dress, my hair, my skin. They spoke to each other in a low murmur, as if I were some animal they were assessing. I thought that perhaps they had never before seen a white woman.

Finally the girl called Mahayna quieted them. The baby on her hip looked close to a year old, with huge eyes and a fringe of curly dark hair. She stood in front of me for so long that my heart beat hard and fast. Was she waiting for something? Finally I reached out and took the baby's pudgy hand. 'Your child is very fine,' I said. 'A boy or a girl?'

I had done the right thing: Mahayna's face split into a wide grin, showing several gaps in her teeth. 'A son. My first living child.'

I smiled back. 'A son. You are lucky. Allah has blessed you.' The baby played with my fingers, and instinctively I put my lips to his little fist.

Mahayna was still grinning, and once more chattered to the women. They all nodded, letting out long breaths that seemed to say, 'Ah – aha,' in agreement with my comment. Babies appeared as if by sleight-of-hand – from under tunics, from slings on hips and supports on backs. They wore tiny muslin shirts, embroidered with flowers, and miniature cloth caps also decorated with fine needlework. The infants and toddlers were thrust towards me, one by one.

'Touch them, please,' Mahayna said. 'The touch of a *ferenghi* woman is said to bring luck.'

Obligingly I stroked downy cheeks and dimpled hands, smiled at each mother. I patted the heads and shoulders of the small children who pranced at my feet. Then Mahayna took my hand and led me to a small tent. The throng of women and children followed closely. Mahayna motioned for me to sit, and I did so carefully in the trampled grass beside the patched tent. All of the women lowered themselves to the ground.

Mahayna bustled in and out of the tent importantly, stirring a battered black pot that hung over a fire. Using a dented tin cup, she ladled a concoction I recognized as *dal* into an earthenware bowl and presented it to me with a flourish. I brushed back my hair, then, using my fingers, spooned the mashed lentils and rice into my mouth. Mahayna watched. When I looked at her and said, 'Good, Mahayna. Good *dal*,' she clapped her hands. The women smiled and talked quietly until I had finished.

When I handed the empty bowl to Mahayna, she made a curious whistling sound. The women fell silent and got to their feet, took their children and moved towards different tents. Mahayna set her baby on the grass beside me. 'They will not get their work done if they sit and look at you,' she

384

said. She pointed to the child, who stared solemnly at me. 'His name is Habib,' she said, and glanced at my abdomen. 'How many children?'

'I have none,' I answered.

Mahayna's face showed sorrow. 'It will be soon, with Allah's will,' she said, with a confident air, her face clearing as she stirred the steaming *dal* in the black cauldron with a skinned stick. 'The chief's women bear sons easily.'

I thought I had misunderstood her accented Hindi at first. But as she continued to stir, I shook my head. 'I am not Daoud's – not his woman. No.' The baby whined, crawling towards his mother.

Mahayna opened the front of her tunic, pulled out a heavy breast and picked him up. He began to suck contentedly, reaching up to swat at his mother's dangling earring. 'I have been here for three years, since I was a bride. Every year Daoud and his men come. I have heard many stories of Daoud's Ghilzai.' She smiled, but it wasn't the open smile of earlier. Now it was teasing.

'I will return to my own people,' I said. The thought of attempting to explain what had happened was wearying. 'I will not stay here,' I said.

She nodded, looking down at her baby. His eyelids were heavy, and his sucking shallow now.

'Your husband is – with the goats?'

She threw her head in a vague gesture towards the hills. 'Some come down once every week for fresh food. There must always be men with the goats at this time of birthing or many are lost.'

I watched her set the now sleeping child gently inside the tent opening.

'Why are Daoud's men here?'

'They keep the horses they catch in the village, readying them to sell or return to Afghanistan. We feed them and clean their clothes. They do not touch us, or our men would not allow us to do their bidding. Our husbands are rewarded handsomely by the Pushtuns for our work.'

I found it hard to believe she had been married for three years. 'How old are you, Mahayna?' I asked.

'I am sixteen years old,' she said, 'but many of the women look up to me.' She told me this with simple honesty. 'I am not born of the *gujars*. My husband bought me from Salenbad, near Srinagar, the largest city of Kashmir. My father was an educated man, and very wise. He instructed my brothers in the languages of India, and I also learned. He beat me when he found me listening, for it was not right that I learn as my brothers. But it pleased me, so I continued to hide, and learned against his wishes. The saying is "A daughter's intelligence is not helpful to the father." This was not so for my father. He was not unhappy when he could command a large price because of it. I am useful to the *gujars*, for I am called upon to deal with the peoples of the south who come to buy our goats.'

She pulled a half-woven basket from the side of the tent and began to twist the tough reeds in an intricate pattern. 'Soon,' she said, 'you will dress in fresh clothing. The women arrange it.'

I watched the shape of the container emerge in her capable hands.

Within an hour, four women came to Mahayna's tent. They carried a pile of clothes, and pulled at my arm, talking loudly. Mahayna had taken the pot of *dal* off the fire, and now a large tin of water bubbled over the flames. She pulled two gathered bags from within the folds of her tunic, and emptied some tiny leaves into her palm from one, then dropped them into the water. As if this were a sign, the women all sank gracefully to the grass and produced a cup from their own tunics, which seemed to be the equivalent of a lady's reticule.

Each woman dipped her cup into the boiling water, and Mahayna opened the second skin bag and passed it round. She handed me a cup of the steaming amber liquid, and I copied the other women, taking a pinch of the white substance that I discovered was coarse sugar. Like the others, I blew on the hot liquid, then cautiously stirred it with my right forefinger. Finally I sipped. It was an unfamiliar but delicious blend of sweet tea. We were taking tea. The ladies chattered quietly among themselves. I remembered the tea parties in Calcutta and Simla, then cursed myself for allowing my thoughts to return to those places. The last tea party I had attended in Simla had been with Faith. We had been invited to the home of a young woman from Lucknow. Faith had been so lovely in a peach-coloured crêpe-de-Chine gown. Her delicate cup had rattled in its saucer, I remembered.

I had to set my own cup in the grass and breathe slowly, for the pain of Faith's death was reawakened, fresh and new. For the last few hours I had forgotten it.

By the time the women had finished their tea, wiped their cups on the hem of their tunics and tucked them away, Habib was stirring. Mahayna picked him up and motioned for the women to enter her tent. I followed, and the minute we were all inside the small space, the oldest woman was pulling at the buttons of my dress.

'You must give us your clothing,' Mahayna instructed. 'We will repair and wash it.'

387

I took off my dress, boots and stockings, and stood in my chemise and petticoat. Mahayna picked up the edge and admired the delicate lace. The other women waited expectantly, their hands outstretched as I took off the petticoat and, finally, my chemise. There was silence as they looked at what was left of my breast, with its crazed and crooked scar, at the fading lash marks of Somers's riding crop on my back, and at the new wound in my shoulder. I wanted to explain to them, so I pointed to my breast. 'A knife in the hand of an evil man,' I said, and they nodded, ah-ahaing as Mahayna translated. I turned to show my back. 'My husband's anger.' They nodded again, and I touched my shoulder. 'By my own people. A mistake.'

It was so simple.

Then I took off my drawers, and pulled away Daoud's sash, gasping as the freshly formed scabs tore off. 'From the big horse,' I said to Mahayna. The women clucked in sympathy, and one dug in her tunic and extracted a tiny muslin bag.

'Daoud gave me his horse medicine,' I said, trying to appear nonchalant as I stood naked among them. I saw some looking at my feathering, pointing at it, and then at the hair of my head, comparing the colours.

'Layla has a similar medicine, but for people,' Mahayna said. She nodded at the hook-nosed woman, who sprinkled a herbal-smelling powder over my sores, talking to Mahayna the whole time. 'Layla makes many medicines from the flowers and leaves of the forest,' she said. 'This powder, if shaken on three times in a day, will heal the skin quickly. But you must not bind yourself — the air will dry and close the sores sooner.'

Layla handed me the bag, and I put my hand on her arm to thank her.

They had brought me clothes. One woman held out a pair of voluminous black trousers, and I stepped into them, pulling the drawstring tightly at the waist. Another slipped a soft burgundy tunic – a *kamis*, they called it – over my head, and still another worked through my hair with a comb intricately carved from scented wood. Finally the oldest woman, her face badly pockmarked, knelt in front of me, holding out two pairs of low boots. I slipped my bare feet into the flexible warm chamois leather, and she laced them. She set the strong outer sandal, with its turned-up toes, to one side.

'You wear the second shoes over the first if you walk away from camp. They will protect your feet from the sharpness of the stones,' Mahayna said.

As they adjusted my clothing, Mahayna, with Habib in his sling, burrowed in a large cloth bag in the corner of the tent, then approached me with a pair of delicately patterned long silver earrings. I thought of the garish jewellery I'd bought on Paradise Street, of the genuine jewels Somers had given me in Calcutta, usually after some unpleasantness. But this straightforward gesture of kindness made my eyes burn. I took the earrings and attached them with silver clips to my ears. 'Thank you,' I said.

Mahayna flashed her disarming gap-toothed smile. 'Now you look like one of us,' she said. 'At least from the back.' She repeated her joke to her friends. They all laughed, and little Habib clapped his hands.

Later that day I saw Daoud as I walked with Mahayna to the stream to fetch water. He was sitting with two men, and they fell silent as we passed. He nodded at me, and as I saw his eyes take in my altered appearance, I felt heat unexpectedly in my face. Something was happening that I didn't understand

389

yet wanted to think about. There was a peculiar stirring in me at the sight of him, the same sensation I had noticed when I felt my breasts against his back, his hips under my fingers. You know what it was, of course, and are probably laughing at my naïveté. I – a girl who had known hundreds of men. But this was new, and it was curiously exciting yet uncomfortable.

That night I slept on soft quilts in Mahayna's tent. The flaps were left open, as the air was warm. Occasionally I heard distant baying; the camp dogs, perhaps, hunting in the nearby hills. I heard Habib's sleepy demanding snorting, which, after a rustle, was replaced by gulping and swallowing. Then the tent was quiet again. I thought of Faith, and of Charles, when he received the news. I realized now that I had barely thought of Somers since I left Simla. Would he think me dead too, if news travelled to him in Calcutta before I returned to Simla? He would outwardly show grief, and despair, but inwardly he might rejoice. Wouldn't it be better for him if I *were* dead? He had his inheritance, and could go on as the grieving widower for many years, with the sympathy and respect of the English contingent. *Poor man*, the matrons would whisper behind their gloves. *So in love with that strange little wife of his that he never got over her death. Chooses to live a solitary life; we could never interest him in another woman. No one could compare with his dear departed.* How disappointed he would be when he heard I was back in Simla; how he would wish it were Faith who had returned, and me lying dead on the cold rocks.

I turned my face towards the open tent flap. I let myself think of Daoud, the shape of his bare back as he had stood at the water's edge, the look of his thighs as they pressed against his horse. His smell. Here it was again, the restless feeling.

The next day I helped Mahayna with the food and played with Habib. I didn't see Daoud. Surely he would come soon to tell me when and how I would return to Simla.

Late in the afternoon, as I was tickling the baby's double chin with a long blade of grass, a shadow blocked the sun. I looked up to see a short, stocky man in a dirty blue shirt and even dirtier trousers. He had a half-grown beard, and his lined brown face and red-rimmed eyes looked tired. He stared down at me and Habib, then ducked his head inside the empty tent.

'Mahayna!' he roared, although it was obvious the tent was empty. Habib screamed at the unexpected sound, and I picked him up and held him to me.

'She brings water from the stream,' I shouted over the baby's howls, but the man stared at me blankly: he didn't speak Hindi. He dropped the sack that had been slung over his shoulder. A woman sitting in the doorway of the tent across from us yelled something at him. He turned his back to me and crossed his thick arms over his barrel chest, standing with his legs apart, eyes fixed in the direction of the stream.

In a few moments Mahayna swayed into view, gracefully balancing a dripping earthenware pot on her head. On seeing the man, she set it down and reached out her arms to Habib.

'It is my husband, Bhosla,' she said to me, her voice breathless. 'He has not been down from the hills for two weeks.' She settled the baby in the sling, then stooped over the black pot and filled a huge bowl with fish and mushroom stew. She handed it to him with downcast eyes, and he barked a sentence at her, tossing his head in my direction. She answered quietly, her tone curiously flat as it never was when she spoke to me or the other women.

Her answer satisfied Bhosla. He squatted, his back still to me, and finished the stew in a few enormous slurps.

I felt the strain. 'I will go for a walk,' I said, seeing Mahayna's expression. She nodded, distractedly, and was already pulling a pile of clothing from the grimy sack Bhosla had tossed on to the ground. I could smell the sweat that rose from it.

I walked through the tents until I came to the low stone wall that contained the sick goat. I leaned on the wall, idly contemplating the flea-bitten creature. A boy climbed up and perched not far from me, whistling to the animal. It was a high, trembling sound that reminded me of a flute and the cry of a hawk. Every time the boy whistled, the goat turned its dull sulphur eyes towards him and circled feebly, first in one direction and then in another, in confused obedience.

I looked to the sloping green hills surrounding the valley. Beyond them were the mountains, their summits hidden, the clouds that floated by caught on those snowy peaks. Were they the same mountains I had seen in Simla, viewed from another direction? I thought of the markings on the maps I had studied in Calcutta, and wondered where I was, and if I would ever know.

I left the boy and the goat and wandered to an open patch of grass where a group of children raced about. It was a cruel game. They chased one boy or girl, and when the victim was caught, he or she was subjected to cruel slaps and hair-pulling by the others, who laughed. From what I could see, the object was to fight back, withstanding as much pain as possible. One small boy burst into angry tears after a hard poke in the eye by a larger girl, and the group walked away from him. Ostracized, his fist pressed to his eye, he tramped to a rock and sat down to watch the continuing game forlornly from a distance.

When the children lost interest and scampered off in different directions, I walked to the horse enclosures. One held a milling herd, and in another, a lone figure stood in the centre, a short-handled whip in one hand and, wound round the other, a rope attached to a plunging, wild-eyed golden stallion. He turned, and I saw that it was Daoud.

He wore only his trousers and high leather boots; his chest and back were wet with his exertions under the warm sun. He had tied his hair back with a leather thong, and I could see the strong, clean line of his jaw, the long smoothness of his neck. He had put larger, wider hoops in his ears. He called commands to the snorting animal as he worked with it. His face was changed; much of the swelling had gone down, although it was still discoloured, but his expression was different. It was not the strained, disdainful countenance I had first seen as he was dragged to the gaol in Simla. It was not the guarded face he had worn for much of the time as we rode to Kashmir. Now it was alive, free, his true face.

He didn't see me. I rested my arms on the top log of the fence and watched. Eventually the horse exhausted himself, and stood with his head low, blowing noisily through flared nostrils. Crooning softly, Daoud approached him, put his palm against the broad forehead. The animal's head snapped up and clots of bubbling foam flew into the air, but he didn't run. Daoud stared into his eyes, and, very slowly, let out a long, low whistle, as he had to Rasool when the horse had trembled with fear in the cave. The stallion lowered his head again. Daoud lowered his, until his forehead was pressed against the golden one. They stood unmoving for at least a minute. Then Daoud lifted his head, gave a gentle tug on the rope and walked towards the gate. The horse followed. At the gate, Daoud slipped off the bridle, and the animal ran across the enclosure, kicking behind him with coltish pleasure. Daoud watched, smiling, then opened the leather latch and slipped through the gate. As he retied the latch, I called, 'A magnificent horse.'

He looked in my direction. 'Yes,' he answered. Something closed in his expression, and I was sorry that my presence had done this. He wound the thongs of his whip round his hand. 'You are well treated?'

I nodded. I wanted to say something, but was confused by the anxiety that overtook me.

'You have the clothes of a *bakriwar*, a goat woman, but your face and your hair – they do not fit,' he said.

He came towards me, and my breathing quickened, but he walked by, and I smelt his glistening sweat-soaked skin.

'Wait,' I said, and he turned back to me. 'I – when will I go back?'

Daoud studied the clouds over my head before he spoke. 'If you wish, I can arrange that you leave tomorrow.'

He waited for me to answer. Why didn't I say, 'Yes, yes, I must go, tomorrow, as soon as possible'?

'Although it would be difficult,' he added unexpectedly.

'Why?'

He played with the soft rawhide plaits of his whip. I watched his hands. 'There is only one *gujar* boy here who can be trusted to lead you through the mountains, and he is our only *syce*. The journey to Simla and back will take seven to eight days. It will take us those eight days – maybe ten – to finish training the horses before we take them to Peshawar. The *syce* will be most important to my men at this time. But

I gave my promise that I would see you returned to Simla. If you are most anxious to go, then I will arrange—'

'No.' Had I said no?

Daoud's face now wore a curious expression. He tapped his whip against his thigh. 'Will your people not worry?'

I didn't answer.

He held the whip still. 'So you will remain longer, here, at the camp? That is your wish?'

Perhaps ten seconds passed before I answered. 'Yes. It is my wish.'

'So be it,' Daoud said, then turned on his heel and strode away, leaving me alone in the still, fragrant late-afternoon air of Kashmir. With him gone, I felt a loss.

And as I watched him walk away I knew now the name of the emotion I was struggling to understand.

Desire.

CHAPTER THIRTY

WHAT HAD I imagined desire to be? I had thought it must be a small thing that arose momentarily and settled in the part of the body that was to be used; when satisfied, it returned, mindlessly, to its lair. I hadn't known that it had its own life, that it would fill all of one's being, that it would infect even the brain. That it was impossible to push away. It had taken me close to twenty years to learn this, even though for seven of those years – between the ages of eleven and seventeen – I had been used as an object of desire. No. I had been used as an object of lust, and it was at this same time, when desire awoke in me, that I learned the difference between the two.

And why had it taken this seemingly disinterested man, this man who had no connection to me or to any part of my life, to make me understand – finally grasp what drove men and women, men and men, women and women, together? Perhaps it is this inexplicable part of desire that renders its victims helpless.

Daoud walked away from me at the enclosure. He had never touched me, other than to put his hands round my waist as he lifted me on and off Rasool. I knew he had rubbed mud – gently – around the wound on my shoulder after he had dug out the bullet, but I had been unconscious.

He had probably cursed his momentary decision to pull me from the meadow, especially when his conscience had made him keep me with him, slowing his journey to Kashmir. His eyes had shown mild surprise at my appearance in the *bakriwar* clothing. I knew how I must appear to him – small and weak, insignificant compared with the strong, capable women surrounding me now. But something about the way the ends of the whip played through his long fingers and his ribs gleamed from his breastbone . . . I felt a movement within, in some deep part of me, low, in my abdomen, that made me soft and pliant.

I stayed at the enclosure, wondering at these feelings, as the air turned cooler and the rich smell of cooking meat sent a rush of saliva into my mouth. I didn't remember when I had last felt hunger like this. I had known the aching gnaw of an empty belly, but this was different. I looked forward to eating with an anticipation that was new and good, a yearning that matched the rest of my turbulent feelings.

I returned to Mahayna's tent. She was sitting by the fire, holding a small bowl to Habib's mouth. 'Bhosla sleeps,' she said. 'He has gone without proper food and rest for many days. Some of the goats fell ill from eating a poisonous shrub, and he and the other men have worked night and day to save them.'

'Is he angry that I am sharing your tent?' I sensed she was explaining her husband's behaviour.

'No,' Mahayna said, shaking her head so hard that the long earrings slapped her cheeks. 'You are welcome.' She said the words with confidence, but didn't look at me, picking at something on the baby's scalp. 'Eat,' she said then, and I pulled stringy strips of meat from the pot with my fingers,

397

tearing at them, feeling juice and grease run down my chin. I ate and ate, as if insatiable.

'I watched Daoud training a horse,' I said, when I had finished. I wiped my hands on the grass, then ran a finger over the etched surface of the silver bracelet Mahayna had given me to wear that morning. I thought of the sweat on Daoud's smooth chest, how I had wanted to put out my hand and press my fingers to it.

Mahayna made a small sound in her throat . . . of amusement. I looked at her.

'You will go to him, I think,' she said.

I shook my head, feeling my earrings swing against my cheeks as Mahayna's had. My face grew hot. 'Why do you say this? He is a chief, and I a *ferenghi*. He has two wives. I have a husband.'

Mahayna shrugged. 'Your husband has not given you children. He beats you. That is reason enough to seek comfort elsewhere.'

She said it, as she said everything, so simply. Seeking comfort. That coupling could be comfort was an odd concept. It meant release, I understood, for men. For women it meant children. Comfort? I looked at the distant silver of the sun, hurrying to rest behind the mountains. Mahayna and I sat in silence as the night sky grew black, and after she had nursed Habib until he fell asleep I followed her inside the tent and bundled myself in my quilt in the crowded space. Mahayna put Habib into a pile of skins in one corner, and lay between me and Bhosla.

I thought the camp dogs had woken me, although this wasn't their usual thin yapping; it was a hoarse, rhythmic barking. I turned over, pulling the quilt round my ears, when a stifled whisper made me tense and wake fully. I opened my eyes, making out the curve of the tent wall. The whisper came again, now angry, from behind me. It was Mahayna. Then the guttural sound started again, and it wasn't the dogs at all, but Bhosla with Mahayna. I listened as his grunting grew louder and more urgent, then culminated in a hissing groan. A few moments later there was a muffled thump.

I lay stiffly, aware that my shoulder was aching; I was lying on the wounded one. Sleep had gone. I waited until I heard Mahayna's quiet, even breathing between Bhosla's snores, then threw back my quilt and crawled silently through the tent opening.

Millions of stars shone brightly in the clear night sky. The light from a gibbous moon outlined the edges of the still camp; a breeze that carried the deep green smell of the mountains stirred the leaves of the tall birch and graceful poplars. I took the goatskin cover off the large earthenware pot of water beside the tent, splashed some on my hot cheeks and took a long drink.

I walked through the camp – I was not the only one awake. In one tent a child whimpered, in another men's voices rose. I heard muffled weeping in a third. A small white dog charged soundlessly at me from the shadows, its hackles standing straight, but after a few sniffs at my feet it trotted away, tail high and rigid with its own importance. Something about the dog's acceptance gave me a heightened sense of belonging such as I had never felt in Liverpool, Calcutta or even Simla.

Finally I arrived at the horse enclosure. It was the only place that called to me. I pressed my forehead against the hard roughness of the wooden fence, thinking of Daoud's against the golden stallion's. The stallion and three smaller horses raised their heads, alert in their corner. I wanted to say his name. 'Daoud.' It was little more than a whisper, but there was a rustle behind me, and I whirled round.

He was sitting on a thick quilt, his back against a red-barked deodar. A *chapan* was thrown beside him. Had he heard me utter his name?

'You pray for your friend?' he asked. At first I was filled with relief, then burned with shame. My thoughts had been base, and all too human.

I stayed at the fence. I couldn't see his face, just his boots and legs, stretched out in front of him.

'And you long for your husband,' he stated. Not a question.

I was so tired of lying, of secrets. 'I miss my friend, and mourn her. Her death is like – like a rock here.' I put my hand on my chest. *But I don't care if I never again see my husband*, I wanted to say, the exhilaration of being able to speak my thoughts growing stronger. 'But it is not true that I long for my husband.'

I had never longed for another person, except my mother. I knew the feeling as it related to her. But had I ever longed to be near a man, to smell his scent? No. I moved closer to the edge of the quilt, trying to see Daoud's face.

Suddenly he stood, and I took a step back. 'You should return to Mahayna's tent,' he said.

I wanted to stay with him. This was what I had hoped to find when I came to the enclosure.

I crossed my arms over my chest. I was trembling, although not cold. 'Why are you here and not in a tent?' I asked.

'I am happier sleeping under the sky. And I like to be near the horses,' he said. He stepped forward and picked up the *chapan*. He handed it to me.

I took the cape and put it round my shoulders. It was

400

warm, thickly woven in myriad colours, heavy with the smell of woodsmoke.

'It is best that you go,' he said, but he came even closer. I looked up at him.

'Go, Linny Gow,' he said, and at the sound of my name on his lips the feelings that were confounding me swept in with such force that I turned and ran through the scattered tents in my soft shoes, making the dogs bay.

The next day I worked beside Mahayna. I was thankful Bhosla was there, as Mahayna didn't speak to me while he was present. I was reluctant to talk, afraid that if I did I would say things I didn't fully understand, afraid I would give away my yearning.

Finally Bhosla left, dressed in clean clothing, carrying a sack of more clothes and an enormous pack of food. Within minutes Mahayna was humming, chattering. I answered, but couldn't stop thinking of the power Daoud held over me.

All the men I had known had wanted something: the endless stream of customers; Ram, for the easy coins he didn't have to work for; Shaker, for love in a needy way that was smothering; Somers, for his inheritance, and a cover for his lifestyle, perhaps also for someone to bully. They had all made use of me. And in using me they had made me into an object.

Daoud wanted nothing; he appeared to need nothing. He was complete. He expected nothing of me, asked for nothing, and there was no need for me to lie about any part of my life, as I had had to since Shaker had brought me to his home on Whitefield Lane. I was so weary of the pretence I had had to keep up with everyone I had met since then, first in Liverpool and then in the false image of England created in India.

Here, in Kashmir, I could be who I was. Nobody cared what had been done to me, and what I had done, least of all Daoud. I felt myself opening, unlocking, the rusty hinges giving way with a sound like the wings of birds as they startle into flight.

I was open. My mind, my heart, my body. I knew what I would do. All my past choices had been made for safety, survival, concealment and acceptance. All had been difficult, fraught with potential consequences. This choice felt easy, and carried no doubt.

The next afternoon I returned Daoud's *chapan* and brought food to him at the horse enclosure. In offering him the rabbit stew from Mahayna's pot, the flask of water from the stream, I felt strong: I was giving him something. He took the bowl and sat on the top rail of the enclosure to eat it. I stood and watched the horses. When he had finished he drank from the flask, putting his head back to drain it. I watched his throat swallowing. I felt stretched, as if there were a bright, high singing in my brain.

As he handed the bowl and flask back to me, he jumped off the fence and looked into my face. 'You are comfortable here now?' he asked.

I nodded. I wanted him to say my name.

'You do not behave as I imagined a *ferenghi* woman would.'

I took a deep breath. 'I am not like the other memsahibs. I only pretend. I am not one of them.'

He leaned one elbow on the rail. 'Why do you do this?'

'I did not grow up as they did. I have a shameful past, kept hidden.'

He hadn't stopped looking at me. A horse neighed, children shouted. 'I have seen sadness in your eyes,' he said. 'I

402

wondered at it. This is the heavy gift of your past?' His own eyes were almost black.

'Yes. I hate it. I'm ashamed of my past.' It was so easy to say these things to him.

'Perhaps you must let those old lights go out. It requires much effort to keep them burning. Let new ones take fire. Today it is not what you have done but what you will do that matters. That is the new light.'

We both looked at the horses. I was shy suddenly, and sensed some feeling – similar? – in him. This gave me courage to say what I had wanted to say. 'Will you sleep under the sky again tonight?'

He turned to me, and I saw him swallow. He nodded.

'I will come to you,' I told him, and he nodded again. My heart thudded so loudly behind my ribs that it brought a strange and beautiful pain.

I understood, that night, more than I had ever understood. I saw what I hadn't known existed. The first time we came together, only moments after I lowered myself beside him on the quilt, was rapid, almost desperate, our clothing merely pushed aside. And then, while we rested and our breathing slowed, he reached out and stroked my face with a delicacy of which I didn't know his scarred, hardened hands were capable, and it was this touch that made me shudder with some combination of joy and grief so immense that I wept. I, who did not weep, was brought to tears by the touch of a hand on my face. And he looked at the tears, then pressed my face to his chest, cupping the back of my head in his hand. He kept his other arm round me. And I thought of Mahayna, who had spoken of comfort.

When my tears stopped I sat up in the moonlight and

drew my *kamis* over my head. He made no sound as he looked at my scar. Then his eyes moved up to meet mine and he put out his hand. It covered the entire scar, and what remained of my left breast; I felt the heat of his flesh against mine. And then he laid me down again on the quilt, and lowered himself on to me. This time our joining was slow and quiet, and the peace grew inside me until it blocked out all sound. I no longer heard the movement of the tree's branches, the tumbling stream beyond the enclosure, the snarls and yips of the dogs, the night cries of hungry babies. There was only silence, except for Daoud's breath, and it was this sound that I would remember, later and always.

Afterwards, my mind and body heavy, languid, Daoud pulled his *chapan* over both of us, and I fell into a half-sleep, his body warm against mine.

It was still dark when I felt him brushing my hair off my face, and I sat up. He handed me my *kamis*. 'Perhaps it is best if you return to Mahayna's tent now.' He said it softly, but I knew it wasn't a question.

I got to my knees and retied the string of my trousers.

'Tomorrow I must work with the horses in the day. And at night,' he was wrapping his sash round his waist, 'I will sleep here again.'

I nodded, and made my way back to Mahayna's tent, stopping once to look at the stars.

For the next ten days every nerve in my body seemed stretched to breaking point. I would bring Daoud food during the day, and he would come out of the horse enclosure, go to the stream to wash, then return and eat. Sometimes we didn't speak, but at others we talked of our lives. I told him of my childhood – all of it – and he told me of his. He didn't speak of his wives or children; I didn't speak of Somers. We didn't speak of him going to Peshawar, or of my return to Simla. At night I would go to him, and stay for a few hours, always returning to Mahayna's tent before dawn.

On the eleventh night he and his men gathered round a fire and two beat goatskin drums. Some of the children whistled a melody, and two of the men danced round the flames. The women stayed back, in the shadows, watching. Habib had been feverish, so Mahayna stayed in the tent with him, but I sat with the other women.

When the men put down their drums they took turns to speak. I couldn't understand their words, but from the rhythm I understood it to be poetry. Daoud spoke, too, in Pashto, then suddenly switched to Hindi. 'When your face is hidden from me, like the moon hidden on a dark night, I shed stars of tears, and yet my night remains dark in spite of those shining stars,' he said, looking at the flames. And then he returned to Pashto, and in a moment the man beside him was reciting.

Such was my emotion at his words, spoken in the language only he and I understood, that everything else was shut out, the words singing in my brain. I could remember nothing else of the evening but those words, and the shape of Daoud's lips as he spoke them.

When I reached the enclosure, an hour after the camp had settled, a breeze blew sweetly. Daoud was waiting with his horse. 'It is a night for riding,' he said, and, as he had on those days of our journey to Kashmir, he put his hands on my waist and lifted me on to the soft blanket on Rasool's back.

Then he swung up behind me, and Rasool walked away from the camp.

'Do you remember the first time we rode together?' I asked.

'Yes.' He urged the stallion on, and Rasool galloped freely over territory he seemed to know, into the broad hills, his pounding hoofs sure of the way. Then Daoud pulled him up, and Rasool walked, and we swayed on his back, I leaning against Daoud, his arms round me, the reins slack in his hands. I felt his breath on my hair. After what felt like an hour, maybe more, we returned to the camp. Still without a word, Daoud dismounted, and I slid off.

After he had put Rasool into the enclosure he took my hand and led me to the quilt spread under the tree. We sat together, our backs against the tree, his arm against mine.

'What were the words you spoke at the fire tonight?' I finally asked him.

'They were written by the Persian poet, Jami,' he said. 'His tomb is in Herat.' And then we lay down together, under the *chapan*. Although he didn't touch me, I could feel the hum of his body, so close to mine. Heat came from him, and with it the smell that I had grown to love, of horse, leather and woodsmoke. After a while I realized he wouldn't reach for me, so I put my head on his chest and slept.

When I awoke I heard Daoud's relaxed breathing. I sat up and lifted the edge of the *chapan*, but Daoud caught my arm.

'I thought you were sleeping,' I whispered. Even though his face was only inches from mine, it was unclear, his eyes shadowed. 'I will go back to Mahayna's now.'

At last he spoke. 'Stay with me tonight,' he said. And then we came together, and this time, the first in all the nights we had been together, he spoke my name as he moved with me, his voice a muffled cry against my neck.

I opened my eyes in time to see the swift beauty of the Himalayan dawn as it flashed over the treetops, turning the sky into a blur of sapphire. Daoud was not on the quilt, although his *chapan* was tucked snugly round me. I threw it aside and sat up, running my fingers through my hair as I glanced at the enclosure.

The horses were gone.

I looked towards the camp. A woman squatted in front of a fire, poking at the contents of a pot. A bony camp dog, tail curled protectively between its legs, snuffled with mild interest at a horse-dropping near a tent. A bold crow swaggered around a cold fire, stabbing at morsels of last night's supper that had fallen to the ground.

The camp looked different. Smaller. Some of the tents were missing. I jumped to my feet, clutching the *chapan*, and ran through those that remained to Mahayna's. She was putting a clean shirt on Habib.

'Where are they?' I panted. 'The Pushtuns – where are they?'

'Their time here was finished,' Mahayna said. 'They returned north, early this morning.'

'No!' I cried – so loudly that Habib looked at me in alarm. 'Daoud wouldn't leave without telling me.'

Mahayna put her hand on Habib's head. 'Did he not tell you in some way, perhaps in a way you did not recognize? Without saying the words? This is often the way of men, is it not?'

I looked into her keen eyes, then sank to the floor, put my arms on my knees and buried my face in them. 'Yes,' I said then, thinking of how he had asked me to stay with him, then of his silence, his gentleness, and the way he had murmured my name. And, of course, the poetry. 'Yes, he did tell me.'

'You know he had to leave, and you know your place is with your people,' Mahayna said. 'I have seen you become a different woman since you arrived. You now possess a kernel of happiness. But you must bury it deep within you and let it rest. You can open it, and touch it, but let it remain a tiny seed. Do not break open the pod and let it grow, to choke your feelings for your husband – for this way leads to discontent.'

I stayed where I was, not looking up, and felt Mahayna brush past me. Eventually I lifted my head and pressed the *chapan* to my face, breathing in its smell. Then I went out of the tent to help her.

The *syce* sat outside, a small but rugged boy with calm sorrel eyes. He jumped up as I came out of the tent, and Mahayna told me his name was Nahim; he would accompany me to Simla.

'Nahim has travelled through all of Kashmir and northern India with *gujars* since he was a small child. No one knows of his parents or where he comes from, but he arrives at different camps and helps with the horses. He is known for his ability to find his way. Daoud has given him one of the tamed mares in return for your safety on the journey, a handsome payment, and more than Nahim would have dreamed of. He is happy.'

The dark-skinned barefoot boy bowed low, then stood, waiting for me to tell him what to do. He couldn't speak Hindi, so we made our plans through Mahayna. He ran off, and returned within minutes, indicating that I would ride his new horse while he trotted alongside on a strong-legged pony, loaded with food and sleeping quilts, all strapped on to either side of the pony's round belly.

I put the *chapan* round my shoulders, swung up into the soft leather saddle and settled comfortably in the moulded seat. My sores were healed, although they had left bright pink scars. Mahayna handed me Daoud's embroidered saddlebag. 'Inside are your clothes and shoes,' she said.

I knew the time had come for me to go, and that my stay in the camp had been little more than a dream. Yet I had felt, so briefly, that I was in my true life, as Chinese Sally had once said. No, not that, I thought, but I had been my true self. Now I would return to the false one, the English enclave, Somers, and whatever hell awaited me. I pulled off the long earrings.

'Please, keep them.'

'But your bracelet . . .' I started, but Mahayna shook her head.

I put on the earrings, opened the saddlebag and yanked out my lacy white petticoat. I handed it to her. 'Perhaps you can make something for your next baby.'

Mahayna smiled. 'My mind will pray to Allah for another son, but my heart wishes for a daughter, even though it would displease Bhosla.' She took the petticoat and smoothed it against her chest. 'I will make a ceremonial dress with it.'

The horse pawed impatiently.

'Now you must leave,' Mahayna said. 'Nahim will take the shortest route, and you will be at your home within three days, perhaps four. He is a good boy, you can trust him,' she said, then turned to Nahim, made a menacing face and instructed him with a few sharp-sounding sentences. 'May Allah go with you,' she said, finally, to me.

'And may He be with you,' I said, then followed Nahim out of the camp, looking back once to wave to the girl, who was now surrounded by a small knot of women. I slapped

409

the horse's neck lightly with the reins and caught up with the trotting pony ahead.

For the next three days I followed the *syce*. When he dismounted to eat, water the animals or relieve himself I did the same. When he tilted his head to the sky to watch a golden eagle swooping overhead in lazy circles, I did so, too. Once when I saw his face break into a sudden smile, I followed his gaze and spotted a pair of little red-brown marmots, sitting on their hind legs on the sun-baked earth in the mouth of their burrow. Nahim whooped and they responded with a whistling reprimand.

He stopped his pony when its ears pricked forward and I reined in the responsive grey mare. He pointed to a cloud of dust on the far side of the meadow we were crossing. As it came nearer, I saw a herd of long-maned wild ponies, mostly mares, with foals prancing beside them.

In the evening, Nahim cooked tough slabs of goat in a smoky fire, and I ate, although I had no desire for food and could hardly taste what I swallowed. As we lay under the stars, wrapped in quilts, I held the *chapan* and fell into a deep, dreamless sleep. It seemed I felt little: everything was reduced to a smallness that had nothing to do with the hills, forests and meadows I travelled through with unseeing eyes. I was still living in that other world of flesh and heat, anticipation and release. The panic and loneliness had not yet surfaced. I did not, in those first few days after Daoud left, fully understand that I was changed and would never again be the woman I had been before I met him. That I was enriched, but would feel pain in a new and terrible way. What I had left behind was still vivid; I clung to it as a child to its mother. That which lay ahead was unreal, far-off and blurred as the waves of heat that rose from the plains under the Indian sun.

On the second and third days we ambled through shadowed cedar forests, concealed by the damp, dense trees, breathing in the honey fragrance of the tiny yellow flowers that bloomed in the spongy moss. We wound upward for hours, plodding over the pathways that Nahim seemed to find instinctively. Some were dry and covered with twisted, protruding roots, others slippery with the damp overflow from shallow serpentine streams. We would emerge suddenly from the darkness of the forests into dipping, sunlit valleys.

In the late morning of the fourth day we stopped at the base of a rocky hill with only a narrow stony path through dense thorn bushes. Nahim climbed off his pony and took the horse's reins. He motioned for me to climb down too, and then, slapping the pony's rear, urged it up the path ahead of him, carefully leading the horse. I scrambled behind, sometimes grabbing the mare's coarse tail when my feet slipped on the steep incline.

After an arduous climb, we emerged on to a grassy knoll. Nahim untied the embroidered saddlebag from the horse. He opened it and pulled out the clean periwinkle dress. He shook it out and handed it to me. I looked at it, puzzled, then back to Nahim. He pushed it into my arms, dug into the bag again, held up my boots and dropped them with the bag into the dust at my feet. Then he pointed down the hill.

I followed his dirty finger, and saw the familiar church spire, the thatched roofs of Simla. Nahim was already leading the horse and the pony towards the bushes we had just come through. 'Wait!' I called. He stopped at the sound of my voice. I ran to the horse and pulled the colourful *chapan* from

411

its strap on the saddle. Within seconds, he had moved on, and the bushes closed behind him, leaving me alone on the hill.

I pushed the dress and boots back into the bag, and then, clutching it and the *chapan*, made my way down the winding spine of the hill towards Simla.

CHAPTER THIRTY-ONE

HALF AN HOUR later I stumbled into the outskirts of town. The streets and gardens were quiet, and it came to me, from the height of the sun, that most families would be at tiffin. As I passed through the almost empty Mall, a few women standing outside the shops stopped their conversations to stare at me. Although I recognized them, and knew they knew me, my sudden appearance after all this time evidently shocked them into silence. One did say, 'Mrs Ingram?', a hand at her throat, and took a few steps in my direction, but I didn't respond, and she remained where she was. I felt dull surprise at what I'd forgotten in these weeks – how pale they looked, how tightly they were held in by their armour of clothes. And their reactions to me – the expressions of disbelief, the murmurs to each other – made the first tiny tear that, all too soon, would widen into a gaping hole of reality in which I could see that I was more alive than I had ever been. In their faces I saw my own, and the jolt brought me back not only to Simla but to my life as Mrs Ingram, and all it represented.

I tried to plan what I would say when I reached the bungalow, but I seemed incapable of logical thought. Would Mrs Partridge still be there? As I turned into the side-street that would lead me to Constancia Cottage, I felt a hand on my shoulder. 'Ma'am?'

It was a soldier in a spotless red uniform. 'Do you need help, ma'am? I saw you walking through the Mall, and you looked . . . I thought you might be in trouble.'

I looked down at my dusty Kashmiri clothes and turned-up sandals; my hair hung in a tangle to my waist. 'I . . . No, not really. I'm just . . .' I gestured at the bungalow.

The soldier said, slowly, 'May I assume you're the other young lady who . . .' He stopped, and I nodded.

'Well, then, I'll escort you home. I imagine a number of people will be pleased to learn that you're safe.' He tried to take the saddlebag and *chapan*, but I held them tightly to me.

We entered the quiet house. I thought perhaps it was empty, but Malti suddenly appeared out of Mrs Partridge's bedroom carrying a flowered china basin. At the sight of me, she stood motionless for a second, then screamed and dropped the bowl. It smashed, and she drew her scarf over her face and ran shrieking from the room, out of the back door.

'I expect she thought you were a spirit, ma'am,' the soldier said. 'They're so superstitious.' He turned at the sound of a whimper, and I glanced back, to see Neel sitting in the doorway of my bedroom. 'Neel,' I said, crouching and holding out an arm, the other still cradling the saddlebag and *chapan*.

He dashed across the slippery floor, wiggling with delirious joy. He had almost reached my outstretched hand when he slid to a halt, whined, and backed away.

'What's wrong, Neel?' I asked. He came towards me again, crouching low, his stubby tail now curved towards his hind legs. As he drew near enough for me to touch him, he bared his teeth, then let out a short, nervous bark. 'Don't you know me, Neel?' I asked.

414

The soldier cleared his throat. 'Begging your pardon, ma'am, but it would be the smell of the things you're wearing and carrying. Those dogs can detect nomad blood – they're bred for it. They'll tear a gipsy to pieces, given the chance.'

I looked down at the saddlebag and *chapan*.

'Once you burn those clothes and bathe, he'll be back to normal.' He looked away from Neel, who was still growling, as loud voices came from the back door.

I stood up as Mrs Partridge stormed in, followed by Malti and the other servants, who hung back and peered at me nervously. Mrs Partridge looked me over from head to foot. 'Where have you come from?' she asked. No joy, no relief, just a matter-of-fact question.

'I was . . . in the hills . . . I don't know. Really, Mrs Partridge, I don't know.' I was suddenly so exhausted that it hurt to speak.

'It doesn't appear that you've come to any real harm,' she said finally, her voice uncertain now, as if she didn't know whether to be relieved or dismayed.

I felt as if a cord were being drawn round my throat. The silence stretched, and I saw Mrs Partridge's flat brown eyes filling with tears, her lower jaw trembling, although I knew her sympathy wasn't for me. I thought of soldiers bringing Faith's broken body to the cottage. A rush of words tumbled from my mouth. 'We just went for a picnic, Mrs Partridge. A picnic. I didn't know she would—'

'Stop it,' Mrs Partridge said, all traces of distress firmly in check now. Her low voice was far more deadly than all the ranting of the past. 'I don't want to hear anything you have to say. We all know Faith would never have gone off like that without your urging. That poor girl,' she said again. 'And now she's dead, dead and buried.'

But Mrs Partridge's grief was false. She had cared little for Faith, and had been just as horrified as Somers that she had joined us. I knew then that whenever she had referred to skin colour in front of Faith she had done so spitefully, to hurt her.

Now she pressed a handkerchief to her nose. 'She didn't stand a chance, apparently.' She took away the handkerchief and stared at me. 'After they retrieved her body, the soldiers, joined by all the men in Simla, spent the next week searching for you, Linny, but finally gave up. None of us expected to see you alive again.' Her eyes were hard as they travelled over my body. 'Well, here you are, looking none the worse for it. Except for that heathen get-up.'

'Charles?' I asked. 'Has he been notified?'

'I sent a message to the John Company offices at Delhi immediately, of course, to Mr Snow and Mr Ingram. The Company would get word to them. I wrote to Mr Snow of Mrs Snow's tragic death, and I reported to Mr Ingram that you were missing. There was no point in them coming here. There was nothing to be done.' She studied my clothing. 'I don't want to hear where you've been for all this time. Don't speak of it.' She started to her room.

I hated her. 'You weren't there on the day Faith died,' I said quietly. 'You don't know what happened. Nobody does. Nobody but me.'

Mrs Partridge turned back. 'Do you think I didn't see the state she was in? How unhappy she was? She needed caring for, true friends who wouldn't drag her out into the wilderness, who wouldn't think more about their own needs than hers. What she needed from you, Linny, was quiet companionship, walks through the Mall, tea at Peliti's, encouragement with her sketching and embroidery. Not a pony ride into the hills. And now she's dead. Thrown over the cliff by that wild man. Oh, it's all been such a terrible business.'

'Is that what you were told?'

She ignored my question. 'Well? How did you convince him not to kill you?' She sniffed, then shook her head as if she couldn't bear to imagine. 'The sooner we leave, the better.' She started through her bedroom door.

'Leave?'

'I had made plans to go home tomorrow. First to Delhi,' she said, over her shoulder, 'where Colonel Partridge is currently working. I'm going to stay with him until his job is done, and we'll return to Calcutta together. It's too distressing to stay here. The Season has been spoiled for me, with all that's happened. First Mrs Hathaway, then you and dear Mrs Snow . . . So you may as well come with me, and go straight on to Calcutta from Delhi. I can't imagine you'd want to stay here on your own. Neither would your husband wish it.' Did she stress 'husband'? Perhaps the word sounded strange because I couldn't think of Somers; I hadn't thought of him for so long. 'To say nothing of the reception you would be sure to receive here. I can't imagine anyone would choose to include you in their plans now. I would think you'd be viewed as quite a . . . Well, I cannot think of a polite expression for what others might think of you. When one considers that you are responsible for Faith's death, and wonders where you've spent all this time, doing who knows what, would you blame anyone for being horrified by your presence?' She closed her bedroom door firmly.

I looked at the huddled servants. The soldier was gone.

'Malti,' I said, seeing her bulging eyes, 'don't be afraid. It's only me. I'm the same as I was.' Although, of course, I wasn't.

But Malti continued to stare at me, still covering her mouth with the soft folds of her mustard-coloured sari. Finally she lowered it. 'But where have you been, Mem Linny? And your clothing . . .'

'Please prepare a bath for me, Malti,' I said. 'I'm very tired, and I want to lie down after I have bathed.' I went into my bedroom. On the little desk in one corner lay a book, a slim volume of Shelley's poetry. I recognized it as one of Faith's favourites. She must have put it there before we left. I held it, running my hand over its soft morocco cover, touching my finger to the pages with their fine gilded edging. There was a ribbon marker; I opened the book to the page. The poem marked was 'When the Lamp is Shattered'. Faith had written, in her small, spidery script, at the top of the page: 'For Linny, dear friend, whose strength I have admired from afar. Always keep your lamp burning. Forever your humble companion, Faith.'

I closed my eyes tightly, then opened them and tried to read the poem.

> *When the lamp is shattered*
> *The light in the dust lies dead —*
> *When the cloud is scattered*
> *The rainbow's glory is shed . . .*

I could read no more. I dropped to my knees, hugging the book to my chest and rocking back and forth until Malti knocked on the door to tell me the bath was ready. As I rose from my knees, I realized I had been crying.

It appeared that tears came easily now.

That evening I went to the graveyard at Christ Church,

accompanied by Neel. He had come into my arms, licking my face and whimpering, once I was dressed in my own clothing, and had hidden the *chapan* and the saddlebag at the bottom of a trunk. I also had the silver earrings and bracelet Mahayna had given me, although Malti had taken away the clothes I'd been wearing.

Faith's grave was covered with stiff, dying floral arrangements. I planted on it a small, perfect laburnum that I had dug up from the garden of the bungalow. It would flower every year with Faith's favourite blossoms, the long drooping sprays of yellow flowers that cover the tree with clouds of gold.

I thought about the other graves I had left behind – my mother's, in the damp, crowded graveyard of Our Lady and St Nicholas parish church, and my baby's, with its holly bush and pink stone. I sat beside the mound and the little tree in the advancing evening, the breeze fragrant, the sky turning silver, the birds settling. In that lovely hour, I felt that those I loved were destined to disappear from my life. And, again, I wept.

Mrs Partridge and I didn't speak to each other on the journey to Delhi. I suppose she thought she was punishing me with her silence; I was thankful to be left in peace with my thoughts, which swirled between sadness and a burning glow that never left. I thought constantly about Daoud, and I also thought of Charles, and how I must see him immediately once I was back in Calcutta.

After her trunks were unloaded on to the *ghats* at Delhi, I thanked Mrs Partridge for her companionship and apologized again for all that I'd caused. She nodded once, imperiously, and I thought she would remain silent, but she couldn't leave without a last remark. 'I hope that by the time Colonel Partridge and I return to Calcutta the furore surrounding your activities will have died down. If there is one thing I can't abide, it's scandal.'

Now it was my turn to say nothing, although I found it difficult. I glanced away so that she wouldn't read the look I knew was in my eyes, put there by her hypocrisy.

And then she disappeared, shouting at the bearers as she made her way laboriously up the slippery steps and into the crowd. I sent Malti to collect her sister and return as quickly as possible. When she was gone I went inside the hut on the *budgerow*, and waited in the dim light, alone, rocking with the movement of the barge and listening to the laughter and chatter of those descending the *ghats* to bathe.

Malti returned with Trupti and Trupti's eldest daughter, Lalita, who looked to be twelve or thirteen, and the *budgerow* set off again. The ride down the Ganges was long and tedious. The water was a milky coffee colour, the air muggy, as if the sky was an inverted copper bowl, trapping me in its damp, smothering heat. The fruit on board was overripe, buzzing with flies, and the spiciness of the curries the bargemen prepared overpowering. Malti, Trupti and Lalita spoke in tones too quiet for me to hear. They treated me solicitously, as if I were an invalid recovering from a serious illness.

I had no interest in walking along the banks, as I had on that other voyage, which seemed years ago now. I didn't read, but sat, much as Faith had, on a chair on the *budgerow*, watching the passing countryside.

It seemed we would never arrive in Calcutta.

But finally, almost four weeks after I had left Simla, I was returned to my old life, back at the house in Chowringhee.

★ ★ ★

420

I arrived home while Somers was still at work, and I was relieved that I had time to gather my thoughts before I faced him. When he came home I was on the verandah, Neel in my lap. He stood in front of me, immaculate in a pearl grey suit and tie, a dazzling white silk handkerchief blossoming from his breast pocket. He had grown mutton chops. I had forgotten how handsome he was, sleek as a weasel.

'It would seem that you're all right, then?' he asked, unsmiling. Without waiting for my answer, he continued, 'A bit thinner, I would say, and your skin is an unflattering sun-baked shade, but you seem none the worse for your escapade.' He almost spat the last few words.

'Escapade?'

He leaned against the stone balustrade, casually crossing one ankle over the other and clasping his hands before him, watching me. 'I want to hear what happened in detail,' he said.

I found it hard to breathe properly. In my head were images of Daoud, his hands on me, his weight, surprisingly light, on my body. 'But didn't Mrs Partridge write to you about—'

'She wrote that you were seen visiting a makeshift gaol, where a Pathan, waiting to be hanged for the rape of a young woman, was held captive. That was the day before you convinced Mrs Snow to leave Simla and go off to some godforsaken place.'

'My visit to the gaol wasn't important. I took Faith for a picnic. We were caught in the middle of the soldiers chasing the escaped prisoner.' I didn't trust myself to say even the word 'Pathan', afraid my voice would tremble. 'And Faith . . . she . . . her pony . . .' I stopped. I had promised myself during the endless voyage from Simla back to Calcutta that I would never tell what I had seen, Faith sailing into the air of her own volition. Better that Charles — and everyone else — believed that she was the victim of a terrible accident. 'Faith fell over the cliff. And I — the man who was being pursued took me with him.'

'Why?'

I stroked Neel's head. 'I supposed he would use me as a ransom. I don't know. I couldn't understand him.' And so the lies continued.

'And where were you, for almost a month?'

I pushed Neel to the floor and stood up. 'Why are you questioning me like this? So coldly, as if I chose — *chose* — this to happen. Do you think I *wanted* to be shot — did you even know that I was shot, in the shoulder? — or to be taken on a wild ride into a gipsy camp in the far hills?'

Now Somers's silence was making it more difficult. I felt his eyes boring into my brain, seeing Daoud and me on the quilt under the deodar tree.

'What did you do, all that time, in the camp?'

'I stayed with a girl in her tent, helped her prepare food, wash clothes and look after her baby. After a while one of the gipsy boys led me back to Simla.' My voice sounded unnaturally loud.

'And what of the Pathan who captured you? And all the other men?'

'What of them?'

'They must have been excited to have you in their midst. You, with your light hair, your soft, white skin.' Now he came close to me. 'Did you like it, Linny? Did they pass you around, night after night?' He put his hand on the back of my head and closed his fingers in my hair. 'Tell me about it. Were they as well endowed as their horses? Do they like it

422

rough?' His fingers pulled my hair so that my face tilted up, forcing me to look into his eyes. His voice was husky, his breath in my face smelt of tobacco and whisky. He pressed against me, and I felt him harden.

I twisted away from him. 'Stop it, Somers. Nobody hurt me. Nobody touched me.'

'Are you sure, Linny? Once a whore, always a whore. Surely you had to do something to persuade them to let you live.'

'*No*,' I shouted, and he raised his hand, open-palmed. 'No,' I said then, dropping my voice and lowering my head. 'Nothing happened, Somers. Nothing,' I whispered.

I knew what he wanted. He was building up to beating me – he was already provoked, excited. Or perhaps he wanted me to live up to his expectations of what I was so he might find a way to be rid of me. It would be easy to convince a few people of what he imagined me to have done in that camp, with as many men as he chose to count, and carry out his threat to throw me out in disgrace. I knew that nobody would have sympathy for me if Somers could find a way to convince them I was a fallen woman. Surely the gossip about me had already started – I had seen a few white women at the docks when I arrived. I would imagine that the story of Faith's death and my disappearance was already common knowledge throughout the community. It was sure to be a topic of conversation at dinner parties for at least a month. And if Somers were to add fuel to the fire . . . Oh, yes. Somers had his ways, and his friends. And I – I had no one, now that Faith was gone. I readied myself for the crushing slap.

But it didn't come. He must have sensed defeat, felt my lethargy, and knew I would accept his cruelty without a fight. And in that there was no pleasure. His hand returned to his side.

'It does go to show, though,' he said, not quite finished with me, 'that you cannot be trusted. I'll have to watch you all the time. You go off to Simla and, because of you, an English woman is dead. When you're here you fraternize with the Indians. Did you believe I wasn't aware of all your sneaking around since we married? I have people who tell me everything, Linny, who have seen you in the most unsavoury places.'

I looked down at Neel.

'From now on only supervised activities, the ones I approve of. You need discipline and boundaries. I've allowed you to go quite tropo, and there'll be no more of that. As it is, I'm sure many women will avoid you after what's happened.' And then he left.

I went back into my bedroom, opened my trunk and unrolled one of my flowery cotton dresses. Inside the folded skirt was the *chapan*. I took it out and pressed it briefly to my face. The smell brought me comfort, but also grief so overwhelming that I hurried back to the verandah, stumbling as if in one of the malaria fevers that plagued Somers. I bent over the wide stone railing and retched drily. Then I fell to my knees, allowing myself to feel what I had held back since that last morning in Mahayna's tent.

I lay on the stone floor for some time, sobbing, curled round the *chapan*. I was filled with grief for that which had been found, and for that which was now lost. And despite all the years when I hadn't cried, since my time with Daoud I hadn't been able to stop.

A week after I had arrived home, I awoke heavy-headed from an afternoon nap. I had fallen asleep on the wicker sofa on the verandah, the hot wind overwhelming. All of Calcutta waited for rain, watching the sky hopefully. I was slow-moving, my skin sticky. I thought of the coolness of Simla, and then of Kashmir.

I was unable to bear the thoughts that came then, so I rose and walked through the garden, although the lacy shade of the neem trees could not keep out the driving arrows of the sun. Under the trees were tended beds of nicotiana and portulaca, hardy enough to bloom even in this weather. I glanced at the servants' godown, the simple building almost obscured by the luxuriant growth of the jasmine hedges I had instructed the *mali* to leave wild.

I wondered how Malti's sister was faring. I had given her a job pressing our clothes. Her daughter Lalita was responsible for the flat household linens – the sheets and pillowcases, tablecloths and napkins.

Restless, I wandered to the godown. It was a well-built wooden structure separated into a few rooms, its open windows covered with freshly watered *tatties*. There was a small ivory statue of Ganesh on a cedar shelf above the doorway. I reached up to touch its smooth surface, for luck, and heard a low groan from inside.

I looked through the open doorway and saw Lalita curled on her side on a string *charpoy*, her forehead beaded with perspiration.

'Lalita?' I said, addressing her in Hindi. 'Are you ill?'

The girl struggled to sit up. 'No, Memsahib,' she said. She pressed her hands to her abdomen.

'Shall I fetch your mother?'

'No, no. My mother sent me here.' Her face was miserable. She fidgeted, nervous or embarrassed. 'I will return to work now, Memsahib. It will pass soon.'

It was her courses. 'No, no, Lalita, stay and rest,' I said.

'Thank you for your understanding, Memsahib. My mother does my job while I rest.' Her round brown eyes widened. 'But you will not tell Sahib Ingram?'

'Of course not. Stay until you feel well enough to work.'

I headed back to the house, but half-way up the slope I stopped, thinking of Lalita. I looked back at the godown, then towards the house. I picked up my skirt and hurried through the steamy air, went to my escritoire and fumbled in the top drawer. I pulled out my engagement calendar, bound in soft calfskin. I opened it to the current month, then flipped back a month, then another.

The book slipped from my fingers as I lowered myself into the padded chintz chair in front of the desk. My hands were shaking as I pressed them against my flat stomach as Lalita had done moments earlier.

I was carrying Daoud's child.

The rains started that night. I sat on my verandah, looking out at the fine mesh of moisture, rain, coming so softly at first that it was almost invisible, almost inaudible. And yet as darkness descended, its intensity grew until it was a drumming presence, making channels in the baked earth. I walked out into it, still in shock. What would I do? How could I keep this child? I fell to my knees in a widening puddle, its surface rippling with the fury of the rain. I looked skyward, letting the stinging drops beat against my eyes, my lips, my neck. I thought of Faith, killing herself and her baby. I thought of Meg Liston, and her embrace of life. I thought of who I had been – not Miss Linny Smallpiece, or Mrs Somers Ingram, but Linny Gow, in Paradise Street – and my fierce determination to create my own destiny.

I stayed on my knees for a long time, until the lashing rain slackened, became finer, and eventually there was only the steady drip from the leaves. The air was washed and pure, and the moon sailed through the ruffled monsoon clouds. It shone on the tiny pools caught in pockets of hollowed earth, and it was as if precious stones glittered around me.

Malti came looking for me, and stood in front of me holding a candle. The slight breeze made the flame dip and sway. 'Mem Linny?' she said, almost a whisper, and put out her hand to help me up.

I put mine into hers, and lifted my chin. I would find a way to keep this baby. It was my connection with my awakening. In the few hours since I had learned of its existence, I knew that I could and would love it, and that it would somehow be my salvation.

CHAPTER THIRTY-TWO

I CLOSED THE WIDE double doors of the house and stepped into the noon blaze of Calcutta in late July. I wore a wide solar topee wreathed with thick tulle and pulled low on my forehead so that the upper part of my face was shadowed. I carried a parasol. Malti followed.

We stepped into the palanquin that now waited outside our house every day. Somers had hired it with four *boyees*; whether Malti and I went out or not they waited, hour after hour, day after day, in our front garden. They were only allowed to take me to the locations Somers instructed them – the *maidan*, Taylor's Emporium, or any of the English homes. I could also attend ladies' activities at the Club, and take books from the library. Today I instructed the *boyees* to take me to the Club for a scheduled meeting of the Ladies' Botanical Society. I told Somers I was thinking of joining it, but this wasn't true.

Since I had returned from Simla I had attended one meeting, but was unnerved by the curious stares of the other women. A few girls I had known from the Fishing Fleet smiled hesitantly at me, asking politely if I had recovered – nobody would give a name to what had happened to me in Simla. I was startled to see what appeared to be genuine concern in the eyes of one woman when I responded that I was quite well now. It made me wonder whether some of the smiles, the attempts at conversation, and the invitations I'd received since I'd arrived in Calcutta had, indeed, been endeavours towards acceptance and friendship. Perhaps there was a woman here – or maybe more than one – who would have been my friend, but I pushed her away.

It seemed that everything I looked at now appeared different, and I knew it was because something had fallen away from me, some fear that hadn't allowed me to look at the English here with anything but suspicion. I realized that I had built the barrier I felt between them and me, to protect myself, sure that my every move was watched and judged.

But now was not the time to wonder about the English ladies. I had a more serious matter to consider.

When we arrived at the Club, Malti settled down to wait for me in the palanquin. 'The meeting should last an hour, the refreshments another hour,' I told her.

She nodded, and I went through the doors, hurried through the main hall, then along a passage, and emerged at the back door. I had searched for and found it a week earlier when I had gone to the library. I opened my parasol and, head down, went out on to the street behind the building. I signalled to a passing rickshaw. The *jhampani* was a skinny little man glistening with sweat, his face as wizened and brown as a walnut shell. When he trotted over, I spoke a single Hindi sentence, then stepped into the rickety box and sat on the hard board nailed between the sides. The bearer picked up the shafts and ran, carrying me down narrower and narrower roads, avoiding the buffalo carts and sacred bulls, *kumkum* on their broad foreheads, garlands of jasmine round their necks. The ancient streets twisted and turned, their paths constructed as an intended labyrinth to confuse evil spirits who might wander into Calcutta's centre.

The man ran through reeking alleyways, nimbly dodging other rickshaws, goats, dogs and hens. Babies screamed, children laughed and cried, women shrieked and men called in a barrage of languages and noise. Beggars and cripples jammed the narrow passages; some tried to grab at my skirt as the rickshaw rolled past. The gutters ran with food slops, animal and human excrement. I saw a naked child of no more than three cradling a dead, stiffened kitten, alive with maggots. My body bounced with the rhythm of the man's short steps.

You will not be ill, you will not, I commanded myself. The rickshaw had no cover, and the scorching wind stirred up choking clouds of red-brown dust whenever we emerged from an alley on to a crossroads, making it impossible to keep my parasol open. The sun beat down on my solar topee, and my stomach churned. I wished I had eaten one of the poppadums Malti had brought me with my camomile tea before we had left. But at the time I couldn't face anything, not even a sip of the cool tea.

Finally the man's veiny pumping legs slowed, and I saw that we had left the squalor and entered a quieter area. Small wooden houses with tiny gardens in front looked refreshingly clean after the filth we had passed through.

I looked at each house carefully, and when I saw one covered with a tangle of Japanese honeysuckle, I called to the *jhampani*. He slowed to a stop, panting heavily, and I slipped out of the rickshaw, but had to steady myself by clutching the splintered side of the rickety cart.

When the ringing in my ears had abated, I looked at the man standing between the shafts of his rickshaw, and he quoted a price. I saw how tightly the flesh was stretched across the bones of his face, the yellowed whites of his eyes. I paid him without bargaining, and he stared down at the extra coins I put in his palm, then back to me, confusion on his face.

I approached the house and called quietly through the mat covering the doorway: 'Nani Meera?' There was a soft reply, so I pulled aside the mat and entered. The room was shuttered, dark and almost cool. For a moment I was unable to see anything, but detected movement on one side of the room. As my eyes adjusted to the dim light, I saw a beautiful young woman in a sari of brilliant orchid and turquoise sitting cross-legged on the clean matted floor. A chubby baby girl lay in her lap, naked except for the charm string round her waist. Her huge brown eyes were ringed with kohl, making them enormous in the little round face. She lay quietly as her mother rubbed her body with gleaming oil in circular motions. The woman looked quizzically at me.

'I'm hoping to find Nani Meera,' I said in Hindi. 'I was given directions to a house covered with honeysuckle on this street.'

'You are in the right place,' the woman answered in English. 'Nani will return in a moment. Please sit down and wait.' She turned her gaze back to the baby.

'Thank you,' I said, sitting on one of two huge wicker chairs filled with soft cushions, wondering how this Indian woman came to speak English so flawlessly.

I smelt the faint odour of sandalwood. A chime made of long thin rectangles of brass and blue oval beads hung beside one of the many narrow windows. Whenever a current of air whispered through a half-opened louvre it emitted a fragile tinkle. A low teak chest carved with birds and flowers stood in front of the two chairs, with a simple white clay bowl filled with smooth grey pebbles on its lid; narcissi bloomed in orange splendour from the pebbles. A doorway, hung with rows of amber glass beads, led into another room, and beside it stood a tall, spare cupboard, also of teak, but devoid of ornamentation except two ivory handles carved in the shape of tiny long-tailed monkeys.

The baby was heavy-lidded with pleasure, and as the woman looked at me I noticed that her eyes were a remarkable lilac, with the same milky opalescence as the panicles of blossom that hung from the chinaberry tree in the garden. I smiled wanly, still fighting nausea, and was about to ask for a glass of water when the doorway beads swayed, creating a cascade of melody. A tall, slender woman, wearing a blinding white sari with a thin gold thread running through it, came in. She was not young, but she carried herself regally, chin high and back straight. Her black hair had a single thick wave of pure white, and her large brown eyes were soft.

I stood, pressing my hands together perpendicular to my chest, and bowed. The woman responded to the ritual *namaste*, and I saw that the palms of her hands were dyed with henna.

'I am Linny Ingram,' I said in Hindi. 'You are Nani Meera?'

The woman nodded. 'I am,' she answered, like the younger woman, in English.

'Charles told me of you,' I said.

Her face lit. 'Ah.' She smiled sadly. 'He has had so little happiness. And Faith, his poor little red nestling. I saw the sickness of the spirit in her. I tried to speak to Charles of it, but he would not listen.' Her voice carried the soft whisper of wind as it stirs long grass.

432

For a moment I closed my eyes. To hear her say that she, too, had known Faith was ill comforted me.

We stood in silence for a few seconds, as if paying tribute to Faith's memory. Then I spoke again. 'I saw Charles yesterday.'

'He suffers greatly. He comes often, although there is little I can do to console him.'

I had found it difficult to see Charles without Somers knowing, but through elaborate planning with many chits back and forth I had managed it. Charles had met me at the door of a near-deserted tea-room used by the uncovenanted civil servants. We looked at each other, tears streaming from our eyes.

Charles had grown thin, and his rumpled clothes hung loosely on him. His hair looked as if it had not been combed that day, and his face was unshaven. Once we had composed ourselves he had steered me to a table near a window, and we made small-talk. But there was no use for pretence. He took my hands in his and asked me to recount every moment of my time with Faith in Simla, every detail of what she'd said, how she'd looked. I tried to cheer him with happy memories, but knew that my presence brought him pain. I told him that she'd spoken of him daily with great love, planning their lives, which she had said would be for ever together. I had to tell that half-truth for Charles's sake. I knew I must not divulge the secret Faith had kept from him – that she had carried his child – for it would only add to his distress. He pressed me for details of her death, saying he couldn't rest until he knew, and I fabricated more, saying Faith would not have suffered, that the fall was quick and her death instant, that she had been singing, enjoying the ride, only moments before the accident.

When, finally, he had no more questions, and I had no more to say, I asked him how to find Nani Meera. He didn't ask how I knew of her, or my reason for wanting to visit her.

Then we parted, and Charles looked into my face with glimmering eyes. I knew – and saw that he did too – that it would be better for both of us if this were our only meeting.

Now Nani Meera turned to the other woman. 'Yali, could you prepare some melon for Mrs Ingram, please?'

The woman rose wordlessly, lifting the child, and disappeared through the amber beads. Immediately there was a soft humming and the chink of crockery.

'Will you tell me the reason for your visit, Mrs Ingram?' Nani Meera asked, sitting in the other wicker chair and motioning for me to sit again.

'Please, call me Linny,' I said, as I perched on the edge of the chair and played with the black silk fringe that bordered the cushion. 'It is difficult for me to speak of this,' I said, finally. 'I have told no one of—' I stopped as Yali returned, carrying a white plate of thick, crimson watermelon slices, another of sugar-coated flat biscuits.

'You may continue. Yali is my assistant, and my daughter,' Nani Meera said, with a smile. The other woman returned the smile, set the tray on the teak chest and left. The quiet humming on the other side of the beads began again.

'Please be assured, Linny, that I have heard every story and I make no judgement.' She studied me. 'Is it that you wish to be rid of the child growing under your heart?'

My mouth opened, and my hands flew to my abdomen. 'No.' I looked down, then back at the woman. 'But it doesn't show. It can't. Not yet.'

'Calm yourself. It is my life's work. I see what others do not. So. The child is wanted?'

'Yes.' Instinctively I trusted her. 'But it is not my husband's.'

'Can you be certain of this?'

'Yes.'

'Your husband knows of the child?'

'No. And he mustn't. Not yet.'

'Then how may I help you?'

'I want my husband to think the baby is his. It's the only way.'

'And the father of the child?'

I took a deep breath. 'He is of . . . another world. We will never be together again. My husband has no knowledge of his existence.'

'If your husband knows nothing of this other man, what is the difficulty? Why will he not assume the child is his?'

I stared at the ivory monkeys on the cupboard door. 'My husband doesn't touch me. He turns to other men for his pleasure. Our marriage has never been consummated.' Something about Nani Meera made the truth slide out more easily than I had thought possible.

Nani Meera looked at my hair, my face, my hands, which were twisting in my lap. I held them still.

'His *lingam* is powerless with you?'

'Yes. Except . . .'

She waited.

'When he hurts me – when he beats me, he wants to take me in a brutal way, but he can never . . . achieve it.'

She nodded, tapping her chin with a forefinger. 'I believe I can help in one way, but the rest will be up to you.' She crossed to the high cupboard and opened the doors, then ran her finger down the rows of small drawers, each labelled with undecipherable markings. 'There are many common herbs and sacred plants in India. Some can be used for either benefit or detriment.' She stopped at one drawer, pulled it out and removed a long flat tin, then took a white linen square from the top of the cupboard. She slid open the lid of the tin and put a large pinch of fine brown powder into the middle of the linen square.

'What is that?'

'This one is *bhang*, a mild aphrodisiac made from hemp, which also promotes endurance.' She opened another drawer and repeated the process. 'Crushed seeds from the banyan tree, also an aphrodisiac. And one other.' She added a third fine powder to the mixture. 'Only a tiny quantity of the powdered leaves of the datura, for it is a powerful intoxicant with deep sedative powers, to be used with care.' She gathered up the cloth, tied it with a small, tight knot and handed it to me.

I stared at the bag.

'You must make sure your husband consumes all of this at one time. I assume, as an Englishman, that he drinks alcohol?'

I nodded.

'Sprinkle the powder into his drink and stir it well. He won't detect it, and the alcohol will intensify the effect. Shortly after he has finished it, you must do what you have to do to bring him to the level you have spoken of. He may be a little confused, but he will not weary at his task, and may even perform successfully more than once.'

I nodded.

'You are in the early stages of your pregnancy, are you not? Six to seven weeks?'

'Yes.'

'You must be careful not to exert yourself and bring it on early, as so often happens to English women. You can deceive your husband by a month or a little more, but if the child makes a healthy arrival too soon, even the most unquestioning male mind may wonder.' She looked into my eyes. 'You said the child's father is of another world. If he is Indian, you must understand that the child may appear—'

'He is not an Indian,' I interrupted. I thought of Daoud's black hair and dark eyes, but also of the paleness of his skin that was not exposed to the sun. I could only pray that the baby's physical attributes would not be too revealing. I concentrated on the fortunate fact that Somers, too, had dark hair and eyes.

'Good. How did you come to my home?' she asked.

'In a rickshaw. It was all I could find. My visit here must be secret.'

'An open rickshaw is not wise in midday heat. I will have Yali summon a curtained palanquin.' She went through the beads and I heard low murmurs; she reappeared with a large glass of thin white liquid. 'Coconut milk.'

I sipped the sweet drink. 'Your daughter is very beautiful. Her eyes are unlike any I have seen.'

'Her father was the English owner of a tea plantation outside Darjeeling,' she said.

'Your husband?'

Nani Meera smiled. 'No. Like you, Linny, I loved a man of a different world.' She sat down again, and I did, too. 'I was *ayah* to his children, although I was already gaining the knowledge of a woman of medicine. His wife had fallen victim to the illness so many English women suffer in India – much like Faith. Over time I grew to be his . . . companion.'

The sound of Yali's baby in the next room made Nani Meera blink, and she looked at my glass. 'Drink. It will settle you.' Her hands were still in her lap. 'I gave birth to Yali. An English overseer and his Indian wife lived on the plantation.

437

Shortly after Yali's birth a son was born to the overseer, but the birth killed the mother. I took the child as Yali's milk brother, and grew to love him as my own.' She smiled at me. 'It was Charles, of course.'

She looked towards the doorway at the jingling of bells. 'Come,' she said, rising and extending her hand. 'Your palanquin is here.'

I set down the empty glass, took her hand and held it firmly. 'Thank you, Nani Meera,' I said, then opened my reticule. 'Tell me what I owe you.' I tucked the cloth bag inside and took out some money.

But the woman shook her head. 'It is my gift to you, for you are a friend of Charles. I wish you success with your husband,' she added, and pulled aside the mat at the front door. 'I am hopeful it will work.'

'My future – and the future of my child – depends upon it,' I said.

CHAPTER THIRTY-THREE

A S I RODE back to the club from Nani Meera's, then onwards to my home with Malti, each jolt of the palanquin was a moment wasted. Time was my enemy. For all I knew, Somers might announce the next day that he was leaving for a few weeks, and my plan would be useless. I had to act that evening, after dinner.

I entered the dining room as Somers finished his pudding. I carried a tray with a glass, three-quarters full. Somers pushed himself away from the table as I approached.

'The *khitmutgar* prepared your brandy *pawnee*,' I told him, and handed him the glass. At the crotch of his tight trousers I saw his outline. I knew what I'd have to do to bring it to life. I felt as if a stone was lodged in my throat, a stone of dread at the physical pain that awaited me if Somers reacted in the way I needed him to . . . a stone of terror that he wouldn't.

He took the glass, glancing at me. 'You are behaving like a servant now?'

I made a tsk of annoyance. 'I passed him in the hall. I'm simply making an effort, Somers.'

He took a generous swallow. 'An effort at what? Playing the dutiful wife? You haven't bothered before.'

It would be simple, I knew now. He had been itching to

beat me since my arrival from Simla. 'You idiot,' I said, putting my hands on my hips as I spoke, letting the Liverpool whore in me come out. 'You'll never give me a chance, will you? You're nothing but an arrogant fool, berating me no matter how hard I try.'

He drained his glass and banged it back on to the table. I saw his eyes brighten, in the same way Neel's did when I picked up his favourite ball. 'How dare you? Are you forgetting where you came from? What I did for you?' He brushed back a strand of hair that had fallen across his forehead, ran his fingers over his moustache. I saw that his hand trembled. *Could the drug work so quickly?*

'I'm tired of your bullying ways, Somers, telling me where I can and can't go. I can do as I like.' It was my Paradise Street voice, coming easily at my bidding.

He narrowed his eyes, but not before I saw that the pupils were dilated. *Yes. It could.* Now his hands were balled into fists.

'Don't touch me,' I said, smirking. 'Don't dare to touch me.'

That challenge was the key. I backed out of the doorway and ran down the hall to my bedroom, slamming the door and leaning against it. 'Out,' I barked at the *punkah-wallah*, and he ran on to the verandah. Somers shoved at the door, and the force knocked me down. He stood over me. 'Ungrateful bitch,' he murmured. He took off his jacket and laid it over the back of a chair. He removed his gold ring, placed it in his waistcoat pocket, and rolled up his sleeves. Then he came towards me, picking up Neel's long leather leash as he passed my dressing-table.

I forced myself to cry out: 'No, Somers! Don't hurt me.' He wound the end of the leash round his hand. Then I threw myself face down across the bed, and the leather strap lashed through the air. He was muttering, but I couldn't make out his words. He brought the leash down across the back of my thighs; its sting was deadened by my clothes. The more I cried and begged, the more violent his blows became. Finally he threw me on to my back, and I saw that his trousers were unbuttoned. In the next instant he had forced my knees open, shoved up my skirt and petticoats, and was ripping at my drawers. Then he gripped himself with a look that combined surprise, triumph and lust, and rammed himself into me. I felt my flesh tear. 'Is this how you like it?' he asked, his hands pinning down my shoulders as his hips jerked. 'This is what you've been wanting from the first time you laid eyes on me, isn't it, whore?'

He closed his eyes and raised his chin, rutting then with such urgency that I worried about the baby – but I knew I mustn't stop him. He went on and on, seemingly tirelessly, as Nani Meera had predicted, his arms shaking with the effort of holding himself above me for so long. I closed my eyes, waiting for it to end, trying to go to the place inside my head that I had found all those years ago in Liverpool. But I couldn't reach it any more. I couldn't make myself float away, disappear from my body. I was no longer sheathed in the internal armour that had kept me sane, that had allowed me to continue to live as I had had to, first as a child and then as a young woman.

Now I knew what this act could mean. I had been touched by its tenderness and shared joy with Daoud. Somers's bestiality was the most horrific rape. Not since my first time, with the man called Mr Jacobs, had I felt so violated. It was as if Daoud's lovemaking had made me clean again, had taken away all the unspeakable memories. I bit my lips until

I tasted blood, bearing Somers's frenzied pounding for what felt like an eternity. At long last he tensed, and then, groaning, collapsed heavily on to me, his body twitching, his breath harsh in my ear. Finally he lay still and his breathing grew soft and steady. Then I couldn't hear it at all.

I tried to shift from under him, but he had grown heavier, and oddly limp, although I could still feel him, stiff, inside me. *What if he's dead? What if Nani Meera put in too much of the datura, and I've killed him?*

'Somers,' I said, my hands under his chest, pushing. 'Somers!' I pushed hard enough to roll him off me. He lay on his side. I slapped his face, hard, and at that he made a sound. His eyelids fluttered. 'Get up,' I said, my voice low and cold. 'Get up and get out of here.'

'What?' he whispered, then opened his eyes. His pupils were huge and black, his face an unnatural red. The leash was still wrapped round his hand.

'You've had your pleasure. Now leave.'

He sat up, looking at my dress and petticoats, bunched around my hips, my drawers torn and hanging off one leg. My hair was plastered to my cheeks.

He eased himself off the bed, jerkily unwound the leash and dropped it. He forced himself into his under-drawers, pulled up his trousers and buttoned them with shaking fingers. He tried to speak, then licked his lips and cleared his throat. 'So you aren't made of steel, after all,' he said. 'I have made you cry.'

I put my hand to my face. It was wet. I tasted salt on my lips.

'You shouldn't anger me, Linny,' he said. 'Perhaps eventually you'll learn.'

I yanked my skirt down and turned on my side. 'I want

Malti,' I said quietly. 'Send Malti to me. I want a bath to rid myself of your slime.'

And then he left, and didn't return until late the next day, eyes red-rimmed, clothing wrinkled. We didn't speak for the next week.

In the first week of September I sat in the cracked leather chair in front of Dr Haverlock's desk. He was a rheumy-eyed old man, his jacket and tie spotted with grease. His high colour suggested gout. He picked under his nails with a small scalpel. He had been one of the English enclave's physicians for over twenty years, Mrs Waterton had told me when I confessed to her that I needed to visit a doctor.

She had grasped my hands, her face beaming. 'Is it . . . ?'

'I believe so,' I said.

She looked so pleased. In fact, she was one of the only women who still invited me to her home for an afternoon call. Despite the anxiety I had caused her, I believe she had a soft spot for me. 'I was becoming quite worried about you, but this climate makes it hard for some. You must be careful not to over-exert yourself. I'd go to bed and stay there for the duration, if I were you.'

Now Dr Haverlock leaned back in his well-worn chair. 'How can I help you?'

'I've been feeling wretched every morning for quite a while, now,' I said, looking at my skirt and speaking in my most modest voice. 'And sometimes I feel dreadfully light-headed for no reason. Only this morning, when I smelt my husband's bacon, I—'

'Quite,' he said. 'Child on the way, I expect.' He took a large pinch of snuff from a small lacquered box on his desk and inhaled it noisily. 'Your first?'

443

I nodded.

'Any questions?'

This time I shook my head. 'But – you won't have to . . . examine me, will you?' I asked, forcing a look of embarrassment on to my face.

'No reason for that. Symptoms are quite clear. We'll just see when it should arrive. Date of last flow?'

I lowered my eyes. 'The beginning of July,' I lied.

The old man studied a grimy calendar. 'Watch for signs in late March.' He stood up, straightened his back, and took a round silver watch out of his waistcoat pocket. He clicked open the cover and eyed the dial. 'That should be it, then, Mrs . . . What was it?'

'Ingram. Mrs Somers Ingram.'

Dr Haverlock's face brightened, and he looked at me with interest for the first time since I'd entered the room. He brushed snuff off his sleeve. 'Ah, Somers Ingram. Well, well, I expect he'll be a happy fellow with this news, then, what?'

'Yes.' I gathered up my gloves and reticule and walked to the door. Dr Haverlock followed me.

'If you experience any discomfort, come to see me again,' he said, his manner warmer now that Somers's name had been mentioned. 'Rest as much as you can. No spicy food, no upset or hysterics, and in about seven and a half months it will all be over.' He smiled in a fatherly way, patting my shoulder. 'Messy business, birthing, but a necessary evil, I'm afraid.'

I forced a smile. 'Thank you, Dr Haverlock.'

He reached in front of me and opened the door. 'Mrs Ingram, when your confinement begins, make sure you call for one of our women to help. Don't trust an Indian midwife.'

'But of course, Dr Haverlock,' I answered sweetly. My smile disappeared at the dull thud of the closing door.

When I told Somers that evening, a range of emotions crossed his face. Surprise, dismay, suspicion. 'What do you mean, a child?'

'Have you forgotten, Somers? That night, with Neel's leash, when you—'

He put up one hand. 'All right, all right. Damn. I don't want a child, Linny. I said there would be no children.'

'You also said you'd never touch me in that way.'

He sat down, his legs stretched in front of him. 'I'm not interested in fatherhood.'

I waited.

'Well,' he said finally, 'we can't do anything about it now. Perhaps it will settle you.'

I nodded. 'Perhaps it will.'

18 September 1832
Dear Shaker,
My congratulations to you and Celina. I was delighted to learn of your betrothal. You didn't mention the date of your forthcoming marriage. Is it to be soon?

I returned from Simla much sooner than necessary; I am sure that the news of Faith's tragic death is well known in Liverpool. It is a terrible thing, Shaker, and I am not sure that I will ever fully recover from it. I think of her every day, and have spoken to her husband. He is constantly in my prayers, for he is a kind and good man who was devoted to Faith, and is numbed by grief.

How fortunate that you are able to travel to London to spend a time of study with the renowned Dr Frederick Quin. I will be anxious to hear of the success

of his planned homoeopathy practice on King Street
(do I not recall it was to open this very month?), and
what you have learned.

In spite of the pall of sadness that hovers over me –
and I'm sure over Celina as well – because of Faith – I
know that the dear girl would want us to look for
happiness within our lives. You sound excited and
pleased at the prospect of this new world of medicine,
and Celina will be, indeed, a wonderful companion.
And I, too, have been buoyed by my own small news. A
child is expected, and in this I am very happy.

My fondest wishes,

Linny

PS An infusion made from the leaves of the *asagandh* –
a modest shrub, known in English as the winter cherry
– is given to those suffering from unspecified fevers
and anxiety.

Somers and I never spoke of my pregnancy, although I
sometimes saw him looking at my growing belly with a hint
of alarm. I sent Malti to Nani Meera with a chit, asking her
to help when my time came, and to arrange for her to come
regularly to Chowringhee, although of course she went to
the servants' godown. It was there, in one of the small, clean
rooms, that she touched me with warm, dry hands, telling
me the pregnancy went well. I told her I had already given
birth once, and she said it would make this birth easier.

I was peaceful as the months passed. I sent notes of regret
to the invitations Somers and I received – he often attended
without me – using my pregnancy as an excuse, and spent
my time sitting on the verandah. In the quick Calcutta

twilight, waiting for the first breath of the evening breeze to stir the leaves, I listened to the whir of the crickets and the frogs' croaks, and wondered if the baby could hear the same sounds. With the heat less intense as we went into the Cool Season, I could hold a needle without it slipping and began to sew, with Malti's help. I worked on clothing for the baby, tiny yoked shirts, vests and petticoats.

Neel was ever at my side. We sat, Malti, Neel and I, and I rejoiced at the first flutterings and stirrings, content to know that the child Daoud and I had created was growing. I refused to imagine what would happen if the baby were too dark. I held tightly to the memory of Daoud's skin, no darker than Somers's, his strong white teeth, his capable hands, his hard, muscled body. I knew that if the physical attributes of the child shouted my deceit, I would have to take the infant and disappear. Where, or how, I didn't know, and I refused to let it haunt my thoughts.

As the air grew cool I became heavier, and I summoned my *durzi* to make comfortable clothes, flowing and unstructured.

Somers hated them, telling me I was a disgusting sight, lolling about uncorseted in loose tea-gowns. He forbade me to wear them, but I continued to do so when he wasn't at home.

One morning, shortly before the new year, he watched me heave myself out of a deep armchair and try to stoop to pick up Neel. 'We're invited to celebrate with the McDougalls. I told them I'd come, but that you weren't leaving the house. You're so large,' he chided. 'You still have another – what? Three months? Dr Haverlock did say the end of March?'

I studied the underside of Neel's ear. 'Yes. But the baby

447

will probably come sooner. He assured me it's unusual to carry a child for the full term here in India, what with the extreme climate. And because I'm small, I probably appear larger than a tall woman would.' I stopped myself. Somers was clever. I couldn't appear to be making excuses.

On the morning of 26 February 1833, I waited until Somers had left for work, then told Malti to fetch Nani Meera.

'It is a good day for a birth,' Malti said, smiling. 'As I arose this morning I saw a flock of the seven brothers in the sky. This is always a sign of a boy child.' She clasped her hands. 'I will inform all of the servants, and have them do *puja* for you.'

Dear Malti. She was my only ally, doing what I asked faithfully. After she left I lay alone, frightened by the remembered intensity of the pain.

When Nani Meera and Yali hurried in, an hour later, I cried out with relief. Within moments Yali was massaging my temples with something cool and sharp-smelling, while Nani Meera laid out cloths, a sharp knife and an assortment of herbs and oils. In the early afternoon I pushed my son into her waiting hands.

'It is a healthy boy,' she said, deftly cutting the cord and holding up the glistening baby. 'From the sound of him it appears he will be brave and headstrong, like his mother.'

I raised my head and studied him anxiously, afraid of what I might see. But he simply looked like a newborn, skin reddish, face screwed into a tight, angry scowl, wailing thinly as if complaining about the discomfort of his journey. His hair was a wet slick of dark gold.

Malti clapped her hands, laughing as the baby's first cries turned to indignant howls as Yali rubbed him firmly with a warm damp cloth. 'Listen to his cry,' Malti said. 'No one will argue with him.' She took the baby, wrapped loosely in soft flannel, from Yali, and when Nani Meera had helped me into a fresh nightdress and I was propped against the pillows, she put him into my arms.

While Malti took away the soiled bedding and Yali packed the bag she had brought, Nani Meera pulled a chair to the side of the bed and stroked the baby's damp head.

'He has your fair hair,' she said. 'Look, it already shines like Surya's first bright rays.'

I took her hand. 'Thank you, Nani Meera,' I said. 'You've given me, and him,' I touched my lips to the baby's velvety forehead, 'a chance of happiness.'

Nani Meera squeezed my hand. 'I have given you nothing, Linny. You create your own destiny.'

Yali set a small packet on the table beside the bed. 'Dissolve this in water and drink it tonight,' Nani Meera said. 'You have no damage from the birth. Do not listen to the urging of the English memsahibs who will come to see you, puffed full of advice. They will tell you to remain in bed for a great while, but you will only become weak if you do so. They will say the child should not be handled excessively, but this is also wrong. The baby has known only your body's warmth and the beating of your heart. To lose this comfort suddenly must be a great sorrow even for a tiny spirit. I know it is the way of your people, but perhaps it is the cause of the hesitancy of the English to respond to others, to back away as if burned when touched. Hold your son, Linny, hold him tight against you. Rock him and sing to him, and let him feel your love. This I did with my Yali, and with Charles, and they are unafraid to show their own love and feelings.'

The baby stirred and turned his head towards my breast.

'You have hired a wet-nurse?'

'No.'

Nani Meera smiled. 'I suspected as much. All the more reason for the English ladies to whisper about you.'

'I don't care.'

'Good. You must be strong with these magpies. Yali will instruct Malti to prepare a daily boiled drink containing cumin and the climbing asparagus. It will increase your milk flow,' she said. 'And now you must do one more thing that requires strength.'

I looked up at her.

'You must help your husband believe it is his child. It may be difficult, when you look at this boy and think of his father.' She touched the baby's head once more, then laid her palm on my forehead. 'May I say a blessing?'

I nodded.

'She is become the light of her house: a red flame in the bowl of a shining oil lamp. She has given birth to his son, whose lands are made lovely with flowers by the pattering rain.'

My eyes were damp. I leaned into her warm hand.

'It is an ancient saying – Ainkurunuru,' she said, keeping her hand on my forehead, and I felt heat and strength flowing from it through me. 'Do you have a name for your son?'

I picked up the baby's loosely curled fingers and kissed them. 'David. His name will be David.'

CHAPTER THIRTY-FOUR

SOMERS STOOD IN the doorway with his hands in his pockets.

'Come and see him,' I said. At this moment I felt such happiness that it extended even to Somers. I patted the bed beside me.

He came to me but didn't sit down.

'Would you like to hold him?'

He shook his head. 'He looks well, I suppose.'

'He is well. Small, because he came early, but healthy.'

'Well,' he said, 'it will be Somers, I suppose.'

'I beg your pardon?'

'His name will be Somers.' His voice was curiously flat.

'I thought we'd call him David.'

'Why?'

'I don't know. I've always admired it as a name. It means "beloved".' I stared at the baby as I spoke, hoping not to appear too determined. If Somers knew how important it was to me that this child was called David – my only connection with Daoud – he would fight me. And win.

'David Somers Ingram, then,' he conceded.

The baby made a face, yawned and opened his eyes, squinting.

'He's got my hair, Somers, but his eyes . . . At the moment

they're dark blue, like so many newborns. But they're murky.' I raised mine and stared at Somers. 'I have a feeling they'll be dark, like his father's.'

Somers stood. 'I suppose they might. Well.' He kept looking at the baby, the same noncommittal expression on his face. I waited, heart pounding. 'I may as well go on to the Club for dinner.'

I smiled and nodded. He had not been thinking about whether the child in my arms looked unlike any other English child.

Later that evening, after I'd fed David, Malti let Neel in from the garden. He ran to the bed and jumped on to the end. He stopped and raised his nose in the air.

'Hello, Neel,' I said. 'Come and see David.' I folded back the light flannel from the baby, who had fallen asleep. Tail curiously stiff, Neel crept up beside me. His kind ochre eyes looked at me, then he sniffed the blanket. Immediately, a low growl started in his throat, and his black lips twitched.

I grabbed David, pressing him to me. He cried out, woken by the sudden movement, and Neel barked in short, angry bursts.

Somers came to the door. 'What the devil is all this caterwauling?' he shouted. 'Neel!'

But the dog kept barking, legs spread and rigid as he backed away from me.

The words of the soldier in Simla came back to me with a heavy thud. *Those dogs can detect nomad blood. They'll tear a gipsy to pieces, given the chance.* 'Take him out, Somers. Take him away.' My voice was high with terror.

'For God's sake,' Somers roared, and grabbed Neel by the

452

scruff of his neck. He carried him away, and returned a few minutes later.

'You're green,' he said. 'Nothing to be upset about. I suppose Neel doesn't like playing second fiddle.'

'Where is he?'

'I tied him up outside and gave him a mutton bone. Give him a few days, and he'll settle.'

'No. Tomorrow I would like you to give him to the Lelands. Ivy's been wanting a dog for Alexander. They're leaving for a new posting in Barrackpore next week.'

Somers blinked. 'I thought you had an affection for him.'

'I do. But I don't want him to be near the baby. I don't trust him.'

'You can do as you like with him,' Somers said, shrugging. 'I'm going to bed.'

An hour later I left David with Malti, and went out to see Neel. I stroked him and held him, kissing his bony head. 'You won't be happy here any more,' I whispered, crying into his fur. He wagged his tail and licked my face.

I stifled my sobs, sitting on the cool stones with him in my lap. I loved him and he me, and now I must lose him.

1 February 1834
Dear Shaker and Celina,

I trust you are settling into your married life with ease and joy. I thought of you over the holiday season, imagining your Christmas wedding.

Your study of homoeopathy sounds intriguing, Shaker, and I wish you continued success.

David's first birthday approaches. It is difficult to

believe almost twelve months have passed since his birth. I find that the year has gone quickly, although the days pass slowly.

I hope it won't be long before you both know the joy of a child, as I do.

My love to you both,

Linny

PS The *gadahpurna* is known by the English as hogweed. It flourishes at the beginning of the rains, and is also known as 'the rain born'. It is used for those suffering from snake or rat bite, and jaundice.

The year had passed in a tolerable way. I was caught up in the physical and emotional demands of David, not letting Malti help except in the most minor ways. I couldn't bear to be apart from my pretty baby, and he slept in my bed with me. I never let him out of my sight for that first whole year. He helped me forget my life with Somers, the suffocating presence of the English enclave, and enabled me to remember my time with Daoud.

But as he passed his first, and then his second birthday, and was running about, needing me less, I found loneliness yawned. There were longer and deeper times of restlessness, of despair, when David's smile made me hunger for Daoud, for the time I had spent with him, the feel of his arms round me, and I developed an inexplicable pain under my ribs that never left.

I was an outsider in my own home, and an outsider in British India. I spent my time now, like the other women, shopping at the English shops, and taking quiet walks in the *maidan* with David and Malti. There were palanquin rides to

454

the homes of the other Company-employee wives too. They seemed to have forgotten my 'ordeal', and there were always new wives from each year's Fishing Fleet, who knew little about me except my senior position, and that I was not overly sociable. But, still, I found their judgemental outlook stifling. They were determined to reinforce the English traditions and rules more strongly in India than they would have at home. Their narrow-minded, unforgiving disposition frightened me when I thought of my dark-eyed son. I dared not imagine the consequences should anyone discover the truth. I grew careful with them as I had become with Somers, cautious not to draw attention to myself or to uspet the fragile confines of their narrow world.

Somers no longer found reason to beat me, although he still struck me occasionally: he was no longer interested in intense beatings because of the difference in me. The excitement had gone out of the game: he considered me broken. I remembered how Daoud, with a gentle hand, had broken his horses' wildness. Somers's tactics were at the opposite end of the spectrum from his and I had grown submissive for the sake of my son.

So I lived quietly, in near-isolation, finding joy in David, but I realized gradually that I couldn't live indefinitely on the edge of my nerves.

When David was close to three I heard, by chance, about a handful of women who met regularly, in a house at the other end of Garden Reach, to produce booklets for newly arrived English women. The content ranged from basic Hindi to use with servants, to recipes that incorporated Indian and English foods, to dealing with minor ailments caused by the climate. Here was something I could be excited about and interested in: the creation of books. The group welcomed me and I began work on a booklet that dealt with the healing properties of indigenous plants. The pages were created on an ancient printing press, sent up from Madras. Mr Elliot – the husband of the woman in whose home we met – ran the press for us. The last time I'd been at the Elliots' I had shown several ladies what I remembered from the bookbindery in Liverpool, and we had worked on simple covers of floral cotton and drawings on white vellum. I had been experimenting on a piece of red silk, embroidering it with gold and coloured threads.

Those afternoons were precious to me. It was so long since I had looked forward to something and felt useful.

One evening I was humming as I sat brushing my hair, thinking about the meeting the next afternoon. It was the beginning of the Cool Season and, as always at this time of year, spirits rose. I breathed in the fresh air from the open window, pinched my cheeks to put more colour into them, and thought about the richness of the red silk cover.

Then Somers came to my room. He stood in the doorway, and I saw his reflection in the mirror. I turned to face him.

'I've heard of your involvement with these people, Linny. The book people.'

I put down my brush. 'I think the booklets are quite useful, especially to new wives. I wish I'd had something similar when I—'

'You're not going back.'

I stood and took a step towards him, my smile gone. 'But – but why not? It's a function for the ladies. You said I could—'

He interrupted again. 'It's a function that includes Indian women, Linny.'

456

'Some of them are Eurasian, but—'

'They're all half-castes. As is Elliot, who works as a clerk in the public office.'

'Mr Elliot is highly educated, very quiet and gentlemanly. His wife is charming. What does it matter that—'

'Did you not learn your lesson with the Snow woman?'

'Her name was Faith.'

'You seem to have forgotten that I do not allow you to associate with anyone unless they are of pure Norman or Saxon blood.'

'Do you think their colour rubs off on the pages, Somers?'

His jaw clenched. 'We're attempting to help the mess that is India, and we're all working together – and that includes you, whether you like it or not – to make this land as proper a place as is possible. We are the superiors. It's our moral obligation.'

'But I feel as if I'm helping in this way – creating booklets for English women new to India, to help them understand the culture and adjust.'

'It's not the booklets, it's the company. As I've said, it's out of the question.' He crossed to where I was standing.

My pulse was pounding with anger. 'So, you expect me to share in this obligation, yet have no responsibility for it.'

'Put it in any way you wish, Linny. The point is that you'll occupy yourself as I see fit. You are the wife of a *burra sahib*, not a lowly uncovenanted clerk. You won't embarrass me again.'

'Why would you be embarrassed by what I create? Mr Elliot said—'

'I'm quite aware of what he said.'

'You've spoken to him?' I looked at Somers's sullen face. 'Are you jealous, Somers, because I'm doing something

457

worthwhile? Perhaps you just don't like it that I have work to do. And they respect me – did you know that? That's it, isn't it?'

He laughed. 'Work? You call it *work*?' His voice grew louder. 'I won't listen to any more of this.' Before I could move he hit my cheek with his open hand. At the sound of the damp smack, there was a small, strangled cry. We turned to the doorway. David stood there, his hands over his eyes.

'David, darling, Mama is quite all right. Look,' I said, trying to smile as he uncovered his eyes.

He ran to Somers and threw his small arms around Somers's legs. 'Don't hit Mama. You mustn't – it's bad to hit.' I reached down, pulled him away and held him against me.

Somers tugged at his cuffs. 'Mama's been naughty, David,' he said. 'She must be punished when she's naughty.'

David struggled to break free of me. 'Mama's *not* naughty,' he said. 'She's not.' His body was rigid, his lips set. There was no fear in his face: instead I saw anger.

'It seems you haven't been disciplined properly either, David,' Somers said now, dull red staining his cheeks. 'That is no way to address your father.'

I held David tighter, trying to shield him from the blow I expected Somers to inflict on him. He hadn't struck David yet, or touched him in any way. In fact, he went out of his way to avoid seeing him, or being near him. I felt it was only a matter of time, though, before something terrible happened.

Now Somers strode past us. For the first time since I'd known him, he had the grace to look abashed. It had taken a child of not yet three to achieve it.

Later that year I found something else to occupy my time, something that involved neither the wrong people nor the wrong area of Calcutta. I found my comfort in the substance derived from the *Papaver somniferum* – the poppy.

In 1836, shortly after David's third birthday, I was pleased to hear that Meg and Arthur Liston had returned to Calcutta after their posting in Lucknow. I hadn't had a chance to see her before an invitation arrived for David, asking him to the second birthday of Gwendolyn Liston, Meg and Arthur's daughter.

Perhaps, I thought, we will resume our friendship; I remembered feeling, at the Watertons' in 1830, that Meg had much the same outlook on life as I.

But I was shocked at the change in her. She was gaunt and sleepy-looking. The pockmarks on her face appeared more visible than I remembered; perhaps it was her pallor that emphasized them. I wasn't even sure that she remembered me; after greeting me politely she told me she had asked Elizabeth Wilton for the names of the children in the vicinity, and Elizabeth had passed her David's. I was disappointed in her apparent confusion over who I was; she appeared vague, too, about her time at the Watertons' six years earlier. I was sure that if we talked alone I would find the irreverent, confident and single-minded woman I remembered.

During the party, the children and their *ayahs* gathered under a large striped tent in the garden, and were entertained by performing monkeys and talking birds. Later, after the cake, the children were given rides on a frisky little pony, the smallest girls and boys – including David – firmly ensconced in a ring-saddle.

The mothers remained inside the shuttered drawing room, eating dainty petit-fours and drinking lemonade. As I looked around the over-decorated room, I noticed a large hookah sitting amid small potted palms and ferns on a round marble-topped table. It had a brass jug and attached cup, with a long snake-like tube wound round it that ended in an ivory mouthpiece. I ran my hands over the jug's smooth round surface. It was warm.

'A pretty hubble-bubble, Meg,' I said, when she came over to me. I found myself using Hobson-Jobson often now with the other women, even though I had told myself I wouldn't slip into the nonsense language created by the English in India. 'Does Mr Liston smoke it?' I asked, picking up the mouthpiece.

She laughed. 'No, it's mine. The water makes it so much easier,' she said. 'It cools the smoke before it reaches your mouth. Oh dear, here's little Gwendolyn, and she's torn her frock!' She rushed to her daughter, who was sobbing. Left alone with the hookah, I put the moulded ivory mouthpiece between my lips. It was smooth and carried a faint sweetness.

After Meg had comforted her child and sent her back to her *ayah*, she returned to me. The other women had broken into small groups, intent on their conversations. 'Would you like to smoke it with me some time?' she asked, smiling distractedly.

'Oh, I don't smoke,' I said. 'I don't even like the smell of Somers's cheroots.'

'Foolish girl,' Meg said. 'You don't have to smoke tobacco in it.' She opened a small drawer under the table's white marble surface, and removed a wooden box. Made of mango-wood, it had a tiny hinged lid. Meg pressed the lid, and it sprang open. Inside lay six black balls, each the size of a large pea.

'What are they?' I touched a sticky sphere with the tip of my forefinger.

'It's White Smoke. Opium. Quite harmless. You know – the ingredient in laudanum. And what would we do without our laudanum? It saved me through three births.'

'Three?' I said, then clamped my lips together. Gwendolyn was Meg's only child.

'Didn't you rely on it?'

I shook my head.

'Surely, when you had your little fellow...' She studied my face. 'Nobody goes through childbirth without great quantities of it. Why would one?'

I made a noncommittal sound.

'Well, the next time you should. You must give some preparation of it to your boy, for his aches and pains, though. Godfrey's cordial, or Mother Bailey's.'

'The herb teas that my *ayah* makes for him when his stomach is upset seem adequate,' I told her.

Meg frowned. 'He's never suffered from boils, or prickly heat, or earache? What about fevers, during the Hot Season?' Her voice was slow, insistent.

I wondered why I suddenly felt guilty for having such a healthy child.

'I've always dosed Gwendolyn with it to settle her, when she's overexcited or won't sleep at bedtime. Much healthier than gin, which some use. I find Godfrey's works like a charm – "A Pennyworth of Peace", as it says on the bottle. She goes straight to sleep. I'll give you a bottle – I brought a small crate with me.'

I remembered Elsie's baby, back on Paradise Street, dead from an overdose of Mother Bailey's Quieting Syrup.

'David's always been an easy child,' I said. 'I've been fortunate.'

Meg touched the hookah. 'Never mind, then. But, listen,

this isn't medicine but sport. Sometimes I have a few puffs in the afternoon when everyone is napping. Lots of my friends in Lucknow used it. We called it Dreamer's Delight. Why don't you call one day next week, and try it with me?'

'I'm not sure . . .'

'Come, Linny, aren't you the memsahib who's the recluse, stuck over there in that great big shut-up house? Wouldn't you enjoy some fun?'

I looked at her heavy-lidded green eyes. I felt the curious pull of their unblinking stare. 'All right. Next week. But, Meg,' I warned, 'I'll only try it once.'

As she nodded slowly, I saw that Meg was no longer the bold creature I remembered, given to wild flights of impulse and outspoken in her ideals. Now she appeared as worn and listless as all the other women who had spent too long under the Indian sun.

CHAPTER THIRTY-FIVE

T HE NEXT TUESDAY I sat in Meg's drawing room, listening to the plunk, plunk, plunk of the ruffled *punkah* overhead. *I shouldn't have come*. But our house was even more stuffy and quiet than usual today. Somers was on a two-week hunt, and David spent most of his time on the verandah with Malti. Today he had played with his small set of drums and tom-toms, and each whack of the stick on the tightly stretched goatskin resonated painfully inside my skull. Even the ticking of the clock on the mantel was unnaturally loud, and I had felt an overpowering urge to flee from what I saw now as a dark prison.

I'd sent our *chuprassi* with a chit to Meg, and she'd replied immediately that she would be delighted to see me. Now she came into the parlour with slow steps, her smile making her bony cheekbones even more prominent. Today it was the smile I remembered from the Watertons', and I was pleased. Perhaps I had been wrong in my first judgement of her. She seemed different today, more aware and responsive.

'Linny! I'm so pleased you decided to come,' she said, her eyes glowing.

'Are you sure you're not busy?' I asked. 'I realize I should have sent my card yesterday but—'

Meg waved a hand. 'Busy? What is there to be busy with? Come, sit next to me.'

'Meg, I have so much to ask you. About your travels with Mr Liston. You must have seen so many sights.'

But again she waved her hand through the air as if what I had said was unimportant. 'One can't spend one's life running about. Surely you've discovered that it takes all our efforts just to keep going here.'

'But did you not pursue your book on shrines? Or your sketches of local customs? You seemed so passionate . . .'

Meg looked pensive, but only for a moment. 'I'd almost forgotten. How is it you still remember those foolish ideas?' She shrugged. 'I was young and impressionable all that time ago.'

'It was only six years.'

'Six years in India – for a woman – is like twelve at home. Surely you've changed too, Linny. Are you the same person you were when you arrived?'

I shook my head.

'Well, then,' she said, almost triumphantly, as if she were pleased at this.

She pulled a small bamboo table close to the sofa, then set the hookah on it. She placed the mangowood box next to it, took a small oil lamp from a corner table and lit it. 'Now we're ready,' she said. She clapped her hands at a boy standing near the door. 'Tell the cook to prepare some tea and have it brought in shortly,' she ordered. The boy bowed and scurried away. 'This makes one terribly thirsty,' she said.

'Watch me, then you can have a turn,' she went on. 'Some people feel, at first, as if they're on a rolling sea, but it soon passes. Ignore it,' she smiled, 'and relax.'

She pulled a long hairpin out of her carelessly piled dark

blonde hair, then scooped a tiny globule of the black opium on to the tip. She held the pin over the lamp for a moment, and when the opium was soft she fitted it into the small opening. She put the mouthpiece to her lips, and there was a loud hissing as she sucked deeply, then silence as she held her breath. Suddenly she released a long plume of vapour from her nostrils. The smoke swirled slowly around my head, and I breathed in its dark, sweet, slightly decayed odour.

Meg rested her head against the shiny sofa cushion, the mouthpiece still in her hand. She looked at something far beyond my sight.

I waited as long as I could. 'Meg?' I whispered.

Her eyes blinked once, then swivelled in their sockets. Only a rim of green showed around the black centres.

'Shall I try it now, Meg?'

Silently, and with obvious effort, she prepared the hookah for me. I put the mouthpiece between my lips and sucked up the warm air through the bead of opium. The smoke went softly into my lungs. I felt dizzy immediately, but it wasn't unpleasant.

After a timeless period I heard myself say, as if from a distance, 'Yes, I see.'

Time emptied into a shadowy twilight, emptying, then folding inward on itself in a gentle pattern, emptying and folding, over and over, without end. I was one of the loose bits of coloured glass caught between the two flat plates and two plane mirrors in the instrument I had held to my eye as a child in Liverpool, standing in a dusty aisle of Armbruster's Used Goods.

I was nothing but a tiny piece of a larger sliding, changing, endless pattern. I thought I felt the very beat of my life in my veins, and embraced that false signal.

★ ★ ★

I fell into the habit of stopping to spend an hour or two with Meg and the hookah every other day. After the first few puffs, we fell silent, and I revelled in the peaceful, dreamy lethargy that spread through me. I learned to set the pattern for my visions, letting myself hover, then float to the beautiful Kashmir valley. That was how it was at the beginning. I could direct the shape of my dreaming.

Sometimes I would be astride a horse in front of Daoud, with the assuring broad warmth of his chest against my back; at other times I felt his arms round me, the hardness of his body against mine. But these sensations aroused no bodily passion in me. It was just a timeless reverie that blended and deepened. Daoud seemed to tell me things, flowing, poetic statements, yet he never spoke. In the communication I felt totally happy, my mind floating in a sea of warmth. Eventually the dream faded, and I returned to the sofa in Meg's drawing room, riding on a favourable breeze of euphoria.

I was grateful to Meg. I thought, in those early courtship days with the poppy, that she had saved my life.

Going home in my darkened palanquin, curtains drawn, I felt that my blood had been replaced by a lighter-than-air, buoyant fluid, and I knew that if I opened the curtains I would fly, weightless, into the still, muggy air of Calcutta.

Best of all, Daoud's face didn't disappear for a number of hours after my visits to Meg: he seemed real and alive, in the front of my forehead, like a portrait in the secret compartment of a brooch.

After a few weeks, I realized it was unfair and impolite of me to visit Meg simply to smoke her hookah, although she didn't seem to mind. I knew she smoked it every afternoon, whether I was there or not.

'Meg,' I asked her one day, before we took up the hookah, 'could I buy some opium for myself?'

'Certainly. There are large English companies that cultivate it in the fields in northern India. Patna produces the best variety. Mr Liston made a trip there, to Patna, on business, and he says that there is a tremendous factory, with halls for drying the opium juice, then balling it – with each ball the size of a small room. Can you imagine? There's also a storage hall with shelves going up to the roof, five times the height of a man, where tons of it can be stored. Most of it is eventually processed into cakes and sold in vast quantities to China. It's the Company's way of levelling a deficit.' She poured the tea she always had waiting. 'Has your husband never talked to you about the problem with the Chinese?'

I shook my head. Somers and I didn't talk about anything. In fact, we didn't speak at all, unless we were in the same room, with David.

'To meet the enthusiasm at home for Chinese silk and tea, England had to pay in silver bullion. Now we want our silver back, and while the Chinese don't want our textiles in exchange, they're all too eager for opium. Arthur says several thousand tons go up to Canton each year. All above board. After all, the results of opium are no more than the pleasure derived from a glass of wine or, for the men, their cigar after dinner.'

'Is it sold here in Calcutta, or did you bring it from Lucknow?'

Meg shrugged, studying me. 'It's as easy to buy as tea, Linny. I'll have my box-*wallah* bring some to you, and you can arrange with him the quantity you want, and when you'd like it delivered. It is quite dear, mind. You can't pay with chits, it must be rupees. Are you allowed your own money?'

I smiled tightly. 'I'll have rupees.'

'All right, then. Look for my man on Friday morning. His name is Ponoo. That's his day to visit me, and I'll ask him to go on to your house afterwards.'

Ponoo was a squinting, neckless little man, and all the fingers of his left hand were missing. As well as opium, he carried tinned anchovy paste, French hair ribbons and cooking utensils. I had occasionally used one of these pedlars when I didn't want to leave the house because of the raging heat or a debilitating monsoon.

Ponoo arrived just after ten on Friday, holding out a small can and naming a price. I quickly placed the rupees I had taken from the safe in Somers's room into his fingerless hand. Somers didn't know that I knew about the safe, but of course I did – and where he kept the key. Did he really think I never ventured into his bedroom while he was away? The safe was behind a false panel in his desk; I had discovered it out of sheer boredom one long rainy afternoon in the first year of our marriage. He never gave me any money; I had to rely on signed chits to pay for everything, as did all the other wives. The chits were all sent directly to him, so he would know exactly what I had bought.

He kept documents, business papers and a locked strong-box in the safe. It didn't take me long to find the key to the box in the pages of a book in his room. I had been stealing from him since the first few months of our marriage, hiding the money where it would never be found, in a tin box to protect it from insects and damp. Every time I took some I

468

felt the same power I had as a girl, slipping tiny objects under my bonnet and down my boots while a puffing man turned his back to wash himself and do up his buttons. Obviously Somers didn't keep track of the amounts he put in and took out. I knew after the first time that he didn't count – if he had, I would never have been able to steal any more: he would have blamed either the servants or me, and I couldn't have let any of them be punished for what I'd done. I would have been beaten, and Somers would have made sure I never saw the strongbox again.

After the box-*wallah* left I gave Malti more rupees and sent her to the bazaar to buy a hookah, ignoring her puzzled look. She returned with a small but splendid one, the stand and cup gleaming silver embossed with intricate dragons, the mouthpiece of exquisitely carved green jade.

I promised myself I would have only an occasional puff, when I was feeling particularly low. I stuck to my resolve for a week, but then smoked more and more. Ponoo became a regular Friday caller.

I was careful to use my hookah only when David was asleep or outside with Malti, and never when Somers was at home. Even with Meg's assurances as to the popularity and acceptability of the magical black balls, I felt uncomfortable about the enjoyment I derived from White Smoke.

Eventually I took up a pipe. It was easier to smoke than a hookah.

24 June 1837
Dear Shaker and Celina,

The Manchester–Liverpool Railway indeed sounds fine, as does your new home in the countryside of Cheshire. It must be lovely to be away from the noise and bustle of Liverpool, and enjoy the fresh air and peacefulness.

I am sorry I have not written as much of late. Time seems to stand still here. The quill slips between my fingers in the heat. The watered *tatties* and thermantidote are no weapon against the heat of the forge that masquerades as the sun. It brings on a lethargy that is impossible to describe. It makes even thinking difficult, a sad statement since the only real weapon to fight the climate is, it appears, the mind.

The heat spreads, covering everything in its path as water over stones.

I feel as if I am one of the leaves of our neem trees, dust laden, faded, hanging by a thin strand to a former steady stem. And should I submit, and drop to the walk below, I would instantly be pushed aside by the waiting broom of a sweeper.

David is growing. He is a lovely child.

With my love,

Linny

PS There is something about the use of cinnamon I meant to tell you.

CHAPTER THIRTY-SIX

Hot Season, 1838

I LOOKED DOWN AT David, asleep, and crooned to him, 'Nini, baba, nini.' Sleep, baby, sleep.

He stirred restlessly, his golden hair stuck to his forehead. I smoothed it back, then wiped his face with a damp cloth and began again. '*Nini, baba, ni*—'

'Linny! Stop that foolishness!'

Somers leaned heavily against the doorjamb. His own hair was damp with perspiration, and his shirt soaked at the front. I rose, pulled the netting down over David's bed, and nodded at the *punkah* boy, who pulled more vigorously on the fan.

'Don't wake him,' I whispered, once I was out in the hallway. 'It's hard to get him to sleep in this heat.'

Somers shook his head. 'Singing those damned Indian baby songs to him, as if he was still an infant. Bad enough that Malti coddles him.'

'All *ayahs* coddle their charges, Somers. That's why they're *ayahs*.'

'And that's why it's a damn good thing the children can't be with them any longer than their first five or six years. It's not good for him.'

I turned away my head; the words had sounded obscene, coming from him.

'He's a great strong lad, past five now, and should be treated as such. The best thing that can happen to that boy will be when he goes home within the year.'

I stopped breathing. I had refused to think about this. It was too overwhelming. I could not bear to be parted from David, but I doubted Somers would allow me to accompany him to England. He had made it clear that I must always be under his supervision, and could have no freedom.

'Yes,' Somers went on now, 'he needs some decent schooling, and to learn how to behave. The way you let him run around barefoot with the servants' children is deplorable. And allowing him to chatter in Hindi . . . The natives' tongues are peppered with improper words and immoral ideas. I don't know how much longer I can tolerate his errant behaviour.'

How dare he call anyone immoral when he was a brute who relished hurting young boys, and thought nothing of raising his hand to me?

'At least he's healthy and strong,' I retorted. 'Isn't that what's most important? The graveyards all over India are full of English children.'

I thought of Malti's words, only yesterday, as we had stopped cutting flowers in the garden to watch David, babbling excitedly with the *mali's* seven-year-old daughter.

'My David-*baba* is not like an English at all,' Malti said, following his every move.

David was darkened by the sun – he often forgot to wear his hated solar topee, yet his skin didn't burn. He had a mass of shining blond curls and his black eyes sparkled as he chattered in Hindi about the huge toad he and the little girl had caught in the garden. She held the squirming creature firmly in both hands as David touched it.

'Yes, David-*baba* is more like a little native, strong and unafraid, is he not, Mem Linny? He does not fall prey to the usual illnesses of the English *babas* here, and is not listless and nervous as they are. Come, my *choti baba*,' she called, 'come. Give your *ayah* a kiss.'

David frowned at us. 'I'm *not* a little baby, Malti. Am I, Mama? I'm a warrior, and I shall ride my horse to battle. The toad is our prisoner, the Emperor of China!' He and the little girl ran off, and I thought, as I did each day now, of how like his father David was, straight and proud and kind-hearted.

I blinked now, looking at Somers in the dim hall. He'd changed so much in the seven years I'd known him. His good looks were gone now: he had put on ever more weight from overeating rich foods, his face was bloated from constant drinking, and he had grown a full beard, which aged him. What would happen to David – and to me?

'Mem Linny,' Malti called quietly at the bedroom door, 'your ladies are come now.'

I opened the door. 'Did you seat them in the drawing room?'

'Of course. You are looking very pretty today, Mem,' Malti added, eyeing my ruffled gown. 'You must wear your fine clothes more often.'

I took a deep breath, then fixed a smile on my face and walked to the drawing room. 'Hilda. And Jessica. How lovely to see you.'

My visitors rose, taking turns to peck my cheek. They were wives of men in Somers's office; it was a wearying game of polite visits back and forth simply because our husbands worked together.

'Are you feeling better now, dear?' Hilda asked, her mouth a concerned *moue*. 'Somers said you were poorly last week. We did so miss you at the Sawyers' musical evening. It was quite a jolly affair, although of course the upper registers of Frederick Jewitt's viola are still rather squeaky.'

'I'm well, thank you,' I said, trying to remember when the Sawyers' party had been, or if I had even heard about it. Somers didn't tell me about events any more, preferring to go alone. I knew he would pop in, then hurry away on the pretence that I was ill, although he rarely came home directly.

'I must say, Linny, if falling ill would keep my weight down, I wouldn't mind. How do you keep your waist so small? No amount of corseting can do that.'

'She's only had one baby. That's what does it, Hilda,' Jessica retorted. 'Believe me, there's no such thing as a tiny waist after six confinements.' She looked down at her massive bulk, a rueful expression on her face, then helped herself to a cream bun from the tray beside her.

'Well, Linny, you must give David a little brother or sister,' Hilda said, tapping my knee with her closed fan. Then she took a tiny hinged mirror from her handbag and inspected the frizzled fringe of orange hair that rose from her high forehead. 'He's what – five now? Before you know it he'll be sent home, and you'll need more children to keep you from being lonely.' She snapped the mirror shut and returned it to her bag. 'With my Sarah and Florence gone, I'd go mad without little Lucy. And by the time she leaves, Sarah should hopefully be returning to us.'

'Yes,' I agreed, shaking my head as the *khitmutgar* offered me a glass of lemonade.

'Did you hear what happened in the *maidan* yesterday?' Jessica asked.

Grateful for the change of subject, I leaned forward.

'It was the oddest thing,' she continued, licking thick white cream from her thumb. 'This . . . dark man, not an Indian, mind you, but dark, was on a huge horse and circling the *maidan*. Some say he was peering at English women. I didn't observe that, but can you imagine? It was quite upsetting.'

Hilda took over. 'I was there,' she said triumphantly, as if she had performed a heroic deed. 'None of us had any idea what he was looking for. A big ruffian, having the audacity to take an interest in us. I suppose he's seen enough of his own sort, and was titillated by white women. I was quite shaken when he looked in my direction.' She touched her faded hair coquettishly. 'Of course, he was driven away quickly, but — oh, what is it, Linny?'

I stood, clutching my abdomen with trembling hands. 'I suppose I haven't quite recovered from whatever has upset me recently.'

'Sit down, Linny. Breathe deeply. Hilda, finish the story.'

'Well, he was bold as brass, not at all a gentleman — of course, he couldn't be. After all, he was one of those foreign breeds. And sitting on his horse as if he owned the square.' They both looked at me.

'I'm sure you'll excuse me.' I hurried out of the room. Faintness overtook me just outside the door, and I leaned against the wall.

'She'll not last here much longer,' I heard Hilda say. 'That frail, nervous sort never does. She's worn to fiddlesticks. And there's something odd about her eyes, don't you think? Very dark. Too dark.'

'It's her husband I pity. She must not be any sort of company for him at all, always so poorly. It's no wonder there are no more children. He probably knows another would kill her. Poor man.'

I steadied myself and went to my bedroom. *When had I become one of India's casualties, one of the frail, nervous sort? They could have been describing Faith. Or the woman Meg was now.*

That evening, after I had tucked David into bed, I walked out into the front garden. Slowly I approached the acacia tree beside the gate, running my fingers over its bumpy bark. I thought there might be a mild suggestion of rain in the air. Could the monsoons be coming early?

At the sudden bark of a jackal from the darkness beyond the houses, there was a rush of rubbery wings, and I tilted my head to watch as bats, big as crows, rose from the acacia, their black ribbed wings cutting the fading sky. Leaning against the tree, I looked down the darkening, empty street, straining my ears for the sound of hoofs. Every so often a Pathan rode through Calcutta. It meant nothing.

I stayed there, my eyes fixed on the street that led to the *maidan*. Finally the fireflies were dancing spots of light and the sky dark and furrowed, the moon resting heavily. Somers called sharply from the doorway that I was to come inside.

The next morning I sat on the verandah reading the same page of my book over and over again. I hadn't been able to sleep for more than an hour or two, and my head ached tiresomely. Malti arrived home from the daily shopping. I saw that her face was dark with dismay, and she was muttering to herself as she placed a new bottle of ink on the escritoire.

476

'What is it, Malti?' I said, coming through the flung-back doors into the bedroom.

Malti gave me a sideways glance. 'Nothing, Mem Linny,' she answered, rearranging the paper, quills and books on the desk. She stopped and looked at me.

'There's something, Malti. You must tell me.' I licked my lips. 'Did you . . . see anything today? Anything . . . unusual?'

'I saw nothing,' she replied, her tone curt.

'Was there any new gossip?'

Malti pushed the bottle of ink back and forth on the polished wood. 'You do not usually ask about the wagging tongues in the square.'

'Well, today I am asking if you overheard anything.'

'It is not worth repeating, Mem. Many of the *ayahs* have allowed their voices to grow as sharp as those of their mistresses. They have too little work to do, and devise stories to pass the time.'

I lowered myself to the chair beside the desk. 'What are these stories, Malti?'

There was pain on Malti's gentle face. 'It is just more silly talk of the man, Mem Linny, from the North West Frontier. The *ayahs* say he continues to ride about the *maidan*, looking at the English ladies. It is said he has spoken a name.' She shook her head, her brow furrowed. 'Can you imagine such nonsense? He will shortly be arrested. This kind of behaviour is not acceptable, and – Mem Linny, what is it?' She looked down, and I followed her gaze. I saw that I was gripping her dark hands in mine.

'Did anyone tell him where I live? Does he know where I am?'

'Oh, Mem Linny, be still. Hush, hush. Do not be worried.

477

It is only the bad memories of your troubled time at Simla that frighten you now. And surely the bitter hens wish to stir up trouble with their simple tale, for . . . Mem Linny? What are you doing?'

I flew to the dressing-table, pinning up long loose strands of hair, my shaking hands scattering hairpins over the floor. I buttoned the collar of my dress and whirled round to Malti. 'Do I look presentable?'

Malti's face closed. 'Of course, Mem Linny. As always.' Her voice was careful. 'But come now, sit down. I will prepare your pipe. That will calm you. And then I will bring you a cup of your favourite tea.'

'I don't want my pipe. There's no time. Come – come with me. David – where is David?'

'He plays with the Wilton children until late afternoon, Mem Linny. Do you not remember?'

'Take my reticule, Malti, and follow me.' I ran down the hall, turning to urge Malti to hurry. She trailed slowly, clutching the small taupe bag to her chest. As I approached the front door the *chuprassi* appeared, ready to open it for me. He put his hand on the brass knob.

'Please, Malti! There may not be much time. Can't you walk any faster?' I gestured to the *chuprassi*, but before he could open the door it swung inward.

I gasped.

Somers's blocky frame filled the entrance. 'Hello, Linny.' He was very still.

I backed away, bumping into Malti, who dropped my reticule.

Somers stared at it. 'You were going out, Linny?' He still hadn't crossed the threshold.

'No . . . Well, yes. Malti and I were going to the *maidan* . . .

478

We often do, at this time, don't we, Malti?' I turned to her. She stood with her mouth open.

Somers stepped in, leaving the door open behind him. 'You were going for a stroll, at the hottest time of day, without your solar topee or parasol – in this apparel?' He had two hectic spots on his cheeks.

I looked down at my limp dress, saw the spattering of grease along one cuff, a button missing at the waist. 'What – what are you doing at home?'

'Fever,' he said tersely. His old enemy, malaria. 'I'm going to bed. Malti, you may not allow your mistress out of the house. Do you understand?'

I grabbed his sleeve. 'But, Somers, I just want—'

He threw up his arm to shake off my hand and caught me across the bridge of the nose. Bright lights burst behind my eyes. 'I forbid it. You'll not make a fool of me, parading around in public like the whore you are.'

I heard Malti's gasp, and the rustle of the *chuprassi*'s clothes.

'In fact, I'm sick of the sight of you. Whore.'

I wanted to spit in his face, to put up my chin and tell him that, yes, I was still a whore. It was tempting, so tempting, to scream at him that David wasn't his, that I was indeed what he had always accused me of, that I had joined with a man joyfully, for my own pleasure, and that David was a child of love and not of his brutal rape. But of course I wouldn't tell him this. What I had kept hidden for these five years was my trump card. I shook with the effort to keep my lips sealed. I tried to push past him.

He grabbed at the front of my dress and as I moved forward, he pulled at the fabric with all his strength. There was a terrible ripping sound, and I stopped, shocked. Somers looked down at the clutch of poplin and cambric in his hand

– he'd even torn away my chemise – then back to me. His eyes were riveted to my exposed chest. The blood drained from his face, leaving him parchment white. He stumbled back, and the *chuprassi* caught him.

Malti stepped in front of me, trying to hold her headscarf over my nakedness.

Somers dropped the fabric and pointed, his finger shaking, at me.

'What's the matter, Somers?' I hissed, pushing Malti away and standing in front of him so that my scar was fully visible. 'Don't you like what you see? I thought you knew all there was to know about me.'

'Mem Linny! Mem Linny!' Malti cried. 'Please! Do not make him angry! Please!' She covered her face and wept.

Somers shook off the *chuprassi* and straightened, his face still bleached, his forehead beaded with perspiration. 'What is that?' he whispered, his finger trembling.

'What does it look like? The touch of an old lover?' I didn't care any longer how I sounded, what I said. The pure hatred I had for him flooded me.

But before he could respond Somers groaned and doubled over; the *chuprassi* helped him down the hall to his room. I lurched through the open doorway and ran, as best I could, down the drive, my boots crunching over the crushed shells. I heard the gasp of my breath, loud in my head, felt the tightening of my chest at the accelerated and unaccustomed pace. I had not yet reached the end of the drive before large, gloved hands gripped me from behind.

It was the *chuprassi*, sent, surely, by Somers to bring me back. I struggled against his hold. 'Let me go,' I muttered. 'You must do as I say.' But the hold remained firm, and his face, as I looked over my shoulder at him, showed nothing as

480

I squirmed like a helpless kitten. Malti was beside us, still crying, reaching up to wipe the spittle from my chin with her fingers, pulling at my dress to cover me, trying to soothe me as I was carried back to the house in the arms of the *chuprassi*.

The small flurry of activity had weakened me: I could no longer fight, and leaned, defeated, against him until he deposited me on my bed.

Later, in my bedroom, I dismissed the *punkah-wallah* and Malti.

'I don't want to leave you, Mem Linny,' she said. 'You should not be alone. You are troubled.'

But eventually I convinced her I was only going to sleep, and she went out, leaving my door ajar. I knew she would remain in the hallway, listening to my every move. I sat at my mirrored dressing-table, looking at my hands on my lap, curled into each other, still and white as dead doves.

Was Daoud really here, in Calcutta, looking for me? I had to know. I would go to the *maidan*, no matter what Somers said or did to me. I would sneak out somehow, and walk all the way there, if necessary. I took a deep breath and looked into the mirror.

Long strands of dull hair fell round my shoulders. I saw how thin my face was, the bridge of my nose purple and swollen from the knock Somers's arm had given it. The skin over my bones was translucent and taut, as if there was hardly enough to cover my nostrils. I had a sudden horrifying impression of my skull beneath the flesh. My lips had grown thin, and lumpy, discoloured pouches stood out beneath my eyes. I thought of my image in Shaker's mirror, nine long years ago. If I had been shocked then, I was doubly so now.

What had I been thinking? Of course it wasn't Daoud. What had I been dreaming of? That Daoud would pull me up on his horse, and we would ride away together? I was a fool, a complete fool. David was here, my child, my life. My fantasies about Daoud were nothing more than that — fantasies. I had known him, almost six years ago, for less than a month. He was, as I had told Nani Meera, of another world, a world that could never be mine.

I looked at myself in the mirror again. I had lost all sight of the bright hope that had brought me to India. I had lost sight of the woman who called herself Linny Gow.

I prepared my pipe, and smoked it until I could smoke no more.

CHAPTER THIRTY-SEVEN

THE MALARIA THAT had held Somers periodically in its terrible grip had indeed returned, and this was the worst episode of the string of his recurrent paroxysms. He had terrible headaches accompanied by nausea and vomiting, followed by chills that were more violent than ever before. The fever raged, leaving his skin hot and dry, and sometimes there was delirium. And then the sweating began: his body was drenched and his temperature fell. Weakened, he sank into deep sleeps that lasted for hours. Dr Haverlock visited every day to check his condition. I was not allowed to leave the house; although Somers might not be aware of where I was, the servants he had paid handsomely watched me at all times. Even as I passed the front door the *chuprassi* would step in front of it, arms crossed over his chest, and when I walked in the garden the *khansana* followed me closely, stopping when I stopped, walking when I walked.

On the fourth evening of his illness Somers sent for me. He was propped up on pillows, alone in the room. He had lost his fevered colour, and his skin had a sticky look in the glow of the lamps lit in his bedroom. The smell of sickness lingered, its stale miasma almost overpowering, but I knew he was through the worst, and he glared at me with disgust.

I felt that he was destined to rise from each attack with renewed strength and venom.

'As soon as this bout is past I shall make arrangements for you to leave here,' he said.

'Leave?'

He flapped a hand weakly. 'You've become too much of a burden. That last episode, with you ready to run out into the streets of Calcutta behaving like a madwoman, made up my mind. Do you really think anyone would be surprised – or care – if you disappeared? Who would notice, Linny, apart from the servants?'

I tried to swallow. I knew my future depended on the next few minutes. 'Will you send us to England, then?'

He stared blankly. When he didn't answer, I thought it was due to his illness. Then he spoke, and his voice was clear and firm. 'Do you realize you're using Hindi, Linny? Are you even aware that you're no longer speaking English?'

'I'm sorry,' I said, and repeated my question.

'Us? What do you mean by us?'

I spoke slowly, carefully. 'Why, David and myself, of course. As you said not long ago, it will be time soon for him to begin his education. I could live with him wherever you choose – in London, perhaps. He could attend your old school.'

He gave a dry cough, then attempted a smile. 'Do you think I'd trust you to bring up my son? You use opium compulsively, Linny. It's all too clear in your decorum. You're disgustingly altered in every way.'

The floor tilted. I put out a hand to hold on to the bedpost so I wouldn't fall, then lowered myself into a chair beside the bed. 'I would stop, Somers. I can stop if I choose.'

'Everyone knows you're nothing but a wasted ruin. I sense that most think you quite mad already. They don't even ask about you or seem in the least curious that you no longer accompany me to social events. My plan is to find a pleasant place for you to . . . rest. Some place — perhaps an isolated post in the Indian plains — where you would be cared for properly, and couldn't hurt anyone or yourself. Or perhaps I should consider another course, if you would like to go home.'

I nodded vigorously, my head still light. 'Yes, Somers. That's what I'd like. To go home.' If I could only get back to England, I would find a way to be near David. Shaker would help me.

'Well, I agree that that is the best plan. A number of places in London could keep you restrained for — well, for an indefinite period.'

'Restrained?' It took thirty seconds for his meaning to become clear. 'A . . . a lunatic asylum?'

'A lunatic asylum, my dear? Is it necessary to use such a harsh term?' He managed a smile. 'You'll be cared for while you have a long rest. It's well known that India does this to some. You wouldn't be the first memsahib who proved unable to bear the strain. Everyone would understand, and not a soul would question my motives. In fact,' he went on, as if pleased with himself now, 'who, besides David and perhaps Malti, would care what became of you? And David is a child — he'll quickly forget. Malti will be dismissed. She's of no importance anyway.'

My dizziness returned. I needed my pipe. I shivered, and sweat rolled from my hairline down my face on to my neck; minuscule insects seemed to be scurrying under my skin. Without thinking, I pulled the gauzy scarf I wore tucked into the bodice of my frock, and swabbed my cheeks and neck.

There was silence, then an odd, strangled cry from the bed. Somers was sitting up, pointing a shaking finger at my chest as he had, days earlier, when he'd torn my dress.

I looked down at my scar. 'Once again, your reaction surprises me,' I whispered. 'Surely you aren't concerned over an old injury. I didn't think my body would be of any interest to you after all this time.'

He slumped back, his mouth opening and closing as he struggled to breathe. 'I know,' he croaked. 'I know now. When I first saw that,' he said hoarsely, his eyes fixed on the scar, 'there was something . . . something. I didn't know what. But . . . yes, I think . . .'

I hardly listened to his raving. I thought of never seeing my son again, of him growing up to learn that his mother had lived out her life huddled on a pile of putrid straw in a darkened stone cell in some Bedlam. Of Somers distorting any memories of me that David might retain from his childhood, and, worse than all of that, trying to impart to him his own twisted values.

The fierce need to protect David from this future gave me a strength I hadn't felt in a long time. I threw the scarf to the ground and pulled my bodice lower as I leaned towards the bed, so that Somers would see all of the destruction. 'Done by one of my old customers in Liverpool,' I said. 'Quite a picture, isn't it? And yet I survived. I survived a madman's blade once, and I'll survive whatever you think you can do to me, Somers. You will not win.'

He made a retching sound and put his fist to his mouth.

'Surely the sight of my ruined flesh should bring you pleasure, not discomfort,' I said. 'After all, my pain is the only thing that *has* brought you joy in our miserable marriage.'

'I know,' he said again, speaking through his fist, that same agitation in his voice, 'I know now why I recognized the fish.'

I sat back, letting go of the front of my dress, trying to understand. The fish? And then I remembered that time in his bachelor quarters: he had identified me as a whore from my birthmark.

He put his hand down, his fist still clenched. 'I'd almost managed to forget my last sojourn at that black spot on the Mersey,' he said. He spoke slowly, as if thinking aloud. He struggled to sit up again. 'And you're right. You did survive. How, I can never guess. You should be nothing but softened bones by now, the crabs using your eye sockets as a home.'

I put my own fist to my mouth as Somers had seconds before. In the quiet that followed his statement, a shocking sense of knowledge overcame me. An understanding too horrific, too unbelievable, dawned at his words. I shivered uncontrollably in the stifling room, my teeth clenched so tightly that my jaw ached.

'Didn't I instruct my man to dump your body in the Mersey?' Somers had regained some of his composure; his voice was low but strong as he stared at me. 'And didn't Pompey swear to me that he had done it? He assured me there was no one left to speak of what happened that night on Rodney Street.'

And suddenly I heard it, the same cold, rational voice that had ordered my death as I lay, a thirteen-year-old girl made blind and helpless, on a thick rug in front of a trunk of glass jars filled with floating hair. The hair of dead girls. The old man with the shears planted in his eye beside me. The stench of rot coming from him, and that of burning hair. I gagged, and my mouth filled with acrid saliva.

This was not what I had expected. Rodney Street. The

old nightmare came to life, reared up, huge and even more terrifying when fed by the light of the glowing lamps in that room. I felt a spinning, a flying apart, and the old vision flooded back: my body, with its broken neck, tossed into the murderers' pit of quicklime. I leaned forward retching drily, then I lowered my head to my knees.

Young Master, Pompey had called him.

'I had to dismiss Pompey not long after the incident in Liverpool. Too many errors. But I suppose it can't all be blamed on him. I saw you too, that night, and believed you to be dead. You were torn open, right down your left breast. I saw muscle. I swear I even saw your heart, unbeating, but of course that couldn't have been.'

I wiped my mouth on the back of my hand, raised my head and looked at him.

He licked his lips, then smiled, as if reliving a fond memory. And that smile chilled me even more than his words. 'If I remember correctly you were little more than a child, your hair gone. Entirely unlike the self-possessed woman I first met in Calcutta – but for that telling fish on your arm. No wonder I couldn't remember where I'd seen it. I put that night out of my mind as quickly as I could.'

I kept my mouth open now, sucking in the muggy air, trying to draw it into my lungs, seeing the illustrations from Shaker's medical books, all those years ago, Albinus's drawings of the two sacs situated behind the breast bone. I knew my lungs weren't plump and full but flat and deflated, shrivelled now. They wouldn't pump, wouldn't fill with the drenched air. My mouth gaped as a fish out of water. I knew I was drowning. The image of that ravaged face, the horror of the flickering tongue, the senseless eyes, stood in the front of my mind as if lit by rows of candles.

Somers was the son of the man I had killed.

'It's too late,' I whispered, finally finding the strength to speak. 'You could never prove it. It's too late to have me tried for murder.' *I must protect David from a future with Somers, and from knowledge of my past.*

A sound like laughter came from Somers's throat, a ghastly crackling noise. 'Tried? For murder? I hardly think so. There was no record of murder, after all. Simply the death of a man riddled with syphilis and driven to insanity. It seemed he would never die. I imagined him living on for years. In fact, you did the job I wish I'd had the nerve to do much, much earlier. Even before he grew so ill he was a cruel, heartless man. I left England shortly after you killed him, Linny. I wanted to leave it all behind, to forget.'

Silence grew in the room. I took short, shallow breaths as if I were learning to breathe.

'Nobody was happier than I to see him buried,' Somers continued, when I knew we had both gone through the details in our minds of that night, 'where the worms could do their final job on what was left of his stinking body. As for his soul – I don't believe he had one. From when I was twelve—'

'I don't want to hear any more,' I whispered, but he ignored me.

'– he took me with him on his prowls. At first he made me watch while he mounted each bitch. He had a penchant for lower-class women. Like you, Linny. After a while I came to enjoy watching the humiliation to which he subjected them.'

I kept shaking my head, wanting him to stop. But it was as if he was enjoying my misery as he recounted the ugly details. I put my hands over my ears, closing my eyes and lowering my head.

489

'Eventually he tried to force me to join in.' He spoke loudly and clearly: it was impossible to shut out his words. 'My father kept me at his bidding like a pet monkey, stroked occasionally, thrown a tasty morsel now and then, but impossibly shackled. And he wouldn't, even in death, allow me to live as I wished. He knew from an early age I had little interest in women. In fact, he supplied me first with the boys I grew to hunger for. But he stipulated in his will that I must be married to receive my rightful inheritance. It was like him to have a final laugh from the grave.

'And so it appears that you really have had a remarkable impact on my life, Linny. First you killed my father, and then you made it possible for me to receive my inheritance. In reality you allowed me freedom. Twice.' With that word he stopped, and was silent.

I removed my hands and opened my eyes. Mosquitoes buzzed at my ears and sweating hairline. Somers was looking at me in an almost jaunty manner, his head tilted and eyes bright, as if surprised at his good fortune.

I dropped to my knees at the side of the bed. 'Then repay me, Somers. Set me free, in turn. Let me take David and disappear.' I grabbed his hands. They were icy. 'You'll never hear from us again. I'll ask for nothing.'

He shook his head gently, as if I were a naughty child caught stealing sweets. 'You don't understand, do you, Linny? Yet you've always been such a clever girl.' He pulled his hands away from mine. 'You can't be trusted to leave me, and you can't be trusted with our son. There is no other way but for you to be put away, properly, lawfully, so there can never be any future questions about you.' His eyes were unblinking now, like a snake's. 'I'll have the papers drawn up by Dr Haverlock as soon as possible. He won't need any convincing,

490

of course. One look at you would be assurance enough that you need caring for. As for David . . . I'll bring him up as I see fit. It won't take me long to have him trained into the shape he should be.' He attempted another of his horrible laughs, but it brought on a fit of coughing, and a chill came over him.

As I stared at him, his body trembling, his moustache sprayed with cloudy beads of saliva, I imagined his face settling into the leering spectre of his dead father. I rubbed my eyes, trying to clear it away, but the haunting wouldn't leave. It seemed that, in the most terrible twist of fate, the evil hand that had brought me to Rodney Street had led me to this room. I got to my feet and stumbled away from the bedside. I looked, in horror, at the man who was my husband. Knowing the power he wielded. Knowing that his twisted hatred, his lecherous ways, and his truly vile nature would continue to grow with each passing year.

This was the man who would destroy me, and who would raise my son.

I had to stop what he was about to do to me. I had to protect my child.

I knew the timing must be perfect. I didn't sleep that night but, nevertheless, arose early in the morning and bathed. I had no weariness. I smoked my pipe, but only to prevent my body going into painful spasms. I had Malti pay special attention to my hair, and I chose my dress carefully. I sat at my dressing-table and studied myself. Now I understood how Faith had felt in her last days at Simla. There is a tremendous lifting, as if a heavy yoke has been taken from one's shoulders, when one knows, with complete certainty, what one must do. That there can be no other way.

Malti looked at me strangely. 'Mem Linny? I don't understand.'

'What don't you understand?' I swivelled to face her.

'Last night you appeared so distressed when you left Sahib Ingram's room. And yet today you are more at ease than for a long, long time. What is it, Mem, that I see in your face? It appears to be happiness. But that cannot be, with the sadness of this house.'

I smiled at her. 'It's not happiness, Malti. Not yet. But there is the future. We must light new lamps for the future.'

Malti shook her head, confused. The rest of that day I sat on the verandah and played with David, my mind whirring, planning. At one point I looked towards the windows of Somers's room and saw Dr Haverlock staring at me. He turned abruptly when I met his gaze.

I went to Somers's room. Dr Haverlock sat at the desk there, writing. Was it the commitment report he worked on? He stopped when he saw me, and looked at Somers, lying on the bed.

'Do you want something, Linny?' Somers asked, his voice deceptively concerned. 'Or have you forgotten something?'

'I thought you might need fresh water.'

Somers gestured to the full pitcher beside his bed. 'But, Linny, it was you who brought this just before Dr Haverlock arrived.'

'No, it wasn't. It must have been one of the servants.' I hadn't been to Somers's room that day.

Somers shook his head, smiling gently. Then, raising his eyebrows, he looked at Dr Haverlock. *You see?*

Dr Haverlock studied my hands. I realized I was lacing and unlacing my fingers. I stopped, but he had already turned back to his paper and started writing again. I left the room, but lingered in the hallway. I heard Dr Haverlock tell Somers it was done; I heard Somers assuring Dr Haverlock that he would receive what had been promised when all matters had been taken care of.

He was making his plans. It was time to finalize mine.

It was easy to acquire a supply of datura from a box-*wallah* that very day. The shrub's English name was thorn apple. It was one of India's indigenous plants, growing wild in rank soil and wasteland. I remembered Nani Meera's caution about using it. In the right amounts it was useful for limiting the coughing fits of pertussis, and maladies of the bladder. Although the large white corollas of the flowers had narcotic and sedative properties, the powdered leaves were stronger. Overdose caused fatal poisoning.

Although ever gaining in strength, Somers was still weak, and there were moments of extreme fatigue and feebleness. While he was recuperating, he enjoyed cooled tea, much sweetened, and called for it many times a day. I took it upon myself to fetch it from the cook and carry it to him each time he requested it, as any concerned wife might. From the way he looked at me the first few times I appeared at his bedside with the tray, I knew he thought I was trying to prove to him that I wasn't mad. I allowed him to think this of me.

I started with minute amounts. I had to be careful: it must look as if he had succumbed to his old enemy.

Within two days he had regressed considerably. His face was dry and flushed. He had difficulty in swallowing, and was given to muttering and restless, purposeless movements. On the third day he fell into a sleep so deep it was impossible to wake him for many hours; I knew it might lead to coma. When he finally stirred and opened his eyes, which were gummy, the pupils were dilated and fixed. I continued to persuade him to swallow a few sips of tea each time he was conscious, crying to the servants that he must have fluid.

As I wrung my hands in front of Dr Haverlock, I said a silent prayer of thanks that the old man was so lacking in medical knowledge. 'He appeared to be rallying,' I said. 'What has caused this turn?'

Dr Haverlock shook his head. 'One never knows how a foreign disease will work on its victim.' I stared, wide-eyed, into his face. 'I fear it's become much more serious. My diagnosis, Mrs Ingram, is brain malaria.'

I put my fingers to my lips in consternation. 'Brain malaria?'

'His slipping in and out of consciousness – as well as the mental confusion – are both symptoms. Should he start showing signs of jaundice, or perhaps convulsing . . .'

'But – but he *will* recover, won't he?'

'Now, my dear, you mustn't distress yourself unduly. Your state is quite delicate.'

'Dr Haverlock,' I stood tall, 'I'm not in any state, delicate or otherwise. Are you telling me that Mr Ingram may not recover from this bout? Tell me the truth, Dr Haverlock.'

The old man took my hands in his, an insincere expression of sympathy on his face.

When Dr Haverlock returned the following day, he made a cursory check of Somers, then led me into the study. 'Please prepare yourself, my dear,' he said.

I waited.

'Your husband's death is imminent. I doubt he'll survive the night.'

I allowed myself to crumple into a chair. I lowered my head and covered my face with my hands. 'Please dismiss the servants,' I said, through my fingers, 'but stay with me.' When we were alone, I looked up.

'I wanted to speak to you in complete privacy, Dr Haverlock,' I said, no longer putting on a show of distress.

'Now, now, Mrs Ingram. You mustn't worry. Very soon you will be at home, where people who know how to care for you can help you through the difficult times you're facing. And you mustn't concern yourself about the child. Mr Ingram left strict instructions as to—'

I stood up, came straight to him and stopped so close to his face that he took a step back. 'Do you really believe me to be mad, Dr Haverlock?

His eyes shifted. 'Your husband knew what was best for you. There are many ways of caring for those unfortunates, such as yourself, who—'

I interrupted. 'And there are many ways, I assume, that a man such as yourself may be – how shall I word it? May be persuaded to see the truth.'

Dr Haverlock's chin jumped, encouraging me. He was so transparent.

'I know you must be weary of working. You've devoted your life to helping people, Dr Haverlock.' The words swam out warmly, slippery, clean. 'You deserve to spend the remainder of your years in luxury, either here or at home. Whatever sum my husband and you agreed upon for writing the . . . recommendation with regard to my future, and that of my son, I will double – if you give that letter into my possession. Then we will speak no more about it.'

495

His chin jumped again, and by that subtle twitch, and his hesitation, I knew I had him. He took my arm and had me sit beside him on the sofa. He glanced around, although the room was empty. 'I may have been hasty in my estimation of your condition, my dear,' he said. 'Your poor husband made his request out of concern for you and for his son.'

'And, of course, Somers has been deeply affected by his constant battle with malaria all these years,' I said, 'so you will know that he has been lacking in clarity this last while. I understand, Dr Haverlock,' my voice grew low with a shared conspiracy, 'how well I understand, the awkward position in which he placed you. I insist you tell me what sum you are owed for the strain this unpleasant matter has caused you. Come, now, what will it be?'

He cleared his throat gruffly. Sly old goat. He was afraid of naming the price in case it was lower than what I was prepared to double.

I went to the desk drawer, took out the wrapped package I had put there that morning and brought it to the sofa. I set it between us and untied the string. The paper fell away, revealing my huge pile of saved rupees, the amount I had pilfered from Somers over the years, and had kept so well hidden. Now it gave the impression of a king's ransom.

The physician licked his thin, dry lips, his breath quickening. I could almost hear the greedy ticking of his brain. 'Oh, my, Mrs Ingram. Dear, dear. I don't wish to appear grasping, but this business has caused me a great loss of time and, as you say, considerable strain on my constitution. I've been quite bilious of late. It would be ungracious to speak of the sum Mr Ingram and I discussed but . . .' Again, his eyes caressed the money so close to his thigh.

I patted his sleeve. 'I understand,' I said, pity in my voice.

'Would you be carrying the document now, Dr Haverlock, that we might make an exchange?'

'Well,' he said slowly, 'I'm unsure to what you refer.'

'The commitment report, Dr Haverlock.' My voice never lost its sweetness. I moved the money an inch closer to him.

Still studying the *lakhs* of rupees, Dr Haverlock reached into his inside breast pocket, and I heard the reassuring crackle of folded paper.

He gave it to me, and once I had read what was written there, I retied the package and passed it to him, then held out my right hand.

He took it as if to bow over it, but I pulled back. He understood then and shook it firmly. We stood, each holding our reward, and exchanged a smile.

We were as good as each other at this game. We had both acquired what we wanted most.

Within the next few hours it was over. And in Somers's last painful moments, I knelt by his bed and stroked his hollow face, appearing to the servants and to Dr Haverlock to be the dutiful wife comforting her dying husband. I kept my own face composed, but in my head I spoke to Somers. *I have tricked and deceived you in ways you will never know. And now it is over. The nightmare is over. I have saved my life and the soul of my child.*

In spite of the depth of his illness I sensed his comprehension of this unspoken fact, that in spite of my past I was the stronger of us. That he was unable to control my future. I knew this from the way his unfocused eyes skittered in their sockets and his lips shook loosely, as if he needed to speak. I put my fingers to his mouth, brushed back his hair and kissed his cold, dry forehead. 'It is all over, Somers. All the hate and hurt to which you have subjected me,' I whispered, so quietly that the only sound the others in the room would hear was a breathless murmur, the last pledge of love from a wife to her husband. 'I have made it so,' I whispered, still more softly, little more than a sigh, and I saw his eyelids move, and I knew he heard me. I knew he understood.

A low rattle came from somewhere within him, and then his eyes rolled upward, to the limp ruffles of the *punkah*, and stayed there, unblinking.

EPILOGUE

1840

I T IS ONE of those glorious spring days when the air
carries the scent of the earth warming. The light from the
open window falls across the floor in soft, buttery squares;
the rustle of the birches that surround our home is a soft
whisper. I rise and go to the window, looking out at the new
growth in our lovely garden – the delicate bluebells and
irises, flowers too fragile to survive India's heat. I have grown
to see the beauty in England's misty weather. The colours of
the garden, without the vibrancy of India's hues, are delicate,
tender. I find them beautiful in a way that was impossible to
me before. I marvel at them.

We live, David and I, in a house that shares its garden with
Shaker and Celina's.

Shaker has opened a small dispensary in the village of
Marigate in Cheshire. Known all over the county for his
quiet, trustworthy manner and acute ability to diagnose
ailments, he discusses symptoms and healing herbs for the
treatment of many physical and mental complaints. The
rooms of the dispensary are always full, and Shaker is often
referred to as a physician, although he always corrects the
misapprehension: he is a lay practitioner of homoeopathy.

On most days I help him in the dispensary, pulverizing, weighing and measuring, discussing cases with him.

I have been amazed at the difference in him since I returned to England last year, after the settling of Somers's will. He still trembles, but at other times – when he sits and watches David play, or listens as Celina reads aloud by the fire – he is perfectly still. I have seen this, but do not comment on it, afraid that if those perceived moments of peace are spoken of they may disappear.

Celina, too, displays a sensitivity I would not have predicted. I remember her as sharp-faced and quick-tongued, but of course that was because she saw me as a rival. Now that fear has long fled; I believe it is the simple and powerful act of loving and being loved wholly in return that has changed her. She now has a quiet beauty; her eyes are filled with a glow I never saw when I first met her in Liverpool almost a decade ago. She welcomed David and me when we arrived at their door, and helped me to adjust to the life I had been away from for so long. It took some time for me to regain my energy and health, but she seemed to find joy in aiding and watching my recuperation. Whether she has learned it from Shaker, or whether she had a natural talent that he has brought out in her, she possesses a healing nature.

Neither Shaker nor Celina knows of David's true paternity; their grasp of my time in India will rely for ever on the letters I wrote. It is all that is necessary.

On Sundays, after church, David and I walk home, hand in hand, along the quiet, tree-lined road from the village. Shaker and Celina walk a few steps ahead, their heads together as they discuss the sermon or whatever news we heard at church. It is at these times that David and I talk about India, and the difference of life here. He remembers

Calcutta clearly, and knows no other place but that and the village here. I describe Liverpool – the buildings, the bustling streets, the train. I have promised him we will soon visit the city together and journey to Manchester on the huge, steaming beast.

A month after I returned to England I went to Liverpool and set a mason to carve a beautiful headstone in pale grey granite. When it was done I returned again, and as it was placed in the graveyard at Our Lady and St Nicholas I arranged for the bells to be rung, and said my own prayers for my mother as I ran my fingers over her name – *Frances Gow* – carved deeply into the smooth surface. And below, in letters just as deep, *Forever Cherished. Beloved Mother of Linny Gow.*

I can wear the pendant with pride now, and I wear no other jewellery.

When the time is right I will take David to visit his grandmother's grave. He will never know of the other grave I visited. The pink-streaked stone is barely visible, sunken into the soft grass, and yet the holly bush still stands, its spiny foliage glossy.

He listens to my stories about Liverpool with interest. He has learned to write, and sends simple letters to Malti. Sometimes he draws pictures of his life in England, and encloses those too. He says he will go back to visit her some day. Malti lives with Trupti and her nieces and nephews in Delhi. They no longer have to work for others, and want for nothing.

David thrives, a healthy, strong-limbed, dark-eyed child of seven, who plays with his friends and complains about his daily lessons. In this way he is an ordinary boy. But he has the love of horses in his blood. Shaker and I discovered this when I decided it was time he had his own horse. We took him to a stable, and he chose a tall, gleaming roan.

I thought the horse too big for him, but he was adamant. And when he was in the saddle I saw his father in him so clearly, in the way he held the short crop but was loath to use it, in his small, capable hands as they smoothed the horse's mane, as he leaned forward and whispered instinctively into the horse's ear. On that first mount, he pressed his knees into the roan's sides and was off across the field, leaving me with my mouth open in surprise and anxiety, yet also with such an overpowering joy that I could not speak.

Shaker gave chase on a quick dappled mare, and within minutes they rode back to me, pleasure unmistakable on David's face, and Shaker smiled the proud, indulgent smile of a father.

He and Celina had not had the good fortune to have children, and they treat David with the love and compassion they would have given freely to their own. They are our family; I am like a beloved sister to them, while David is the cosseted child of us all.

Unlike me, who too early lost a mother, my son blossoms in the love of two women. David has his memories of the man he believes to have been his father, although they are thin and fading rapidly; soon they will be reduced to the small likeness painted on a cameo. Shaker, who stands in for his father, is kind and loving. And the one who truly fathered him will remain — at least until David is no longer an impressionable child — unknown.

When he is fully grown, will I give him the missive I wrote at the end of that terrible time in Calcutta, in the days following Somers's death? Who can say? At times I take out the shakily written, ink-blotched pages and read them, seeing myself – as I was then – as if through someone else's eyes. I keep it safe, for I believe it may be important to David one day. I have come to realize that there are no certainties in this life, no promises – to others, or to oneself – that can always be kept.

There are days when the longing for the poppy is so strong I endure physical pain. I know now that it is likely I will never lose it, but I also know that nothing can ever again drive me to become its slave. At odd times, unexpected times, perhaps when I am waking, I feel a sense of the old ebb and flow of the White Smoke in my head. At these times I am confused, saddened, when I think over my life and see it as a litany of errors, lies and deception. But then I hear the sound of my son murmuring to his puppy in the other room, and I know that the long journey I took has brought me to this place, with David, in the way it was meant to be. I can bear to look at my reflection now: although my eyes are deeper, the skin around them finely lined, they are clear. I look like a mother, an ordinary woman.

Celina has suggested that perhaps I shall soon find someone – an ordinary man – to share my life. Perhaps. I have learned that I am capable of passion, of giving and accepting love. I am twenty-eight. There is time.

For now I have my dream – the dream that has nothing to do with the poppy. This real dream, the one I can bring at will, is the memory of the copper sun, of the Kashmir valley, its carpet of flowers. Of passion, and completeness. This dream has replaced the nightmare. I am free of all that kept me prisoner for so long. And who could wish for more than this?

My book on the medicinal plants of India, which I began to compile when I first arrived back in England, using the notes I had collected over my years in India, is finished. It shall be published within a few months by Carruthers of London. Although I am known as Linny Ingram here, I put the name Linnet Gow on the book. The publisher strongly suggested that I use as the author name 'A Lady', which they prefer, or Mrs Somers Ingram. Of course, I think of myself as neither.

I wrote back that I would like it published under the name I originally indicated – Linnet Gow. They resisted politely, suggesting L. Gow.

I replied in my finest hand, stating that I insisted on my choice: with all respect, I do insist.

They will come round to my bidding, of course, for I have never been one to back down. And no matter what names have been appointed, I will continue forever to think of myself as Linny Gow, the name my mother gave me, and the only name of which I am proud.

ACKNOWLEDGEMENTS

I AM GREATLY INDEBTED to my agent, Sarah Heller, for all her help with this project. I would like to thank my editor, Harriet Evans, for her instinct, her insight and her questions, and for pushing me to go further and dig deeper. She truly was instrumental in helping me make this book as close as possible to the one I envisaged. Heartfelt thanks to Catherine Cobain for all her assistance and to Hazel Orme for her astute suggestions. I must also thank Donna Freeman, Shannon Kernaghan, Irene Williams, Anita Jewell and Kathy Lowinger, who read the manuscript in its original form, and encouraged me. Lastly, I thank my children, Zalie, Brenna and Kitt, for their understanding and constant support. No matter how difficult the journey, they are always willing companions.

Now you can buy any of these other bestselling
Headline books from your bookshop or
direct from the publisher.

FREE P&P AND UK DELIVERY
(Overseas and Ireland £3.50 per book)

None But the Brave	Joy Chambers	£7.99
The Beekeeper's Pupil	Sara George	£6.99
The King's Touch	Jude Morgan	£6.99
Killigrew and the Incorrigibles	Jonathan Lunn	£5.99
Virgin	Robin Maxwell	£6.99
No Graves As Yet	Anne Perry	£6.99
A History of Insects	Yvonne Roberts	£6.99
The Eagles and the Wolves	Simon Scarrow	£6.99
The Accomplice	Kathryn Heyman	£6.99
The Seventh Son	Reay Tannahill	£6.99
Bone House	Betsy Tobin	£6.99
The Loveday Scandals	Kate Tremayne	£6.99
The Lamplighter	Anthony O'Neill	£6.99

TO ORDER SIMPLY CALL THIS NUMBER

01235 400 414

or visit our website: www.madaboutbooks.com

Prices and availability subject to change without notice.